A SINGLE BULLET FIRED IN ANGER; A COMMUNITY OUTRAGED BY THE ACQUITTAL, AND A SECRET MORE DEADLY THAN THE CRIME . . ."HE CONFESSED BUT WAS ACQUITTED." THE VERDICT SENT A SHOCKWAVE THROUGH THE COMMUNITY

"I'm not making any accusations," Gavin finally said.

"Well, it sounds like you're pointing fingers at an awful lot of people," the reporter said, "from the entire original trial team to the new district attorney."

"I'm not pointing fingers; I'm simply echoing what the community has been screaming for all along, justice. This isn't about someone dropping the ball. Those boys lied, and got away with murder. They have the evidence against them. If I were in charge, I wouldn't hesitate, and I'd guarantee a conviction. You can quote me on that."

Samoan gang members, fired a fatal shot into the car of an innocent teenager. Tyler Tutuila confessed to police, but changed his story at the last minute. The gun disappeared, the jury was confused — it was enough for reasonable doubt. The acquittal gained national attention, and rocked the prosecutor's office to its core.

Two years later the tragic memory has faded, until Gavin Brady, an ambitious young civil attorney, inadvertently receives a secret internal memo that stirs up puzzling questions about the original criminal trial. Gavin's discovery threatens not only to reopen old wounds in the community, but expose a cover-up between the D.A.'s office and the police department.

The more Gavin digs into the past, the more perilous his own present becomes. Even his firm bows to the political pressure, and turns against him. Gavin's pursuit turns into a fight for survival, blurring the line between justice and greed.

D1566514

"Gripping legal thriller that will keep you on the edge of your seat, a can't-put-it-down must read...."— *Wendy Ladd, journalism professor, Farmingdale State College.*

"... Stone Grissom's knowledge of the legal system shines ... a must-read for anyone who enjoys lots of twists and turns ..."—*Susan Mustafa, co-author of The New York Times bestseller The Most Dangerous Animal of All—Searching for My Father and Finding the Zodiac Killer.*

"Move over John Grisham and make room for Stone Grissom."—*Chris Hahn, syndicated radio host and national political analyst.*

"... a skillfully crafted thriller ... Stone Grissom has truly mastered the art of suspenseful storytelling."—*Rich Everitt, author of Fallen Stars: Air Crashes That Killed Rock and Roll Heaven, and president of Medialine and Talentapes.*

"Grissom is poised to be well on his way to rival the giants in the genre ... A Cry For Justice hits every mark."—*Andreas Kyprianou, former national marketing director, MGM, and professional script doctor.*

"A Cry for Justice is an unforgettable, compelling story of power, greed, and the choices that we make. Once I started reading the book, I couldn't put it down."—*Thomas McDermott, Jr., Mayor of Hammond Indiana.*

"... smartly written ... breaching the mystery becomes an itch that must be scratched!"—*Amy Miller, Host of Detroit Today, WDET.*

" ... crackles with energy, suspense and young Gavin Brady's passion for justice from the very first paragraph ... Ultimately, this book is a tale of redemption and forgiveness, set against the backdrop of the rain-soaked, pine-scented Pacific Northwest."—*Vicki Gruber, attorney and writing professor.*

" ... as riveting and engrossing as any legal thriller ... Stone Grissom's first-hand knowledge of the inner workings of the legal system – both good and bad – shine brightly through. A tremendous debut. Well done!"—*Jason Schauer, civil trial attorney, Seattle, WA.*

A CRY FOR JUSTICE

Stone Grissom

Moonshine Cove Publishing, LLC

Abbeville, South Carolina U.S.A.

FIRST MOONSHINE COVE EDITION JULY 2017

ISBN: 978-1-945181-17-7
Library of Congress PCN: 2017910200
Copyright © 2017 by Stone Grissom

Front cover design by Gregory Stevens, back cover design by Moonshine Cove staff, author photo by Michael Shekian Photography.

For my wife and daughter,
who taught me that the hour billed is
far less valuable than the one lived.

Stone Grissom is an Edward R. Murrow winning journalist and prime time news anchor in New York. Grissom has won multiple awards for his work as a journalist, has more than a dozen Emmy nominations, has been named one of the top TV reporters by the Long Island Press, and has been recognized for his journalistic enterprise by the Associated Press, the Fair Media Council, and The Press Club of New York.

Additionally, Grissom boasts a distinguished background as a successful civil rights and criminal defense attorney. He has appeared as a legal analyst on a variety of local and national stations, including Court TV, MSNBC, CNN, Headline News, and Fox – and covered such national and international stories as the Sandy Hook shooting, numerous presidential and local elections, the civil trial of Michael Jackson, the sentencing of the Green River serial killer, and the trial of Saddam Hussein.

Grissom earned his law degree from the University of Notre Dame Law School. He was awarded the Louis A. Powell Medal for Excellence in Trial Advocacy by the American College of Trial Lawyers, was named a "Rising Star" three years in a row by the Washington publication, Law and Politics, and co-chaired the trial advocacy division of the Washington State Bar Association. He has authored numerous articles on trial tactics and constitutional issues for various legal publications and teaches News Media and News Writing at the State University of New York at Farmingdale. He lives with his wife and daughter on Long Island, and is currently working on his second thriller, *Bonds of Friendship*.

Read more about his interests and writing approach at his website:

https://www.stonegrissom.com

A Cry For Justice

PROLOGUE

THE COOL BRISK air pricked her face as she stepped out the door, a sobering refreshment for the ride home. The moist grass gently gave way to the weight of her diminutive frame as if to secretly memorialize the few final marks she would ever make on this earth. A thick line of large broad-leafed rhododendrons ran parallel to the gravel driveway. Mounds of sprouting red and purple flowers sparkled in the dewy moonlight and camouflaged the sea of parked cars along the street.

Slam! Sara flinched as she turned around to see the back door violently bounce against the back of the house sending a loud shockwave throughout the neighborhood.

"We didn't scare you, did we?" Casey said through his laughter as he spilled out of the threshold along with Katie and Paul. Sara was visiting her girlfriend, Katherine Zuckert, from Virginia. The two girls grew up together in Alexandria, and became instant friends the day Sara's family moved next door. Katie made Sara's transition to the fifth grade in a new school easier and less frightening. Sara's family only moved a couple of blocks away from her old house, but it was far enough to cross into a new school district, which, to an eleven-year-old girl might as well have been another country. Meeting Katie, however, made all that disappear.

The small pangs of trepidation in Sara's body immediately dissipated at the sight of her friends coming outside to join her. Katie grabbed her by the arm and pulled her toward Casey's car. The two girls were more like sisters than best friends. During field trips in school, they always made a point of being in the same group despite their teachers' efforts to organize the students by last names. Normally, a Katherine Zuckert would never have a chance to be in the same cluster of students as a Sara Harrington. However, secret trading with the other students or blatant cutting in line in the wrong group ensured a place together.

This was Sara's third trip to Tacoma. She was contemplating attending the University of Washington after receiving a scholarship offer. Her parents wanted her to stay closer to home and attend the University of Virginia. However, Sara loved the idea of moving to a new part of the country. Plus, since Katie's family had moved to

Washington three years ago, Alexandria didn't have the same appeal as it once did.

"How do you feel?" Paul asked as he caught up to the girls.

"I'm fine." Sara smiled. "The breeze feels good." Although Sara and Paul weren't officially dating, he always managed to show up whenever she came to visit.

"You okay to drive?" Katie said turning to Casey.

"I better be — I'm in no shape to walk." He laughed. Katie feigned a half-sarcastic smile. "I'm fine, really."

The four of them were heading home from a spring break party. Sara wasn't a drinker, but made an exception this evening in honor of seeing Paul. The crisp night air seemed to give her a boost of adrenaline. Casey, on the other hand, never seemed to get enough of anything, especially Katie. Sara watched as he pawed at her best friend on the way to the car.

Sara glanced at Paul, who pretended not to notice Casey's lustful displays. She could feel goose bumps forming on her arm and prickling her skin. She decided to write about this later tonight.

"After you, babe," Casey said to Katherine as they reached his car. Katie climbed in the front seat through the driver's side while Paul walked around to the back seat behind Katherine and held the door open for Sara. Before Paul could close his own door, Casey slammed his foot on the gas pedal and made a sharp right onto the road jerking Paul across his seat into Sara.

"Sorry," he said bracing his right hand against her window for balance.

"It's okay," she replied.

The car jerked as Casey slammed on the brakes. "Fucking country roads," he said, covering for his failure to see the sign.

"Isn't it the next right?" Paul said.

"Here we are," Casey said pointing at the street sign.

He turned right and headed down the four-lane road that was illuminated solely by the shadows of the night. This was only Casey's third time driving down this dark road. However, he knew every inch of the one-and-two-eighths mile street. This stretch of the road was a favorite of Casey's football coach. Every summer for the last two years, he suffered its endless and unforgiving pavement with his teammates. Two times a day, his team ran this particular path on the way to and from the school field. He paced the distance like any good runner, by breathing. One breath every two seconds, which turned into twenty breaths per minute, and one hundred forty breaths per mile. Even after several beers, Casey caught himself counting each exhalation as if pacing the road as he drove.

He stopped counting and looked in his rear-view mirror. A car rapidly approached. Its high beams shot a blinding light through the back of Casey's car bouncing off the mirror into everyone's eyes.

"What the hell!" Casey yelled as the car came closer to Casey's back bumper. Sara heard music blasting from inside the vehicle.

"Assholes!" Casey said, looking in the rear view mirror again.

"Don't worry about it," Katie said. "Let's just keep going."

Casey tapped his brakes. "Tailgate the bull and you get the horns," he said. The car behind him locked up its tires letting out a high-pitched screeching shrill.

The car shut off its headlights. Sara could feel the blood rush to her face in panic.

"What the..." Paul muttered.

"I don't like this," Sara said. The car's engine raced behind them. It moved to the left-hand lane, shrouding itself in the darkness.

"What's he trying to do?" Katie squinted and tried to focus on the outline of the car.

"Why'd he turn off his headlights?" Paul asked.

The mysterious car revved its engine and pulled alongside Casey's car. Sara reached over and gripped Paul's hand for comfort. Casey looked to his left to see who was driving. Without headlights, the car looked like a bulky shadow pushing itself through the black air. The invisible engine rumbled with great force as the car sped by them. The inside was as dark as the outer shell, but Casey thought he could make out the outline of four people. The passenger seemed to raise his hand and wave at them as they passed his window.

"Assholes!" Casey stuck his hand out his window and flipped them off. As if in response to Casey's gesture, the car's headlights came back on as it continued on ahead of them.

"Who were those guys?" Katie asked.

"They were probably mad because they weren't invited to the party," Paul said. He always seemed to know what to say, Sara thought. Paul turned to her. "You all right?"

"Yeah." She loosened her sweaty grip on his palm.

"Is that them?" Casey's voice regained a serious tone. About fifty yards in front of them at the stop sign, the mystery car's brake lights pierced the night sky with its left blinker flashing. "It's okay, we're turning right," Casey said with a semi-assured tone.

"Don't use your blinker," Katie said. "They might change their mind."

Sara's heart began pounding again. 'It's okay,' she told herself. Each thump drummed against her chest as if it were trying to escape her body. 'It's okay,' she told herself again. 'There are four of us. We can speed away if they try anything.' Like a scared child, her thoughts turned to the warmth and security of her parent's home. She would be eighteen in less than four months, and all she could think of right now was running back home and snuggling deep into her father's welcoming shoulders, burying her entire body into his comforting and protective embrace. 'It'll be fine,' she told herself as they approached the stop sign. 'It'll be fine.'

Casey gripped the steering wheel with both hands exposing his façade of self-confidence.

"This doesn't feel right," Paul said.

"Just turn right," Katie said. "Let's just get out of here."

"Don't worry," Casey yelled back. The darkened vehicle sat patiently at the stop sign. Its bright red tail lights glowed like an ominous fire piercing the solitude of the Northwest night.

"You don't think they saw you flip 'em off, do you?" Sara said.

"What? Shut up." The cracking in Casey's voice no longer masked his angst at the situation.

"You shut up," Katie said. Casey's car began slowing down as it approached the stop sign in the lane to the right of the mystery car. It hadn't moved. Nearing the vehicle, Casey's headlights confirmed that the inside contained the outlines of four people.

"Just don't look over at them," Katie said as they approached.

"Don't worry." Casey came up even with the other car. He could hear the music blasting out its open windows. "I don't owe them an explanation." A sole streetlight across the road offered just enough illumination to backlight the four figures into large shadowy silhouettes as Casey pulled to the right of the car.

A faceless figure in the front passenger's seat turned his head toward them. His features were drenched in the blackness of the night. Casey locked his head toward the road to avoid any eye contact. He couldn't be sure, but he thought he saw the passenger smiling at him in his peripheral vision.

"Go!" Katie cried. Casey turned the wheel to the right and gunned the engine. The mystery car seemed to match them in velocity as it turned in the opposite direction.

A blast ripped through the night. "What the hell was that?" Casey yelled and looked around at Katie.

"It sounded like a gunshot."

"It sounded like back fire to me," Paul said. The mysterious car was already out of sight in the opposite direction.

"At least we're away from them," Katie said in relief. "That was crazy."

"It's okay now," Paul said looking over at Sara. "Sara." Her eyes began to glaze over and roll back into her head. "Oh, my God!" He reached over catching her as she slumped back in her seat. "Stop the car," he shouted moving his hand behind her back to support her. His heart stuttered as he felt the warm pulse of her lifeblood spurting from her. Dry-mouthed, he realized it was bad, really bad.

"What's wrong?" Katie twisted around.

"Oh my God!" Paul lifted up Sara's shirt and moved his hand across her lower back until he found it. He pressed against the gaping hole.

"Oh my God. She's been shot."

CHAPTER 1

GAVIN FIDGETED IN his seat trying to stay awake as the professor droned on about the development of jurisprudence. He had one week to go before his law school career was finally over and he couldn't wait. Gavin chose Notre Dame because he wanted a school that would place a great deal of emphasis on the practical applications of the law. He wanted his day in court, and he wanted a school that took trial advocacy as seriously as it did citation checking.

By the end of his first year, it was clear that he was a natural at oral advocacy. He barely showed for class, but could argue with the most obstinate professors about legal policies as well as the global reasoning behind decisions. He fidgeted in his seat trying desperately not to listen to the professor lecture on the coinciding shift from natural law to legal positivism.

Gavin's classmate, Seth Douglas, raised his hand to ask a question. Gavin shook his head in disgust because Seth had an innate knack of finding the most obscure useless point and harping on it until the only way to shut him up was for the entire class to acknowledge his insightfulness. Seth was grooming himself for a career in academics, and a question from him would prompt the professor to continue droning on for the remainder of the period. Seth had connections that reached the very pinnacle of the judiciary. His life had been mapped out since the day he was born. In contrast, Gavin had been forced to defer his undergraduate student loans when he entered law school and was facing close to a two-hundred-thousand-dollar debt when he earned his juris doctorate. Still, he had nothing to complain about. He not only had a wife whom he adored, but he already had a great job lined up for himself.

The past year had been a blur of interviews, job offers, and congratulatory parties. Gavin had been pretty lucky. He knew that he didn't want to work in New York amongst the Seth Douglases of the world. He didn't go to law school so that he could get out and write memos for partners on obscure issues that only had meaning in the abstract theoretical debate. Gavin wanted to *practice* law, not sit back in a library postulating arguments. He wanted to stand in court. He wanted to argue for justice. He wanted to look his clients in the eyes and see the appreciation on their faces when he won.

Interviews came easy. He was in the top five percent of his class, and he had won every trial advocacy award imaginable. He knew he could go anywhere in the country, but he had focused his interviewing to several middle-sized firms in San Francisco and Seattle, mostly environmental plaintiff firms.

He'd almost given up hope of finding a firm that fit his finicky requirements until early in his last year. The second week into the semester, he received an invitation to interview with a small boutique firm in Tacoma, Washington that specialized in both plaintiff and defense practices. The firm's letterhead read, Stewart, Meridiam & Smithwick. The invitation seemed odd because Gavin hadn't sent them an inquiry letter, and they weren't on any of the on-campus recruiting lists. It wasn't until he scrolled down the list of partners that the answer came to him — *William T. Hanson, Of Counsel.* Gavin recognized the name immediately. His father must have been behind this.

Gavin's father was a semi-connected political consultant in San Francisco. His parents were divorced when he was only nine, and his mom decided to move out of California and back to the mid-west. Gavin grew up as more of a pen pal to his father than a son. They saw each other for only brief periods on major holidays when his father's work allowed.

They became closer when Gavin turned his attention to the study of the law. His father asked for some advice on a legal matter involving an out of state attorney and his political campaign. It seemed that a Washington attorney had retained Gavin's father to help him with his campaign in the San Jose area for a Superior Court bench that just became vacant. The problem was that this attorney, Mr. William T. Hanson, had been admonished by the Washington Bar early in his career for missing the statute of limitations in one of his cases. Normally, such a disclosure to the judiciary was mandatory for a potential candidate, but Gavin's father had done some checking with his own sources, and it seemed that the Bar Association no longer had record of the admonishment due to a fortunate administrative clerical error.

Gavin advised his father on the potential ethical dilemmas that were involved, and his father pretended to heed the advice. In the end, the bar association admonishment was never revealed, and Mr. Hanson won the election after engaging in a rather brutal smear campaign against his opponent who had the political damaging fortune of being caught leaving an under-age club with one of his daughter's friends.

Gavin's father proudly sent him a copy of the press release for Hanson's appointment. Instead of congratulating his father, Gavin reacted sharply by writing a distasteful letter calling him a sell-out. It was the last time he ever wrote to his father. He even stubbornly refused delivery of all return correspondence for the next six months, ten letters in all. Then, the mail stopped. Just before spring break of Gavin's first year at law school, he received the news. His father had been hospitalized for the past three months with advanced brain cancer. He died on a Saturday morning after an unsuccessful surgery to remove a tumor from his cerebellar region. Gavin never forgave himself.

Now, it seemed that his father was reaching out from the grave. Gavin wiped away the forming tears as he read the letter:

You are cordially invited to come to Tacoma, Washington to interview with the partnership of Stewart Meridiam & Smithwick for an associate position with the firm.

Also enclosed was a first class ticket.

Gavin went to the interview and was hooked within five minutes of arriving. The firm had a distinguished reputation. Three of the partners had gone on to the United States Senate, and four partners were now federal judges. The list, of course, did not include the one infamous partner, who had successfully reached out of state to secure a superior court judicial position. The partnership had twenty-six attorneys in all. Two-thirds of the firm's practice was a mix of corporate securities law and high end land use development, which generated more than enough income to subsidize the remaining one-third of the practice. It was this remaining third that excited Gavin.

The firm's wealthiest partner was a gray-haired man whose presence commanded the entire space when he entered a room. Jonathan Winston Stewart IV, or "Duke" as everyone called him, had been with the firm since its inception. He came from a long line of trial attorneys, and had grown up in the Delta area of Mississippi before following his legal ambitions out to the Northwest. He picked up the name Duke during his fraternity days in college, and it followed him through law school. He kind of liked the nickname and even played it up by prominently placing a framed movie poster of John Wayne from True Grit on his office wall opposite the door. The name fit him well. He was confident and cocky, yet had a charm about him that made him also extremely likeable.

Duke's law practice involved governmental liability, and he was on every hit list of every attorney general in Washington, Idaho, Oregon, and California. He loved to sue municipalities and was personally responsible for emptying out one hundred thirty-eight-million in jury verdicts in the Northwest in the past five years, and was known as the Robin Hood of the underrepresented amongst the legal community. He was also a regular speaker at trial lawyer conventions all over the country.

As he sat amongst the cherry wood beams and dark leather chairs in the firm's front lobby, Gavin went through his pre-planned speech on why he loved the law, detailing the one moment in his childhood when he figured out that he wanted to be an attorney. For some reason, that one question seemed to be an interview staple, and every recruiter wanted to hear that law students dreamed of becoming lawyers as far back as the childhood days in the sandbox. Gavin had recited it many times along with a canned speech about why he would like to make his home in Milwaukee or San Diego or San Francisco or wherever the particular firm was located. It was an interviewing tradition that went back as far as recruiting itself, and Gavin knew it well.

"Let me stop you right there," Duke said in a slight southern drawl after leading him back to his office.

"Yes, Mr. Stewart?"

"Whoa. I think we need to clear the air a bit before this meeting goes any further."

"Okay." Gavin was not sure how to respond.

"Only creditors and banks call me Mr. Stewart. Now, I can live with Jon, but my friends call me Duke. You can decide what you want to be," he said with that hint of Southern charm.

"All right Duke, what else would you like to know about me?"

It was the moment Gavin needed to break the ice and help him relax. Duke seemed experienced at putting people at ease, and the two of them began chatting like old friends. The meeting lasted less than an hour, and then Gavin was shipped off to another office where he went back to his old stand-by speeches. The cycle was repeated several times that morning before he was whisked away to lunch with a whole new set of partners and young associates at a restaurant overlooking the picturesque Puget Sound.

"Do you think you could get used to this?" One of the partners asked.

"Absolutely," Gavin replied, "I'm thinking about staying in school just so that I keep interviewing."

The table politely chuckled, and the attorneys noticeably loosened up. Soon, horror stories of interviewing became the topic of discussion, and some of the younger associates began telling tales they heard in law school.

One associate told a story of the student who was handed his rejection letter after the first interview before he even left the room. Then, there was the student who took all his suits with him, and had his hotel dry clean them all on the interviewing firm's tab. Recycled stories passed around to ease the tension of the interviewing process. Gavin laughed anyway. After all, they were funny, and he was the center of attention — a role he heartily enjoyed.

After lunch, he spent two more hours interviewing with various partners before being released for the remainder of the afternoon to check out the surrounding area on his own. The firm hired a chauffeured car to take him to Point Defiance Park, a seven hundred acre wooded preserve that overlooked the water and contained a zoo, a botanical garden, a beach, and a five-mile running path. Gavin walked through the old growth forests that hovered around the manicured paths of the park's botanical garden that housed one hundred twenty-five varieties of colorful fuchsias, assorted colors of Pacific Coast iris hybrid flowers, and a rainbow of more than fifteen hundred rose bushes. The sweet tangy fragrance of fresh bark infiltrated his nostrils scrubbing and cleansing his senses.

At the end of the day, Gavin observed the commuters making their way home across the bridges in the distance. The burnt sienna sunset added soothing hues that dribbled across the sky and danced off the water. He looked at his watch. He had been there for three-and-a-half-hours. He made his way back to the entrance where the firm's car was waiting. The driver took him back to his hotel and waited while he showered, ate, and checked out. He was then driven to the airport where he took a red eye back to school.

His offer came one week later. In true litigator style, Gavin had taken photos of the most picturesque areas during his trip. He then had his wife, Hannah, pick them up from the photo lab knowing that she wouldn't be able to resist peeking at them. She was already sold on the area before she even got home. Gavin sent the firm his acceptance while Hannah updated her resume for a teaching position at one of the local colleges.

That night Gavin went for a run. He liked this part of the year. The warm Indiana evening air was heavy and stimulated his sweat glands, like a baptismal cleansing of the day's problems. Gavin's nightly run was his alone time. The first mile was spent counting his breaths and getting his cadence. After that, time melted away, and each rhythmic step allowed his mind to wander.

Mostly Gavin thought about what it would be like when he was allowed to practice law for himself. He knew he had a gift, at least his mother always told him so. He was blessed with boyish looks that gave him an air of innocence and purity. This played well in front of a jury. At least he was hoping it would.

Gavin's shins began to hurt with each pounding blow to the concrete. The warm sweat streaming into his eyes began to sting as he blinked to regain focus. The pain meant he was halfway home. He began to count his breaths again. He could feel his heartbeat, and turned his focus toward slowing it down. Each hurried breath was followed by a practiced tempo that was in synchronicity with his stride. His whole life to this point was nothing more than a series of countdowns, and he had become very skilled at performing them. *Two miles to go. One week to go, thirty minutes to go.* His goal was drawing closer.

Soon his life would begin.

CHAPTER 2

"WHERE IS HE?" Duke's voice yelled out of his office and into the hallway where his secretary sat. With the training of a good infantry soldier, Becky was on her feet with her head poking through Duke's door.

"Where's who?"

Duke didn't wait for a response as he charged by her. "Do you have my motion notebook?"

"Of course, I have your notebook. Have I ever not had your motion notebook ready?"

"No, you haven't." Duke's voice softened exposing just enough of his Delta roots to disarm her. "That's why I'm the luckiest man in the world." Although four years at Harvard and three more at Columbia Law School had almost eviscerated Duke's Mississippi ancestral roots, he worked hard to accentuate certain moments with either a soothing country phrase or an old wise country saying. It was a trick that he used to warm up to juries and judges, and Duke was a master at using it effectively.

"Where's who?" Becky wasn't letting him off the hook that easily. She had been Duke Stewart's secretary ever since he joined the firm. She watched him grow from an overly zealous associate to a prominent and powerful partner in the firm. As Duke won victory after victory molding the firm into his vision of success, she was always sitting outside his door. She was also the only one who could handle him and the only one who could tame his increasingly large ego.

"What?" He feigned ignorance.

"Where's who? You said, 'where is he.' Where's who?"

Just then, Gavin came around the corner into sight. He was carrying a thick stack of materials he received during his in-house training session on how to access the firm's computer system and document database.

"Our new boy here." Duke turned to Gavin and smiled.

"Hey, Duke." Gavin stopped.

"I see we have you buried in papers already in your first week. How's the bar studying coming along?"

Becky looked inquisitively at Duke. He was not one for small chitchat with new and, especially, unproven associates.

"Well, between my bar classes at night and the firm's afternoon tutorials, if I fail, I deserve it." Gavin waited almost two weeks for this opportunity to talk with Duke. He practiced his responses almost every night in front of his mirror. He thought out each potential enthusiastic and confident response that might result were he to bump into Duke in the hallway.

"It's too bad. We seem to be working you so hard that you keep forgetting where your office is located."

Gavin's face went flush. Duke was on to his little charade. Gavin's office was on the other side of the building and located just three doors down to the left of the computer training center. Gavin purposely chose to take the opposite more scenic route. A path that forced him to walk the entire circumference of the building and directly in front of Duke's office before reaching his own.

"Yeah, I'm still learning the layout." *What a stupid response.*

Duke smiled. "Thinking on your feet is the most important characteristic of a trial attorney." Gavin looked at him as if wanting to find an appropriate response. "Look we'd better hurry," Duke continued. "I've got a ten a.m. motion. Now you can stay here and learn about proper billing procedure or you can tag along and begin to immerse yourself in how this firm really operates."

Gavin stood frozen. All that practice in front of his mirror at home didn't adequately prepare him for this moment. He stood there like a little boy on his first day as school. Becky finally took pity on him and broke the ice by handing Duke his motion notebook. Finally, Gavin took a silent deep breath.

"I think I'd rather see how the firm really operates."

"Let's walk and talk then," Duke said as he began briskly heading down the hallway toward the elevators. "You can drop off that stuff in your office on the way," he said motioning to the armful of training materials Gavin was holding.

They walked down the hallway together as Duke began to explain to him how opposing counsel had made a motion to change venue in a feeble attempt to gain some type of home court advantage.

Halfway to the elevator doors, they stopped so Gavin could drop off his training materials. He entered his office still feeling like the nervous pre-schooler who needs his hand held by an adult while crossing the street. Despite the fact he hadn't had time to hang anything on the walls, Gavin's office was already nicely furnished. The firm provided him with a maple desk and a matching bookcase, complete with treatises on every subject tested on the bar exam already tabbed out for easy reference. Gavin's freshly painted walls were eggshell colored except the wall opposite his desk, which was accented in a rich burgundy hue. All new associates were allowed to choose between five approved colors. These were Gavin's choices, meaning Hannah had chosen them and Gavin had agreed.

"Nice wall."

"Yes, it is." Duke didn't have to make that comment. It wasn't about the paint. This was Gavin's first year, and Duke had invited him to watch his motion.

Gavin quickly dropped off his armload in his in-box and turned to leave. Next to the door sat two banker boxes.

Duke pointed to them. "Good, I'm glad they delivered them already. It's a wrongful death suit and a potential gun manufacturer's liability case. I'd like you to take a look at it."

Gavin removed the lid from one of the boxes. His eyes glowed in the exuberance of the moment. Inside were neatly stacked rows of manila folders, each labeled in type print with the words, *Harrington v. Tutuila, et al.* The smell of paper perforated his nostrils as he took in a breath.

"Ab- Absolutely. I'll get right on it."

"I haven't decided to take it yet. The clients live out of town, Virginia or some place and – I just don't know yet. I'll talk to you about it on Monday after you've had a chance to immerse yourself in the case."

Gavin fingered the manila files in the box, still basking in the moment. Duke turned toward the door to exit. "You're still interested in coming, right?"

"Yeah. I'm right behind you."

He glanced down at the open box as he began to exit with Duke. His hand grabbed the closest folder, and he tucked it into his suit jacket. The label was marked, *Research.* Duke caught the move out of the corner of his eye and silently smiled to himself at the enthusiasm of his new protégé.

Although the courthouse was only three blocks from the firm, Duke always drove. He said it gave him a chance to think, but it was really so he could show off his car d'jour. Gavin sat quietly in the front seat as they pulled out of the firm's parking lot and drove the football field distance to the courthouse. He pulled out the manila folder he had tucked away in his suit and cracked open the file. Inside was an article titled, *Gun Industry, Marketing Through Lethality.* The article looked as though it had been photocopied out of a legal magazine. On the front was a post-it note. On it, someone had written, *we need the gun.* His curiosity was getting the best of him. What did that mean? What gun? Gavin was intrigued. He could already see himself in front of the appellate court arguing the finer points of the law as a team full of attorneys sat behind him defeated by his overpowering advocacy.

Duke looked over and saw him playing with the folder. "Here, read this before we get there." He reached in the backseat and handed him his black motion notebook. "I want you to know what the argument's all about so you can follow along."

Gavin put the folder back under his suit jacket against his shirt and opened the notebook. They were only a block away, so Gavin was forced to skim the arguments as quickly as he could. The law of venue could be described in many ways, but on the legal excitement scale, it's right up there with watching paint dry. Venue deals with the actual location where a particular suit is brought. It's a game attorneys play during litigation to gain tactical advantage, but it's also dull, technical, and dry. It couldn't compare to the idea of going up against the entire gun manufacturing industry in a heated battle in the courtroom.

THE COURTROOM was packed and the back pews were lined with men and women in dark suits all clutching briefcases.

"Friday is motion day in Pierce County," Duke whispered as they made their way up the center aisle.

There were attorneys filling both sides of the pews, some reading their files, some taking last minute notes, and some just reading the newspaper. Duke waved to a few of the attorneys, who responded with forced, artificial smiles. There was a lot of jealousy in this room. After all, a lot of these people, at one time or another, had been on the losing side of one of his cases. The others were simply envious of Duke's winning streak. The adversarial system fosters a level of competitive spirit that rivals any professional sport. Attorneys are hired for one reason and one reason only, to win. They win or they don't practice very long, and Duke won a lot. They reached a standing table in front of the judge's bench where the court clerk sat.

"Hi Suzy," Duke said cordially. She rotated a white sign-in sheet toward him.

"I see you brought help with you on this one." She smiled at Gavin. "It must be a big motion."

"Yep. I wouldn't want to lose it." Duke signed his name.

"Well, you'll find out soon enough. It looks like you're first up on the docket this morning."

"Excellent." He turned to Gavin to introduce him. "This is Mr. Brady, a new associate in our firm."

Gavin quickly reached out his hand toward Suzy.

"He'll be arguing the motion today." Duke's eyes locked on to his young protégé.

Gavin pulled his hand back, and looked at Duke waiting for the punch line.

"A good trial attorney thinks on his feet," Duke said turning to Gavin. "You might as well start today." He winked at Suzy as if they were in on the same inside joke, and then walked back toward the pews.

Gavin was right on his heels. "Are you kidding me? I can't argue this."

"You read the briefing, right?"

"Yeah, but once, about ten minutes ago in the car."

"You know their arguments. You know our response. Look, tell me in one sentence why the other side wants to move this case to another venue. More importantly why they want it in Thurston County."

"The state capital is there."

"Exactly. Why is that important for them?"

Uh, the jury pool will more likely produce people with relatives or friends who work for the state."

"And —"

"They would be less likely to award a large verdict for us when a state agency is a defendant."

"So, what's our response?"

"Uh, what's our response. Uh, there's been a lot of publicity about this case in the local paper down there, and both sides have thrown a lot of mud back and forth. Plus, we're only thirty-five miles away so the witnesses wouldn't be unduly prejudiced by litigating here versus there."

"There you go. Now listen to their argument, remember our response, and go fight for your client."

"All rise," the clerk announced. "The honorable Judge Thurenberg presiding." Gavin could hear his heart pounding in his chest. He could feel sweat forming on his palms. He looked around to see if anyone else heard it echoing in the room. The judge called the first case. Duke nudged Gavin to stand up.

"Are the parties ready?"

Across the aisle, a gentleman stood up. "The defense is ready to proceed, your honor."

"Mr. Stewart, are you ready to proceed?"

Duke nudged Gavin again. He slowly rose to his feet. "The plaintiffs are ready, your honor," he said with a pubescent crackle. He meekly stepped forward next to opposing counsel, opened Duke's motion notebook, and took out a notepad. He could feel a slight nervous tremor in his hand as he removed the cap from his pen. *Breathe,* he thought. He took a deep breath and visualized the long road that he ran each night. He began to silently count his breaths. •

There was a THUD. Gavin looked down. His pen had slipped out of his hand and hit the table. The sound pierced Gavin's fog. He began to feel himself regain control. His opponent had already begun to argue. *Hopefully, he didn't hear the pen drop.* It sounded like it reverberated throughout the courtroom. The rush of energy focused his attention on his opponent's words. He grabbed his pen and feverishly wrote notes and counterpoints. Soon, he would be standing in front of a real judge before his peers and advocating for his client. As his opponent wrapped up his argument, he took a deep breath. His moment had arrived.

"Counsel," the judge interjected, still focusing his attention on Gavin's opponent. "It seems to me that you're not disputing the fact that Pierce County is a permissible venue."

"Well, your honor, the, uh, truth is, technically Pierce County is one of many permissible venues, but that doesn't mean —"

"I know," the judge said. "I know it's more convenient for your clients to be somewhere else, right?"

Defense counsel was silent for a moment. "Well, your honor, like I said before."

"Yes, I've heard the arguments and I think both sides' briefing illuminates the issues in your motion. I'm not convinced that it would best serve the interests of justice to move this case out of the county." He turned to Gavin. "Do you have anything to add, counsel before I make my ruling?"

Gavin stood there looking at his notes. Of course, he had things to say. He had several pages of things to say. It was his turn, his moment. But had he heard the judge correctly? Was he about to rule in his favor?

"Counsel," the judge reiterated. "Do you have anything to add before I make my ruling?"

Was he kidding? He was finally standing in a courtroom with a captive audience and Duke was one of them. He looked around, took a deep breath and, with a disappointed sigh, finally threw in the towel. "No, your honor, nothing."

"Then the motion is denied and the case will remain in my court." The judge banged his gavel and called for the next case.

Gavin turned around, vanquished by the judge's expedited decision in his favor and walked back to his seat next to Duke. His moment of glory had come and gone without a single word from his mouth. His eloquent arguments sat there voiceless, silently staring back at him. They were just words now on a page, arguments that would never live.

"Good job. You won." Duke's victorious smile seemed almost inappropriate.

"I didn't say anything."

"You thought on your feet."

"But I didn't. He had already made up his mind."

"And you didn't say anything that might have ruined it. You knew he was about to rule in your favor, and you chose not to give him the opportunity to change his mind. Sometimes the winner is the one who knows when to shut up."

He was right. He had sensed it when the judge turned to him, and his instincts were right. Gavin felt better about his performance. He silently played out the arguments he would have made in his head as they walked back to the parking lot. The only person who would ever hear it out loud would be Hannah that evening when she would be forced to endure the unabridged version of his brilliant counter-arguments.

"You know, Duke, that guy was pretty lucky I didn't get a chance to speak," Gavin quipped as they reached Duke's car.

"So is our client," Duke quipped back with a smirk.

GAVIN DIDN'T REALIZE the significance of the day's events until seven that evening when he finally took a break to forage for food in the break room vending machine. When he and Duke returned to the office, Gavin was immediately whisked away to his afternoon bar review; a three-hour tutorial on the ins and outs of the uniform commercial code. An area of law governing commercial transactions, transfer of funds, commercial paper, bank deposits and a variety of other corporate transactions. In other words, money law.

The tutorial was given by one of the firm's transactional partners, Walter Pendleman, who had a unique talent of not only being able to recall statutes and codes verbatim, but also of extinguishing any latent sparkle of excitement that corporate finance might have to offer. He lacked the presence of a "Duke" with his monotone voice and absence of gesticulation of any kind while he spoke.

Walter took a similar track to Gavin's old nemesis, Seth. After graduating summa cum laude from Tulane, he clerked for two years for Justice Kellogg, a maverick jurist, in the Fifth Circuit Court of Appeals. Justice Kellogg was, simply put, hubris gone amuck. He was infamous for his brazen opinions and his clerks always got noticed. There was a rumor that, at one point, some unnamed politician started a drive to have him impeached after he wrote in one of his opinions, *"Our higher court seems to forget that not only do two wrongs not make a right, but they, instead, create destructive precedent that oozes into the fabric of reason resulting in legal genocide."* The Supreme Court was not amused and agreed to hear the case for the sole purpose of reversing him in what became the fastest appeal in federal history. However, Judge Kellogg was already a legend and a favorite amongst lawyers who loved to plagiarize his pithy quotes in their legal briefs. It would take more than a few embarrassing reversals to knock him off the bench.

Walter certainly did not possess Kellogg's flamboyance, but he, nonetheless, clerked for the most notable judge in the Fifth Circuit. For Walter, the law was not about presentation or dramatic license, rather it was driven purely by economics. Presumably, that was the reason that banking transactions and securities appealed to him.

Three hours of Cliff's Notes on the highpoints of subrogated interests in secured transactions, and then Gavin was shuttled to his office to digest the material and memorize it before the next day's lecture. By seven, his stomach was telling him to take a break.

The vending machine didn't offer much in the way of nutrition. He pushed the button for a candy bar, grabbed a fresh cup of coffee, and headed back to his office. The banker boxes were still sitting next to the desk, tempting him to take a peek. This was the first assignment that Duke gave a brand new associate in years and the buzz was already flying around the office. No one could believe that Duke allowed someone else to speak in court. Most of the secretarial staff congratulated him on his victory that day. Gavin didn't have the heart to tell them that he never uttered a word. He just thanked them, and pretended to be embarrassed. He actually felt a little uncomfortable. He hadn't really done anything.

Gavin turned his attention to the boxes and the secrets that lay hidden within the folders. The anticipation was killing him. He knew he had another hour to digest the inner workings of today's lecture and then he could start reviewing the file. He would start tonight so he could sort through the material and map out a schedule to save time this weekend. He picked up the phone and called his wife to tell her he'd be late, very late. He knew she'd be disappointed but he hoped she would understand. They'd met at Notre Dame where she had been a graduate student, and she'd been with him during exam week when he lived at the library. Besides, what could he do about it? This was the profession.

CHAPTER 3

THE ALARM SCREECHED like a dying animal as Gavin turned his head into his pillow to muffle the sound.

"Turn it off." Hannah was not amused.

Gavin flicked off the alarm and sat up in bed to stretch. He hadn't slept very well. The new case Duke gave him to review was still spinning around in his head. He had stayed at the firm until about two in the morning outlining the facts for future review. On the way home, he hardly noticed the police officer, who followed him through downtown mistaking him for one of the last call crowd. He found a note from Hannah on the table that directed him to a plastic bowl full of spaghetti in the fridge. He ate a few cold bites out of the bowl and then headed to bed, setting his alarm for five.

Hannah rolled over and yawned.

"Go back to sleep," Gavin said as he gently stroked her hair.

"I'm awake now. Besides I haven't seen you for awhile. I don't want to sleep through your visits home."

"I'm sorry."

She was right. Beginning in the last semester of law school, he had become increasingly scarce. On top of his classes, he was also the undergraduate debate team coach. In college, Gavin honed his skills as an orator by competing in debate. It was one of the activities that solidified his decision to go to law school, and coaching help defray some of the high costs of tuition. This meant juggling long evenings in the law library with the preparation for weekend debate practices with the team. The time he spent away bothered Hannah but she rarely complained. She was a professional herself and knew the demands of a competitive career. However, her schedule as a Psychology professor was more of a nine to five. He always promised her that it would get better once he established himself.

Gavin stroked her hair again. "Want some breakfast?"

"In bed?"

"It'll have to be. We don't have a table yet." He jumped out of bed. "Come on, I'll make the pancakes if you start the coffee."

"It's not breakfast in bed if I have to help make it." It took some cajoling, but she finally pulled herself into the kitchen.

Saturdays were always their time, the day to relax with each other and share the events of the past week. The smell of coffee blended perfectly with the sweet aroma of hot fresh blueberries singing in their own juices as the pancake batter coagulated around them in the hot griddle. Gavin flipped the last fruit-filled doughy frisbee onto a large steamy stack of freshly made pancakes and headed back upstairs. The coffee was already brewed and waiting for his arrival in a thermos by the bed. Hannah had tucked herself back under the covers.

"My lady," Gavin said presenting the morning platter.

Without delay, the coffee was poured, and they immediately began to eat. Gavin devoured his food as if it were his first meal in months.

"So, you start," Hannah said, "tell me about your week."

"I thought you'd never ask."

He began by telling her about his office and the other associates in the firm. He talked about the in-firm gossip and how his training was going. Finally, he steered the conversation to Duke, and how he had been chosen to accompany him to court to stand before the entire room to perform what would have been his first oral argument. He acted out his rebuttal argument complete with hand gestures and anticipated questions by the judge. He even stood in front of her for effect. Hannah lay in bed enthralled at Gavin's retelling. She seemed to love listening to him. She always told him that his passion was contagious, and one day he would do something great.

"And I got a new case."

"What do you mean? Already?"

He explained the banker boxes to her and what Duke said about immersing himself in the case. "I have to go back today."

"What?" The words hit her like a bullet. "Today is Saturday. At least tell me what the case is about." Her face softened.

"It's complicated." He refilled her coffee cup. "Or at least it's complicated to understand all of what's going on. I just started my initial review so I'm a little fuzzy on the facts."

That wasn't entirely true. Gavin had spent several hours last night taking copious notes and had most of the information already memorized. He loved reciting cases and class details to Hannah, because it gave him the chance to explore what he actually knew and had retained. He took a sip of coffee for momentum. "It's like a case within a case. It starts with this seventeen-year-old girl who was shot to death in some type of drive-by." He outlined the tragic events that began as an innocent drive home from a party, and ended with an unexplained shot that left Sara Harrington dead on the side of a dark, lonely road.

"Are you defending someone?"

"No. Apparently four Samoan gang members pulled up behind her car and shot into it."

"Samoan gang members?"

"Yeah."

"Samoa has gangs?"

"I guess they do." That was a good question. Gavin couldn't think of one country that didn't have gangs. Why wouldn't Samoa? "They had been drinking and smoking pot pretty heavily earlier that evening and were on their way to drop someone home."

"The girl who got shot?"

"No, she was just some honor student driving with some friends."

"Just?" Hannah snorted. She loved to point out the contradictions in Gavin's idealism every chance she got.

"You're right. There were four people in her car. On the way home, the gang members came up behind them in a silver or gray car, and began taunting them by tailgating them and flashing their headlights. Then they passed her car and waited for them at a stop sign. When Sara's car pulled up to the sign, the driver told police that he heard a gunshot as he turned right. A nine-millimeter bullet went through the backseat and into Sara's back. It ripped apart her aorta and most of her small intestine."

"Oh my God."

"I'm sorry. Today's our Saturday, not the day to tell you this."

"No, it's just so awful."

It was awful. Gavin was so busy trying to memorize facts and organize his review schedule that he forgot to actually listen to what he was reading. He saw the painful expression on his wife's face. For a brief moment, he allowed his senses to feel the tragic horror of Sara's death. His heart beat slightly faster as he imagined what she might have been doing that evening or what she was thinking about just before she felt the searing heat tearing through the small of her back and ripping apart her internal organs. Then he shook his head. *An attorney must maintain objective passion in his advocacy for his client.* This was the golden rule of trial work. Every one of his professors preached that attorneys cannot allow themselves to feel their client's pain, or their emotions will begin to govern their strategies and lead to hasty and rash decisions. Much like a physician, who objectifies the trauma patient while preparing to reattach a severed limb, the attorney must rise above the pain and emotions of the client in order to zealously advocate and counsel on the best course of action. Gavin could not allow himself to feel too much for Sara. Otherwise, he wouldn't be able to properly represent her memory.

"I'm sorry, keep going."

"No one in Sara's — this girl's — car saw any of the perpetrators. All they could tell police was that they thought they might have been Polynesian. The police got some early tips that led to the arrest of a known Samoan gang member, Tyler Tutuila. He confessed to the shooting and the other passengers in the car confirmed that he was the shooter."

"Well that's good."

"You would think. However, on the eve of opening statements, he changed his story. Then two of the others in the car changed their stories, and all of them turned the blame on the fourth guy in the backseat."

"Why'd they do that?"

"The driver of Sara's car, some guy named Casey, was initially interviewed on audio tape and told police that he knew Tyler. They played football on the same high school team, and he told the police that he couldn't have been the shooter. The police never bothered to transcribe the tape recording to the prosecutor's office until close to trial when Casey asked to review his statement. Once Tyler got wind of what Casey had said on tape, he recanted his confession. He told his attorney that he had confessed to protect one of his best friends, Marcus Kiuilani."

"The fourth guy in the car," Hannah said.

"Yes, his new story was that Marcus was actually in the front passenger seat where the bullet came from and that Tyler was in the back seat."

"So, he switched places with this Marcus person."

"Depending on whom you believe. I mean Marcus said that Tyler was the shooter, the other boys in the car changed their stories too, so everyone ended up pointing the finger at Marcus. It was enough to create reasonable doubt and Tyler was acquitted."

"So, he got away with it completely?"

"With the murder charge, yeah, pretty much. Double jeopardy set in, he can't be tried again."

"Wow. So, what's your case about?"

Gavin took a breath. "I'm not entirely sure. Duke wants me to research civil liability against the gun manufacturers, but, I don't know. I have some more reading to do." He wasn't sure if a gun had ever been found, and he knew Hannah would ask about it if he went into detail so he skipped over that part. He made a mental note to look for the recovery of the gun in the file.

"So, you represent, the parents of the murdered girl?"

"Well, we don't represent anyone yet, but yes. If and when we decide to take the case, the parents would be the clients." He smiled as he answered. He liked the fact that he was actually in a position to recommend whether his firm would take a case.

"What are they like, the parents?"

Gavin looked at her for a moment. "Truthfully, I don't know. They live in Virginia." He hadn't given them much thought. "Their daughter was out here looking at colleges."

"That's terrible, Gavin."

"Yeah, I guess."

He wrapped up his story, and asked her about her week. Hannah's week hadn't ended the same way as Gavin's, but she, nonetheless, obliged with a recount of her activities. They talked and caught up for a couple of hours over lukewarm coffee. Gavin tried to concentrate on the morning but he couldn't stop thinking about that gun. Where was the gun?

CHAPTER 4

THE DOORS TO the tiny church opened as if breaking a tight seal to the cool breeze outside. Two hours of prayer and rhythmic Polynesian gospel had given the inside air a weighted density. The final "Amen" rang out announcing the end of services and the beginning of the feast. The children and some of the men awoke from their heat-induced slumber just as the congregation rose a final time to rhythmically sway to a quartet of ukuleles playing in harmony with the church organ.

The children were already running around the legs of the adults, who were now standing together behind the pews in fellowship. The bronze-skinned women were chatting. The men huddled together along the back wall socializing in a more reserved style. The chattering skillfully flowed between broken English and Samoan as the group relayed news from the homeland as well as the local community. The older generation spoke only Samoan to each other, and only switched to English in front of the children, who were not as well-versed in their parents' native tongue, having been born and raised in the United States. Most of the teenagers had American girlfriends or boyfriends, and were quickly slipping away from the traditions of their past. They were the generation stuck between two worlds, the world in which they grew up and the world of their parents and forefathers. The latter was quickly being chipped away and limited to family stories and traditional aigu meetings.

Samoan culture has always been organized around the concept of extended families. In Samoa, several families would band together as a group called an aigu, which was then headed by a chief, usually from the most powerful or influential family. As the families immigrated to the United States, the aigu concept helped to preserve their heritage and pride as a people. According to tradition, Samoa was the home and birthplace of the entire Polynesian race. Samoans cherished their role as the gatekeepers of their genesis, and their place in their aigu not only defined them as a people but also legitimized their existence as a family. There was nothing more important to a Samoan family than its place in the aigu.

This was disrupted as economic tensions forced many Samoan families to emigrate to other more industrial countries such as the United States. Mostly unskilled by American standards, proud and important families in Samoan culture were forced to take less-cherished and sometimes thankless jobs as janitors and delivery people. Although an insult to their heritage, a Samoan could tolerate working as a menial laborer to support his family as long as he could hold on to his rightful place in the aigu, which didn't judge him on his occupation or income. Church gatherings became even more important to preserve their dignity. Most aigus were inter-connected not only within the United States, but also had ties back to Samoa where the chief usually resided.

Outside the church, several groups were unfolding picnic tables and lining them with enough food to feed even the hungriest army. The smell of sweet and sour pork lingered in the air as large bowls and trays were brought out and set on the tables. The women and children began to align the food for better access as the mass moved toward the tables. In the background, Polynesian music played on a portable stereo. Normally, family gatherings occurred on Wednesday evenings. But occasionally, they threw in an extra one on a Sunday to keep the aigu traditions alive. The feast wasn't limited to specific aigu divisions, rather it was simply a convenient excuse to dance, eat, and swap stories about the islands. The food would last several hours, and no one would leave until it was all gone. A blend of pineapple and mango juice with sweet dark rum was placed in pitchers on each table and helped to deliver the initial courage to dance.

Kauni Tutuila looked around for his father. He had a worried look on his face. He had missed the services and wasn't necessarily interested in partaking in the aigu fellowship time. He needed to speak to his father. He quickly spotted him at one of the tables and made his way over to him.

"Father, I need to speak to you." He would never think about calling him Dad. They were a very close family, but Samoan culture required a level of courtesy that would preclude such informal terms.

"Talofa, my son." Talofa was the Samoan form of hello. "Where have you been all day? You know your mother worries when you don't show up to church. How do you think it looks?"

"I'm sorry. I have to speak to you."

"You will. First sit down and eat." Kauni's father had already consumed several grogs of the pineapple mango rum and wasn't in the mood for a serious conversation.

"I just spoke to the lawyer."

The conversation at the table dropped off immediately, and everyone became interested in Kauni's presence.

"Palolo, I thought that was over," one of the men at the table said to Kauni's father. The criminal trial had torn their community in half, and no one was eager to relive another legal battle.

Palolo took a large slug of spiced juice from his glass. "It is. Mind your business." He turned to his son. "Let's go get you a plate of food so you don't starve to death."

The two of them walked over to the buffet table, and Palolo began dishing out large portions of food onto his son's plate.

"Why do you come here talking this nonsense in front of everyone?"

"I know, I just got scared and the lawyer told me to let you know what's going on."

"What do you mean, what's going on? I thought that this was over."

"Apparently not."

"Well, what do you have to tell me?"

"Someone's re-dredging the sound looking for the gun."

Palolo's face twitched as his son finished his sentence. The police tried to locate a gun before the criminal trial and found nothing. His youngest son, Tyler, spent almost two years in jail awaiting trial, two years away from his family, two years of allowing himself to be falsely accused to protect a friend. That's what Tyler and his brother told him, that's what was said in court, and that's what a protective father wanted to believe.

"I thought they couldn't do that." He had a limited understanding of the American legal system, but he understood the concept of double jeopardy. No one could try his son again for murder. No one.

"It's not the prosecutor's office. The lawyer said that the girl's family hired someone to look for the gun."

THE SMELL OF freshly brewed coffee kept Gavin focused on his reading. He had successfully gone through all but one box on Saturday, and was hopeful that he could finish his review before the work week would officially begin again tomorrow. Thankfully,

Hannah was also busy preparing Monday's lecture, so he didn't feel like he was completely abandoning his family.

There were bits and pieces of the prosecutor's investigatory notes stuffed between many of the trial transcripts. These documents were normally privileged and confidential, not accessible to the public and certainly not accessible to civil attorneys, who were contemplating bringing a lawsuit. Someone must have inadvertently misplaced the notes in the stack of documents requested by his firm. It was a pretty big oversight, but not surprising to Gavin after he began reading the trial record. The trial had been riddled with oversights and missed opportunities. The prosecution allowed the defense to gain tactical advantage when Tyler Tutuila changed his story and blamed someone else for the shooting. It was a fatal move. They didn't contact any of the witnesses who could contradict his new version of events. They just sat back and played catch-up for the remainder of the trial. Gavin found himself playing Monday morning quarterback as he read each cross examination. He tabbed each of the prosecutor's notes accidentally provided to his office so he could easily find them later.

He pulled out the remaining seven manila folders and placed them on his desk. The labels were marked: *Investigation of Vehicle, Trial Exhibits-Defense, Trial Exhibits-Prosecution,* and *Jury Questionnaire.* He stopped when he reached the one marked, *Gun Search.* He opened it and pulled out a single sheet of paper. It was an invoice from an investigation company, D & A Investigations. Gavin recognized the name. Duke's desk was littered with invoices from D & A on other cases. The bill was for twenty-five hundred dollars to be paid on receipt for dredging a two-mile radius of the Thea Foss Waterway. He recognized that area. Flipping through the several legal pads of his notes, he found the section referencing the area. This was the same section of waterway where the boys initially claimed they ditched the gun after the shooting. He looked back at the bill. *To commence August 28th at 10 a.m.* That was today's date. It was already 3:30 in the afternoon. Gavin slammed the file shut and ran out of the office.

It didn't take him long to reach the right spot. The firm was only a few miles away, and on a Sunday afternoon there was little traffic. The waterway stretched for almost six miles along the Tacoma city coast, and was lined with a nice walking park and several restaurants. In recent years, it had become a haven for joggers and young professional couples out for a stroll. As Gavin drove toward the area marked on the invoice, he began to feel a little guilty. He and Hannah strolled along the same stretch of water while they were looking for a place to live. Now he was here again enjoying the view on a weekend without her. He pulled into a parking lot and saw Duke's BMW with a vanity plate that read, *Justice.*

Gavin made his way to the edge of the water. From a distance, he could see an entire crew of workers bobbing up and down in the sound. Two side-by-side boats were slowly motoring about ten yards apart in a series of straight lines. Between them, a tightly woven dredging net was being dragged along the bottom of the sound pulling up all kinds of marine life, empty beer cans, old shoes, and other discarded trash. A larger tugboat style vessel was docked off to the side. Gavin watched as the net was taken to the larger boat and hoisted up to the deck, spilling its contents onto a conveyer belt, where five men furiously sifted through it, immediately throwing overboard anything that seemed to put up a fight.

"I wasn't sure you'd make it." Duke's voice rose up from the water and surrounded Gavin. Duke was dressed in jeans and a polo shirt and walked from the shoreline to where Gavin was standing. "You're late."

"It was the last box."

"Have they found it yet?"

"No," Duke shrugged. "It's a shame too. This would have been a good case. She was a good plaintiff."

Gavin knew what he meant by "good plaintiff." It was sometimes called the dirty side of Plaintiffs' work, but was also the unfortunate reality of the legal system. In the civil justice system, people's worth is measured by the maximum amount of recovery possible in every case. It's not a simple matter of how much a human being is worth, it's how sympathetic you can make your client sound to the jury and how tragic the loss? Ultimately, juries must put a monetary figure on the emotional void caused by the injury or death. For example, jurors will not be as sympathetic to the tragedy of a known drug dealer with a long criminal history as they would be to the housewife with two kids. An elderly, retired woman who dies in a nursing home as a result of medical malpractice is worth less money than an upper middle class man killed in the prime of his earning years as the result of a physician's negligence.

Gavin had taken an entire class on damages in law school, the legal system's attempt to reconcile the need to categorize victims by their monetary worth with society's disdain for reducing justice to simple economics. Gavin could hear his old professor's arguments as he thought about Duke's comment. Sara was the perfect plaintiff. She was an honor student with everything going for her. She was a cheerleader from a solid family, and she was on her way to a bright successful future. She was a shining candle that was brutally extinguished with one stray bullet. The loss was immeasurable and easily worth eight figures.

"You thinking about dropping this?"

"It's not a matter of want to. It's a matter of economics."

There was that word again. "Economics? What about justice?" He didn't even realize that he said it out loud.

"Justice? Justice is a matter of perception. It depends on who we're trying this case against. Right now, all we got is a potential lawsuit that'll cost us minimum sixty grand against four boys with minimum wage jobs and no future prospects. That means the verdict is meaningless because we'll never collect a dime. Our clients don't get any money, and we don't get our fee and to top it all off, we're out sixty-thousand dollars. You call that justice? What we need is a deep pocket."

"They can't get away with this."

"I hear you. Sometimes justice is nothing more than being slapped by life in a way that makes us want to fight that much harder next time."

"But —"

"I know you want to help her. I want to help her. But we need the gun. You see those guys out there in the water? They cost money. Investigators cost money. The time you spend researching and working this case up for trial costs the firm money that could have been spent on other cases that actually pays. Someone's got to pay our costs. Without the gun, what do we really have?"

"We have a case against twenty-one gun manufacturers on a market share liability theory." Gavin had done his research.

"I'm glad you've at least started to get into the game." Duke's tone turned condescending. Gavin had been told about Duke's colder side but this was the first time he'd seen it. He had been eating and breathing this case for the last couple of days. More than that, he resented Duke's tone.

"I'm in the game. I've been researching gun liability, and we have a market share liability case. The forensic team had only been able to recover a partially mashed bullet from the crime scene that had first penetrated the back tail-light and ricocheted off the side of the vehicle before entering Sara's back. They were able to conclude that the bullet was most likely a nine-millimeter."

"An impressive start, but tell me the make and model."

"You're right. They couldn't narrow down the make and model of the gun used to fire it. However, they did narrow it down to twenty-one separate manufacturers that could have crafted the weapon."

"Including three models of World War II German Lugers." Duke had done his homework as well.

"It's been successful before." He blurted it out without thinking, but he was mad and on the ropes. "In the Southern District of New York, there is strong precedent for the proposition that, even absent the actual gun, a market share liability theory could apply to the potential gun manufacturers. Recovery would be based upon their share of the market. If we obtain a ten million dollar verdict and a particular gun manufacturer owns ten percent of the market for nine millimeter guns, then he would be responsible for ten percent of the verdict."

"Yes, but what you failed to consider is that twenty-one gun manufacturer defendants will come to the table armed with twenty-one different law firms, all making motions and conducting discovery all over the United States. Do you realize how expensive it would be to litigate a case against twenty-one separate law firms? It wouldn't be worth the recovery. We need the gun or there is no case unless you have a better idea."

Gavin was stunned at how easily his argument was shot apart. He hadn't thought it through.

"Do you have a better idea?" Duke wasn't letting him off the hook.

Gavin was already beaten down. He wasn't sure if his response would result in another verbal pummeling, but he had to say something. It was an idea that he thought of as he was reviewing the file late Saturday night or maybe early Sunday morning. "What about the parents?"

"What about the parents?"

"They have a homeowner's policy. They were negligent in letting their son drink at home and then go out driving, right? What did they think was gonna happen? Let's go after them."

CHAPTER 5

WHAT STARTED OUT as an upbeat day had ended with Gavin feeling confused and beaten down. He typed his password on the office computer trying to forget how hasty he was in believing that Duke and he were becoming friends. Gavin got a good taste of Duke's colder nature and wasn't anxious for seconds. He picked up the phone and checked his messages. He punched a button to bypass his greeting. He hated hearing the recorded version of his voice. Most of the partners had their secretaries create the greeting for them. It added an extra level of prestige and power when one's greeting came from an assistant. It would be a long time before Gavin was in that position.

There were two messages. The first consisted of ten seconds of dead air and the faint sound of music in the background before hanging up, probably a wrong number. The second was a message from Hannah telling him that she missed him and asking when he'd be home. He took a weary breath as he thought about how much work he still had ahead of him. He picked up the phone to call her.

"Hello."

"Hi, it's me. I just got your message."

"Oh good. I just wanted to let you know that I missed you and ask when you're coming home."

"I don't know. I have some research to do on this case." He didn't want to tell her about the disappointment at the pier or the conversation with Duke. "I'm sorry about this. I promise I'll make it up to you."

"I know you will. You do what you need to do and then come home to me. I miss you."

"I miss you too. I'll call you in a little while, I promise." He hung up the phone and sat back. Hannah was so understanding about the situation. It made him feel even worse for putting work ahead of his home life. She deserved to spend time with him. After all, he promised to be her partner for life. It was this case, he told himself, and soon it would get better.

Quickly, his mind turned to the gun. Duke's hired squad never found it even though they ended up spending all day dredging an area six times larger than where it was allegedly discarded. Truthfully, the whole dredging idea was a long shot and everyone knew it. The police searched the water two years earlier and found nothing. If those boys truly threw that gun off the pier that night, it was either already buried deep under years of shifting sandy muck, or it drifted with the currents to some cold and distant resting place under the water. Of course, that presupposed the shooters were actually telling the truth the first time when they admitted to throwing the gun into the water. Three of them had since changed their stories, and blamed the fourth occupant for the shooting while disavowing any knowledge of how he disposed of the gun. At any rate, the gun was lost, and Duke was becoming cooler on the case. He gave Gavin one last chance to find him some liability when Gavin mentioned the parents.

It was an intriguing idea and certainly not the easiest argument to make, but Gavin needed a break. He needed another *in* with Duke. Gavin clicked onto the online legal research site used by the firm, and began typing in his search terms, SOCIAL HOST, PARENTS, NEGLIGENCE, DANGEROUS PROCLIVITIES. He clicked another button and, almost instantly, a list of a hundred case names appeared on the screen, complete with summaries and bolded entries matching his search terms. He perused the list finding facts involving little kids beating each other up and minors sneaking alcohol at parties. Gavin made himself comfortable. He would be here all night.

MONDAY MORNING BEGAN punctually at 6:30 for the Stewart Meridiam & Smithwick partners with a weekly meeting on potential cases and an update from the Board of Directors on the firm's state of affairs. Larry Smithwick was usually the cause for the meeting to last until 8:45 a.m. even though it was fifteen minutes past the agreed upon cutoff. Larry was already well-established in commercial real estate transactions when he merged with the blossoming Stewart & Meridiam in the early Seventies. He brought his partners a whole new clientele of upscale corporate developers, and tossed aside the fledgling mom and pop businesses that had been responsible for the stability and steady growth in the Tacoma area. The recently merged partnership quickly embraced their fresh stream of revenue, which also allowed a young rising star by the name of Duke Stewart to properly fund his contingency fee cases.

Traditionally, the Monday partnership meetings were for the firm to get together and review the increasing cost advances on Duke's cases. Larry felt responsible for the sudden insurgence of capital into the firm, and he wanted a detailed accounting of each instance that money flowed out. Once Duke began hitting eight figure verdicts at trial though, the agenda focused more on how to build the practice and tighten the costs so named partners could keep more of the money and work fewer hours. Larry ran unsuccessfully for the state legislature twice and managed to make some valuable political connections. He also discovered a weakness for young blondes. As the firm grew exponentially in stature, Larry's discretion seemed to diminish in equal proportions. Many Monday meetings served as nothing more than strategizing sessions to defend against the series of Larry's sexual harassment suits. Attorneys fees and confidential settlement agreements kept the coffers relatively tight, and although the firm was stable and always in the black, everyone remained cognizant of the bottom line.

After a lengthy two hours, the partners were dismissed and left the conference room in true mob style leaving only the three named partners, Duke Stewart, Larry Smithwick, and Fred Meridiam in the room. They always stayed an extra thirty minutes to reflect and scrutinize how the meeting unfolded, and to discuss the junior partners as well as the upcoming associates.

"Today was painless for a change," Fred said. He was the straight-laced of the group. His father had made a fortune in copper smelting in the early nineteen hundreds until the environmental protection groups discovered that the plant was also polluting the South Sound waterways. Fred's family received an anonymous tip on the eve of an exposé investigation. They immediately sold the business for enough money to retire and became instant philanthropists in the community. He owed favors to no one and didn't care whom he offended.

"That's not what your wife said to me yesterday," Larry said with a grin.

"What's that supposed to mean?" Fred was as humorless as he was wealthy. He and Larry had been known to have some knock down drag out arguments in the past.

"Nothing. It doesn't mean anything except that Larry's being a pain in the ass," Duke replied.

"Yeah, that's right. I'm being a pain in the ass. All right, enough chit chat, let's get this over with. I got a late morning tee time."

"Who's got the list?" Duke asked this every time knowing full-well that Fred had already spent hours pouring over the list of current junior partners and associates.

"As you know," Fred began right on cue, "we've raised salaries more than sixty-five percent in the last three years."

"It's called inflation and the job market," Larry said.

Fred was used to ignoring Larry and continued. "However, we haven't seen a dramatic increase in productivity from them. With our monthly draws, we run a tight ship. I think we need to re-evaluate some of our decisions."

"The list Fred, let's just go over the list."

"I have to agree with Larry. We're a small boutique firm, not a sweatshop. Let's just get to the list and table this discussion for next week."

Fred flipped open a legal ledger with a list of all the current associates. One by one the three of them nit-picked each person's billable time, caseload, and overall attitude. The meeting lasted exactly thirty-seven minutes and, by the end, three associates had lines through their names, Monty Colbert, David Chesterman, and Raymond Kildeer.

Larry was already at the door by the time Fred finished marking through the third name. "Are we done finally? Fred, you should be happy, you just saved us almost nine hundred twenty thousand dollars in salaries and benefits."

He turned the knob as a knock came at the door. It was Gavin. "Who are you?" Larry asked.

"I'm sorry to barge in, Becky said it was okay if I—"

"Are you a lawyer?" Larry's tone was a mixture of impatience and condescension.

"Uhm, I just started."

"Well, you're off to a brilliant start." Larry arrogantly turned to his partners. "You ask this kid a straight question and he dances around the answer. Must be a litigator." He turned back to Gavin.

"Your name?"

"Gavin Brady, and you're right I am a litigator." Gavin recovered his cool quickly. He was quickly learning that hesitation and self-doubt were not what his bosses were looking for in a future partner.

Larry turned to the other two, who slightly shook their heads as if to convey that Gavin was not one of the crossed-out names on their list. Larry paid so little attention to the day-to-day operations that he had already forgotten the names of the three associates he had just voted to fire.

"Gavin here just won a rather large motion Friday on a case of mine," Duke said.

"Well that's always good news for our bottom line, eh, Freddy?" Fred sneered back at Larry.

"What can I do for you?" Duke said ignoring the two of them.

"Sorry to interrupt. I just wanted you to look this over for approval before I filed it." He handed him a pleading. Larry was already standing halfway out the door, and Fred was placing his papers back into their respective folders as he walked out. Duke studied the papers. It was a complaint and a rather thick one at that.

"You drafted a complaint? Steven and Louise Harrington, individually and as Personal Representatives of the Estate of their daughter, Sara Harrington. You got the parents and the girl's estate, good." He looked at the defendants. "I see you named the four shooters in the car, but who are Palolo and Mauuaua Tutuila? I can't even pronounce that name." He tried but had little success.

Gavin tried to correct him, but even his version was nothing more than a guess. "Mau-uu-ah-uu. It's Samoan. They're Tyler's parents. He's the shooter."

"I know him. At least our bad guy has an easy name."

"Not necessarily."

Duke looked at his partners. "Gentlemen, our young fledgling is about to regale us with jurisprudential brilliance. Mr. Brady, why don't you tell us what our theory of liability is?"

Gavin felt a little caught off guard. "Ultimately there's a market share liability case against twenty-one gun manufacturers. However, it's a tough and expensive case to bring, so to fund it, I thought we could first go after the parents of the shooter on a theory of negligent supervision."

"Negligent supervision."

"Yeah, they have a homeowner's insurance policy that covers negligent acts and has a policy limit of half-a-million-dollars."

Fred perked up whenever the discussion turned to large amounts of money.

"The best part of this is that it allows us to conduct discovery without the slew of attorneys that would otherwise be involved if we immediately named the gun manufacturers. By the time we turn our guns, so to speak, on them, we'll already be sitting in the driver's seat."

"I'm listening." Duke smiled. "And why would you hold the parents accountable for the actions of their almost grown child who committed a crime outside their presence?"

"Yes, I'd like to know the answer to that one as well," Larry said. He liked money, but he also had very conservative sensibilities, and holding parents liable for the acts of their kids threw up red flags in his mind.

Gavin took a short beat. "All of the boys were under eighteen at the time of the shooting. Tyler was still living at home even though he was starting college in the fall. According to the record, he still had his bedroom and hadn't put a deposit down on a dorm room yet. This was a wild party with illegal drugs that took place at their house, a party that took place right under their noses. In essence, the parents encouraged and even helped facilitate their behavior, and it was this behavior that directly led to the death of a young girl."

"Oh God, not another one." Larry put his hand on Duke's shoulder. He could see Duke's passion in Gavin's rhetoric. "As long as you get their forty percent. It was nice meeting you, Mr. Brady. Keep up the good work," he said disappearing down the hall.

Fred waved the legal pad with the list of names on it in the air as he, too, headed for the door. "Well, I'll take care of this and leave you two to the task at hand." He exited right behind Larry.

"Don't mind them. Anything that involves a disagreement scares the hell out of them." Duke seemed intrigued not only by the new theory, but that Gavin had handed him the complaint with the idea that it was on its way to being filed. Associates usually didn't take that type of initiative. Associates wrote memos and asked permission to go to the bathroom. Gavin had just handed him a complaint, and was asking for the firm's stamp of approval. "You weren't through, were you?"

"No."

"Good, give me the ten cent version."

"Okay. The night Sara was shot, Tyler had his friends over for a party — like a going away party before he left for college. They got drunk. They got high and then went out to cause damage on the community."

"The parents were home?"

"Not at first. They were at church, but then they came home while the party was going on and, yet, didn't do anything to control the

46

situation. There was alcohol and illegal drugs being consumed by underage kids who —"

"Not kids, known gang members." He held up the complaint and waved it. "Remember, you're a story teller now. You have to capture your audience."

"Underage gang members, exactly." Gavin made a mental note to substitute the language. He was trying to soak up every morsel of wisdom that poured from Duke's mouth. "Just as the bartender has a duty to not serve an obviously intoxicated patron who might foreseeably get in his automobile and cause an accident, Tyler's parents, as parents, had a duty to control their minor child. After all, they're in the best position to guard the public against any known dangerous proclivities."

Duke flipped through the complaint without actually reading any of the nine pages. He looked at the last page. The signature line listed both Duke's and Gavin's name underneath as the attorneys of record. Duke tapped the complaint with his hands. "Do we win?"

"I think we have some good —"

"No." Duke handed the complaint back. "I don't want it unless we win."

Gavin looked at him. Win? No, the case against the parents was tenuous at best. They couldn't even prove the illegal drugs without someone admitting to it under oath. It was all hearsay, based upon the police investigation materials, which consisted of written inadmissible statements that were not taken under oath and would never be put forth in front of a jury. Duke's expression was serious and to the point, and Gavin didn't want to disappoint him again. He swallowed hard before answering. "Yes, we win. You wanted liability, I got it for you." He held out the complaint again.

"Then, you sign it." Duke waited for Gavin's hand to collapse under the weight of his words. "Sign it, then file it. Welcome to the big leagues." Duke patted Gavin on the shoulder and left.

Gavin was speechless. He really was in the big leagues. He was also in over his head. His mind was racing. Had Duke just told him to sign a pleading and file a case? He envisioned second chairing his first trial alongside Duke, making masterful arguments before an enthralled jury. His clients would be seated behind him smiling at his brilliant speech. Then it hit him. They hadn't even signed up the clients yet. They didn't have a fee agreement. How could he file a complaint on behalf of a couple whom he'd never met and whom the firm did not yet represent? He turned back to call after Duke, but there was no sight of him. He ran down to Duke's office.

"Can I help you, Gavin?" Duke's secretary was typing up a rather large handwritten document. "I'm afraid you missed him. He always takes the day off after the partner meeting. You'll have to catch him tomorrow." She resumed her typing. Gavin looked back down at the complaint in his hand and thought about what Duke had told him, *you sign it, then file it.*

CHAPTER 6

THE PIERCE COUNTY Prosecutor's Office was teeming with activity, and there was no dearth of attorneys to work on the incoming cases. Jenny came barreling down the hallway clutching a case file. As a third-year deputy prosecutor, she already had five felony trials under her belt. She made her way up a flight of stairs and into Randy's front office.

Randy was the head Pierce County Prosecutor, an elected official whose sole purpose was to run the office and publicly put as many people behind bars as possible. Randy had never actually tried a case before, but his uncle was a successful trial attorney as was his great uncle. In fact, he came from a long line of trial attorneys in the area. Randy's real claim to fame was his last name, Bougainville. The name, itself, was synonymous with trial attorneys in the South Sound area of Washington. It seemed that every small town boasted at least one Bougainville district attorney or district court judge, and Randall Bougainville didn't care that he hadn't earned the reputation himself. He was a legacy and, like royalty, enjoyed the spoils of his lineage.

Randy may not have been a litigator, but he was an exceptionally savvy politician who knew how to capitalize on a moment. He had followed Pierce County politics since the first day he entered law school waiting for the right opportunity to run for office.

Immediately after graduation, Randy took a clerk position with the state supreme court, where he solidified many of his political connections. While other clerks were buried in the library, Randy was finding ways to get himself invited to legislative power lunches and talking with special interest lobbyists. He had his sights set on the Pierce County D.A.'s office because it was just small enough that it didn't matter whether he had any real experience and, yet, large enough to be a stepping stone into the judiciary. When his clerkship was completed, he elicited his family's support and applied for a position with the Pierce County Prosecutor's Office. His last name had not only secured him a spot as a deputy prosecutor, but a position in the felony division. Still, he spent more of his time seeking out the judges and promising his family's support in their reelection campaigns than he did lobbying to get in the courtroom.

Randy was climbing the political ladder quickly and it wasn't long before his real opportunity arose. The current district attorney just barely weathered a media storm after being accused of hiding documents in a discovery battle around the same time that Sara Harrington was shot and killed. Randy volunteered to do some case work for Frank Gilreath, who was the first chair on the case. The investigation and trial was covered by the media on a daily basis. The entire community was outraged and shocked when it was reported that four gang members had committed the murder. Gangs were not supposed to exist in Washington let alone Pierce County. Sara's parents campaigned for justice against the boys in their home state of Virginia and next door in Washington D.C. They made a national cry to the Northwest in the name of their slain daughter. The media loved the human interest angle and began covering the investigation. Almost nightly, cable news stations began asking, *how safe is Washington State for tourists?*

A nation held its breath when Tyler, after spending sixteen months in jail awaiting trial and after confessing to the shooting, reversed his confession along with two others in the car, and pointed the finger at the fourth occupant. The prosecution didn't have time to react. The truth is they never saw it coming. Only Randy was smart enough to keep his hands clean. He organized the case files for Frank, and then slipped away into the background. No one even remembered that he worked on the case.

Casey Goodman, who drove the car Sara was in, gave a taped statement to investigators at the hospital the early morning of the shooting. He stated that he was driving Paul, Katie, and Sara home when a car pulled up behind them. He brake-checked them because they were tailgating. The car swerved to the left, passed them, and then stopped at the stop light about fifty yards in front of them. He pulled up alongside the car to turn right and briefly looked at the passenger. All he could see was that the shadowy outline of a person; he couldn't really see his face because he was backlit by a street light. Then he made a statement that buried the prosecution. He stated that although he couldn't identify the passenger, he knew that it wasn't Tyler Tutuila. He knew Tyler. They went to the same school and played football together.

The taped statement was filed with the prosecutor's office and, then, misplaced. The prosecution wasn't even aware of its existence until Casey mentioned that he wanted to review his statement before testifying. Then the statement curiously resurfaced in the file. Once the defense heard about the tape, they screamed loudly in the media of prosecutorial misconduct and bad faith. It was after the tape was turned over that Tyler turned on the fourth occupant, Marcus Kiuilani. He stated that he had originally confessed in order to protect Marcus and to give him time to put his affairs in order. The other two passengers in the car changed their stories as well.

The entire trial became about Casey's original statement and it was enough to create reasonable doubt in the minds of the jurors. The outrage from the community swept over the district attorney's office with a fury. There was a short-lived internal investigation to figure out how the taped statement had disappeared, then reappeared. However, by that time the damage was done. Randy immediately called in his outstanding favors from his time at the state supreme court and announced his candidacy for the district attorney's office. He won by a landslide. Now, he was biding his time until a cushy state judge position opened up.

"Excuse me, is he in?" Jenny stopped at the secretary's desk outside Randy's office.

"Yes, but he's busy," a pretty middle-aged woman behind the desk responded. Jenny knew that wasn't true. Everyone in the office knew that wasn't true. Jenny didn't know what he did all day, but it wasn't anything that kept him busy.

"Please, it's very important. Tell him it's regarding Sara Harrington and the Tutuila murder trial."

The lady picked up the phone and whispered into the receiver. After a few muted sentences, she hung up the phone. Her tone seemed to change. "You can go right in."

Jenny stepped through the door and into the lair of the County Prosecutor's Office. It was exactly as she had imagined, deep mahogany wood shelving surrounding a cherry desk. The shelves contained new and old legal treatises likely never touched since Randy's predecessor left office almost two years earlier. Randy sat behind his desk leaning back in a brown leather chair like a county despot. The state and federal flags framed him on the back wall.

"Who are you again?"

"We've actually never met. I'm Jennifer — Jenny Garrett. I'm one of the — your assistant deputy prosecutors. It's nice to meet you finally." She was lying through her teeth but some type of introduction seemed appropriate. She walked over to the desk, held out her arm to shake Randy's hand. He barely leaned forward to accommodate her gesture.

"Well, Jenny Garrett, to what do I owe this honor?"

She pulled out some papers from the case file she was so closely guarding and tossed it on Randy's desk. The word "FILED" was stamped across the top.

"What is it?" He picked it up. "Complaint for Damages." Then he recognized the name. "Where did you get this?"

"It was filed this week. One of the clerks recognized the caption and gave me a call." Randy read Sara's name. It was the complaint that Gavin had drafted.

He seemed to shrug it off, trying not to show any emotions. "Well, good for the family, they're suing the bastards. I don't see our name in the list of defendants. Why bring it to me?"

"Sir, it's not so much the fact of the suit, it's some of the allegations. I think you should read them."

GAVIN NERVOUSLY TAPPED his pen on his desk. "Ring damn you, ring," he said as he skimmed over the stack of projects and potential case reviews from Duke. He was happy to get them, and the rumor around the firm was that Duke was grooming Gavin for partnership. Still, he couldn't keep his mind focused on anything but that phone. His intercom light lit up.

"Hello."

"Have you heard anything yet?" It was his secretary.

"No. I mean Hannah said she'd call when the mail came." Today was the day that the bar results were supposed to come out.

"Well, let me know if you hear anything."

Gavin hung up the phone and impatiently stared at it. Five hundred twenty-eight people sat two to a table lined up in a drafty auditorium furiously scribbling out legal answers for three days, eight hours a day — all for the opportunity and privilege to be one of the keepers of society's laws.

For Gavin, it was achievement of a passion that drove him to law school, a passion that drove him to moot court, and a passion that drove him to civil rights. He wanted to champion the rights of the unrepresented in society against those in power — those willing to step on the weak to maintain their own positions. He wanted to walk the same path as Atticus Finch and Clarence Darrow, giants who roared and battled in the courtroom as the gladiators of the oppressed, and who shaped our legal institution and our own beliefs toward a more humanistic and introspective viewpoint. The phone came alive as Gavin jumped to pick up the receiver.

"Hello."

"How's your day going?" Hannah said.

"Did it come?"

"What?"

"Don't be a shit."

"Oh, you mean the mail. Oh that, yeah, it came."

"Well?"

"I bet you'd like to know if you got a letter or not."

"Jesus! Yes, did it come?"

"Okay. Yes, you got a letter and it's from the Bar. Do you want me to open it?"

"Yes. No. I don't know, what do you think? Is it thick?"

"I'm opening it." He could hear the envelope tearing as she removed the contents. "You ready?"

"Yeah. Hold it." Gavin put the receiver on his chest and took a deep breath. "Okay, go ahead."

"Dear Mr. Brady, on behalf of the Washington State Bar Association, I am pleased to announce that you successfully passed all portions of the examination earning full rights and privileges as a counselor at law."

Gavin let out a yelp of excitement.

"Congratulations. I knew you'd pass. You want me to read the rest?"

"No, unless they change their mind somewhere in there."

"I think you're safe. I love you sweetheart. I'm gonna have a special licensed-attorneys only dinner for you when you get home."

"I look forward to it. Thanks for calling. I'll see you later." He hung up the phone and took another deep breath. Gavin was too restless to continue sitting so he strolled out into the hallway, which had been nick-named *associates row*. It was called that because all new associate offices were lined up along the same hallway so the partners could easily recognize them and, more importantly, easily find them from year to year. Gavin looked up and down the row. Four associates looked happy and relieved. One had a somber almost shocked expression on his face as his secretary tried to console him.

Gavin went back into his office and closed the door. He had a lot of work to do.

CHAPTER 7

THE NEXT FEW days were a blur. Now that Gavin was a full-fledged attorney at law, the firm began to get their money out of him. His nights at the firm grew in proportional length to his caseload. Whenever a partner wanted an issue researched, there was an available associate to oblige, and Gavin was no exception. He did, however, try to stick as close to Duke's docket as possible. Gavin looked up to Duke as a mentor. Duke was one of the wealthiest men in town, but, in Gavin's mind, the money was nothing more than a fortunate residual consequence of helping victims against a system that had grown too large to care about any one person.

Gavin sat at his desk reviewing a settlement agreement that a partner handed him earlier that morning when Susan came into his office. Susan was a senior associate with the firm and focused on health care law.

"Gavin, there's a gathering in the library to celebrate our associates passing the bar."

"Great." He started to get up as the phone rang.

"I'd leave it, that's what voicemail's for," she said.

Gavin wasn't used to ignoring a ringing phone, but Susan outranked him. As the phone clicked over to his voice mail, he disappeared out of his office following Susan down the hallway.

RANDY'S SECRETARY LED the last person into his office. Jenny stood next to the desk rocking back and forth nervously waiting to jump into her speech as Randy closed the door.

"Thanks for coming everyone." Randy turned and faced his audience.

Two men, Frank Gilreath and Harold Benoit, were seated on a leather sofa against the side wall. Frank was a senior deputy prosecuting attorney and was first chair at the Tutulia murder trial. He had taken a lot of grief from the media's attacks on the office. After Randy's election, he took pity on the defrocked prosecutor and re-secured his position in the office by becoming one of Randy's whipping boys. Harold, on the other hand, didn't owe anything to anyone. He was a retired police officer and now worked as an investigator in the office. Both men reeked of stale cigarette smoke masked only by the aroma of the coffee.

"We have an issue that Jenny has been looking into for me and I wanted to go over it with you. Jenny, why don't you begin?"

She glanced at Randy with disapproving eyes. "Thanks, Randy," she said biting her tongue. In his first sentence, Randy took full credit for all of her hard work. "As you know, our division does not concern itself with civil litigation."

"Only if our name is on the pleading as a defendant," Frank Gilreath piped in with his usual inappropriate one-liner. His subtlety and tact was outdone only by the mediocrity of his litigation skills.

"You're close. We all remember the Sara Harrington murder, don't we?"

Frank looked around quickly as if to head off any snide remarks. "What's that supposed to mean?" Frank stood up confronting Jenny. "What are you trying to infer here, Missy?"

"Missy? Excuse me?" Jenny thought about correcting Frank's grammar faux pas, but swallowed her disdain.

"All right people, let's calm down here," Randy said.

"No, Randy, this isn't right. I'd like to know what she meant by *don't we*? You said, 'we all remember the Harrington murder trial, *don't we*? Then you looked at me."

"No, I didn't, Frank," Jenny said.

"It's not like it was the first case we ever lost in this office. I don't have to take this crap from some junior case-pushing greenhorn. I want to know what she's inferring."

"Come on Frank —," Randy started, but Jenny cut him off.

"Greenhorn? First off, my name is Jennifer Garrett, not Missy."

"I know your name."

"Then try using it. Second, I wasn't 'inferring' anything, you were. I would have been 'implying' something — I 'imply,' you 'infer,' which I wasn't."

"That's enough, both of you!" Randy had a commanding voice when he needed it.

"Can I say something?" Harold Benoit stated in his trademark calm matter of fact voice. He had a no nonsense approach not only to his work, but to life in general. The police force had taught him that the world was black and white, right and wrong. People either committed crimes or they didn't commit them. The gray areas were for lawyers. He knew the Harrington investigation, and had been outspoken in the media, openly voicing his disdain and astonishment that twelve people could have been tricked by such a stupid defense strategy.

"Yes, Harold, what?"

"As much as I enjoy seeing Jenny rake Frank over the coals, I'm sure there was another point to this meeting."

"There was." Randy took the complaint from Jenny's hand. "Sit down, Frank, you too, Jenny. Outside the grammar police, no one's attacking anyone's legal skills or abilities here. We're all on the same team. Let's get back to the matter at hand." Frank grudgingly sat back down on the couch and Jenny leaned back up against the wall.

"I'm sorry," Frank said. "It's just I've been hearing about that damn case for a long time. It's just one case out of a thousand for Christ sake."

"Well, we're not here to discuss the trial, it's something else. Last week, a complaint was filed that caught the attention of an astute clerk who contacted our office." He waved the complaint in the air. "We're not here to rehash the criminal trial or point fingers at each other. It seems the Harrington family has brought a wrongful death suit against the four Samoan Gang members in the car."

"And the parents," Jenny said.

"I hope they named the jurors as well," Harold said.

"Does the complaint name our office?" Frank asked.

"No. It's not the suit. It's what's contained in the facts section." Randy pressed a button on his intercom. "Why don't you bring 'em in." Randy loved dramatic effect and used it every chance he got. The door opened and his secretary reentered with three copies of the complaint, which she then passed out to Harold, Frank, and Jenny.

"The reason I called this meeting is because of what is alleged on page four." Everyone turned the page right on Randy's cue. The moment was building just as Randy planned. "If you look down to paragraph six." Jenny watched Harold and Frank read the paragraph silently to see who would discover it first. She knew what it said and what it meant.

Harold flipped to the last page. "Who filed this?"

"A first-year associate at Stewart, Meridiam & Smithwick," Jenny answered. "His name's Gavin Brady. He's smart."

"Not this smart," Harold replied turning back to the page in question.

"Will someone clue me in because I don't get it?" Frank said.

"Am I correct that we never released this information to the public?" Harold asked still staring at the page.

As usual, Frank was the last to see the obvious. "Am I reading the same paragraph? It says that at approximately 10:45 in the evening, the defendants, along with a fifth occupant, Chillie Ki, stopped to purchase more beer at a local convenience store. After making the purchase, the defendants drove Chillie home before heading toward the area of — oh, my God. The fifth occupant."

"That's right and they named him," Randy said.

"What does that mean for us?" Frank asked turning toward Harold.

"Don't look at me. I didn't have anything to do with this or we wouldn't be sitting here right now trying to figure out how a bunch of civil attorneys found our mystery man."

"We spent months trying to figure out if there really was a fifth person in that car," Frank said resuming his defensive tone. "One clerk claimed that there were five boys in the car, but everyone else denied it. We should have busted that guy for selling them the beer to begin with."

"Frank." Randy tried to interrupt.

"It wasn't even an issue until their stories changed. I mean we had an air-tight confession. By that time, the Samoan community shut up tighter than a clam, plus the trial had already started."

Late in the investigation, the detectives received an anonymous call that the car involved in the shooting stopped off at a small convenience store that was known for selling cheap beer and wine to minors. It was a haven for teenagers on Friday nights. With a slight amount of pressure and a threat to tip off the state liquor control board, one of the clerks at the store came forward, and told the investigators that five boys were in the car that night instead of four. The clerk only recognized one of them, Chillie Ki, the mystery boy. He gave the information to the detectives in exchange for them looking the other way on the underage sale of beer charge. Frank's team made the search for the fifth boy a low priority. After all, they had a confession and a slam-dunk win. However, when their stories changed, placing Tyler in the back seat and Marcus in the front seat, Frank found himself in a situation where he couldn't prove who was actually in the front seat.

"It's okay, Frank. Like I said, we're not here to point fingers. We just want to know where they got their information."

"This is Duke Stewart's firm, right? He likes the limelight," Harold said.

"Déjà vu. Another public relations nightmare." Frank got up and started pacing the room.

"That's not going to happen," Randy said. "That's why we're having this meeting." The Tutulia trial secured his election, and he wasn't about to let it all unravel now.

"You want me to get the little bastard on the phone and ask him?" Frank continued to pace, working himself into a frenzy.

"No, we don't want to go looking for a fight here. I'll handle contacting him." Randy was a good talker. He managed to win a position as district attorney without ever stepping into a courtroom, and could handle this situation. "I just called his office and he wasn't in. I left him a message."

"Probably out playing golf already in that ivory tower."

"Didn't I overhear you just say that this Gavin Brady character was smart?" Harold asked Jenny. "So, you know him?" Harold didn't miss a trick. He was smart and a very good listener.

"Yeah, I met him during a moot court competition my third year in law school. He was acting as a witness for the team we were competing against in Chicago."

"Would he remember you?"

"Sure. Who could forget me?" She gave a sly smile.

"We got to shut this kid up." Frank was still pacing.

"What do you want us to do, put out a hit on him?" Harold joked. "You're an attorney, not a killer."

"I'm just saying."

Randy said, "Look, it's important that as we move forward on this, what's said in here, stays in here. This matter needs to be handled with kid gloves. I don't want to be talking to reporters on the way to my car over this case. Agreed?"

They all nodded.

"Good. Unfortunately, there's not much to do right now except be aware of the situation. I'll talk to this Gavin guy, and then we'll decide what to do with this new information. For now, go back to work and keep your ears open and mouths shut."

Harold got up and grabbed Frank's arm to avoid any last-minute confrontations with Jenny.

Jenny stopped at the door after Frank and Harold had left. She closed it and turned to Randy. "I think I should clarify a couple of things before we go any further."

CHAPTER 8

THE LIBRARY AT Stewart, Meridiam & Smithwick was nothing short of opulent. The entrance was adorned with a white Romanesque style archway, eight-foot mahogany French doors, and opened to reveal a gothic style vaulted ceiling suitable for any ivy league law school. Long, dark, wooden tables stretched across the center of the room dividing it in half. Around the circumference, stood towering bookshelves that spanned several lifetimes of legal history. Slender windows allowed light from the outside world to streak across the room. The whole spectacle was mainly for show now. The modern age of online research had made these books archaic and obsolete. The only hands that touched these pages anymore belonged to the old-timers, who were either too afraid or too obstinate to embrace modern technology.

Gavin was met by his fellow junior associates at the entrance of the library.

"Where's Alex?" Gavin asked. The last time he saw Alex was in the hallway the morning of the bar results and he didn't look happy.

"Didn't you hear?" Hunter said.

"No."

"They canned him. Just like that."

"It was not cool the way they did it." Another associate added his two cents.

"Come on. He failed the bar. This isn't a charity."

"They told him at lunch and by two o'clock, his office was bare."

Gavin liked Alex but he also agreed with Hunter. This is a competitive profession. The very basis of the adversarial system is that there must be winners, and there must be losers. His trial advocacy professor had always said that the goal of litigation is not to uncover the truth. The truth only lives in our hearts and can never be measured. Litigation is simply two sides zealously pulling against each other on behalf of their clients for the purpose of uncovering the best *version* of the truth. Alex knew this and as harsh as the consequences might be, it was reality.

The doors opened and the associates were led inside. The partners, all dressed in conservative dark suits, were inside scattered around the room. In the center of the table sat a food tower with several layers filled with fresh fish, oysters, shrimp, calamari, and various other types of seafood. Waiters in tuxes weaved in and out of the crowd passing out champagne flutes on silver trays. Duke, Larry, and Fred were standing together in front of the seafood tower, each holding a champagne flute looking over their minions. Larry waved one of the caterers over to him, and pointed toward the group that just entered. Duke picked up a spoon from the table and tapped his glass until he had everyone's attention.

A polite and respectful hush came over the room. Duke was known for his eloquent rhetoric that served to inspire and persuade his audience. He was as equally comfortable in front of a room of corporate CEOs as he was in front of a box of jurors, whose academic degrees came not from a university but from the school of hard knocks. Gavin, along with his classmates, looked over at Duke anticipating what he would say as they each grabbed some champagne.

"Thank you for coming," he began. "As we look out among our newest associates, we are reminded of our profession's great history and the tradition that connects and binds us with the past while gently steering us toward the future. From our very founding, lawyers such as Thomas Jefferson and James Madison have championed the nobility of our profession by literally forging a new nation whose strength is derived on being subject to it. Twenty-four lawyers signed the Declaration of Independence and forty signed the Constitution. It was a lawyer who held our nation together as a civil war was tearing at its very fabric, and it was a lawyer who stood against tyranny of the times and said, 'the only thing we have to fear is fear itself.'"

Duke took a step to his side to accentuate the moment. His face showed an introspective contemplation worthy of the weight of his message. Larry rolled his eyes. After years of practice together, he knew Duke's moves, and had heard variations of this same speech many times in the past. The room, however, was enthralled. They were right where Duke wanted them, in the palm of his hand. Larry sipped his champagne but was stopped by Fred's elbow in his shoulder. Duke continued.

"I wish you all a long and prosperous career." Duke raised his glass. "Be proud of what you do and be worthy of our past deeds." The light glistened off their raised crystal flutes casting golden rays across the room.

"What do you think of the digs?" Walter Pendleman came up to Gavin, who had made his way over to the seafood tower.

"Well, it's better than hamburger helper, I'll tell you that."

"And it goes better with the Dom Perignon."

Gavin scooped up a plate of food. "You can say that again."

"How's the workload? Have you found out that litigation isn't all it's cracked up to be?"

Gavin smiled as he popped a shrimp into his mouth. "Nope, I'm still investigating."

"You know, it's not idealism when you fight harder simply because you're getting a third of the cut."

"What?"

"Litigation." He eyeballed the room. "Do you see any idealistic warriors here? We don't help people because it feels good or it's our passion."

"Why do we help people then?"

"Simple, there's a lot of money in it. We're the privileged few that can truly turn the heat up when it gets chilly outside."

"Wow, I didn't know you had such a cynical view of your own profession."

"Gavin, I'm a transactional lawyer," he said gulping down his champagne. "It's not cynicism. It's not even apathy. It's envy. My curse may be the fact that I don't fear being complacent with a scheduled day to day work load, but I'll tell you one thing, I'll never have to compromise my morality for my paycheck."

Those words echoed inside Gavin's head as he contemplated Walter's inebriated philosophical insights. Gavin quickly shook it off as traitorous ramblings.

"Well you passed and that's all that matters," Walter said.

"I will say that I owe you a debt of gratitude for grilling securities into my head."

"It's all part of the package. Look around. There isn't a single partner here who failed the bar."

Gavin immediately thought of Alex, that look of despair on his face in the hallway, and his empty office. *No wonder,* Gavin thought to himself. Walther's remark seemed more like a callous comment than idle conversation.

"Hey, you're not trying to steal away my guys, are you?" Duke walked over with a newly replenished glass. "Enjoying the party?"

"Beats working for a living." Gavin was relieved that someone came along.

Walter grabbed a plate and quickly dumped some food on it. "Well, congratulations."

"Thanks," Gavin replied.

"And there's always a seat open over at the corporate table when you get tired of ruling the world." He winked at Duke and disappeared back into the crowd.

"That should tell you something right there," Duke said as he gulped down half his glass.

Gavin fought back a smile trying not to broadcast his agreement. He knew that he was not in a position to chide other partners' practices, even in jest. He took a sip of champagne to clear his expression.

"So, you like that Harrington case, huh? That was good work bringing in the parents."

Gavin smiled at the compliment. He knew that the boys in the car didn't have any money, and a judgment against them wouldn't be worth the paper it was written on. He also knew that a suit against the gun manufacturers required money, and the parents had a homeowner's insurance policy that covered negligent acts that occurred on their property. The way Gavin saw it, Tyler's parents were home when he and his friends got drunk and high in his room. Therefore, because the boys were in no shape to make rational decisions, the parents were negligent for not supervising the boys and ensuring that they didn't go out afterward and kill someone. The case law was not well developed on the issue because it was rarely pled in lawsuits. But without it, Duke would have already thrown in the towel.

"You want to run it?" Duke asked.

Gavin almost choked on his champagne. "You mean it?"

"Why not? You know the facts better than anyone else and it's time for you to earn your keep around here."

Gavin looked around first to make sure this wasn't a practical joke. "Absolutely. I think this is a great case."

"Now, I'm not looking for a homerun here. That was nice bringing in the parents so let's not lose sight of the ball. We settle with the insurance company and we get out."

"Whatever you say. What do you want me to do first?"

"I want you to tell me when the check is in the mail. Maybe I'm not making myself clear. This is your case, so go out and get it." Duke patted him on the back as if he were one of his fellow donors at a gala function. "Enjoy yourself today. Then get on a plane to Virginia and sign that couple up."

"Get on a plane?" Gavin gasped. "You want me to fly to Virginia?"

"Yeah, it's not Syria, though its proximity to D.C. politics may make it feel like it sometimes. Besides that's where our clients live."

"Can't I just fax it to them or mail them the agreement to save money?"

Duke smirked at his comment. The professor was about to impart some invaluable knowledge on his young naive pupil. "Yes, you could. You could do that and you'd save a little money, and it would be fine if you represented a faceless corporation or an insurance company. Phone calls work, faxes work. But our clients are not insurance companies. They have faces and stories — stories that ultimately must be played out in front of a jury." Gavin could feel chills running down his arm as he soaked up every word. "A jury that will never get a chance to know the case the way you do, and you will have one shot to give them your side. It has to be simple and straight-forward so that even a child could understand it. It's like a play. It's a live performance and you have to become its playwright and main actor. A good plaintiff's attorney burns his clients' expressions in his mind. He breathes in their whole tragic tale and then exudes it every time he exhales in litigation. The side that's not scared of trying the case in front of a jury is the side that controls the litigation and the settlement. Let the defense argue the law, you argue the tragedy and the law will follow you."

Gavin was nodding during Duke's diatribe. "You're right."

"Of course, I'm right. We need to know if these people are as good in person as they are on paper. Now tell Gladys to get you a ticket — coach — and bill it to the file."

"When do you want me to leave?"

"I'd sober up first, but sooner than later."

Gavin's face went flush at the horror of Duke thinking he was intoxicated in front of a partner. Duke gave him a reassuring smile, and grabbed two more glasses as a steward made his way past them.

"Tell Gladys to get you a deal. You can wait until tomorrow." He walked off leaving Gavin alone with a tower of dead fish and a thousand unanswered questions. The bubbles of the champagne slowly directed his attention upward to the magnificent bookcases that wallpapered the room like skyscrapers.

Despite the lack of use by the newer associates, the library had an unspoken enticement in its papered shelves. Among these walls, presidents fought with justices, states fought to solidify their own power, a nation was torn apart and rebuilt again, and a simple woman stood up and said, *I'm tired of moving to the back of the bus.* Such history was undeserved for any single eye. Yet, there it was, exposed and accessible to those few who had access to this room.

Gavin was now one of the elite. He felt like a child gripped in a loving parental embrace. He tried to block it out but his father kept popping into his head. His father must have spent time in this room while consulting with his client, the now Honorable William T. Hanson. He must have seen many rooms like this one and met many men like Judge Hanson and Duke Stewart. It was something they had in common and yet could never share. He looked around at the other associates. Many of them had not yet seen the inside of the courtroom. Gavin spent three years in classrooms with professors and students who did nothing more than simply distinguish facts and philosophize about the policy reasons behind each decision. They were destined to become spectators in the fight for justice. These walls held the names of those who were truly destined for greatness. Their names were listed at the beginning of each case and Gavin had tried to memorize all of them. For them, the law was not about stagnate rules. The law was about social justice, an elusive concept that would yield only to the fiercest challenge. The battle wasn't fought in books. It was fought on a daily basis in depositions and in the courtroom. Those shelves surrounding Gavin rewarded the maverick trial attorneys by proudly displaying their names as an introduction to each decision. Gavin imagined how it would feel to ultimately find his way inside one of those books for future desk warriors to ponder.

The party lasted another hour. Gavin, along with the other newer and more established attorneys, stumbled out of the library and dispersed down the halls to their respective offices. As Gavin reached his door, he could hear the elevator ding several times to haul people down to the lobby for an early retreat home. The afternoon was a bust. There was no way Gavin was going to get anything of substance completed after four or five glasses of champagne. He made his way over to his desk, and collapsed into his chair. The leather felt cold and helped to revive him.

"How was the party?" His secretary, Gladys, stuck her head into his doorway. She handled two partners along with Gavin, and was considered one of the senior secretaries in the firm. Gavin was not the first new associate she had worked for, and she was well accustomed to whipping them into shape.

"Great. Thanks." He was bursting with the news of his first case and desperately wanted to tell someone. He also needed to ask her to book him a flight to Virginia. *Where in Virginia?* He couldn't remember where they lived. He started to move toward his desk to look for the complaint.

"There's a message for you," Gladys said noticing that he was heading toward his phone. *Probably Hannah.* He couldn't wait to tell her about the news. "Let me know if you need anything." She smiled at him in a motherly fashion. "Congratulations." She disappeared back to her desk.

"Thanks," Gavin said, even though she was clearly out of ear-shot. He looked over at his phone and saw the message light blinking. He looked back at his in-box at the myriad of papers that were waiting for his immediate attention. Rubbing his eyes, he took several deep breaths to clear his mind and concentrate on not swaying back and forth. Nothing was of much help at the moment. The champagne bubbles were seeping through his brain, hindering his cognitive abilities. *I need some coffee.* He calibrated his movements thinking out each one before executing it as he made his way to the break room and back to his office. The steam from his cup was already making him more alert and focused.

HE SAT IN his chair and took several large sips of coffee allowing the steam to infiltrate his nostrils and wake him out of his libation-induced trance. The stack of papers from his in-box sat in front of him on his desk. He began thumbing through them making two piles, one for the sheets confirming service for each defendant and the other for notice of appearances and answers to the complaint. He counted five notices of appearance and five answers to the complaint. Five notices meant that there were five different law firms and five different attorneys on the other side. In addition, he saw that there was one pleading titled, *Motion to Dismiss.*

His thoughts were getting jumbled so he took another sip of coffee and tried to focus on the papers in front of him. The answers were typical, *Defendants deny all allegations in paragraph one and have insufficient knowledge at this time to admit or deny allegations in paragraphs two through six.* He opened a file drawer on the side of his desk and pulled out the complaint so he could reference what they were actually denying. On the first page, the parties were listed. Alexandria, he thought to himself. *I have to make reservations.*

He reached for his phone to call Gladys and get the ball rolling but then thought better of it. The coffee did a good job of sobering him up, but he didn't want to slur any of his words in front of his secretary. He took another sip and then practiced the phone call a few times before dialing her extension.

"Gladys, hi this is, uh Gavin."

"Yes, what can I do for you Mr. Brady?"

Gavin thought about the next sentence before answering. "Duke wants me to fly to Virginia. I mean to Alexandria, which is in Virginia." He shut his eyes and gulped down another swig of coffee.

"I'll get right on that. When would you like to go?"

"Tomorrow, if possible."

"And how long will you be staying?"

He hadn't thought of that. How long would he be staying? How long would it take to burn someone's tragedy into his mind? There was a pause on the phone as he contemplated this question.

"Are you still there?"

"Oh, yeah. I — don't — know how long. I'm just signing up a new client." He was holding his own in the conversation but just barely.

"Well, why don't I make it for the earliest flight out the next morning and you can fly stand by if you're done sooner. I'll go ahead and book your room as well."

"Thanks." She had already hung up the phone. Her efficient nature meant that certain niceties were unnecessary. *I'm going to Virginia tomorrow. I'd better call Hannah.*

As he reached for the receiver, he noticed the message light still blinking so he pressed it.

"Mr. Brady, this is Randy Bougainville over at the Prosecutors' Office." His voice had the slight tinge of a country lawyer. Gavin wondered how ironic it would be if Randy were from Virginia. "I'm holding a civil complaint that you filed on behalf of a Sara Harrington's estate against some Samoan boys and some of the allegations caught my interest. If you would, give me a call at your earliest convenience so we can discuss it. By the way, congratulations on passing the bar, I'm sure you'll make a fine addition to the profession."

The message clicked off without leaving a phone number. Gavin pressed the button again and listened to the message. What did he mean by congratulations on passing the bar? It was a subtle technique used by seasoned attorneys, a way of calling them out as a rookie and inexperienced. Maybe the prosecutor's office knew that he had filed a complaint on behalf of people he didn't represent yet. He thought for a moment and then shrugged off that last thought with his last swig of coffee. It would have to wait until he got back. He had to prepare to go to Virginia and had to sign up the Harringtons since the complaint was already filed . . . and he had to tell Hannah.

CHAPTER 9

"HOLD THE DOOR," Jenny called out as she made her way down the hallway toward two clerks, who were holding the elevator doors open for her. "Thanks," she said as she shifted a briefcase from one hand to the other and pressed the button for the basement. Jenny hated riding in elevators. It wasn't so much the uncomfortable silence, rather the idea that perfect strangers would choose to confine themselves together in such a small area only to pretend not to notice one another. It seemed ludicrous. Everyone huddled against the side walls looking up at the numbers blinking by each floor, trying to mentally make the car go faster. Jenny made eye contact with one of the clerks sharing the car just as he blinked and looked away. She looked up to see where they were. The car stopped on the second floor and both of the clerks got out. *Thank God.*

The elevator quickly dropped two more floors to the basement level. Jenny jumped out and headed down the dank and dimly lit hallway toward the room at the end. At the entrance, stood a security officer reading a newspaper. A plaque hung next to the doorway reading, *Pierce County Archives, Criminal Division.* She flashed her badge and the guard waved her through without even looking up.

Once inside, she made her way to a cubicle where an elderly robust looking gentleman was typing on a computer.

"Are you Gordon?"

The man looked up with a pleasant smile on his face. "Gordy, yes."

"Hi, Gordy. I'm Jenny Garrett, deputy prosecutor. I called earlier to look through the State v. Tutuila file."

"Right. That's Frank's case, isn't it?" Gordy continued typing.

"Well, it's the county's case, but Frank was the trial attorney on it." She detected a twinge of territorialism in his voice.

"Yeah, that's what I thought. I tried calling him, but he wasn't at his desk."

"Why would you do that?" Jenny was a smart prosecutor and knew that the "boys" protected each other. However, she had moved up the ranks pretty quickly, and wasn't afraid of taking on anyone who was offended by her gender.

"Well, I just thought he'd be coming down here with you."

"No. Randy Bougainville sent me." There was only one Randy in the building but she wanted to use his last name to punctuate that she had received her orders from the top. She didn't actually need Gordy's permission or his approval to view any file in the records room, but he made her mad and she wanted to watch him squirm.

Gordy fiddled with the keyboard without making eye contact. "Randy, huh? Must be important." He acted unconcerned.

"It is, but I can't really go into it. You understand," she said as if to flaunt her status in the hierarchy.

"I'm here." Jenny turned around and saw Harold Benoit in the doorway.

"What are you doing here?"

"I was told we were looking through the Tutuila file."

Jenny glared at Gordy who gave her an innocent shrug of his shoulders and continued typing.

"It's in the back room." He pointed behind him. "Second table to the left. I pulled everything out from the shelves. Looks like someone's been through 'em recently."

"I know," Harold said shaking his head as he walked past Gordy into the back room. Jenny continued her intense glare at Gordy, who was completely ignoring her at this point, and then joined Harold in the back room.

The files were spread out along the top of a folding table in red expandable folders. Some of them were labeled and some were blank.

"I see Frank's organizational skills are still up to par," Jenny remarked as she eyed the mess before them.

"So, what are we looking for?"

Jenny half-sneered at Harold. She never intended him to join her. Randy sent personally to sift through the file, and she didn't like the idea of someone else intruding on her turf. Harold was a good guy though, and she knew that he didn't want to be there anymore than she wanted him there. Jenny tried to bury her annoyance and pulled out a sheet of paper from her briefcase. "This." She showed the paper to Harold.

"This is a public records request."

"Yes, it is."

"I take it that this request and your presence here has something to do with our little meeting in Randy's office."

"You don't file a wrongful death case without first doing your homework." Every civil case that is filed must contain a good faith basis for the allegations in the complaint. Otherwise, an attorney might find himself in front of a judge answering some embarrassing questions and fighting off a potential disbarment proceeding. Jenny knew Gavin was smart and, more importantly, she knew that Gavin's firm wouldn't file a lawsuit without first doing some initial investigation.

"So, they did their homework."

"I want to know what we gave them." What Jenny really wanted to know is how they found out about Chillie Ki and the fact that he was the fifth occupant in the vehicle.

Harold skeptically eyed the stacks of files on the table. "How are we gonna do that unless you got a magic wand to figure out which documents were copied?"

"Actually, I do." Jenny smiled. "I'll show you how we figure this out."

Harold looked at her half-embarrassed half-insulted. After all, Harold had been a forensic detective for many years before retiring and moving to the investigations division of the prosecutor's office.

Jenny saw his look. "There's no reason you would know this. It's a little lawyer's trick we use in this office." She began thumbing through one of the expandable files as she spoke until she found what she was looking for. "You see, it's pretty common for civil actions to be filed after a criminal trial. In fact, we expect it and plaintiff's attorneys always want our files. Hell, why not? We already did most of the work for them."

"I'm following you so far."

"Not everything we produce is discoverable. Some of it's protected — like our notes and strategies. But plaintiff's attorneys are under the impression that they should get everything. Usually, it ends up in a fight in front of a judge. Sometimes we win, sometimes we lose and have to turn over more than we'd like. Several years ago, long before I got here, an attorney sued our office for hiding documents. We didn't know what we'd given and what we hadn't. Anyway, the file was turned over to a judge who found several key documents that he considered discoverable and had not been turned over. The press had a field day and our office became a target."

"I remember that, Orlich, right?"

"Yeah, something like that. Anyway, someone had a good media consultant because after the judge was through with his ruling, we had to turn over the entire file, all our notes and outlines and strategies for trial."

"That was a year or so before the Tutuila criminal trial."

"Weiss never recovered. Two scandals while he was manning the ship. Randy ran against Weiss that year and beat him by a landslide. Anyway, Randy's first order of business after taking office was revamping the way we turn over discovery, which, by the way, was a pretty good idea."

Jenny held up the sheet she pulled out of the file and turned it over for Harold's inspection. On the back was a stamp with several zeros followed by the numbers one, three, seven, and four.

"When our office gets a request from a civil attorney to turn over the files from a criminal trial, the entire file is secretly bate-stamped on the back of each sheet of paper. After that is done, an attorney in our office — usually the attorney involved in the case — goes through the file and determines which documents are privileged and which are discoverable. A privilege log is produced to reflect which documents are being held back so in case we're taken to court, we're not blind-sided again because we now know which documents we're dealing with. The plaintiff's attorney is none the wiser because the bate-stamp is on the back, he never pays any attention to it. Pretty smart, huh?"

"You saying that each paper is stamped on the back?"

"Each and every one." She pulled out a file from her briefcase and opened it. "This is the privilege log from the Tutuila murder file. These are the documents we held back. The rest we gave them. What I want to know is whether we held back the sections that named Chillie Ki. If we did, Gavin got his information from another source. Otherwise, it came from us."

"Doesn't someone go through this stuff first before we send it off?"

"Yeah." She held up the back page of the privilege log. It had Frank's signature on the bottom.

"Wonderful." Harold took a deep breath and grabbed one of the folders. "Let's get to it."

HANNAH AWOKE TWO hours ahead of Gavin and already had breakfast ready by the time his alarm went off. He hit the snooze button. The details of the night before were sparse, but he recalled that instead of responding with anger when he told Hannah he needed to go out of town, she hugged and congratulated him on his first professional trip. It was quite an honor to have bestowed upon a first-year associate.

When he told her, she immediately opened the good bottle of Merlot that they had been saving for a special occasion, and they toasted to their future. One glass quickly turned into two, and one bottle turned into a short trip to the grocery store to get another. He remembered lighting a fire in their sparsely decorated living room and lying in front of it with Hannah. He adjusted himself to sit up straight.

"It's five fifteen in the morning by the way," she said.

"Oh my God." It started to come back to him. He faintly remembered getting a message from his secretary early in the evening, something about an early flight.

Hannah sat the breakfast tray across his lap. "That's right. 'Oh my God' is what you'll be saying if you don't call when you arrive and when you get checked in your hotel. Now eat, we've got to get you to the airport." She shoved a piece of toast in his mouth. "You're already packed and ready. I packed your suit to change in at the hotel, and you have khakis and a polo for the flight out."

Now he remembered. He had a seven a.m. flight out of Seattle to Washington D.C. From there, he would take a rental car to Alexandria, Virginia, which was less than an hour away. He remembered that at the time, he was excited at the prospect of flying to the nation's capital, but, now, all he could think about was his throbbing head and how badly he wanted to sleep. The eggs and bacon helped to soothe the pain.

The ride to the airport was uneventful. Gavin kept the passenger window cracked so that the early morning breeze could hit his face. Neither he nor Hannah noticed the black Trans Am following them. It had been with them since they crossed the mile-long Narrows Bridge, but Hannah never saw it and Gavin was too busy trying not to concentrate on the movement of the car to notice.

Hannah pulled up to the front entrance directly across from the baggage claim to let him out. Although it was only six a.m., the police were already out patrolling the area; a solemn reminder of lost innocence and a new world era. The Trans Am pulled in one car behind them. The windows were tinted, making it impossible to see anything beyond one's own reflection in the glass. Gavin got out of the car and met Hannah in front of the trunk. Both doors on the Trans Am remained closed as it silently sat parked observing their every move.

"I'm very proud of you," she said as she brushed his sandy hair out of his face.

"I'm proud of me too. Now you won't forget me, will you?"

"I think I'll last twelve hours." She kissed him. "Just don't forget to come home to me."

Gavin looked at her in surprise. "Where else would I go?"

A cop knocked on the Trans Am's window signaling it to move on. It revved its engine briefly drawing Gavin and Hannah's attention to it before speeding off. Although it came uncomfortably close to them as it passed, neither of them noticed. Hannah stroked Gavin's cheek as he picked up his suit bag.

"I'll miss you."

"I'll call you when I get there." He made his way into the airport and to the gate. The image of the Trans Am revving its engine popped into his head again as he checked in at the front ticket counter, but it was a fleeting thought, a normal occurrence for a busy airport.

The plane was on time and boarding occurred almost immediately after he got there. It was a four-and-a-half-hour flight to Washington D.C. and a three-hour difference in time, which meant that he would arrive at 2:30 in the afternoon. He was scheduled to meet with the Harrington family at five, which left just enough time to rent a car, get to his hotel, shower, and find their house.

After an uneventful flight, he checked in to his hotel at 3:45. The Harringtons didn't live far from his hotel. In fact, nothing in Alexandria was very far from his hotel. He stood in front of the mirror and straightened his jacket. His front pocket had something sticking out of it. He pulled it out to see that it was a card from Hannah. The front was simple, a road leading to the horizon. Inside it was blank, only a handwritten note that read, *the road home is only a phone call away, Love Hannah.*

Gavin was always amazed at how lucky he was. He gently caressed the words letting the emotions and intent behind them sink into his pores. He knew he had a few minutes before he had to leave so he picked up the phone and called Hannah. The conversation lasted only a few brief moments but it was enough to sustain him for the rest of the evening.

CHAPTER 10

Although the Harringtons were not far away, the drive over felt like it took an hour. Gavin wasn't exactly sure how to begin the conversation. They obviously knew he was coming. His secretary had called and made arrangements for the meeting. Maybe he wasn't ready for this. He took a deep breath as he made the final turn and pulled the car to the curb. At the end of the street sat the Harrington house with a solemn aura around it. Gavin slowly made his journey down the boulevard and pulled into the driveway.

There were no more chalked outlines of hop-scotch on the pavement, and the indents from the swing set in the front yard were already overgrown with newly planted grass buds. The house's red brick exterior was a brave façade of security and permanence. An oak tree stood in the middle of the front yard swaying in the breeze, each turning leaf carrying the silent cries for an era now long past. Everything else was slowly being erased by time. Although the lawn was neatly manicured, the work that went into it was no longer out of love, rather out of inertia. The neighboring houses all seemed to stand around the street half-turned in pity and disbelief of the tragedy that had befallen their friend.

Gavin grabbed his briefcase and went to the front door. Before he was able to knock, it opened.

"Hello, you must be Mr. Brady." The woman at the door was in her late forties but bore a remarkable resemblance to Sara. It was something that Gavin hadn't counted on, and it took him by surprise.

"Yes," he said trying to gather his composure. "Are you Mrs. Harrington?"

"Louise. Please come in." Her smile was warm and inviting. It was exactly the way he had imagined Sara. He began to relax a bit as he stepped across the threshold of the door. She led him into the family room. The walls were littered with framed photos of their family, frozen moments in time. There were shots of three girls smiling together on a swing set. Gavin recognized Sara immediately. She was a toothy, blond, little girl who dominated each photo with her smile. "My husband's in the study, would you like some coffee?"

"Coffee would be great, thank you." Gavin had been taught early by his father that you should always accept any opportunity to break bread with a potential client. It builds a bond, and chips away at the business aspect of the conversation.

Louise disappeared leaving Gavin surrounded by the pictorial past of the Harrington family. As he looked around him, there seemed to be an order about the arrangement of each picture as if someone had taken the time to chronicle their time on earth. A television was mounted on one wall and a sectional sofa against another. Everything looked lived in and cozy. His mind turned to the last thing that he read in the case file, the medical examiner's report. The bullet had ripped through Sara's abdomen nicking the small intestine before exiting her body. She had lost control of her bodily functions due to the shock and trauma. The doctor conducting the examination noted that her underwear showed evidence of defecation. That was her last act before leaving the earth. It was something Gavin regretted knowing as he looked around the room. The photos seemed to cry out to him. There were dreams and hopes on these walls, frozen glimpses into the private world of a happy family before it had been reduced to a medical examiner's report and police statements.

She died alone in a hospital room while her family helplessly sat on a plane, rushing to comfort their daughter. They were one hour too late. He knew intimate details about the horror of her death, details that her family would likely never know. Gavin felt the weight of the room. He didn't want to know such horrific things about this beautiful little girl swinging in her front yard with her sisters. He felt like an intruder. He thought of his father and what his last minutes must have been like. Alone in a room desperately hanging on to each fleeting moment, hoping someone would come and take away his pain.

The coffee cups clanked together as Louise and her husband made their way into the room. Gavin felt a cool tear on his cheek, which he quickly wiped away before turning around.

"I hope you found us okay." The father's deep voice demanded respect. "I'm Steve." His handshake was firm.

"Nice to meet you, Gavin Brady."

"How long have you been with the firm?" Steve asked as he passed Gavin his cup.

"Since Spring."

"How long have you been a lawyer?"

Gavin paused for a moment. He wasn't sure how to answer that question. How could he instill confidence in his abilities when they were still untested? He was there to ask them to put the life of their daughter's memory in his hands — hands that had yet to weather from the maturity of defeat and success.

"To be honest with you sir, this is my first case."

"Ours too."

"I know what you're thinking. This is a low priority case worthy only of a new associate. But that's not true. I wish I could tell you to trust me because I have a successful track record handling these matters. I can't. I can tell you that I work with Duke Stewart, and that he does have a successful track record handling such cases. The firm has dedicated its resources to effectuating justice for Sara, and the best I can do is tell you that I won't rest until that is accomplished."

"I appreciate your honesty. You know we hadn't heard from Duke or your firm for the past six months, and we didn't know what was going on."

"Well the investigation process can take some time."

"We contacted another attorney last month." Steve showed Gavin a retainer agreement. "We were all set to go with him too but then these showed up in the mail." He showed the complaint that Gavin had filed. Gavin's expression barely hid his surprise. His secretary must have sent copies to them as a matter of course without knowing that they hadn't yet signed them up as clients. Steve's tone grew serious. "Why'd you file this without consulting us first?"

Gavin put down his coffee cup and looked him straight in the eye. "That was a mistake I made. I should have consulted with you and I'm sorry." He wanted to tell them that he was under the impression that they were already clients of the firm. He wanted to say that it really wasn't his fault, but, in the end, it was his fault. He was the attorney, and he should have known the full story before moving forward.

"Why did you fly out here?"

"Pardon me?"

"We asked the other attorney to meet with us, but he didn't hop on a plane. He sent us this agreement instead. Virginia is a long way from Washington, Mr. Brady. We could have talked over the phone."

Gavin thought for a moment. "There's only so much I can learn from a file." This was the first time that he began to think about his clients as people and from the moment he stepped through their front door, he knew that he didn't know them at all. "Before today, Sara was nothing more than a stack of photos and investigative reports. I could have called you. It would've been cheaper, but I want to be your attorney, I do. I understand if you think I'm too inexperienced and, in your shoes, I might feel the same way. You see, I never knew your daughter. I need to breathe a life into my case and my legal arguments, and I thought that I needed to meet you in person to do that."

Steve's eyes began to well up. "A life into your case?"

"Yes, your daughter's life. I can only promise to work every day to bring some type of justice to your daughter."

"You promise? You want to know what promises I made when my daughter was born?" There was a short pause as Gavin's eyes were locked on his face in fear of what he might say. "Never to leave." Steve got up and left the room into the kitchen.

"It's still so hard for him. Excuse me." Louise followed her husband into the kitchen.

Gavin could see them consoling each other as they stood framed by the entryway of the other room. Steve was in the center of the kitchen with his back to the family room. Louise gently laid her hand on his shoulder.

"It's just that I can still feel her," he said fighting through the tears. "God, how I feel her still."

"I know. She's here with us."

"It's like she's embracing me with her spirit, trying to be strong for me. Oh my God I miss her." His body collapsed into his wife's embrace as if a thousand lifetimes of grief were pouring out of him. His heart that had once beat with such revitalizing pleasure and joy, could no longer find its cadence. It beat out of habit, aging with every blood cell that passed through its chambers. The two of them embraced each other as the rising moon from the kitchen window blanketed them with the beginnings of the evening's light. Gavin could see Steve's hands strain and turn white as he gripped his wife. His sobs echoed through her body rocking her up and down.

Gavin stood up not sure how to react. Before him, a proud stoic man lay totally exposed to the universe, beaten down by despair and tragedy. It was a pain that only a parent could know, a pain so powerful that language simply could not define it.

As the Harringtons tightly gripped each other, Gavin stood in the background empty and alone, witnessing the love of a daughter reaching beyond the grave to aid her grieving parents. He wished he knew how they felt and, yet, was glad that he couldn't fathom such pain. Still, part of him wanted to share the moment with them. He wanted to feel that Sara was smiling on him as well. He was fighting for a young woman whom he would never meet and would never feel her presence the same way they did.

His thoughts turned to his own father and the loneliness he must have felt before he died. He had never thought he might be somewhere smiling down on him, proud of his legacy. In his own way, he silently commiserated with the Harrington's pain of loss. However, the dead took no comfort in him. His own personal emptiness remained juxtaposed against the couple before him. Gavin couldn't stand it anymore. He didn't deserve to be there, and he was pretty sure that they were about to fire him before he was even hired. This was a mistake, he thought to himself. He wasn't ready for this and he knew it.

"I'm sorry Mr. and Mrs. Harrington. I know this is a bad time," he said as he picked up his briefcase and headed toward them. "I'll just let myself out."

"No wait." Steve stopped him. "She was a precious gift to our family."

"Yes, I can see that."

"She brought you to us," Steve said looking directly at him.

Gavin took a moment to reflect on Steve's words. "I'd like to think so."

"That's all I have left of my daughter are the memories of a life, my life. It's funny what you remember, fleeting moments that you never bother to put words to at the time, like walking down a hallway or a quick smile as she left a room. They were moments that I never knew would be so important. Sometimes that's all you're left with."

The tears began to well up in Gavin's eyes. "I'm so sorry for your loss." His legs were feeling heavy.

"You know, I can still sometimes smell her perfume in the hallway?" His eyes blankly reached through Gavin as if he were a window separating Steve from his memory. "It's true. Sometimes, I'll walk down toward the bathroom, and, as I pass her room, I swear that I can smell the lingering fragrance drifting from her dresser out her door." Steve's eyes welled up again. "I always turn to look. But it's just an empty room."

Gavin was unable to speak. He desperately wanted to run away. He wanted to convince himself that his father didn't sit in judgment upon him.

"Tell me Gavin, can you feel her presence now?"

Gavin's eyes could no longer shield his emotions. A single tear had already dried on his cheek leaving a salty trail down his face. He'd been fighting back the tears since he entered the house. He swallowed the growing lump in his throat. "No, but I can see that you do." It was the truth, and all he could do to retain some type of control. Maybe it was a residual effect of his hangover breaking down his resistance, or maybe it truly was Sara's spirit. Whatever it was, in that moment, he knew what Duke had meant when he told him that he needed to meet his clients in person. The Harringtons were now real and they brought Sara alive in their emotions. The pain was real, and the depth of their grief burned a hole through Gavin's chest. This was no longer a case, this was a quest.

They stood silent in the kitchen for awhile, then made their way back into the family room, where they began to talk about the case. Steve tore up the agreement from the other lawyer and officially hired Gavin. He had his first case and he would from here on exude their story.

JENNY AND HAROLD spent the after noon and into the evening sifting through papers. Each stamp was carefully compared to the privilege log to show which documents were held back when Gavin's firm made their public records request. Gordy had long since gone home and left the key with Harold to lock up.

"I don't see anything unusual here," he said.

"What about this?" She held up a handwritten investigative memo.

"What's the number on the back?"

"P,C,one, zero, zero, one, two, four."

Harold began flipping through the pages on the list. "I don't see it here."

Jenny was already reading the memo. "Son of a bitch," she mumbled to herself as she continued reading, "son of a bitch. You sure it's not on the list?"

"Suit yourself." He handed her the list. She began looking through it, not because she didn't trust Harold, but because she was a good attorney and not willing to take another's word when she could look for herself.

80

"Son of a bitch."

"So if it's not on the list, then we didn't hold it back, right?"

"That's right. That's how they got the name." She flipped to the third page of the memo. Two-thirds down the page was the name 'Chillie Ki' with a circle around it.

"We even circled it for them so they'd be sure to see it," Jenny added. "Wow. This looks like a memo that corroborates that Tyler was in the front seat. I wonder why Frank didn't use this at trial."

"Hey, doesn't this stuff get sent to you guys before it goes out?"

Jenny began to make a snide remark about Frank and his legal abilities, but thought better of it. Harold was no fan of Frank, but she knew that things had a way of getting back to people. Besides, there was something else in that memo that bothered her.

"I'm gonna make a quick copy of these before we leave."

"Can you do me a favor? Don't tell anyone about this for now."

"Hey, I'm just here for the good company. No sweat off my back."

"Thanks." She took the memo and slipped it in her briefcase along with the privilege log.

"What are you doing?"

"I'm going up front and make a copy of these."

"Why don't you just tab'em and have Gordy do it?"

That was the procedure. The records custodians didn't like outsiders handling the original files, and they developed a system that required all copy requests to be submitted to the custodian along with the requested pages neatly adorned with sticky notes. Within a few days, the copies would be routed to the attorney's desk by interoffice mail.

"He's already gone." Jenny hesitated at Harold's disapproving comment as if she'd just been caught by the hallway monitor smoking in the bathroom.

"Today. Isn't this how things get lost?"

"No, you're right." She gave in not wanting to raise any red flags. "I'll leave these pages flagged for Gordy to copy for me tomorrow. Besides, it feels good ordering the prick around a little. Can you put this mess back?"

Harold faked a smile. "Sure, why don't I just clean up after you."

"Thanks. I'll see you later." Jenny disappeared toward Gordy's desk to request copies to be routed to her office.

It was two days before she saw Randy again. Harold did keep silent about the discovery as promised. Randy's secretary led her into the office after waiting for fifteen minutes in front of his door. Randy enjoyed the air of importance that came with the position and took full advantage of it. He was finishing up a conversation when she walked in, and signaled for her to sit down. She was used to waiting for Randy. She smiled when she overheard the word "dry cleaning" just as he was hanging up the phone.

"I take it by your demeanor that you have some news," he said turning his full attention to her.

"Well, I'm pretty sure I know how they got Chillie Ki's name." She explained finding the memo leaving Harold's name out of it as he requested. Randy listened attentively.

"It looks as though we need to find this Chillie fellow before they do, doesn't it?" He seemed overly concerned.

Jenny was thrown off guard. "Well, certainly it wouldn't be the best thing for this office if it got out that we had the other occupant's name, but we're not involved in the civil suit."

"Let's not get ahead of ourselves here. This office had nothing to do with that debacle. My predecessor, the all mighty Weiss, dropped the ball on that one." Randy's demeanor became tense.

"You're right." Jenny was not in the mood to agitate him. He was a charmer, but had a reputation for also having a short fuse, and he was her boss. "I still don't know why we need to contact this Chillie person."

"Maybe, but we do need some damage control." Randy stood up and walked to the window. "Just like you said, if this gets out, no one's gonna care who was in office at the time. The fingers are all gonna be pointed here at me, at us." He turned to her as he finished his sentence wanting her to feel the impending danger as well.

There was some logic to what Randy was saying. The prosecutor's office did have some responsibility to maintain its integrity, and he was right about one thing. No one would care that it was a past administration's mistake.

"Who else knows about this?"

"You mean the complaint?"

"I know who knows about the Goddamn complaint." Jenny could see a vein beginning to pop out of Randy's forehead. "This memo, who else knows about this?"

Jenny began feeling uneasy again. It was the same feeling she had when she found that memo. There was something that bothered her about that memo and she couldn't figure it out. There was obviously something that was bothering Randy as well.

"Just you and me." She thought about mentioning Harold but Randy was scaring her, and she figured it would be better to leave him out of it for now.

"Good. Let's keep it that way." Randy was looking out the window again. "I want you to stay on it. We don't need to open a new file yet. Let's keep this between you and me for now, okay?"

"Absolutely, mum's the word."

"And you're probably right anyway about Chillie. We don't need to find him. What do we care about some silly civil law suit? As long as your friend, Mr. Brady, doesn't do something stupid like try and embarrass this office."

"Why would he?"

Randy faced her. "I don't know. I don't know this Gavin fella. But you do."

Now Jenny was feeling really uneasy. What did Randy mean by that comment? She told about her encounter with Gavin during a mock trial competition in Chicago. Gavin was in his senior year at Cornell and part of the undergraduate debating competition that was taking place at the same location. Jenny was in her second year of law school. After a lengthy cross examination during the first morning, he approached her to congratulate her on tearing the witness to shreds, and to arrogantly offer her some pointers on her cross. She thought he was self-centered at first, but he was very friendly and seemed genuinely interested in how she'd prepared for the trial. They talked over several beers that evening about law school and the competition. They debated public policy and laughed about the silliness of fake competitions. The next morning, they both woke up in her hotel room. Gavin didn't even look at her as he dashed out of the room. She never saw him again, and also never forgave him for his rude departure.

She really didn't know him very well. She didn't even know where he was originally from. She didn't really want to know anything else about him after he ran out of her room without even saying goodbye. He made her feel like some cheap one night stand.

She told Randy about meeting Gavin. She didn't care how it looked to him. She was a liberated woman who grew up with the knowledge that what was good enough for a man was also good enough for a woman.

"That was a long time ago. I knew him for about a day."

"You know he's married now?" Randy had done some checking of his own. He had connections and could find out information on people all over the country with just one phone call.

"No, I didn't."

"How do ya feel about that?"

Jenny began to see where this was going. "What do you mean, how do I feel? I'm not some cheerleader crying over being dumped by the captain of the football team, and I don't like being used as a trump card." Her anger was focused and sincere. She wasn't about to give Gavin or any man all her power by playing the woman scorned. She was stronger than that. Besides, he hadn't hurt her. They barely knew each other. She forgot all about him until she saw his name on the complaint.

"Take it easy, Jenny. You have a bright future here. You're no one's trump card, but let's face it, you're smart, ambitious, and you know this Gavin Brady better than I do — and I need your help. I want you to stay on this case. Who knows, it might be a nice stepping stone."

Randy knew exactly what to say. She was ambitious and this wasn't the first time it occurred to her that her involvement in this matter might lead to bigger and better legal opportunities in the office.

The two of them continued to talk for a while about the criminal trial and Frank's mistakes. Jenny never produced the memo, and Randy never asked to see it. She did find it odd that he appeared to know all about it. As far as she knew, he had never seen it. It was created before he took office, and the file remained in storage since the acquittal. At the end of the meeting, Randy assigned her unofficially and privately to the case. She left the office with the same uneasy feeling. Everything revolved around that memo.

She headed back to her department to catch up on the stack of paperwork starting to overwhelm her desk. It wasn't very far, one floor down to the criminal felony division. Her desk was exactly the way she left it, a sea of white and manila. She would begin to investigate this case next week for Randy, but first, she had myriad motions waiting for her response. She made a mental note to review the memo again once it was routed to her.

CHAPTER 11

THE PRESS RAN a short op-ed piece on the last page of the local section about the civil suit the day after Gavin returned home from Virginia. It was a small article, only one column, and there was no mention of Gavin's firm or the attorneys involved. Gavin didn't care. It was his first bit of press, and he latched onto it like a kitten to a ball of yarn. He bought every paper at the newsstand in the lobby of his building.

Gavin was not the only one who noticed the small publicity that the civil filing received in the paper. Lance Penderson stuck his coffee mug underneath the cappuccino machine in the front lobby of his office. He pressed the button for double strength as he skimmed the folded newspaper in his hand. It mentioned the filing of a wrongful death case stemming from the acquittal of Tyler Tutuila.

"Not a good day for the plaintiff's attorney. Didn't get your name in the paper," Lance said with a smirk under his breath.

Once the machine quit spewing coffee and foam, he headed back to his high rise office. The interior décor looked more like a marina gift shop than an attorney's office. Lance was an avid sailor and enjoyed surrounding himself with aquatic trinkets. Several sailing photos hung on his dark wood paneled walls, and his credenza proudly displayed a scaled down model of a Gokstad Viking battle ship that he had purchased during a vacation in Roskilde Fjord, Denmark. It sat under his window and seemed to float above the indigenous low Seattle winter fog that draped the outside skyline. He plopped down in his leather chair when the phone rang.

"This is Lance," he said leaning back. Lance always made a point of answering his own phone even though he had a secretary, three paralegals and six associates at his beck and call.

"Mr. Penderson, James Lapp from National Insurance."

"Yes, how's the Florida weather doing?" Lance's main client was National Insurance. He had never met anyone from their headquarters in St. Petersburg, but talked to them at least three times a week.

"The weather's fine. It's dropping to the mid-sixties, but we'll ride it out."

"That's a shame," Lance said looking out his rain-drenched window overlooking downtown Seattle. A ferry horn bellowed in the backdrop as winter raindrops pounded against the outside of his window. "What can I do for you?"

"I'm sorry to bother you, but I needed to update you on the Tutuila matter."

"Let me guess, you got wind of the article in this week's paper? You guys are good. I'll never understand how you get your information sometimes, but I am impressed." Lance knew exactly how they received their information. They ran on-line searches for each local newspaper where litigation was pending involving one of their insureds. Lance was very familiar with this tactic because he did the same thing. Each article that was found was categorized, summarized, and added to the file. Lance liked to be as informed as possible and did not like surprises.

Most good plaintiff's attorneys like to use the media when filing a suit. Publicity scares defendants and can usually force a quick settlement, even on frivolous claims. No business likes to read about accusations against them in the morning news.

"Well, we figured you already read about it, but my boss just wanted to make sure."

"I did read something about it, but didn't pay too much attention since they seemed to fail to mention my name." Lance chuckled into the phone. He was known nationally as one of the top-notch corporate insurance defense attorneys. "I learned long ago not to get too worked up about these things."

"Well, that's what we like to hear."

Lance didn't care what this person liked to hear. He knew the game. Insurance companies are in the business of paying out the lowest amount of money for claims filed against the people they insure. They hired Lance because he was consistently the best defense attorney around.

"One more thing that our office wanted to discuss with you. The complaint is from Duke Stewart's firm, but his name was conspicuously absent from the pleadings. What do you make of that?"

This was the first astute observation made by the voice, and one that Lance had made as well. He already had one of his associates checking into the matter. "It seems that Duke's passed this case off to some attorney who just passed the bar. The kid's in over his head, and I don't think Duke's gonna bother himself with this case."

"Have you met your clients yet?" The voice asked. Lance was hired by the insurance company, but his actual client was the insured. In this case, National held the homeowner's policy for Tyler's parents, Palolo and Mauuaua Tutuila.

"Nope, I can't even pronounce their names. I don't even know if I'll have the chance. My guess is that this Brady character is just trying to impress someone in his firm by fishing around for a quick score."

"That's what we're afraid of."

"Don't be. They're way off base on this one. I don't see this case sticking around for the long haul." Lance knew that the only reason to sue Tyler's parents was to get at the homeowner's policy, which had a policy limit of five hundred thousand dollars. None of the four boys who actually did the shooting had any money, so the only way to recover anything was to sue the parents and collect from the homeowner's policy.

Lance motioned his hand as if he were about to hang up the phone. "Anything else I can do for you today?" He was already tired of the conversation.

"No, I think that's it. I appreciate your time and we'll let you know if anything comes up."

Lance had already hung up before the voice stopped talking. He pressed down on the intercom. "Brian, could you come in here?"

Within seconds, Lance's door burst open. Brian Thomas, one of Lance's associates, entered the office wearing a dark suit and holding a legal-sized notepad. He was in his mid-thirties with sandy-brown hair parted neatly on the side of his head. His brown-rimmed glasses gave him a scholarly look that enhanced his corporate demeanor. Like the other associates in Lance's employ, Brian graduated cum laude from the University of Washington Law School, and had sought him out as a potential employer.

"Brian, I want you to bring me all of the cases in our motion to dismiss in this Tutuila case and not just the ones you cited in the brief. All of the cases."

"How soon do you want them?"

"I would assume you already have a file with all of the cases in it, right? I assume you looked at every possible case on point before drafting our motion to dismiss?" Lance was not one for discussions or debates unless he asked for it in advance.

"Of course." Brian scribbled some notes on his pad.

"Good, then make sure they are all still good law, then bring me a summary of each case. I don't want any mistakes on this one."

"Right away." Brian got up to leave.

"Oh, and set up a meeting with our clients, Mr. and Mrs. Tutu something."

"Tutuila. It's the same as that big mountain in Samoa." Brian threw that small tidbit of information to show Lance he had done his homework.

"Let's set up a meeting with them before oral arguments. I want to make sure we're all on the same page."

Brian jotted down a couple more notes on his legal pad and left the office.

GAVIN WAS ALMOST out of sight when Gladys called after him. He returned from Virginia with a renewed vigor and sense of purpose. Duke was right about the importance of meeting the Harringtons, and Gavin was more determined than ever.

He spent the morning creating a list of witnesses he needed to interview and depose. He wanted to talk to Casey, Katherine, and Paul. Afterward, he would move to the occupants of the shooter's car as well as the family members. Gladys had some names, and was spending her time trying to contact them to set up appointments for interviews. The remainder of the time was spent reviewing Penderson's motion to dismiss until he had to leave for his morning associates meeting.

"Mr. Brady," Gladys called. She had a way of shouting with an air of professionalism and courteousness.

"Gladys, why don't you call me by my first name?"

"Because that just wouldn't be proper, Mr. Brady," she said matter of factly.

"Okay, what is it?"

"A call just came in that I thought you might want to know about."

"That's fast." He was expecting to hear from some of the witnesses, but not within the first morning.

"It's from the prosecutor's office."

Gavin stiffened. He was already late for his meeting but this was the second call from their office.

"I'll take it in my office." He walked back inside and sat at his desk. He wasn't sure what to say. He didn't even know why Randy Bougainville would be calling him on a civil case that didn't involve the prosecutor's office at all. Gladys put the call through to his phone. Gavin took a deep breath. He was ready to deal with Mr. Bougainville.

"Hello, Gavin Brady speaking."

"Mr. Brady, this is Jenny Garrett at the prosecutor's office."

The words hit him like a cinder block. He knew the voice and the name. He'd carried around the pain and guilt of that evening for years.

"Jenny Garrett?" He wasn't sure what to say.

"Yes, we actually met once before — in Chicago I believe it was."

"Oh yeah, sure. How are you?" He knew that was a stupid thing to say after all this time, but it was all he could come up with on the spot.

"Great. Anyway, I'm one of the deputy prosecutors at the office, and we noticed that you filed a wrongful death case arising out of the murder of Sara Harrington."

"Yes, we did. Is there something wrong?" He still was unsure of what her office's interest was in the case.

"No. As you know, our office handled the criminal trial several years back and we did a lot of the initial investigating."

"Yeah, I think we did a public records request, and your office was kind enough to send over your documents."

"Yes, I see you got some of them." She crumpled a sheet of paper next to the receiver to simulate the sound of papers rustling.

"We didn't get them all?"

"Well, of course not."

"Why not?"

"I can't comment on an open investigation. However, if there are any questions you may have, I've been assigned to handle the case from our end so you can call me directly. We'd also appreciate it if you could share with us anything you uncover as well."

Gavin took a deep breath. "What do you mean handle the case from your end? Is there still an investigation going on?" Part of him thought that she was toying with him, but part of him thought there must be something else. After all, Randy had called him as well.

"I'm sorry but I just can't comment. I wanted to introduce myself or re-introduce myself to you in case you needed to contact us during your case."

The phone call ended as abruptly as it began. Gavin sat in his chair for what seemed to be an eternity replaying the phone conversation in his head. Something was going on and he was completely in the dark.

On top of everything else, he had to get started on the response to the motion to dismiss.

CHAPTER 12

THE AFTERNOON SUN remained hidden by the dark brooding clouds blanketing it. Tyler was the first to speak.

"No one changes the story."

"Why don't you shut up," Danny said. He wasn't as big as Tyler and certainly not as intimidating, but he kept a straight face and didn't back down. *"Ua tautalagia le uma lapalapa,"* which loosely translated as 'we're here because someone screwed up.' For Tyler's and Danny's generation, the language of their parents was less a form of communication as it was a means to accentuate moments.

Tyler understood what was being said to him. "What's that supposed to mean? You got something to say to me?" Tyler stood directly in front of Danny towering over him. Both boys wore heavy frames, but Tyler's body was built like a front lineman.

The music started back up in the distance. It was Wednesday and the Samoan community was gathering together again for family night to celebrate their aigu and each other lives. Danny and Tyler were second cousins. Their parents grew up together on the island of Samoa and their fathers joined the U.S. Army at approximately the same time. Although they completed their service in different parts of the world, their aigu was very strong and pulled them both to the Pacific Northwest upon retirement.

"We don't talk about that night. It's over," Tyler said.

"It's not over." Danny wasn't backing down. "We're being sued. What if the police decide to get involved again?"

"So, what if they do?" Sal said as he approached the two. Sal was the same age as Danny and although the two of them considered each other cousins, they weren't actually related by blood. They all grew up together in the same aigu and were as close as any family.

"I'm not going down for this, Sal." Sal's real name was Aleni Saulo Ga Fuatimau after his father, but everyone just called him Sal because it was too hard to pronounce his real name.

"Neither am I," Tyler stated emphatically.

"None of us are. Look, the police already investigated this once. Marcus is the shooter, end of story."

Danny shook his head. "Freddie said that he heard they found a gun in the Puget Sound. Last week, I got served with a lawsuit for wrongful death. I didn't shoot nobody."

"Hey, uso." Kauni Tutuila's voice rang out as he approached the three young men. Uso was Samoan for brother and a pet name he used for Tyler. "What's up here? You fellas are missing the festivities." Kauni overheard them talking and wanted to warn them that their voices were drifting within listening distance of the crowd. The music was playing loudly in the background, but some members of the community couldn't help but notice them squaring off with each other. The lawsuit was no secret by now. Stories had a way of spreading even without a word being spoken.

Tyler's acquittal had been received with mixed reaction. The community celebrated the fact that one of their children was freed, but the criminal investigation and the accusations of a cover-up surrounding the changing of their stories disrupted their peaceful loving community, forcing families to take sides against each other. The scars still ran deep within their neighboring homes.

Marcus' parents, the Kiuilani family, albeit from a different aigu, were beloved in the Northwest Samoan community and had never caused any disruptions since they arrived. The Tutuila family, however, was the largest and most connected family in their aigu. They had strong ties to Samoa, and were related in one way or another to most of the families in their area. This meant that families were forced to end friendships and draw the lines of loyalty that divided and separated aigus. Palolo campaigned hard every Sunday at church for donations for the lawyers and for support of his son. He was adamant about Tyler's innocence calling him a loyal friend and hero. He also publicly blamed the Kiuilani family for causing the growing division within the community, calling for Marcus to finally step forward and take responsibility for his actions.

Secretly, people's opinions were split. No one really thought of Tyler as a saint. He, along with Danny and Sal, had made a name for themselves early on as troublemakers. Tyler sprung up quickly and, by the time he entered high school, he was already six feet five and weighed close to two hundred sixty pounds. They were the school thugs, a group of middle class punks who used their size to intimidate the other school kids.

On the evening of the shooting, Danny, Sal, Marcus, and one of Sal's friends, Chillie Ki, had came to Tyler's house to celebrate the fact that Tyler just been accepted at a small local college. Marcus' family had only moved to the Northwest two years earlier, and he was the youngest member of Tyler's entourage. The boys hung out in Tyler's basement smoking pot and drinking beer. They went out twice that evening to get more beer at a local mini-mart that was known in the area to pay more attention to the method of payment than the validity of one's identification. Freddie was working late that night. Otherwise he would have been with them when the shot was fired.

"What are you guys talking about?" Kauni said in an earnest voice. He was six years older than Tyler with a similar build and shared his love of football. In fact, he was something of a role model for his younger brother. Kauni played second-string football in college before making a short-lived run for the NFL. When he failed to make the cut, he moved to Canada and eventually Germany, where he played three years in the European Football League until an injury to his knee extinguished any hopes of going pro in the United States. He worked odd jobs when he returned and eventually trained as an air conditioner technician.

"What do you think we're talking about?" Danny said.

"Not here."

"Where then?"

"Tomorrow, the driving range at Lakewood Golf Course." Kauni looked at each of them. They all had frustrated yet scared expressions on their faces. "Until then, keep your mouths shut. We're at church and this is supposed to be a party, remember?"

Kauni took Tyler by the shoulder. "Come on, uso, Dad's been looking for you." Before walking off, he turned to Danny and Sal. "Tomorrow, ten o'clock at the driving range."

"Okay." Danny said.

"Okay?" Kauni said turning to Sal.

"Whatever. Tomorrow." Kauni walked off pulling Tyler by the shoulder. Palolo could see his sons walking away from Danny and Sal through the church's sliding glass door. A band played soft Polynesian music behind him.

Palolo was a proud and stoic man. He silently tolerated Tyler's volatility. He saw his son's erratic behavior as part of growing up in this strange country, which seemed to celebrate violence and guns. He and his wife both spoke only broken English and communicated in Samoan at home.

Tyler's generation understood most of what the elders said, but none of them were fluent in the language. He was born and raised in America, and the Samoan heritage was nothing more than a distant part of his ancestry. Palolo shook his head quietly to himself. He had also been served with the lawsuit. He knew that it wasn't over.

As usual, the festivities lasted most of the evening. No one said a word about the lawsuit until the next morning. Sal picked up Freddie at nine, and the two of them stopped at the Burger King drive thru for breakfast.

"You still down for this?" Sal said without even looking at him.

"Yeah." That was the most that the two of them had said about the murder or the lawsuit since Tyler had been acquitted. Freddie was the group's drug connection during high school. That, however, came to a sudden halt after the shooting. They acted tough and wore the right clothes, but deep down, they were just scared, troubled kids. Tyler was in real trouble, the kind of trouble that couldn't be solved by beating someone up.

Freddie was the last one to hear about the arrest. It was only fate and a conflicting work schedule that kept him out of the car that night. He showed up late to Tyler's house arriving only five minutes before they returned. He saw who got out of the front seat. He knew Danny was driving and that Sal was sitting behind him in the back seat. He also saw Marcus exit the car. Once the police found him, Tyler confessed and was in custody. Danny, Sal, and Marcus also pointed the finger at Tyler as the shooter. Freddie confirmed their story, a story that would last more than sixteen months while Tyler sat in jail awaiting trial, a story that would eventually change.

"Where are we going?" Freddie asked as Sal handed him a bag full of breakfast croissants and hash brown nuggets.

"We're meeting at some driving range."

"You golf?"

"I do today. That's where Kauni said to meet." Sal spoke between mouthfuls of sausage and egg as he drove.

"I thought this was over. Wasn't he acquitted? They can't retry him again can they?"

"This ain't criminal. It's some lawyer suing us all for lying or something."

Freddie didn't respond. He remained loyal to his friends once and saw no reason to stop now. However, time had turned him into an adult and his life was different now. He had a young wife and baby and a new job at a local department store. He had almost forgotten about the entire trial until Sal called him last night to show up this morning. He soothed his uneasy stomach with the heavy food as they drove back toward their dubious forgotten past. Kauni would know what to do. He always knew what to do.

GAVIN WAS ARRIVING to the office earlier and earlier each morning. The unexpected phone call from Jenny had reignited pains of guilt regarding his past behavior as well as his relationship with Hannah. He loved her so much. How could he even begin to face her with the threat of Jenny always around the corner? He tried to tell himself that he didn't actually cheat on her. They weren't married. They weren't even engaged. In fact, they had only just met a couple of weeks earlier. The moment he met Hannah, he knew that she was the one. Then he ran into Jenny in Chicago a week later. He was swept up in the moment, and before he knew what was happening, the morning sun was peeling back the night sky infiltrating Jenny's hotel room.

Gavin pushed all of that to the back of his mind and tried to concentrate on his case. He had set up two interviews for today. One with Casey, who drove the car that Sara was in, and the other with Paul, who was sitting in the backseat with her when she was shot.

Like clockwork, his phone rang right at 9:30. It was the front desk telling him that Casey had arrived. He asked to have him wait in one of the conference rooms while he got his notes ready. Next to his phone sat a glowing glossy print of Hannah standing on a beach holding her wedding bouquet of flowers. Gavin grabbed his notes and left to meet his first witness.

When he entered the room, Casey was already sitting down with a mocha from the firm's machine, and looking out one of the windows. There was a long table in the center of the room with twenty-four leather chairs around it. A conference phone sat in the center. The firm's conference rooms were all encased in frosted glass. It allowed the privacy needed during meetings while taking advantage of those rare occasions when the Northwest sun would fight through the gray skies and permit natural light into the interior of the firm. The conference room walls were a dark burgundy giving a feeling of power to the space, offering a nice subliminal home court advantage during depositions or negotiations with opposing counsel.

Larry Smithwick always took credit for the frosted glass. One of his architectural clients designed the entire interior in exchange for representation on a commercial dispute with one of his employers. The fact that the design wasn't costing the firm any out of pocket expense other than Larry's regular fee was the only way that Fred would give his consent to the remodel. It also gave him some secret satisfaction to know that Larry's economic column for the year was going to be diminished by the amount of the remodel.

"Hi, are you Casey?" Gavin said, "It's Goodman, right?"

Casey turned around and looked at him. "Yes."

They both shook hands. Casey had shaved brown hair and stood about five feet nine inches tall. Gavin was surprised by Casey's age. Gavin knew from the file that he was only a couple years older than Casey. However, the similarity in age seemed more pronounced now that he stood face to face with him. Gavin was playing the seasoned legal expert. He quickly shook off his uneasiness and poured himself a cup of coffee.

"Good, I'm glad you got some coffee. Feel free to help yourself."

"Thanks," Casey said. "Who do you represent again?"

"I represent the estate of Sara Harrington as well as her parents." As soon as the words escaped his lips, he realized how callous and stupid that sentence had sounded. After all, Casey knew Sara and was less than two feet away from her when she was shot. She was not an *estate* to him. The word itself disrespected her memory and reduced it to a mere legal term.

Casey didn't even notice the faux pas or, at least, pretended not to notice. "Well, I don't know what I can tell you that I haven't already said before."

"I understand you testified at Tyler's murder trial."

"More like fed to the wolves. I turned for a split second and saw the car out of my peripheral vision and it all got used against me."

"Tell me about that." Gavin made himself comfortable and was taking notes on a legal pad. "You knew Tyler, right?"

"Yeah. We played football together in high school." Casey didn't have an extremely muscular build, but he was big enough to play high school ball. "I knew him and he knew who I was. That's why I didn't think it was him that night."

"Did you see anyone in the car that night?"

"No. I wasn't looking when they passed us and I only got a split-second shot at them at the corner."

"What did you see?" Gavin was getting into the flow of his questions.

"I saw a large head, but it was dark. That's what I told the cops."

"But you couldn't finger Tyler until after he confessed."

"That's right. Why is that so weird? I mean he was looking right at me, I wasn't looking at him. It wasn't until the memorial service that I was able to put two and two together."

"The memorial service?" Gavin had not read anything in the trial testimony about the memorial service. He began flipping through Casey's transcribed testimony.

"Yeah. You're not gonna find it in there. No one asked me about it at trial about being approached." He figured Gavin already knew what he was talking about. "I told the cop about it, after it happened."

"Okay, let's back up. I want to make sure I don't miss anything." He wanted to hear what happened at the memorial service. He remembered Jenny telling him that he hadn't received everything from the Prosecutors' Office. His mind was already working on his motion to compel. What were they hiding? "Tell me what happened there."

"I showed up with Paul and Katherine. Sara's parents were there as well though I'd never met them before."

"Did you talk to them?"

"No — yes — I said hi. But I didn't really know what to say to them. I may have said something, but I can't really remember."

"Okay, tell me about what happened for you to put two and two together."

Casey sat up in his seat and looked at Gavin. "You don't know, do you?"

"No, I don't know."

"Fucking cop. I told him everything. No wonder they didn't ask me at trial."

"What happened?"

"The memorial service was pretty somber. I didn't really want to be there, cause it had just happened. Anyway, I was standing next to a tree, and this guy came up to me and started talking about that night."

"What guy?"

"He seemed to know things about what had happened. He's the one that told me about Tyler."

"Was he Samoan?"

"No, he was some Asian guy. He said he was with them that night. He said Tyler had a gun and had been waving it around all night. He said he saw Tyler in the front passenger seat."

Chillie Ki, Gavin thought to himself. He was Asian and had been in the car earlier that night. "What else did he say?"

"Nothing. I never saw him again. He just disappeared."

"What was his name?" Gavin was pretty sure he already knew.

"I don't know. Look, I told a cop the next day what happened, and I never heard back until the trial."

"Was this the same cop that you gave a statement to the night of the shooting?"

"No. It was a different cop."

"Does the name Koblenz sound familiar?"

"Yeah, that's the cop I talked to the night of the murder. It wasn't Detective Koblenz. It was another cop."

Gavin was puzzled. Detective Koblenz was the chief investigating officer up until trial. Everything he had read was either signed by Koblenz or approved by him. If Casey was right, there was another cop, who dropped the ball somewhere along the way. Maybe Jenny was holding something back. Maybe there was more to this story than he originally thought.

He continued to speak with Casey for about an hour, and the two of them went through the drive home from the party in painstaking detail. He told Gavin about the gunshot and his statements to the police.

They talked about the trial, and how no one ever mentioned the fact that Chillie Ki told him about Tyler being in the front seat. It was an important fact because forensics determined from the trajectory of the bullet that the shooter had to be in the front seat of Danny's car. By the time they were through, Gavin was exhausted. They were winding down their conversation when the front desk buzzed Gavin. Paul was in the lobby waiting to meet with him.

Gavin thanked Casey for coming and for talking with him. He took a fifteen minute break between interviews giving Casey and Paul a chance to briefly catch up. Gavin made several notes to himself regarding his interview before calling Paul into the conference room.

Paul's interview lasted almost two hours because he needed to take several breaks to gain his composure. Paul wore his feelings for Sara on his sleeve, and was still deeply hurt by her loss. Unfortunately, he never saw anyone in the car. His only heard the gunshot and watched Sara life drain from her body.

TYLER, KAUNI, AND DANNY were already on the driving range with a full bucket of balls when Sal and Freddie showed up. They took a few minutes to check out a bucket of balls in case someone was watching.

Kauni picked out a spot on the far left section of the range where no one was around. Most people liked to hit down the middle of the fairway or as close to it as possible. On the edges, a slight turn of the wrist could turn a still decent drive into a fence slamming disaster. Kauni's choice ensured the group that no one would be listening.

"Thanks for showing up." Kauni was never afraid of speaking first.

"What the hell is going on with that bitch's lawyers?" Sal asked. They all knew why they were there. Kauni called them together to talk about their strategy.

"Nothing's changed," Kauni said.

"What do you mean nothing's changed? That's easy for you to say. You're not in the middle of this like the rest of us," Danny said. He wasn't afraid of anyone and wasn't afraid of saying what was on his mind.

"What you say? I'm here ain't I? My brother's in the middle of it. My parents are in the middle of it. My people are in the middle of it. I got the same stakes as you, uso."

"So, what do we do?" Tyler asked.

Kauni answered without hesitating. "We don't do anything. Lawyers are involved. Let'em fight it out. We stick to the same story. Nothing's changed."

"These are different lawyers," Sal said.

"It doesn't matter. Don't worry, I got it covered."

The boys trusted Kauni. He helped them the first time around. He was the one who suggested changing the positions of Tyler and Marcus in the car. "We flip the script, keep it simple. Everything stays the same except we put Tyler in the backseat and Marcus in the front." No one liked doing that to Marcus. After all, he was their friend. However, Tyler was in jail and facing a murder charge, and Marcus was the newest member of the community to move to the area, which meant he was the closest to being an outsider. Someone had to be blamed, and he drew the short straw. After the acquittal, the whole ordeal was supposed to be over. Now, some lawyer decoded to stir up the past bringing them back to yet another clandestine meeting to decide what to do.

It seemed so simple at the time. Somehow, Kauni got word that Casey couldn't identify Tyler just before trial. None of the boys knew where Kauni got his information, and no one asked. Everyone knew that the defense attorney told Tyler's parents about Casey's statement. Kauni then arranged for the boys to meet at the defense attorney's office. The rest was easy. One by one, they told the attorney what he wanted to hear. They told a story of loyalty and friendship. They flipped the script just like Kauni told them. They told Tyler's attorney that they were protecting Marcus until he could get his affairs in order and make peace with his family. They told a story of protecting one friend while sacrificing another.

"I heard they found a gun," Sal said to the group.

Everyone uncomfortably looked at each other. Their expressions displayed so many unspoken fears.

"Nobody found anything," Kauni said.

"How do you know?"

Kauni looked over the young men's faces. They were worried. "I got a call about it. It's taken care of."

"The lawyer?"

"No." Kauni wasn't sure how much he should reveal about what he knew. None of their attorneys had been retained at the time Duke was having the sound dredged, and Tyler's old criminal defense attorney was now living back east working as a legal correspondent for some cable news network. "I got it covered. Let's just say nobody wants to see this thing go forward. We gotta just stick to the script. Everything the way we said before and Marcus was in the front seat. As long as they can't shake us on that, we're good."

"How do you know they didn't recover the gun? How come you seem to know so much?" Danny asked.

Kauni always knew more about the case than the boys, which was one of the reasons they grew to trust him. He was older than Tyler, and was actually born on the island of Samoa. After the murder, he was the one who convinced them that flipping the script would work, and that the community would support them if they told the story correctly. He was right. Once again, he seemed to have more information about the lawsuit and what was going on.

"What gun you talking about, uso? You know something about a gun?"

"No," Danny said.

You think I'm lying?"

"No, I know you're not. I just want to know how come you know so much when you're not involved." Danny was simply vocalizing a question that each of the boys wanted to ask for a long time.

Kauni looked at the group. "It's better that you don't know. It's safer for everyone."

"How can it be safer? We're already in it?"

"Okay." Kauni looked around at the group. "I got a call from this guy who is close to the case and he lets me know what's up."

"What guy?"

"A guy. Someone who's close to the case."

"An attorney?"

"Na."

"A cop?"

Kauni didn't answer. "You guys keep your mouth shut. There's nobody, you got it? That's all I'm gonna tell you, and it's too much already." Danny and Sal tried a couple more times to get information about Kauni's informant, but he wasn't talking anymore. They talked about the plan for awhile between swings, and how it should stay simple. The conversation turned almost joyful as each of them began to take comfort in the fact that they had a secret informant feeding them information

CHAPTER 13

THAT EVENING, GAVIN decided to go home early. He was emotionally and mentally exhausted from his first couple of interviews. Casey waited in the front lobby for Paul and the two of them left together. Gavin spent the rest of the afternoon writing a response to the defense's motion to dismiss. He originally thought that he would have more time to dig up facts to support his theory, but Lance Penderson was tenacious and moved quickly.

Lance represented Tyler's parents, and argued in his brief that the parents of a minor can't be sued for negligence unless they are aware of the child's dangerous propensities. Tyler had no criminal record before the murder. The only thing that the plaintiffs could point to was the fact that Tyler and his friends were drinking alcohol before they went out that night. Lance meticulously outlined the legal shortcomings of Gavin's complaint section by section. It was well written and very persuasive.

When Gavin first received Lance's motion, he put a copy of it in Duke's in-box hoping to get some advice. Instead, he received the copy back in an interoffice envelope with a handwritten note stating, *He's right, but don't lose.* The response was due by four p.m. tomorrow, and Gavin had been working on it all week. By late afternoon, his brain shut down. Deadline or no deadline, he needed a break.

He called Hannah at around noon and told her he would try to be home early, which meant he would be home before the late-night talk shows were on television. This would give them at least an hour together before they fell asleep.

Even with the endless distractions of the day, Gavin still couldn't shake the thought of Jenny's ominous phone call and her cryptic message regarding the prosecutor's involvement in the case. There was something that Jenny was hiding, and yet, he was terrified to confront her because of their past.

Gavin stood in front of his window next to his desk looking out at the Tacoma skyline. The evening sun was quickly overpowering the afternoon daylight turning the sky a majestic red. To the right of his office, hidden behind one of the city's hills, lay the mile-long Tacoma

Narrows Bridge and Hannah. He tried to imagine what she was doing. She would be home from work and probably watching the news or winding down with a book. Perhaps she was enjoying the same sunset.

He stood there silently for a bit stretching out his back as he allowed his mind to drift before turning his attention back to his desk and the response he was writing. It wasn't his best work, but it was almost finished, and he could clean it up tomorrow before he filed it.

He breathed in the ventilated air piped through the overhead vents pretending that he was really smelling the fragrant scent of the mountains outlining his sunset. He inhaled in several more before sitting back down to spend the next couple of hours finishing his written response to the court. Afterward, he cleaned up his desk, organizing his research and notes into neat piles, and wrote himself a note to review certain sections of his legal brief tomorrow. He then called Hannah to let her know he would be home soon.

As he headed down the hallway toward the elevators, he noticed several other associate offices still glowing brightly under the fluorescent lighting. He smiled to himself because tonight, he wasn't one of them. Tonight, he was going home to see his wife while she was still awake.

The drive seemed to take longer than usual. The bridge didn't have any traffic on it this late, but the highway felt as it had been stretched out lengthening the distance home. A couple of times, Gavin glanced back in his rear-view mirror. Behind him was a black Trans Am. There was something familiar about the vehicle. He couldn't put his finger on it, but he thought he'd seen it before.

The car stayed behind him for the length of the bridge, and Gavin wasn't sure how long before that. He put on his turn signal, and took the second exit past the bridge. The Trans Am didn't follow, passing him on the left as he turned off the highway onto the road leading home. Gavin put the image of the mysterious car out of his mind, and chalked it up to déjà vu. He was troubled by Lance Penderson's motion to dismiss. His response was weaker than he would have liked and oral arguments were next week. A judge would then rule whether the case would be allowed to move forward or if it was to be lost forever.

Gavin pulled into the parking stall in front of their house and hopped out of the car. He almost galloped up the front drive. Before he had a chance to put his key in the lock, the front door swung open.

"Hi, stranger."

"I've missed that smile." Gavin could feel the day beginning to melt away as he looked at her natural radiance.

"Can I offer you some wine?" She asked. In one hand, she held a bottle of Merlot and, in the other, two empty wine glasses.

"Wait a minute," he said stopping under the frame of the doorway, "this isn't a ploy to get me drunk and take advantage of me, is it?"

"Only if you're lucky." She handed him a half-full glass of merlot.

He swirled the merlot around the edges to watch the legs of liquid streak back into the reservoir. He stopped when he noticed Hannah's silent pause.

"What's wrong?" She glanced over Gavin's shoulder to the street, which was visible from the entrance to their house.

"What's the matter?" He asked again.

"Nothing I guess. It's just that car seems familiar for some reason."

Gavin turned around. On the far side of the street sat a black Trans Am, like the same one that Gavin saw on the bridge. The windows were tinted, blackening out the inside. The engine purred softly, and a steady stream of gassy steam rose out of the tail pipe in the cool Northwest evening.

"I've seen that car."

"I know, isn't that weird? I swear it looks familiar."

"No, I mean. I saw it tonight."

"That car? Are you sure?"

"It was behind me on the bridge."

"It followed you home?" Hannah's voice was filled with apprehension.

"Yeah. Well, I didn't think so but..." Gavin headed toward the street.

"Gavin."

"Don't worry."

"No, don't do anything." Hannah tried to pull him back but he was already out of reach.

He walked several steps toward the car. His glass dropped to his side spilling several drops on the pavement. The Trans Am sat quietly as if daring him to come closer. "Excuse me," Gavin called out. "Can I help you with something?"

The car allowed Gavin to take a couple steps closer before the engine revved up and disappeared into the blackness of the night. Gavin picked up speed and jogged to the edge of the street. It had disappeared before he was able to get a license plate number. "Did you see a plate number?" He called back to Hannah.

"No. Maybe we should call the police."

Gavin stood there looking down the street into the blackness of the night. He didn't know why that car followed him home or where he'd seen it before. The familiarity of it haunted him.

Hannah was already inside on the phone with the police. Within ten minutes, a patrol car pulled up in front of their home. The two deputies were mechanical. This was routine to them. They hurriedly took Gavin's and Hannah's statements without offering any emotion or sympathy. One of the officers even grilled Gavin about the wine stains on the pavement, more concerned about how much alcohol he consumed that evening.

The investigation, including the time it took to respond, lasted roughly fifteen minutes. Before leaving, the deputies recommended that the two of them go down to the courthouse and take out a restraining order.

"Against whom?" Gavin asked, exacerbated by the entire ordeal.

"That's a good point," the deputy said. "Let us do some preliminary investigating, and then we'll let you know what we find."

Gavin knew that it was a virtual impossibility to trace a non-descript vehicle without a solid license plate. The deputies were going through the motions of a low priority investigation that was destined to lead nowhere.

"Thanks officers." Gavin shook their hands and pretended to be optimistic. He watched them leave down the street in the same direction as the Trans Am before marching back inside.

"What's wrong?" Hannah asked as he continued toward the kitchen. There was a definite purpose in his movements. He snatched the phone off its base and rummaged through his briefcase until he pulled out a folder. It was a manila folder labeled Tutuila Case notes.

"What's wrong? What are you doing?"

He opened the folder and began rummaging through the pages. "I don't know, but I'm gonna find out." On one of the pages was Jenny's direct number at the prosecutor's office. He wrote down after her phone call about an on-going investigation. It seemed odd to him at the time that there might be an investigation pending almost three years after the jury acquitted Tyler. Plus, her call rattled him. What did she want after all this time? He dialed her number.

"Who are you calling?"

"The prosecutor's office."

"Why? Is there something going on that you're not telling me?"

Gavin paused before answering. Her question brought back the flood of secrets that Jenny's phone call had unlocked. There was a lot that he didn't want to tell her, a momentary detour down a sully path that filled him with regret every moment of his life. "No, I just want to make sure it has nothing to do with this case I'm working on."

The phone was ringing and then stopped as Jenny's voice mail answered. "This is Jennifer Garrett at the Pierce County Prosecutor's Office, I'm away from my desk or in court at the moment so please leave your name, number, a brief message, and the case number you are calling about."

He turned away from Hannah as the message played. He felt uncomfortable hearing Jenny's voice in the same room as Hannah. There was a short pause at the end of her message before the beep.

"Yes, Ms. Garr — Jenny." He wasn't sure if he could call her by her first name under the circumstances, but he thought that Ms. Garrett sounded callous and cold. "This is Gavin Brady. I just had a vehicle follow me home and scare my wife and me. You mentioned that there was an ongoing investigation involving Tyler Tutuila. I don't mean to overreact, but if there is something I should be aware of, then I'd appreciate a call back." He left his direct number at work and then hung up.

"Do you think that car had something to do with your Samoan case?"

Gavin took a deep breath. "No."

"Oh? You just thought you needed to call the prosecutor?"

Gavin took another deep breath. As he exhaled, his nerves turned into a dull laughter. "Yeah, that was pretty stupid, huh?"

"This isn't funny."

"I know." Gavin was calmer now. He wanted to reassure Hannah that everything was okay. He probably did overreact. "I'm just being a lawyer, just covering all the bases. Don't worry about it."

She wasn't fully satisfied, but Gavin hugged her until her body relaxed. She confronted him a bit further, but he kept reassuring her that there was nothing to worry about. He poured them some more wine, and they tried to begin their evening all over again.

That night, Gavin couldn't sleep. He tossed and turned for several hours, and finally got up and paced in the living room. There was something he was missing or wasn't being told. He finally lay down on the couch and slept, but had a terrible nightmare of being trapped inside a dark box unable to find the door. He could hear someone knocking, but the walls felt too solid and too heavy to budge. The knocking grew louder and was accompanied by a voice. He was growing desperate, trying to escape. It was dark and cold. The voice grew louder and the knocking heavier. The voice was familiar now, less echoed. It was Hannah.

"Gavin."

He shook himself awake.

"Gavin, wake up." Hannah was standing over him shaking his shoulder. He was on his own couch in his own living room.

"I didn't even hear you get out of bed," she said softly. "You better get up, you're late for work."

"What?" He said coming to his senses. "What time is it?"

"Seven-thirty."

"Seven-thirty," he said repeating her words.

"I figured you needed some rest after the hours you've been putting in."

"Oh my God! I'm late." Gavin jumped off the couch, kissed Hannah, and ran to the shower. Today of all days was not the day to go in late. He had a brief due and several hours of revisions still to make. Furthermore, he wanted to follow up on the Trans Am.

Within minutes, Gavin was showered, dressed, and out the door. He ran an electric razor across his face while driving to the office. Small beads of wetness seeped through his dress shirt exposing the spots where he hadn't fully dried off. He didn't care. No one would notice behind his desk. He had to get that brief out. As he weaved in and out of the late morning traffic, his mind replayed the events of the previous evening as well as the impending deadline for his brief in response to Lance's motion to dismiss his case.

The firm was already in full swing when he entered. Larry was handling a rather complex commercial dispute for one of his clients that turned sour at the last minute. This meant late nights and weekends for Larry and his staff to prepare for trial. This also meant that everyone else in the office had to either stay out of his way or suffer some form of verbal retribution.

"Morning Gladys," Gavin said as he raced into his office.

"Only for those who have the luxury of staying away from here."

"Busy day, huh?" Gavin said popping his head back into the hallway.

"Mr. Smithwick's preparing for trial. God help us all."

"Well, I'll keep a low profile today. I have this brief due and —"

"I know, by noon today at the courthouse," she said, cutting him off.

"Noon? I thought it was due by four."

"Used to be that way. The rules have changed and now all responsive briefs are due by noon at the clerk's office."

Gavin looked at his watch. It was eight-thirty. "Great!" He closed his door without saying a word, and rushed to his computer to turn it on. Before his sign on screen popped up, Gladys was in his office with a cup of coffee.

"Gladys, you don't need to give me coffee."

"You're right and don't expect this again. It's not part of my job description."

Gladys had a directness about her that commanded respect. "I wouldn't dream of it," he said, smiling.

She put the coffee mug in front of him. The steam rose up to meet his eager nostrils reminding his body of its need for the rich caffeine filled liquid. He didn't sleep very well. "It'd be best to keep your door closed this morning, and, when you're done with that brief, it might be better to make yourself scarce this afternoon. Mr. Smithwick's in trial prep and that means —"

"We're all in trial prep."

"Exactly. This should tide you over for awhile."

"Thanks Gladys." She was a good secretary. She knew how to put him at ease and make his routine smoother during the times that he was rushed.

"I suggest using the back hallway if you want a refill." She smiled and left.

Gavin quickly opened the brief he'd worked on the day before. He'd planned to spend the early part of this morning carefully re-reading it, but now didn't have time. He quickly skimmed the brief for typos, and began revising it in the sections that he already knew needed work. He paused briefly to take a sip of coffee. He was in a rush to finish his brief and each momentary gulp of coffee added much needed and welcomed fuel.

CHAPTER 14

THE MORNING WAS almost gone and Gavin was still revising the first draft response to Lance's motion to dismiss. It was lengthy but cumbersome and confusing. He found himself completely reworking each section several times. It was a nightmare. The truth was that he was on the losing side of the law, at least with the evidence that he possessed. He had a strong moral position but the law didn't support him, and the law is what counts. Time was becoming a fateful foe. Each ticking second served as a painful reminder that the deadline was fast approaching.

Gladys poked her head in several times to see if he needed anything.

He appreciated her gesture, but needed every moment to finish his brief. Despite his efforts to the contrary, it was slow going, and the words were sounding the same in his head. He broke his argument down into three sections. Originally, he had only two, but his legal writing professor had always taught him that the power of "three" is paramount. Judges and juries are more likely to be convinced if there are three arguments rather than one or two. There was some psychology behind it, but he couldn't remember what it was. Gavin needed all the help he could get right now so he took his second section and divided it in half to create a third and final reason to support his case. He was just beginning to revise the last section when he heard the knock at his door.

"Hey killer, how's the fight?" Duke popped his head in the door.

"Tough." Gavin's mind was racing and he struggled to find words for idle chit chat. "I have this response due at—" He glanced down at his watch. "Oh my God, It's due in forty minutes."

"Let me read it," Duke said marching inside his office. Gavin was timid about showing it to Duke, but he couldn't refuse. Without hesitation, Duke snatched up a copy from his desk.

"No!" Gavin blurted out as he jumped up ready to wrestle it from Duke's hands. "I mean, that's an old version. I'll print you the latest one." He took it back and hit the print key on his keyboard.

"Nervous?"

"Sorry, yeah, I guess I'm a little nervous."

"Good. Nerves make you think harder," Duke said with a sadistic smirk.

Gladys walked in with the copy of the brief that Gavin had just printed out. "Here you go, Mr. Brady," she said in her professional voice.

"Thanks, Gladys."

Duke took the copy and began leafing through it. Gladys was already back at her desk and out of ear shot. Gavin was happy about that. He didn't want to be chastised in front of her.

"I know it's — I could've used a couple more days."

"Why? It's the argument I'd make."

"Really?"

"It's the only argument you got." He continued to peruse the brief. "I didn't realize our case was this thin. Wow." Duke laughed to himself. "I don't know what I was thinking when I let you talk me into this." He handed it back to Gavin. "Oh well, live and learn."

"You think it's thin?"

"It's nothing you did. That's a good creative argument, and this is a learning experience for you. That's what we do, we're plaintiff's attorneys. You're doing what you were told, argue the tragedy and the law will follow you. Our job is to find something that'll pay, something that'll push the envelope."

Gavin didn't even hear his explanation. He was still processing Duke's word about his brief being *thin*. "Don't you think we have a shot on this?" Gavin was looking for some encouragement.

"I think we'd have been better off without someone like Lance Penderson on the other side. We might've been able to bide some time, conduct more discovery before dealing with a dismissal motion. It's just litigation. That's the way the chips fall sometimes. Besides, you're not a real plaintiff attorney until you lose one." He said it so matter of factly.

"It's not over yet." Gavin didn't think all was lost.

"You're right. You're in it until the judge slams down that gavel." He handed the copy back to Gavin. "How was the trip by the way?"

"The trip." Gavin tried to look at his watch without being obvious. He only had half an hour to print a final version, sign it, make copies for opposing counsel, and then get to the courthouse to the clerk's office for filing. "It was good. They're a nice couple."

"Good. They understand the risks here I assume. That's always the hardest part."

The risks? No! He hadn't explained the risks to them. Duke never prepped him on what to say or explain. He was over his head the moment he stepped on that plane, and had spent most of his time trying to get the Harrington's not to fire him. Flashes of malpractice hearings and complaints ran through his head as he looked back down at his brief.

"Well, go get 'em. Got to cut your teeth sometime." Duke patted Gavin on the shoulder and left.

Gavin stood in the middle of his office in complete silence. The seventeen pages in his hand felt heavy and awkward. He wasn't sure how long he stood there and didn't even notice Gladys enter.

"Mr. Brady."

The words shot through the dizzy fog in his mind and jolted him back to reality. "Yeah, Gladys. Sorry, I didn't see you come in."

"You have to leave."

"Leave?" Images of being fired sent chills through his body.

"If you're gonna make it in time, you have to leave now."

"Right." He looked down at the pages still clutched in his grip. The entire left side of the brief was crumpled and wet from his hand perspiring.

Without blinking an eye, Gladys held out another freshly printed copy. "I just need your signature and then I'll make copies for the court while you get ready to leave."

"Thanks." He took the brief and quickly signed it. He wanted to do a quick revision of the last section, but time was gone. He leafed through the pages one last time before handing the document back. *Seventeen pages — such an inadequate amount of space to encapsulate a human life.*

Gladys disappeared into thin air as soon as he gave her the brief. Before he could put on his suit jacket and grab his briefcase, she returned with several copies. She explained the filing procedure to him, one copy filed with the court, one with the judge, each copy stamped with the court clerk's seal, etcetera. It would have been easier to let their messenger service handle the filing, but he didn't have time. Gavin listened as she walked him to the elevator trying to keep the Harrington's out of his mind.

Traffic was light. The three block drive to the courthouse didn't take long. He pulled into the parking lot and grabbed space number thirty-five. It was the spot that Duke always superstitiously took when he came up for motions or hearings or trials. The rumor was that when

Duke was just starting out at the firm, he parked in this space the day his first favorable verdict was read. Ever since that date, he made it a point to park in that same spot designating that small area of the parking lot as his lucky space. Today, Gavin was hoping for some of that magical charm to rub off and help carry his cause to victory. He looked at his watch, less than ten minutes left.

THE HALLWAYS IN the courthouse were crowded with people leaving for lunch and delivering last minute filings with the court. Gavin made his way through the metal detector and down the corridor to the clerk's office with several minutes to spare. Jenny spotted him as he was leaving the clerk's office. She was already on a lunch break from her trial. She made her way through the crowd of people clamoring in and out of the various courtrooms that lined the hallway.

"Gavin!" She called through the crowd. "Gavin Brady!" She composed herself, ready for their inevitable reunion.

He noticed her standing in the entrance of the hallway waving her briefcase at him. He regretted the phone message. Maybe he had overreacted. Maybe he was reading too much into last night's events. He took a deep breath and headed her direction.

They met in the middle of the hallway near one of the courtrooms. People were filing past the two of them, many wearing white laminated juror badges on their lapels. These were the citizen jurors, temporary officers of the court sitting in judgment of their peers. They walked down the corridors absent of pretense and armed only with the look of their solemn duty. Lives were altered and futures were carved by their decisions. It all seemed so simple. All it took was convincing a dozen of these individuals that one's side of the story was correct.

"Mr. Brady."

"Look, I know that my phone call may have sounded a bit —"

"You've got a lot of explaining to do," she said interrupting him. Her voice was cold and direct.

"What?" She had caught him off guard.

She signaled him into one of the empty courtrooms for privacy. "Come here." The judge and judicial assistants were undoubtedly at lunch gearing up for a long afternoon of dry legal arguments regarding some commercial dispute between developers.

"What are you talking about? What are you so mad about?" Gavin figured her anger was personal and, if so, he knew it was also probably deserved.

"I want to know how you got this." She pulled out a copy of the handwritten memo routed to her by Gordy and handed it to Gavin. He recognized the memo that referenced Chillie Ki. It wasn't a secret as far as Gavin was concerned.

"From you. Wait a minute, is this about my message last night? I'm sorry but I was a little upset. Some asshole followed me home. He scared my wife to death."

The unresolved history between the two of them seemed to surface when he mentioned his wife. They both felt it. Jenny's eyes tightened and Gavin tried to keep his face from going flush. He could feel the muscles in his cheeks twitch.

"No," she said breaking the silence. "This is not about the phone call. I'm sorry about what happened to you and your family." She paused. "It's about you trying to extort our office into filing charges against those men and using this memo against us."

"What are you talking about?" He said looking down at the document in his hands.

"It won't work."

"I'm not extorting anyone. Maybe you should talk to your cops about Chillie Ki."

"What about Chillie Ki?"

"I had an interesting chat the other day with Casey Goodman, the one driving the car Sara was killed in?"

"I know who he is."

"He said he told the cops all about Chillie."

"Who?" She seemed genuinely surprised.

"He didn't know, just some cop."

"Well, that's not very helpful." Jenny looked around. Gavin could sense she was uncomfortable discussing this in such a public setting.

"Why do you guys care anyway?" He asked. She turned to the door.

"That memo was supposed to be privileged."

"I didn't steal it from you. Your office sent it to me."

"Well, that was a mistake."

"Why is this stupid memo so important?" He asked, not realizing they were seeking the same answer.

She paused at the door way. "I don't know, but it is." Her tone was direct and honest. She opened the door and disappeared back into the sea of laminated badges.

Gavin didn't follow her. He was confused, more confused than ever. There was a message in her voice. This wasn't a vindictive conversation. He looked at the memo still in his hands. He was missing something. He quickly flipped through it again. Chillie's name was circled. That was too obvious. The front of the memo had some scribbling on it that read *route to AB.* It looked more like an *R* than an *A*. What was RB? Perhaps, it was some internal procedure directing the memo to the right department. The sounds of the courthouse grew louder drawing his attention to his surroundings.

He replayed the entire conversation in his head on the way back to the office. She mentioned charges, but he was unaware of any charges pending, and he hadn't run across anything in the file that mentioned a current investigation. Besides, he was a civil attorney. He wasn't involved in any type of criminal prosecution. Maybe they were contemplating charges, but which ones?

Tyler had been acquitted of murder. Double jeopardy precluded re-filing on that charge or even any lesser included offences such as manslaughter or negligent homicide. Any first year law student knew that. They wouldn't file murder charges against the other boys in the car, because all the evidence pointed to Tyler, and they would be conceding that Tyler's second story was the truth. Jenny had given him a message, that much he knew. Now it was time to figure out what she was trying to tell him. He pulled out his cell phone and called Gladys.

"Gladys, this is Gavin. Will you do me a favor? Pull the Tutuila case files and put them on my chair. Thanks." He hung up the phone and continued to run the conversation in his mind. One thing was certain. *Jenny knows more than she's telling me. She's hiding something. Maybe she's protecting something or someone.* He reread the memo again as he walked toward his car. His eyes kept coming back to the circle around Chillie's name and the notation, *route to RB.* The memo was important, Jenny confirmed that much. Now he needed to know how it fit into his case. At any rate, the meeting with Jenny helped to take his mind off the motion to dismiss and the creatively written response brief he just filed.

CHAPTER 15

JENNY COULDN'T HELP but second guess her decision to confront Gavin with the memo. All afternoon, as she confidently tore apart the defense's case witness by witness, Gavin's phone call, the memo, and Sara's murder bled into the cracks of her mind during the brief pauses between her questions. Gavin was smart. She was counting on it. He was beginning to ask the right questions, and it was up to him to uncover whatever truth was out there.

Gavin's civil suit was scratching at old wounds, but they were open wounds that had silently festered under the lies that prevented them from healing for years. She didn't want to think about the implications of her suspicions. Gavin mentioned that cops were involved, and Randy was extremely disturbed by the case. She had done all she could. If there was such a thing as justice, if the word meant something more than a criminal defense attorney chiseling away at the burden of reasonable doubt placed upon the shoulders of the prosecution each day in court, then it was up to Gavin to uncover it.

Until now, Jenny thought of justice as nothing more than the pieces of evidence admitted before a jury. That's what drew her to Gavin long ago. She wouldn't admit it to herself, but she was still drawn to him — perhaps not to him personally, but to his passion for the law.

She hammered the table during her closing argument, demanding justice for the community, demanding accountability for the defendant. Gavin was there, in her mind, smiling at her, and ready to debate the philosophy of the law. As she continued her memorized speech, her thoughts transcended the walls of the tiny courtroom, piercing the arrow of time to revisit their first conversation in Chicago. She still remembered that night as if it were yesterday. Gavin was droning on about the evils of big business, and how they stifle civil justice and the individual's access to the system. It wasn't arrogance, rather a fanatical empathy for humanity and society that boldly showed through each word he spoke. It was contagious. Jenny laughed and countered with startling runaway verdict statistics due to what she considered to be frivolous lawsuits. They talked for hours, neither one of them yielding an inch and gaining even less.

Perhaps that was what had bothered her all these years. She was seduced not by Gavin the person, but by an unobtainable ideal that Gavin seemed to intuitively grasp with the ease of a savant. And yet, in so many other ways, he was nothing more than a childish, self-serving male. She wasn't hurt, and, perhaps, she used him as well, but her actions were at least more honest in nature. She shook her head, clearing it of all the remnants of Chicago, focusing on the last bit of her rebuttal closing argument.

"I ask you for one thing ladies and gentlemen. The community demands but one thing, Justice. Thank you." She confidently walked over to her chair and sat down.

The judge began reading his final instructions to the jury. Jenny straightened her papers and prepared for the excruciatingly painful wait while the twelve members retired to the back room to deliberate the defendant's fate. She knew she had done the right thing in confronting Gavin and pushing him in the right direction. She'd done her part. This wasn't her fight. It was up to other people to stir up the hornet's nest.

HANNAH BRISKLY MADE her way across the university campus when one of her students came up behind her. She had just completed her lecture, and was heading back to her office.

"Professor Brady?" David tapped her gently on the back shoulder.

Hannah jerked a bit, startled by his presence. "Oh, my God, David. Sorry, you scared me to death," she said smiling a breath of relief.

"Sorry about that, professor." David was a gentle spirit. He wore a bright multi-colored knit cap that covered most of his dreadlocks. When not studying Psychology, David worked with an outreach organization taking troubled youths on backpacking excursions. It was easy to become annoyed at his incessant questions during class, but he'd grown on Hannah during the semester, and she admired his kind-hearted nature.

"What can I do for you? We can walk and talk. I'm just beginning office hours."

"Well, yeah, sure we can discuss some stuff."

"Any stuff in particular or do you wanna just cover the entire subject of Psychology?"

"Well, actually I got another class right now."

Hannah stopped. She sensed something odd in David's voice. He was usually so calm and direct when he spoke. His hesitant behavior concerned her. "What's up?"

"Something weird just happened. I feel a little uncomfortable about this."

"What wrong, David?"

"I was sitting in your class, right? Which was great as always."

"David, tell me what's wrong."

"Anyway, I go to the bathroom after class. I'm standing at the urinal doing, well you know, when this guy comes in and starts using the one next to me. No big deal, just two guys in the bathroom. But then he says, 'you in Professor Brady's class?' Which is already weird cause guys usually don't talk to each other while using the bathroom."

"I've heard that," Hannah said smiling. "Someone really ought to study that phenomenon."

"Especially guys that don't know each other. So I said, 'yeah,' and then this is where it got kind of weird. He shoved a manila envelope under my arm and said, 'give this to your professor.'"

David pulled out a manila envelope from his backpack. It was sealed. There was no name on it and no return address.

Hannah looked at the envelope in David's hands not quite sure how to react. "Did you say anything?"

"No. I just kept my head down. I mean he shoved it between my arm. I couldn't move or anything. I was kind of busy at the time."

"Did he say anything else?" Hannah asked still not reaching for the envelope.

"Nothing. Oh yeah, this is the weirder part. He wasn't even using the bathroom. I mean, I didn't see him zip up or anything. It was like he was following me or something."

"What did he look like?"

"I don't know. I mean I don't look at anyone in the bathroom, and I was just so freaked out by this already. I just kept my head down. I didn't get a good look at him."

Hannah slowly took the envelope from David's grip. It was heavy and solid as if it had several pages of cardstock inside.

"Do you think we should tell someone? I mean, should I report it?"

Hannah stared at it momentarily. "I don't think so. If it's something of concern, I'll take it to the administration, but I'm sure there's a reasonable explanation for this."

"Like I said, I feel kind of weird about this. I wasn't sure what to do."

"You did what you should've done. Don't worry about it. Thanks." She smiled and patted David's shoulder reassuringly.

"But don't you think that's kind of weird?"

"It is a little weird, but I'm sure there an explanation. If not, I'll take care of it," she said feigning confidence.

"Okay. I should go to class, but let me know if you need a statement or something."

"I will. Thanks." She waved as he turned away and headed back across campus. She looked back down at the envelope. It looked covert and secretive. Who would pass an envelope to her? She was a professor and a new one at that.

She looked around the campus. There were scattered groups of students walking between the gothic style buildings. A group of students were laughing at something, a joke perhaps. There were large Douglas Fir trees that dotted the area giving the university a natural Northwest feel, but also obstructing the view. Perhaps the man who slipped the envelope to David was hiding behind one of those trees staring at her. Perhaps it was another professor, who was benignly passing her an interesting article. She brushed aside the thought as ludicrous. Professors don't sneak into bathrooms and accost students.

She thought about opening the packet right there on the sidewalk. She looked around again to see if anyone stood out, if anyone reacted to her. For a moment, it seemed as if the entire world was staring her down. Each group of students seemed to turn her way, as if mocking her briefly before resuming their discussions. Hannah kept searching the campus. If the man was still out there, if he was watching her, he would want to see her reaction when she opened it. He would want to watch her as she ripped open the seal and took out whatever was inside. *No,* she said to herself. *I won't give the bastard the satisfaction.* She tucked the envelope firmly under her arm and marched to her office. She would open it there, in private. Whatever was inside, she would need to digest alone.

Along the way, she kept a nonchalant eye out for anyone who might be following her. Today was much like any other day. The afternoon breeze carried the scent of fresh pine through the air. Most of the students were clad in sweaters and half-shorts, taking advantage of each brief drop of sun that successfully fought its way through the blanketing Northwest sky.

Because she was relatively new, her office was temporarily located in the Philosophy building until one came available in the Psychology department. The hallway was empty as she made her way to her office door. She was hoping that someone would be there to distract her a little while longer. At least someone could be in the area when she opened the envelope. She had no such luck. Her fellow professors were either in class or at home.

Her office door was locked, which gave her some comfort. On the front of the door was a Calvin & Hobbes cutout from the newspaper. It was her favorite cartoon, and she had been cutting them out and saving them since college. Gavin used to make fun of her for hanging them all over the place, but it seemed such a waste to her to only enjoy something once. She didn't even notice the cartoon as she fumbled with her keys in the lock. Once inside, she put down her papers, and set the envelope on her desk ready to open.

Now that she was alone, she could examine it closer. Both sides contained no markings and no return address. The flap was securely sealed. Whoever sent this even took the time to latch the brass brads through the small eye hole on the flap. *This is crazy. What could it be?* Reaching in her drawer, she pulled out a long metal letter opener and sliced one end of the envelope. She paused a moment after exposing the end to the contents inside. She half-expected an explosion and was ironically disappointed in the anticlimactic result.

The envelope contained eight by ten inch photos of something. She decided that the wait had been long enough. Turning the envelope upside down, she poured out the contents on her desk. The pictures scattered along the top of the wood staring back at her. She skimmed them quickly. There were seven in all, each one black and white. At first, she didn't know what she was looking at, but, as if the photos were developing right before her eyes, she saw something that shocked her. In the middle of the small stack was a photo of her in a grocery store. She was at the checkout line. She even remembered the day. It was last week.

She picked up the others. One of the photos showed Gavin alone by the water. He was on the Tacoma pier leaning over the edge near the spot where the gun that killed Sara allegedly had been discarded. The next two photos showed their house from the street. There were no lights on inside, and it didn't look as if anyone was home at the time. The last three disturbed her the most. The photos showed Gavin with a young professional and attractive looking female. They were talking about something. One shot was taken outside the courthouse, and the other two were taken inside the building.

Chills ran down her entire body as she looked back through the photos. She picked up the phone and dialed Gavin. There had to be an explanation. Perhaps, this was a joke. If it was, it wasn't funny. The phone rang three times before Gladys picked up.

"Mr. Brady's office," she said in her usual matter of fact voice.

"Hi, Gladys, this is Hannah. Is Gavin around?"

"Hi, Hannah, how's the new job?"

"Oh, it's fine." She didn't have time for polite chit chat. "Do you know if Gavin is available? It's kind of urgent."

"I'll check for you dear." Gladys wasn't easily insulted. The business of law was driven on stress and impossible deadlines, and she had survived in this environment for more than twenty years. For a woman in Glady's position, an impatient wife was almost a relief. She put Hannah on hold and buzzed Gavin's office. There was no answer. She clicked back on the line with Hannah.

"There's no answer in his office. Let me just pop up his calendar on my computer."

"Thanks, Gladys." She tried to hide the anxiety in her voice, but Gladys could sense something was bothering her.

"Yes, here it is. He's in a document review in our south conference room. I can page him if you'd like."

"No — yes please," she said changing her mind in mid-sentence. "I probably need to talk with him as soon as possible." She thought for a split moment that she could wait, but then decided that she needed to have Gavin informed now. This was too weird as her unwitting deliverer had put it, and a little unnerving. For all she knew, Gavin had received similar photos and had an explanation already.

Gladys put Hannah back on hold to page Gavin. It only took about two minutes for Gavin to come to the phone, but it seemed like a lifetime to Hannah. Gladys only told Gavin that he had an important call, not that it was his wife. Partners didn't like associates to feel as though they could maintain a normal life without first satisfying the needs of the firm. The law is a jealous mistress, and most of the partners took that saying to heart. It probably also explained why most of them were either sleeping around or on the down slope of a second marriage.

Gavin picked up the phone outside of the conference room. "This is Gavin," he said in his new found authoritarian tone.

"Gavin, thank God they found you."

"Hannah?" His voice immediately softened. He walked the same hallways as his hardened peers but, deep down, Hannah always came first. "What's wrong?"

"I'm not sure. I just needed to talk with you."

"Are you okay? Were you in an accident?"

"No, nothing like that. Look, I think you should come over here."

"Hannah, I'm at work. What's wrong?"

She told him about David's encounter with the stranger in the bathroom, and about the envelope. She had been so brave up to this point, but the stress of the moment finally got to her. As she told her husband of the photos, she broke down crying. Gavin asked if she'd called the police. She hadn't even thought of that. The police, of course. That would be a smart idea.

He calmed her down and then hung up the phone after she promised to lock her office door until the police arrived. He took a deep breath and dialed Gladys.

"Mr. Brady's office."

"Hi, Gladys."

"Did you get in touch with your wife?"

"Yes, could you do me a favor, call the police, tell them to meet me at her office on campus?"

"Of course, is everything all right?"

"Yeah, I'm sure it is. It's just precautionary, but better safe than sorry. Do you have her address?"

"I do. I'll call right now."

He hung up the phone and turned to the conference room. He was tempted to have Gladys tell them that he was called away, but there were two partners in there, and he wasn't sure what type of impression that would make. He took a deep breath and walked back inside. He told them that there was an emergency on one of his cases, and he needed to handle it right away. They seemed to accept the explanation, which surprised Gavin. He'd heard too many horror stories about partners becoming territorial with associates and cases. No one liked to be second-bested, especially to other partners.

He ran to his office and grabbed his keys. It only took him seventeen minutes to get to her office from his building. When he pulled into the parking lot, he could see two police cars already parked. He was relieved. He sprinted to her building and down to her office. Hannah was standing outside her door talking to one of the uniformed officers.

"Hannah." He called out as he approached.

She embraced him. It was a relief to have him finally there.

"Are you okay?"

"Yeah, I'm fine. I just didn't know what to do."

"Are you Mr. Brady?" One of the uniformed officers asked.

"Yes."

"Perhaps you could go talk to sergeant Mozol over there, and see if you recognize the photos while I finish taking a statement from your wife."

"Sergeant Mozol?"

"He's inside the office. I'll just be a minute." The officer was kind but direct. This was an investigation, and they had a job to do.

Gavin hugged Hannah again and walked inside the office. Mozol was young. He looked to be the same age as Gavin. This bothered him. He was picking up each photo with tweezers and placing them inside plastic evidence bags. Gavin could see that the envelope was already sealed in a bag. "Sergeant?"

"Mr. Brady, nice to meet you. Your wife said a student gave her an envelope that had these photos inside."

"Yeah, she called me right after she opened it."

"Are you the one who called the police?"

"Yeah, well, my secretary did. I rushed over here as fast as I could."

"Why don't you come over here?" He signaled for Gavin to come beside him for a better look at the photos. The first two were almost identical shots of their house.

"What the hell is this?"

"Well, usually it's some kind of message. Maybe whoever sent these is telling you and your wife that he knows where you live."

"Knows where I live?" Gavin looked up at him. He couldn't think straight. He wanted to ask a million questions but couldn't find the right words.

Sergeant Mozol could see the fear in his expression. "Look, this could be nothing."

"Nothing?"

"It happens all the time on college campuses. It could be some pissed off student trying to scare your wife over a grade or not letting him in her class or something like that."

"Well, that's reassuring."

"Let's go through the photos and see if you recognize anything."

He turned over the next photo. It showed Hannah in line at the grocery store. She had a contemplative distant expression on her face. The next photo showed Gavin standing on the pier.

"Oh my God."

"Do you recognize something?"

"Oh my God."

"Mr. Brady, what is it?"

"That's me on the pier. I was there all alone. I didn't see anyone around."

"Your wife tells me you're a lawyer?"

"Yeah."

"Could this be a past client or something like that?"

"I just started. I'm an associate at Stewart, Meridiam & Smithwick."

"What type of law do you practice?"

"Uhm, right now everything." He was only half listening to the questions. He picked up the bagged photo of him on the pier.

"Why were you there?"

Gavin started to answer and then stopped. A wave of insight rushed over him. His face flushed as he continued to stare at the photo. Sergeant Mozol saw the expression change in his face.

"Is there something that you recognize?"

"It's this case." Gavin looked at the sergeant with an expression of recognition.

"What case?"

Gavin took a moment to gather his thoughts. He then told the sergeant about the Trans Am, and how it appeared in front of their house. He told the story of Sara's murder, and that he represented her and her family in a wrongful death suit against the boys in the car and against Tyler's parents.

Mozol remembered the murder. Every cop in Pierce County remembered this case. It was front page news in the area, and it shocked the verdict shocked the community. The last three photos confirmed Gavin's story. They showed him talking with Jenny in front of the courthouse and inside the crowded hallway.

"What's this?" Gavin asked as he flipped the photo over. On the back was the number two in black magic marker.

"Well, that's interesting," Mozol said scratching his head.

Gavin turned over the other photos as well. All of them had numbers except one of the photos of the house. On the back of that photo was a capital A.

"What does this mean?"

"You got me."

"Could it be some type of categorizing or something to do with where it was developed?" Gavin asked.

"I've never seen this before. My guess is that the perp probably developed these photos himself, and I say that because I do a little amateur photography as well. I don't use anything like this, and I've never heard of putting numbers behind photos, but I tell you what, I'll call around the photo houses to see if anything turns up."

Gavin picked up the clear bags that housed each individual photo. "Can I make a copy of these?" He wanted to have a chance to study them, and once the police had possession of the evidence, he would no longer have any access to them.

"The photos?"

"Yeah." His mind raced for a legitimate reason. "I'm working on a civil case, and if these are related, then I might need them. Plus, I might find something out to pass along to you guys." *That sounds good.*

Mozol reluctantly nodded his head. Gavin took out his phone and walked over to the copy machine and placed each bagged photo face down on the glass first copying the picture and then the back side with the magic marker writing. The photo of him at the pier had the number seven on the back. The photo of Hannah had the number two on the back. The photos inside the courthouse contained the numbers zero and two respectively, and the photo outside the courthouse also had a zero on the back. One of the photos of their home contained the number seven, while the other one contained the letter A. There didn't seem to be any pattern or purpose for the markings. However, these photos were sent for a reason and the markings might be part of the message.

The sergeant took down the rest of Gavin's statement after he was finished copying, and promised to call if they turned anything up. He reassured Gavin that there probably wasn't too much to worry about. He told him that it was most likely some type of prank or a stupid message. Dangerous people usually don't warn first.

Gavin wanted them to dust for fingerprints around the office even though there was no evidence of a break-in. He wanted to be thorough, to cover all the bases so they wouldn't miss a potential lead. Mozol and his partner humored him, and gently tried to explain that it would be a waste of time. There were eight professors with permanent offices in this area and one revolving office for visiting lecturers. On any given day, fifty students came through this hallway past Hannah's door. The number of prints they would turn up would likely be staggering and completely unhelpful. They did, however, promise to dust the photos and envelope for fingerprints. If they found a match, they would call.

When the police left, Gavin called Gladys and told her what happened. She promised to cover for him the rest of the day, and threatened him if he came back to the office. Hannah was in no condition to be alone right now anyway. They left her car in the faculty parking lot and drove home together in Gavin's car. Hannah was uncharacteristically quiet. She kept one arm on his shoulder the entire trip. Gavin remained silent as well. He didn't know what to say and was pretty sure there was nothing he could say that would put Hannah's mind at ease.

What was it about this case that caused such a stir? Duke handles wrongful death cases all the time without this type of reaction, Gavin thought to himself as he drove across the bridge. He began rethinking his role. Someone was threatening his family now. That person knew where he lived and followed him. Then again, maybe the police were right. Perhaps this was nothing more than a sick college prank. After all, they didn't seem to be taking it too seriously. He looked over at Hannah.

"What's going on?" she said.

"What do you mean?"

"People are parked in front of our house. Now they're sending photographs of us and our home, you with some woman." She stopped herself and looked away.

"Is that what this is about? She's a prosecutor." He felt terrible trying to justify the photo. He felt like a cheating husband who got caught. There wasn't anything going on between them. It was the memory that haunted him. "She's investigating this case at the prosecutor's office."

"I don't care who she is. It's not about her."

"Look, the police are right. It's probably just some asshole trying to scare me."

"Well, he did a great job. What's next?"

125

"I can't just stop every case just because the other side gets mad or does something rash. Anyway, whoever this is, he'd be stupid to try anything else now that the police are involved. I wouldn't let anything happen to you. I promise." Hannah didn't respond. She was angry and with good reason.

Maybe he'd talk with Duke tomorrow. Duke always seemed to know the answers, and, after hundreds of wrongful death cases, he must have run into this situation before.

They were quiet the rest of the ride home. The day's events stifled any hope of talking about anything benign, and they were mentally exhausted. As they pulled around the corner to their house, Gavin tried not to let Hannah see him scan the area for unfamiliar faces or cars. She was too busy looking around herself to notice.

She made him walk through the entire house and search all the closets before she would relax. He assured her that this was a one-time event. She was not convinced. How could he guarantee such a thing when he didn't even know who was behind it? He knew that the memo had something to do with it. Jenny was trying to tell him something today, and he needed to figure it out. They silently watched television together before turning in for the night. Gavin made one last check around the house. He checked the windows and then joined Hannah in bed.

The night offered only temporary solace, and sleep was brief and untamed. The events of the day churned around in their thoughts infiltrating their dreams. Gavin woke up twice. Each time, he could see Hannah's eyes twitching back and forth underneath her eyelids in a tumultuous slumber. After several hours of restlessness, he got up and went into the living room.

He pulled out the copies of the photos and turned on the television. He tried to concentrate, but all he could think about was what Jenny said to him. *It's about you trying to extort our office into filing charges against those men, and using this memo against us.* What did she mean by that?

He adjusted himself on the couch as he studied the photos, turning each one over to find the connection between the picture and the number on the back. There were two zeros, two twos, the numbers seven, nine, and a capital letter A. *002279A.* He ran the sequence in his head. Nothing made sense. There didn't seem to be any rhyme or reason to the numbers, but there had to be. Whoever sent these meant to mark up the back, and meant for him to see it. His mind wrestled with the case as he finally drifted off to sleep. Tomorrow would be a new day and, hopefully, a new opportunity to discover the truth.

CHAPTER 16

THE NEXT COUPLE of days went by without any news from the police. Both Gavin and Hannah tried to put the mysterious photos out of their minds. Meanwhile, Gavin's days continued to grow longer as partners flooded him with research projects and legal memos on everything from subrogated interests in land contracts to the environmental protection act. Duke continued to take an interest in him, and he was regularly sitting in on new client meetings. As he listened to Duke talk about the contingency fee arrangement and what to expect throughout the course of litigation, Gavin wished that he would have had this experience before going out to Alexandria. He tried to balance his time between the projects due for the partners, who held his future in their hands, and the one case that Duke had entrusted to him.

Along with the oral argument that was scheduled for the end of the week on Lance's motion to dismiss, Gavin had depositions coming up in the case as well. All the boys in the car were scheduled to appear over a two-day period. Gavin had never actually taken a deposition before other than simulated ones in law school. He knew the drill and technique, but didn't yet have the experience. Depositions, his law professors always told him, are as much an art as they are a skill. A good attorney should know more about the case than the person being deposed. For every scheduled hour of questions, the attorney should be spending two hours preparing, because it is important to lock the witness down to certain pre-determined statements that will advance the attorney's theory at trial. Additionally, good attorneys know when to stop questioning so that the witness isn't given a chance to wiggle out of an answer.

Gavin's class practiced deposing each other using mock cases, but it was not the same. There was little pressure and nothing but a grade at stake. In contrast, the real world put a tremendous amount of pressure and importance on the performance in a deposition. A young innocent girl was murdered and these boys held the key to unlocking the cover-up. Gavin did his best to prepare. He sat in on two depositions that Duke was taking on another case and took copious notes. Duke made it look so easy. He only used a rough outline as a guide, and his questioning style seamlessly weaved around a windy path of seemingly innocuous topics until, before the witness knew what was happening, he was trapped into Duke's theory of the case like a helpless insect in a spider's web.

Additionally, Duke was a master at utilizing silence to his advantage. He would comfortably pause during the dead space between the end of an answer and the beginning of the next question. In court, he would stand before the witness methodically sizing him up with his stare, and creating enough uncomfortable dead air that the witness would continue giving up every last morsel of information. If he thought the person was too prepared or not forthcoming enough, Duke would pause after an answer and stare him down, bathing himself in the awkward silence. Time would bend and the spaces between each second would serve as caverns that echoed each ticking moment. Finally, after the witness couldn't take it anymore, he would continue talking just to breathe life back into the air. "People will admit to almost anything. They'll tell you everything just to avoid the social awkwardness of silence," he told Gavin.

Gavin had been doing his homework and he knew the elements of his case. He knew that they were drinking the evening of the shooting, and that it was important to lock them all down to that fact. Not just social drinking, but power drinking, the kind of drinking that makes people do negligent things. It was also critical to somehow tie the parents into their party.

He had read in the investigative materials that Tyler's father, Palolo Tutuila, was a big shot in the community. The parents knew that their son was a troublemaker. He wasn't a hardened criminal but he had been in and out of juvenile detention since he was eleven. Each time, his father put up his bail and hired a lawyer. Each time, it was the same lawyer, Mike Davies, an ex-federal prosecutor, who quickly earned a reputation as an experienced criminal attorney.

Davies was involved in several high profile death penalty cases as a federal prosecutor before coming to the defense side. He was charismatic with jurors and, more importantly, quotable with reporters. He had an uncanny knack for being available to comment on whatever legal issue popped up around the community, and made it known he aspired to become a nationally recognized legal expert. The Harrington murder trial gave him that opportunity.

The case was front page news for almost a full year. The associated press picked up the story because it had a human interest element and involved families on both sides of the country. The fact that Sara was a beautiful victim didn't hurt either. Even several United States Senators used the case as a pulpit to talk about the growing problems of random violence in the country and the need for tougher gun legislation. The case received so much publicity that Senator Donaldson from Sara's district in Virginia asked Congress for one minute of silence to honor her during his election campaign. In a brilliant cliché of political promises, he vowed not to rest until her killers were held accountable for their dastardly deeds against humanity and the sanctity of life. Unfortunately, it was one campaign promise that was forgotten after the acquittal.

The entire time, Davies countered with his own spin on the morning talk show circuits and the national news organizations. Once the boys changed their stories and Tyler was acquitted, Davies was touted as the attorney with the Midas touch. The calls came pouring in, and it wasn't long before he had his own weekly segment on one of the national news programs. Everyone seemed to use this case to their advantage, everyone except the Harringtons, who were left empty-handed while the system coldly abandoned them.

The case bothered Gavin from the beginning. It was all too perfect and neat. Tyler originally confessed to the shooting. The three other occupants also confirmed that Tyler was the shooter. Within days of hearing that Casey couldn't identify anyone in the car, Tyler and two other boys changed their stories and pointed the finger at Marcus. It was simple. The boys' testimony remained unchanged except for one fact. They switched the places of everyone in the car so that Tyler was now in the back passenger seat and Marcus was in the front passenger seat. It matched the forensics.

They were arrested within hours of each other and without notice to the others. How could they have come up with such a scheme before they even knew the police were on to them? It was too contrived to have been a spur of the moment plan. Finally, there was the Chillie Ki factor. Chillie was in the car thirty minutes before the shooting. They bought beer at a local store, and then dropped Chillie off at his mom's house. The memo that Jenny was so upset about in the courthouse detailed this event. It stated that Chillie positively placed Tyler in the front seat the entire time that he was in the car. When Chillie got out of the car, he saw Tyler re-take his seat in the front passenger side of the vehicle. This was the last stop before they came upon Sara's car. How could they be so sure that Chillie would not testify to this fact, ruining their plan? The memo was clear that Tyler was in the front seat and Chillie knew it.

The memo had been bothering Gavin for days. He knew it was significant and he knew that it struck some nerve not only with Jenny, but with the entire prosecutor's office. What he couldn't figure out was why. He was working on his notes for the upcoming depositions when Gladys buzzed him.

"Mr. Brady?"

"Yes, Gladys."

"You asked me to find the address for a Mr. Chillie Kwon Ki."

The investigation file had a lot of names, but the addresses and phone numbers were redacted. It was typical for attorneys to do that for privacy reasons. Gavin had the option to go to court and get a judge to order the prosecutor's office to give him unredacted copies, but he didn't have time to do that. Besides, given Jenny's comments to him, the prosecutor's office could argue that the records were now privileged because there was an active investigation going on.

It didn't help matters that Lance filed his motion to dismiss very early in the investigation, and Gavin was desperate to find enough information from the witnesses to keep the case alive. He was feeling the weight of this case on his shoulders, and was beginning to doubt whether he was even cut out for litigation.

He couldn't stop thinking about the case. He knew that the Harringtons were taking a chance on him, a chance that was less than deserved. Had he been honest enough with them about his lack of experience? He thought he explained it to them, but he was so desperate to keep the case, desperate to make a good impression on Duke. Now it was beginning to keep him up at night and, more importantly, it was affecting his home life. How could he drag Hannah into this? She didn't need to be involved. It wasn't her fight, but someone was bringing the fight to his home and making it personal.

He needed to prioritize his tasks, and focus on one thing at a time, and forget about the fact that the entire case seemed to be crumbling around him. Gavin gave Gladys a list of witnesses to locate that he got from the file. It was cheaper than an investigator and Gladys was a master at tracking people down. Chillie was the hardest to find. He didn't testify at the murder trial, and the prosecution never listed him as a witness. The only document that referenced him at all was the memo. That bothered Gavin. Chillie seemed critical to rebutting the changing of the stories, but somehow was completely ignored by the prosecution. It was as if they didn't even know about him. Why not? They had the memo.

"I think I have an address for you." Gladys' voice brought Gavin back to reality.

"Did you find him?"

"I've haven't been able to find him, but I did find his mother."

"His mother?"

"I think so. She wasn't listed, but it was the last known address for a Chillie K. Ki. I assume it's the same person."

"Is she local?" Gavin didn't want to travel out of town again. Not with what happened at Hannah's work, and with the strange car following him around.

"Not only local, but home at the moment. I called her house and confirmed that she was there."

Gavin looked at his watch. It was already 6:30 in the evening, and he was in the middle of preparing for the depositions coming up.

"Would you like the address?" Gavin quickly picked up on Gladys' insistent tone.

"Thanks, I would. I just need to finish what I'm working on and I'll head over there."

He was annoyed at the interruption, but he knew that this was a break. He hadn't been able to find Chillie since the beginning, and now he might have an opportunity to talk to him, and find out why he didn't testify. The problem was that everything was happening at once. The oral argument was coming up and the depositions were right around the corner. This was litigation and if he wanted to become a good trial attorney, he had better get used to the pressure of unobtainable deadlines. He quickly jotted down the address and hung up the phone. This had better be good.

THE WAITRESS WEAVED through the crowd with perfect precision as she balanced two overfilled beers on her tray. She was dressed in a short sleeve shirt and jeans that hugged the bottom of her hips, and partially revealed a tattoo on her lower back. She continued through the bar past several tables to the back where Randy and another gentleman were seated. The man was dressed in an old polo shirt and khaki pants, and wore a cloth windbreaker that looked at least two decades out of style. He fiddled with an unlit cigarette in his hand.

"Here you go, gentlemen," the waitress said as she replaced their empty glasses with two more beers.

"Thanks, Darlin'." Randy flashed a friendly grin. He was almost twice her age but his disarming demeanor allowed him to get away with calling women things like Darlin' and Honey. It just sounded natural coming from him.

"Now, you're not going to light that up are you?" She asked jokingly to the man sitting next to Randy. "I don't wanna have to call the law on you."

He didn't seem amused by her playful banter. Without looking at her, he put the cigarette into his jacket pocket. Unfazed, the waitress gave Randy a polite wink, and walked off to her next table.

"Lighten up will ya, she's just a kid," Randy said after she was out of earshot.

"I'm not here to get laid. I'm here to discuss our mutual problem." Nate continued to fiddle with his cigarette. Nathaniel Bridges was a private investigator. He did not much like Randy but tolerated him because of their history together, and because Randy came from an influential and powerful family.

"How much does the kid know?" Nate asked.

"Nothing. What's there to know? He's just meddling into an old wound that I don't want reopened." Randy was a politician to the end. He had an uncanny ability to vaguely talk around a subject so that he could never be pinned down to a solid statement or position.

"Cut the crap, Randy. There're no cameras or recorders around, unless you're wearing a wire. We gonna talk or what?"

Randy took an uncomfortable sip of his beer and glanced around the room. "Somehow, the memo from the Tutuila murder case was leaked to the kid's office and he put some info from it in the complaint."

Nate smiled. "That must make you real nervous right about now?" He enjoyed watching Randy's discomfort.

Randy let out a nervous chuckle and looked around the bar again. He had picked the location well. The room was filled with mostly blue collar workers who were winding down from the second shift. No one noticed Randy and Nate sitting at their table, and no one would recognize either one of them. Still, Randy was not taking any chances. He reached over to Nate's chest and began rubbing his hand up and down his upper torso looking for a wire. A thick bearded man in the corner turned his head briefly to witness the display, but soon lost interest.

"What the — you think I'm wearing a wire? You're pathetic."

"It's a dangerous world, can't be too careful."

"You want to feel the gun I got strapped to my shoulder as well?" Nate was as short tempered as he was direct.

Randy tried to dismiss the indirect threat by rolling his eyes. "We need to do something, don't you think?"

"Damn you, Randy," he said with a calm voice. "Why'd I get tangled up with you, you're a snake, you know that?" He shook his head and looked away.

"Oh, now I'm a snake? What do you think that makes you then?" Randy's smooth political demeanor dissipated. "You need to stop playing the victim here cause you got as much, if not more, to lose than I do."

Randy called Nate a week earlier but he was out of town on an assignment. When Nate finally returned his call, Randy refused to discuss anything over the phone. He demanded they meet face to face, and somewhere that no one would recognize them. Nate chose a bar next to the old docks in Tacoma that catered mainly to commercial construction and ship workers.

"What we need to do is not fight each other, okay?" Randy said.

"Well, what do you want me to do?" Randy just looked at him. "You want me to kill the bastard?" Nate said to force a reaction.

"Are you kidding? No." Randy wasn't sure if Nate was serious or not.

"I'm not going down for your mess."

"Nothing's happening to anyone over this, just calm down. We just gotta think carefully and make sure that we're at the head of it and not the back end. You think I'm out lookin' for a scandal involving this case? This case was my ticket in and I'm not going anywhere."

"And yet you called me." Nate was Randy's henchman. He had set Nate up in his own surveillance and security business, and had even put in a good word for him with a lot of his political friends in congress and at the state capital. There was no shortage of politicians and judges who needed personal matters handled discreetly. Nate would then keep Randy informed on all the dirt he learned. Randy figured that in a couple of years, he'd start cashing in on the embarrassing information he was collecting, and make a run for the governor's office.

"This is an easy one. The kid's a rookie and besides, he sued the entire world over this case. He's dealing with lawyers from each person in that car as well as Tyler's parents. By the time they're through with him, he'll be wishing he was back in school playing pretend law."

"Okay, smart guy. If he's not our problem, then why blow up my phone with calls for the past week, and then make me come out to this dump to meet you?"

"Because there're five attorneys besides him looking at this case now. I don't want someone accidentally becoming a super sleuth."

Nate finished off his beer. "Okay, then, what do we do?"

"This is a time for thinking. We just need to be very careful and cross all our ts on this one."

Nate signaled the waitress over for another round as she passed by their direction. "The kid's still the key. He's the only one who'll be asking questions, right?"

"What makes you say that?"

"Look, the others are just defense attorneys. They're not out to prove anything. They just want to minimize damages and poke holes in the kid's theory."

Nate was right. After all, these particular attorneys represented the boys who were actually in the car that killed Sara Harrington. None of them would be interested in finding evidence that tended to prove their clients conspired to lie under oath in order to free Tyler. They wouldn't even be looking in that direction.

"Yeah, you're right. The kid's the key. He's the only one ambitious enough and stupid enough to poke his head down the well. If he falls in, I don't want him to make a splash if you know what I mean."

"Tell me everything you know."

Randy started from the beginning. He explained about the complaint that Jenny found and that, somehow, Frank overlooked the memo, and allowed it to be released to Gavin's office. Since that date, Randy reopened a dummy investigation to block any additional documents from being released. Prosecutors are entitled to seal any and all documents pertaining to an active investigation. The memo was already out, but Randy wasn't taking any more chances. Double jeopardy precluded re-trying Tyler for the murder, and he didn't want any type of public spectacle surrounding this case. It was too dangerous.

"This one's gonna cost you," Nate said as Randy finished bringing him up to speed.

"What the hell do you mean, cost me?"

"You want me to follow him, right?"

"Yeah, that's right."

"I don't work for free. Equipment's expensive. I got other cases that I'd have to put on hold for this. That costs money."

"Well, doesn't that beat all. The man's sitting here sinking in quick sand and he's asking for a handout."

"I'm pretty sure it's your hand I feel gripping mine in the puddle. I mean what are we doing here?"

"Don't start getting too big on me. You forget who gave you this life. Who do you think is going to take the fall if this thing goes south?"

"Maybe your memory's not very good anymore either. I don't think your family's gonna want to circle the wagons around you on this. If you want my help, it's gonna cost you."

The waitress came over with the next round interrupting their stare down. Randy was gripping his glass so tightly that his knuckles were turning white.

"Wow, you two," the waitress said. "No need to fight, there's plenty of me to go around."

Randy turned to her and tried to crack a smile. His face was beet red, and a vein was popping out of his temple. The waitress knew better than to overstay her welcome. She plopped down the beers and continued on her way.

Randy contemplated the dilemma they were both in. Nate seemed to have him. Randy had a lot to lose, maybe more than Nate. After all, Nate was lucky to be where he was, and did not have the ambition that plagued a man like Randy.

"How much?" He finally asked, breaking the tension.

Nate cracked a smile and took a swig of his beer. "I figure that the rate should be the same as last time."

"Agreed."

"Adjusting, of course, for inflation."

"What?"

"You don't think I can do this for those prices. Things are more expensive now, cost of living and all that bullshit."

"You greedy bastard. I hope I get the chance to repay you one day."

"And ruin all that we've built together, Counselor? You hurt my feelings."

"All right asshole. You'll get your money."

"We might as well do cash again, avoid all those banks and signatures."

"Cash it is. Now, you screw this up or step off the line at all, and I'm gonna enjoy taking my time destroying your career piece by piece."

"Calm down. Tell me what you want me to do."

The waitress only visited them two more times delivering them the liquid courage that helped plan their continuing conspiracy. When Nate finally took a last gulp of his beer, he stood up robotically and promptly excused himself, leaving Randy to order another pitcher and pick up the tab. In the corner of the bar, a shadowy figure stirred from the bar stool, and followed Nate out of the bar.

TRAFFIC WAS LIGHT in the area in which Gavin was driving. He called Hannah and told her he would be late. She told him she understood but Gavin could tell that she wasn't happy. It became a typical conversation. They spent maybe an hour together in the evenings, and she almost never saw him in the morning. He kept telling her that it would get better. He kept telling her that once he made partner, things would change. He would be home more often, and they would be able to spend time together the way they used to.

Part of him knew it was a lie. It seemed like every partner in his firm was either on his second marriage or secretly seeing someone on the side. In trial advocacy class, they don't teach students that litigation ends at five. Sometimes the difference between winning and losing a case can be as simple as one obscure and overlooked piece of paper buried in a stack of documents. Sometimes it is as small as a single sentence that goes unnoticed until one side finds it and takes the time to dissect it with meticulous detail. Usually this occurs very late at night while staring at a wall, and after the hundredth review of the thousands of irrelevant pages that are always produced in civil litigation.

The demands of firm practice require long hours. Most attorneys in Gavin's firm only saw their families between cases or on whichever weekend day the attorney decided to take off. They were like temporary renters, coming home to fill up the empty spaces between work hours and give some normalcy to their existence. The spouses accepted their lot in life by spending a lot of money, and planning expensive trips on the off chance that a trial was continued or a case was settled.

Gavin tried to put Hannah out of his mind as he rounded the corner to the address Gladys gave him. Although Gavin had not formally prepared for this meeting, he was ready to ask Chillie all the questions needed to prove his case. Most importantly, he was interested in finding out why no one from the prosecutor's office contacted him to testify at Tyler's murder trial. He was such an important witness, and certainly could have rebutted the testimony of everyone who changed their story.

He pulled up to Chillie's house. The homes on the street needed painting, and almost every house had several cars parked in the yard. A group of men stood on the corner staring at him as he pulled up. The grass needed cutting and there were remnants of plastic wrap still on the windows from last year's cold front. For a brief moment, he looked around for the Trans Am that followed him home. It was nowhere to be seen. *How silly.* He got out of his car and pressed the door lock button on his key fob. He saw the porch light was on but the house looked anything but inviting. Even the landscape fighting to survive in this tough neighborhood had a sense of foreboding.

Hesitantly, he knocked on the door. After a few moments, An Asian woman answered. She was approximately the same age as Sara's parents, and carried the same sadness in her face.

"Good evening, I'm sorry to bother you like this."

"You Mr. Brady?" Her voice offered no warmth to her words.

"That's right."

"Some lady called an hour ago. I didn't think you was gonna show up." She moved aside as if to invite him in. Her accent offered no hint of her ethnicity, rather it was an insight into her lack of education and social status. "May I come in?" Gavin didn't want to presume anything. "I only have a few questions."

"Sure."

He followed her into the house. The inside was small and plain. The walls were mostly bare except for several plain landscape paintings that looked as if they were bought at a second-hand store. She led him to a small living room that was just off the front door. Two windows faced the front yard, and provided enough light in the room to amply supplement the lamp in the corner.

She silently directed him to a cloth chair across from the sofa. A coffee table separated the two of them, and there was a television to their right sitting on a brown wooden stand with a small photo of a smiling Asian boy on top of it. The photo was the only bit of life in the room.

"So, you a cop?" She pulled out a cigarette and lit it.

"Me? No." Gavin was surprised at the question. "I'm a lawyer."

"A lawyer, huh? You look like a lawyer." She drew heavy on her cigarette. The end grew red hot and crackled. "You definitely don't look like no cop. What can I do for you?"

"Well, I'm really looking for your son, Chillie."

Her face went stone cold. Smoke slowly crept out of her mouth and rose up her face. "Why, you want your money back?"

"Money? I'm not sure I understand."

"You a lawyer right?"

"Yeah."

"Why do you want Chillie?"

"You see, I'm working on a case that he has some information about."

"You here about that little girl who got herself murdered a few years back."

"Yeah, how'd you know that?" Gavin was sure that Gladys told her nothing over the phone. She was a professional and left those details up to the attorneys. It was always better to hold all the cards when going into a meeting.

"You think you the first person to come over here with your big talk and threats?"

"Ma'am, I just want to talk to your son. I'm not threatening you."

"What are you, the new junior prosecutor in the office?"

Her words hit Gavin like a bullet. Chills shot through his body. He tried to control his eyes from flickering, giving away his surprise. It was important that she not realize his shock if he were to get any additional information from her. He knew this was important. This was a clue. He spoke calmly. "When was the last time someone came by here about the murder?"

She stared him down as she continued to take long draws on her cigarette. "Who are you?"

"My name's Gavin Brady."

"I know your name. You work for the prosecutor's office?"

The gig was up. He couldn't lie. Not only would it be unethical, he would lose any credibility left with her.

"Get out of my house."

"Ma'am, please, I just need a few."

"Get out!" Her voice was instantly loud.

"Okay." Gavin got up and walked to the door, which was only about fifteen feet behind him. He stopped at the doorway. "Please, Mrs. Ki, I need to speak with your son."

"I ain't no Mrs. My ol' man run out on us when Chillie was two."

"I'm sorry." Gavin was desperate to stay. He needed information, and she knew something important. He could feel it. He couldn't just leave. "If I could just talk with your son."

"You can't."

"Please, it's important."

"He's dead."

Gavin was speechless. The coldness drained from her face. She was a woman hardened by the losses in her life, and saying the words only dredged up the agony of the past. He felt just like he did when he was with Sara's parents. He could see the pain seeping through her stone face.

"I'm sorry, I didn't know."

"Yeah, well I guess your bosses forgot to tell you that. He's been dead almost two years. Imagine that." She regained her cold expression. Her eyes offered the only evidence of grief left.

"Can I ask you something?"

"What."

"Was he murdered?" Gavin wasn't sure if that question was appropriate, but he needed to know and it was the only question he could think of that would allow him to continue talking to her.

"I guess you could say that. Drugs killed him, an overdose. He'd been messed up in that shit for years. I kept telling him to stop that." She had more to say, but stopped in mid-sentence. "Who do you work for?"

"I'm a private attorney. I represent the young girl who was murdered. The girl you mentioned earlier. Her family just wants some answers."

"Well, that explains why you don't know shit. I ain't got no answers, and Chillie can't tell you nothin."

Gavin stood there trying to formulate his next question. He wanted to talk about the money and the threats, but he didn't know how to ask the question.

"You want to know about the money, don't you?"

"Yes, I do."

She looked at the street quickly. "I don't know anything about it."

"If you're afraid of someone."

"Sonny, I'm not afraid of anyone. I just don't know nothin."

"Chillie was in the car that evening. He was in the car before the murder."

There was a short pause as she sized him up. "Look, if you want to keep talking, come back in. I need a cigarette."

She led him back to the living room and sat down on the couch. Gavin took his original seat across from her. She lit another cigarette before talking.

"Yeah, he was there, so he said. I never knew what that kid was into. He was in and out and always going somewhere."

"Did he tell you about it?"

"No. I didn't know nothin' until a cop came around investigating, wanting to talk to him."

"Do you remember who it was?"

"No. It was a cop. I didn't speak ten words to the man. He wanted to talk to Chillie. He came around a few more times until he caught him at home. They talked and that was it."

"Did Chillie tell you anything about the night of the murder?"

"No. Chillie didn't say nothin.' He was in his own world."

"What about the money?"

She paused and looked him over. "You say you represent who?"

"The murdered girl and her family."

"You ain't no cop?"

"No."

"You got a card on you?"

No one had ever asked for a business card before. Gavin just received his cards last week. He forced several on Hannah just to get the feel of giving one out. He reached in his jacket pocket, and pulled out one of his cards and handed it to her. She looked it over and then discarded it on the coffee table in front of her.

"Okay. All I know is that Chillie came by one day and told me that some guy gave him a lot of cash to get out of town for awhile. He didn't say who."

"Was this before the trial or after?"

"Before. That's why he was supposed to get out of town, to miss the trial."

"He told you he was supposed to miss the trial?"

"Didn't have to. I knew what was going on."

"What was going on?"

"Somebody was making money off this trial. Chillie knew something that they didn't want anyone else to find out about, so they paid him off."

"How long was he gone?"

She took a long draw on her cigarette. "He never came back. He went down to California to visit his dad and he got mixed up with heroin, and then I heard he overdosed."

"How much money did they pay him?"

"I don't know. I do know that he paid my utility bills up to date and then six months out before leaving. I hope you find the bastards. They all deserve to rot in hell."

"Did you see the people who paid him off?"

"Never saw em,' never asked."

Gavin continued to talk with her for the next hour before leaving. He exhausted her memory of the subject but she either didn't know who paid Chillie off, or was not willing to tell him. Talking with her did confirm that the memo was important to the case. Chillie was paid off by someone to disappear and not testify. That still didn't explain why the lead prosecutor, Frank Gilreath, acted like he didn't even know of Chillie's existence. He didn't make a motion for a material witness warrant or even an extension of the trial to locate him. The case was getting stranger by the day, and, yet, he was no closer to any answers. Plus, he had oral arguments coming up on Lance's motion to dismiss.

On the way home, he drove by the site where the gun was supposedly thrown in the water. It helped him think and to connect with the case in some strange way. It was dark already, and the streetlights along the road sparkled off the Puget Sound. His mind was racing about the interview with Chillie's mom and the case. He was missing something. Chillie was an important figure and one of the reasons that the prosecution was unsuccessful at trial. His mom mentioned a cop who came by and paid Chillie money. His mind clicked. He slammed on the brakes, and pulled his car over to the side of the road. The moonlight bouncing off the water illuminated the inside of his car as he furiously flipped through his working file on the seat next to him.

He pulled out a file labeled *Attorney Notes* and opened it. Inside he found his notes from his interview with Casey. He remembered Casey mentioning a police officer who took his statement at Sara's memorial service.

My God. Casey had told him about an Asian kid who came up to him at the memorial service with the information about Tyler being in the front seat. He figured it was Chillie. Casey also mentioned that he relayed this information to some cop. Probably the same cop who paid Chillie to disappear. The question was why? The more he dug into this case, the more questions he uncovered. He was no closer to the answer than he was the day Duke gave him the file. To make matters worse, Chillie was dead.

Gavin looked out the window. It seemed somewhat ironic that he was parked at the pier where Tyler and his group threw the gun into the icy waters of the Puget Sound. Here he sat trying to solve the mystery of this case at the very location where the first cover-up occurred. *Maybe that's not irony, but it's certainly weird.*

He checked his rearview mirror to see if it was safe to pull back out into the street. Hannah was probably worried about him despite growing accustomed to the fact that he didn't get home until well after dark. In the mirror, about one hundred yards back, he saw a dark vehicle parked on the same side of the road with its lights off.

Gavin turned his car back on and pulled out onto the road. The car behind him began to leave its spot, and head in the same direction keeping a safe distance. It was too dark for Gavin to see the model or color. He sped up to see what would happen. The car also accelerated as if to maintain the same distance behind him. He made it around a bend in the road temporarily disappearing out of sight of the other car. Once the other car's lights were gone, Gavin slammed his foot on the gas pedal. He only had a four-liter engine but it had quick acceleration. It took several seconds before the other car appeared around the bend. By this time, Gavin had gained a tremendous amount of distance. He watched as the lights grew brighter and brighter. The car accelerated to the same distance it kept before the bend, and then slowed to maintain its speed.

Gavin's heart pounded. His headlights drenched the path in front of him with light flooding the night roadway. He could see that there were several cross streets coming up and he needed to act quickly. His revelation about Chillie and the cop had him flustered. What had he stumbled upon? Whatever it was, he was in the middle of it and all alone on this street. He looked back in the mirror. All he could see were the car's lights. It stood to reason that the car behind could only make out his lights as well. He had a thought. Looking ahead, he tried to memorize the road. After a couple of seconds, he clicked off his headlights cloaking himself in the blackness of the night. He knew there was a cross street coming up and he squinted his eyes to find it.

The lights behind him began to grow increasingly larger as the car sped up to find him in its high beams. The road was coming up. He could barely see it but the moonlight offered just enough light to reveal the green edges around the name of the street on the pole at the corner. Hopefully, the moonlight wasn't betraying him as well. The lights behind him continued to grow more intense, but was still too far away to pierce the black blanket around Gavin's car. He waited until he was directly at the corner before turning the wheel sharply to the left. His tires let out a high squeal as they hugged the pavement barely making the turn in time. Gavin immediately made a u-turn and pulled his car to a stop at the edge of the road, ready to spring back out onto the street if the other car followed him. He could see the lights searching the road as the car approached. The engine purred loudly with no sign of slowing. Gavin gripped his chest trying to muffle the thundering beats from his heart. The car behind him gunned its engine and roared past the side street disappearing in the night. Gavin's heart slowly regained its rhythmic beat. He only got a glimpse of the car as it sped past the road, but he recognized it.

It was a black Trans Am.

CHAPTER 17

IT DIDN'T TAKE long for the news of the photos to travel throughout the firm. By the time Gavin came into work following his meeting with Chillie's mom, it was obvious everyone knew. There were a lot of sympathetic hellos and nods as Gavin made his way down the hallway to his office. Even the security guard seemed extra nice to him as he entered the building.

"What's with all the looks?" Gavin said as he reached Gladys' desk.

"You're the talk of the office. You and those nasty photos that some degenerate gave your wife."

"How'd they all find out?" She was the only one who knew as far as Gavin was concerned. Gavin intended to keep this quiet. As bad as he felt about Hannah's unfortunate involvement, he didn't want to give anyone an excuse to pull him off the case. He wasn't quite sure what to do about the photos. However, it would be wrong to stop moving forward with the case. He owed the Harrington family that much. He owed Sara's memory that much.

"It wasn't me. This is a law firm after all. People here get paid to be informed. Today you're news, but don't worry, tomorrow it'll be someone else and you'll be forgotten."

Gavin turned away not entirely satisfied with her answer and headed to his office.

"Mr. Brady?" Gladys called after him. "Here's your mail."

She handed him a small stack of letters along with a couple of legal magazines. He took them and disappeared into his office. By the time that he made it to his desk, Hunter was at his doorway.

"Hey, Mr. famous new associate." Even though they were in the same class at the firm, Hunter was a couple of years older than Gavin, and one of the few attorneys who didn't take himself too seriously.

"What do you mean, famous?" The mysterious photos had been haunting him for days. He knew that Hunter wasn't being malicious. Gavin liked Hunter although he was too busy to really get to know any of his fellow associates very well. Unfortunately, that was true for everyone in the office. Unless the attorneys worked in the same area of law, they would never have enough time with each other to become friends. Hunter fit into that category. He worked with the junior partners in Larry Smithwick's department on land use issues, so he and Gavin didn't have a lot of contact.

"The photos." Hunter's tone turned serious. "How you doing?"

"I'm okay, thanks. It was probably just a stupid joke. You haven't heard whether they're thinking about pulling me off the case have you?"

Hunter snorted a laugh. "Don't worry, you're safe. Stewart's out of town for the next couple of days and the other bigwigs wouldn't go near you without asking him first."

Gavin nodded his head. He knew that Duke was giving one of his usual speeches to the National Trial Lawyers Association on the evils of caps in medical malpractice suits. It was election time again, and the American Medical Association was out in record numbers lobbying senators for federal caps on lawsuits. Excessive verdicts were causing medical premiums to skyrocket, they would argue, and were pricing doctors out of the profession. One of Gavin's mid-week research projects was to correlate whether states with caps on damages actually had lower medical premiums, and to write an argumentative memo advocating why the opposition was wrong. It was a relatively straight forward argument but time consuming nonetheless.

"You sure you're okay?"

"Yeah, I'm fine. Thanks."

"Well, I got a bunch of stuff to review and respond to by noon, so I'll let you get back at it. We gotta have you and Hannah over some night for dinner."

"Sounds good." He thought about the idea of spending a relaxing evening with friends as Hunter left his office, but he knew there was no time. He spent six days a week at the firm, and he never got home before dinner. Hunter's schedule could not have been any better. This was the life of a new associate.

Gavin sat down and began leafing through his mail. There were mostly advertisements from different court reporting services and legal expert referral companies. It did not really matter to Gavin. He was happy to see the *J.D.* at the end of the name, and pretended not to notice that every other associate received the exact same advertisements in their in-boxes.

As he leafed through the flyers, he noticed a letter addressed to him. The return address read, Penderson & Associates. It was some type of legal correspondence from Lance. Gavin tossed the rest of the mail aside on his desk, and opened the envelope. He leaned back in his chair as he read the three-page letter. The introduction was benign enough with a general salutation between counsel. However, the letter immediately began to take on a litigious and adversarial tone as Lance outlined the weaknesses in Gavin's case against the parents. Each paragraph pointed out another flaw in the case. It almost looked like Lance's reply brief that Gavin received the day before. By the time Gavin reached the bottom of the second page, he could already feel a headache starting from the back of his head to the front brow. Gavin turned to the last page. His heart began pounding as he read the last paragraph.

I doubt Judge Velez will entertain your novel theory in this matter. However, if he decides to turn away from legal precedent and allows this case to go forward to a jury, I still do not see liability being crystal clear as you put forth in your briefing. Give me a call to discuss this matter and, hopefully, we can come to an equitable resolution.

The letter infuriated and terrified him at the same time. Everyone in the legal community knew Lance and his reputation as a top-notch corporate attorney, and Gavin did not feel entirely comfortable negotiating with him, especially after Lance had read his brief. Duke was out of town and the oral argument was fast approaching so Gavin was left to handle this alone. Besides, Duke had made it crystal clear that this was Gavin's case. He could still hear Duke's words, *if I wanted to make the tough decisions on this case, I'd litigate it myself.*

Gavin closed his office door before picking up the phone and dialing the number on Lance's letterhead.

"Good morning, Penderson & Associates, how may I direct your call?" A sweet voice said on the other end of the phone.

"Mr. Penderson, please." Before he finished his sentence, he was being transferred to another extension.

"Brian Thomas, may I help you?"

"Uh, yes," Gavin said thinking he got the wrong person. "I'm trying to get in touch with Mr. Penderson."

"Junior or senior?" The voice said quickly.

"Uhm." Gavin wasn't sure. He didn't know that there were two Mr. Pendersons. He didn't know how long the firm had been around. He didn't know anything about Lance or his firm other than Lance was a good attorney. "I don't know. This is regarding the Harrington — Tutuila case."

"Oh, you need Penderson senior. He's not in the office today. Can I take a message for him?"

That was a relief for Gavin. He really wasn't excited about talking with Lance, and now it looked as if he was off the hook.

"Yes, this is Gavin Brady at Stewart, Meridiam & Smithwick."

"Oh, yes, Mr. Brady," Brian said cutting him off, "Mr. Penderson left instructions to forward your call to his cell phone. Hold on, I'll put you through."

This seemed like a good sign. Lance was awaiting his call, and wanted to speak to him about resolving this matter. Duke told him that a good plaintiff's attorney never initiates settlement negotiations. He should always look and act as if he wants to go to trial. In the end, defense attorneys always pay. It's simply a matter of how much.

The phone began to ring again after a couple of clicks by Brian. Gavin was beginning to feel better about his position. The brief wasn't all that bad, and the case law could go either way. Lance must've realized this and wanted out. He was beginning to look forward to regaling Duke about the settlement when he returned.

"This is Lance."

"Mr. Penderson." Gavin swallowed hard. "This is Gavin Brady."

"Yes, Gavin, I'm glad you called." His tone was informal and conversational. He sounded like a reasonable guy. "I wanted to talk to you over the phone instead of the impersonal formal nature of a letter to see if we couldn't get this matter wrapped up quickly."

"That sounds great," Gavin said with confidence. "I think my clients would like to resolve this matter so that they can get on with the healing process."

"Good, I'm glad." A foghorn bellowed in the background almost drowning out his voice. "Sorry about that, can you hear me?"

"Yeah, no problem."

"I try and take one day a month and get out on the water regardless of the weather." Lance was sitting on the deck of his thirty-three-foot sailing yacht with one hand on the steering wheel and the other on his cell phone. It was unusually sunny for the Northwest and the wind wasn't strong. Lance had the sail up, but most of the movement was caused by the yacht's diesel engine. "Today was such a nice day that I couldn't resist. Do you sail?"

"No, I scuba dive but I've never sailed." Gavin was feeling right in his element. He was speaking to Lance not as an adversary, but as a civil professional.

"Well, you've got to try it. Maybe when this case is over, you and your wife can come out sometime and get your feet wet so to speak."

"That sounds great, I'd appreciate that." Gavin was surprised that Lance knew he was married. He was new to the area, and had never met Lance before. Gavin thought about it briefly and then brushed it aside as Lance began to speak again.

"Well, look Gavin, let's get to it. I sympathize with your clients but I've tried a lot of similar cases and I've come to realize that juries, although empathetic to the tragic loss, are reasonable and astute to the randomness of such an act as we have here."

This wasn't what Gavin had expected. This sounded more like his letter than a defense attorney looking to settle the case.

"Randomness? Someone pulled out a gun."

"Not my clients."

"But your clients knew their son was a troublemaker."

"Of course, and it's a clever argument, but at the end of the day, you're asking to hold the father accountable for the sins of the son. That's a tough sell, and let's not forget that their son was acquitted. But I'm gonna put all that aside for now. The reason I originally called was I don't like what's going on here, and I've had a long talk with my clients. I'm satisfied that the Tutuilas had nothing to do with the unfortunate incident with the photos."

"How'd you know about that?"

"Gavin, you'll find out that this is a small community and word travels fast."

"Well, I'm not worried about the photos. The police said it was probably some prank or something." He believed that explanation less every time he repeated it.

"Good. We're civil attorneys, not street thugs. Anyway, I do sympathize but the law's not on your side on this one, and I've got an obligation to my clients. Having said that, I'm prepared to make a fair and final offer to your clients to avoid any further and unnecessary litigation."

"I'm sure my clients will appreciate that." He'd heard that Lance was a tough negotiator but also a straight-forward attorney. Duke told him that defense attorneys always pay to avoid the risks of trial.

"I'm willing to go as high as ten thousand dollars. I know it doesn't divide by three very well." Lance chuckled out loud. It was a joke at Gavin's expense referring to the one-third contingency fee agreement between plaintiff's attorneys and their clients. "But I wanted to start at the top figure to save us from going round and round and beating around the bush."

Gavin felt the blood drain from his face and rush to his feet. That was such a low number. He imagined the painful expressions on the Harrington's faces as they heard the figure.

"Your clients' insurance policy is half a million," Gavin said without masking the shock in his voice.

"Gavin, we're both professionals here and we're both advocates for our clients. But you don't want to go forward on this one. I respect your moxy, kid, but this is a gift. I'm holding four aces and willing to fold for a small outlay of cash that'll satisfy your clients and let mine go back to their world."

"I don't think your position is that solid, why else would you call me?" Gavin tried to reach out and take the words back as he spoke. Never let the other side think you are on to them when they call. He knew that. He had read all the books on negotiations. Now, in his first one, he broke the golden rule.

"I'm calling you out of professional courtesy. I'm calling you because I don't like seeing my colleagues stalked even if they are opposing counsel." Lance's voice grew harsh and loud. "I think something stinks and I don't want to be a part of you getting hurt. You're over your head, kid. I've been doing this a long time and I've dealt with Duke many times. Don't play the man in the white hat with me. We both know what's going on here. You're lookin' for some seed money to finance the suit against the gun makers that's just around the corner. Am I right?"

Gavin's heart sank. Was it that obvious? Gavin originally come up with the idea to go after the parents in order to make the larger suit easier, but things were different now. He had met Steve and Louise Harrington. He now believed in this suit. More importantly, he wanted justice for a teenage girl who never had a chance to stand on her own feet in this world.

"That's unfair and you're wrong." Gavin's voice was raised and not hiding his emotions. "I don't see their names on the complaint. I do see your clients' names."

"Under normal circumstances I'd agree with you." Gavin could almost hear the pinstripes in his suit squeak against his starched shirt. "But I just found out that the prosecutor's office might be starting a criminal investigation."

"So. That doesn't relieve your client from his responsibilities under my subpoena."

"You're right. However, if the prosecutor's office begins investigating my client criminally, then he's not making any under oath statements regarding that night or any night leading up to the death of your client."

"He can't do that."

"Sure, he can. He has an absolute right not to incriminate himself under the Fifth Amendment, and he's told me he's invoking it. That means no deposition."

There was a long pause. His entire case was being played out in the silence on the phone.

"You still there?"

"Of course, I'm still here. I don't agree with your assessment. I have a subpoena and I want to depose your client as is my right."

"I'm sure you do, but not at the expense of my client's constitutional right."

"What makes you think that there's a criminal investigation going on?"

"I got a call this afternoon from Randy Bougainville himself. He wanted to know if I was defending Danny criminally as well as civilly."

Gavin felt as though he was on a roller coaster that was out of control. The news kept getting worse. Why would Randy call Dennis and inform him of a potential criminal investigation? Law enforcement didn't normally give people advance warning that they were going to investigate their activities. Plus, Randy was an elected official and in charge of the entire prosecutor's office. He didn't have a caseload of his own. His role was administrative. Why was he taking such an interest in this case? Gavin thought about the message that Randy left on his machine early on, and the fact that Jenny yelled at him about extorting the office into filing charges. What charges? "What investigation?"

"Excuse me?"

Gavin didn't realize that he had spoken out loud. "What investigation? Did he tell you what he might be investigating?"

"Nope. Just that they were looking into things. Sorry about this but my client's not opening his mouth at all until the criminal investigation mess is over."

"I assume this is going to hold true for the others as well?"

"Well, I can't speak for them, but if I were a betting man, I'd be anticipating more calls."

"Okay, I guess your position is clear. I guess we'll just have to take it up with the judge."

"That's your prerogative of course, but what judge is going to violate someone's Fifth Amendment rights just for a civil case?"

Gavin tried to hold in the anger. "I guess this is just a civil case." He hung up the phone before Dennis could respond. The message light was blinking. He saw it suddenly illuminate during his conversation with Dennis. Before hitting the button, he already knew what the messages were going to say. They were from Sal's lawyer and Tyler's lawyer. Both attorneys parroted Dennis' position. Gavin was just about to pick up the phone and call the prosecutor's office when Gladys buzzed his line.

"Yes, Gladys."

"I have Mr. Thomas McCullough holding. Do you want to speak with him?"

"Who's that?"

"He's the attorney for Marcus Kiuilani I believe is how you pronounce it." Her pronunciation was perfect. Marcus was the fourth occupant in the vehicle the night that Sara was shot and sat behind Tyler in the backseat. At least that was everyone's account until Tyler, Sal, and Danny all changed their stories and pointed the finger at Marcus instead.

"Okay, put him through." Gavin took a deep breath, and prepared himself for the already ubiquitous objections to tomorrow's depositions.

"Mr. Brady?" Thomas said as Gavin picked up the phone.

"I assume you're calling to cancel the deposition tomorrow?" Gavin was not in the mood to beat around the bush any longer.

"Well, sort of."

That wasn't the answer that Gavin expected. "Sort of?"

"You see, my client's in a bit of a predicament here and I see this situation as one that may be advantageous for both our interests."

"Go on."

"Look, my client's not wealthy by any stretch of the imagination. I'm not getting paid for this, so I'd like to get him out as fast as possible."

"You're not getting paid?"

"Nope."

"Really." This was unusual for any attorney and certainly in this case. There was no moral cause to fight on the defense side, he thought to himself. Why would he take this case pro bono?

"Not a dime. I'll be honest with you. I'm doing this as a favor to my paralegal, who's married to one of Marcus' cousins."

"Okay. What can I do for you?"

"I've talked at length with Marcus and he's got nothing to hide. His story's been the same since the beginning. However, he is being sued by your client and if no one else is talking, then it's best if he stays silent as well."

"I've been hearing a lot of that today. Let me guess, the prosecutor's office gave you a call?"

"You're getting the idea that no one wants this case to go forward."

"I'm getting there."

"My client wants vindication and he's willing to talk to you but not under oath. You don't want him. You want Tyler, your clients want Tyler, and my client wants you to get him."

"What's he gonna tell me?"

"He'll tell you what happened that night."

Gavin was intrigued. He already had Marcus' trial testimony, but the focus from the prosecution and defense was on the events after they were in the car. Gavin was interested in what happened earlier that evening at Tyler's house, and what took place to make the boys change their stories.

"What does he want?"

"He wants to be dismissed from the suit. He can't afford my fees and pretty soon, I'm going to have to withdraw if he can't pay me."

"I can't do that." Gavin knew that it was critical to have all the boys as parties in the lawsuit. Otherwise, Marcus would be an empty chair at the trial, and the defense would be free to argue to the jury that he alone committed the murder without their knowledge or cooperation. They could argue that he secretly brought the gun and, by the time they saw him holding it out the window, it was too late. Marcus needed to be in the case if for no other reason than to keep the issues simplified for the jurors.

"That's too bad. How do you think your case is going to go after Penderson's motion? I don't want to play hard ball with you, but my client is out of the suit anyway if you lose. You and I both know the reality here. If there's no money, there's no suit. But my client has been living with the stigma of being considered a liar and murderer in his own community."

"Come on, Tom. You also know that I can't just dismiss your client. Without your client as a defendant, I'd get crucified at trial because everyone would argue that Marcus shot her."

"What if we could come to some sort of amicable agreement that would allow Marcus to stay in as a defendant and protect him as well?"

Gavin was desperate for a break. In the last hour, he'd seen his case, which was already built on matchsticks, go up in flames. He thought for a moment. "Okay, I'll cancel the deposition if your client comes by my office tomorrow."

"You won't regret this."

Gavin hung up the phone. The life preserver that Tom threw him only reminded him of how mad he was at Jenny and the prosecutor's office right now. How dare they interfere with his case! There was something he was missing, some elusive clue that was staring at him, mocking his blindness. Lance's motion was just hours away, fast approaching and he was no closer than when he began.

CHAPTER 18

THE ENGINE ROARED as Jenny slammed her foot on the accelerator. It was mid-afternoon and her trial schedule opened up due to a two-day judicial conference. She took the opportunity to leave town and drive to the coast. It was a two-hour drive, and she needed to be back in the office in the morning, but there was still plenty of daylight and the weather was unusually calm and sunny. The trees along the windy road rumbled softly in the breeze as Jenny's sporty Mini cut through the afternoon air.

State highway three was empty with large uninhabited forested areas on each side, which allowed her to unleash the car's full potential. The area was mostly home to loggers and fishermen, and the highway, for the most part, was used by logging trucks hauling bulging loads of trees, and vacationers heading to the ocean during the summer months.

Her car kicked up a cloud of dust as she rounded a sharp corner. She glanced at her speed, sixty-five, pretty fast for such an unkempt and windy road. Her cell phone began ringing. She slowed down to fifty-five while she answered it.

"Hello."

"Good, I'm glad I got you before you left."

"Who is this?" She asked into the phone as she rolled up the window to drown out the outside air.

"Benoit," the voice said.

"Harold?"

"Hello." There was static over the lines. "Are you still there?" The area was getting out of range of Jenny's cell phone service. Her provider guaranteed reception anywhere in the state. However, there were very few transistor towers near the ocean. This was a slower paced environment. Payphones still dotted the landscape, and people enjoyed communicating face to face.

"Yeah, I'm still here."

"Hey, it's Harold Benoit."

"What's up?" The reception was still fuzzy.

"I wanted to touch base with you and ask what you wanted done on this investigation."

Harold never asked for direction on a case from a prosecutor. After almost twenty years as a police officer and seventeen in the homicide unit, he was usually the one who assisted the office in determining which angles would pan out in an investigation. He was involved in several serial killing investigations and was the lead investigator on three death penalty cases.

"You're gonna have to give me more than that, Harold." Jenny knew this phone call was unusual. "What investigation?"

"The Tutuila investigation. Given what's been going on, I assume you want me to follow up on some things," he said fighting through the periodic static.

Jenny thought for a moment. What did Harold know that she didn't? Perhaps, Harold overheard her talking to Gavin about the memo. It was a stupid thing to do, especially in the courthouse. She had to tread lightly.

"What's been going on?" She wanted to take the words back as soon as they left her mouth. If Harold had overheard her conversation with Gavin, then he would know that she was suspicious about his question. If he heard it from another source, then he would think that she was stalling to get more information. She put herself out on a limb just by talking to Gavin.

"I just thought you'd give me some instructions since Randy was involved."

Randy was involved? How was he involved in this matter? Everything seemed to be unraveling in her mind. She knew it was risky to talk to Gavin, and she was very careful not to give out any privileged information.

"Harold, I can barely hear you. Tell me what's going on?" Jenny figured she could use the lack of good reception to her advantage. She wanted information and, apparently, Harold had more than she did at the moment.

"I heard that Randy has informed all of the civil defense attorneys that our office is looking into the possibility of opening up an active investigation."

"What?" The words came out before she had a chance to process the information. Randy was calling the civil defense counsel? Why would he be interfering with that suit?

"That's right."

"Have you talked to anyone about this?"

"No. I just found out about it myself. So, I thought I'd give you a call since you're in charge of the investigation. What would you like me to do?"

Jenny clued in to Harold's purpose immediately. There was no investigation. Jenny was in charge of keeping an eye on Gavin's actions and reporting back to Randy, but nothing more. Jenny was caught in the middle of one of Randy's political maneuverings and Harold was warning her.

"I found out something else that you might find interesting involving your new nemesis Brady. Apparently, someone's been spying on him."

"You mean the car?" Jenny remembered Gavin mentioning something about a car near his home.

There was a pause. "No, I hadn't heard that one. Someone dropped off some eight-by-ten glossies to his wife to scare him off."

Jenny shifted the phone to the other ear. She and Harold had not known each other for very long. However, his reputation preceded him. If there was an individual who could be trusted, it was Harold. Jenny didn't know what to say to him. After all, this was an unusual situation. Here was a twenty-year veteran homicide detective asking a rookie deputy prosecutor what to do on an investigation that didn't yet exist. If Jenny was going to find out what was going on, she needed to take a chance.

"Well, Harold," she said with some hesitation, "what do you suggest?"

"Oh, I don't know." There was a slight pause before he continued. "I thought I'd snoop around a bit. See what I can dig up."

"That sounds like an excellent idea." Jenny realized and she and Harold had just brokered a secret pact. Both of them knew there was no investigation, and both of them knew Randy's actions were beginning to rise to the level of suspicious. "Did you talk to Randy about this?"

"No. I assume I report to you and to you only. After all, you're in charge of the investigation, right?"

"Of course, I'm in charge. As far as I know." She tried not to laugh.

"Good, are you around today at all?" Harold's last couple of words drifted off in the static.

"I'm sorry are you still there?" Jenny said into the phone.

The static grew momentarily loud and then faded.

"Yeah, I'm here. Can you hear me?" Harold's voice grew stronger again.

"Yeah. I hear you. What did you say?"

"I asked if you'd be around today."

"Not today. I'm out all afternoon. I'll be back first thing tomorrow morning. Do what you feel necessary though. Whatever you can do will be much appreciated, especially since this is an active investigation."

"Tomorrow let's talk." Harold's tone turned serious. "Can you make time?"

"Yeah, sure." Just then the connection gave way to the static on the line. She clicked off the phone and hit the accelerator. The engine roared releasing her inner tension as she sped down the empty highway. Her trip had turned from a relaxing getaway to a strategy session. Gavin had inadvertently stumbled onto something big with his complaint. He must be completely unaware of the trouble his lawsuit was stirring up in the prosecutor's office. A chill shot down her back charging each hair on her arm with static electricity. The memo was beginning to seem not just suspicious, but also dangerous. She picked up her phone again and dialed the office.

"Catie?" She said into the phone.

"Hi, Jenny. What's up?"

"Can you do me a favor? Will you forward my phone calls to my cell phone? I'm gonna be out of the office for the afternoon, and I'd rather not have to check my messages every five minutes."

"Sure, no problem."

"You know how to do that?" Jenny had confidence in Catie, but also knew how it was to be a young intern wanting to please everyone and being reluctant to admit when you didn't know something.

"Absolutely. I'll do it right away."

"Thanks." She clicked off the line. The thick pine scented Douglas Firs stretched for hundreds of acres on each side of the road. The prickly needles blanketed the world around her as she cut her way through the sea of green. It allowed her to mull over the continuing developments. Perhaps a call to Gavin was in order. She needed to think about that a bit more. Harold's call had ratcheted up the stakes and brought everything to a new level. She would spend the afternoon going over her options and planning her next move. Hopefully, Harold would call with some news or insight into what was going on with this case.

KAUNI AND TYLER were headed out the front door when the phone rang. Tyler's gelled hair was still wet and gleamed against the outside rays as they crossed the front entryway. The driveway was empty. Their mother was at her sister's house playing bridge and their father was at work. Kauni grabbed Tyler's shoulder.

"Wait a minute, uso."

He turned around and headed back into the kitchen to the phone on the counter. Normally, he would ignore it and let the machine pick it up, but something told him to answer it.

"Hello."

"Kauni?" It was a male voice on the other end.

"Yeah, who's this?"

"It's me." The voice was familiar to Kauni. Just then Tyler came to his side. Kauni gave him a nod of reassurance.

"What's up? We were just headed out to see the lawyer. I was waiting for you to call."

"Good, I'll save you the suspense. Tell your friends that their testimony won't be needed tomorrow."

"Who's on the phone?" Tyler asked.

Kauni waved his brother off. "What do you mean?" Kauni said into the receiver. "Is the case over?"

"Just stay the course and it will be." The phone clicked off.

"What's going on?"

"Calm down, uso. That's my guy on the inside, the guy I was telling you about."

"What'd he say?"

"He said your lawyer's not gonna make you show up tomorrow for the deposition."

"You sure about that?"

"Didn't I say I'd take care of you on this one?" Kauni smiled at his little brother.

"Who is this guy?"

"Don't worry about him or who he is. I got it all under control." Kauni had told the boys about his man on the inside before. He was supposed to be someone with knowledge about the lawsuit, and someone who was working to make sure that none of them got in any more trouble. Kauni never gave any hints about the person's identity. Tyler was just happy for the assistance.

Kauni dialed both Sal and Danny and told them the good news. They were all overjoyed, not having heard it from their lawyers yet. Kauni was making good on his promise that he would take care of the matter. Danny, who had been his greatest critic, was even beginning to trust him. Tyler was especially pleased. He had spent close to two years in jail already, and was not excited about a lawsuit that would potentially dredge up the past.

Kauni reminded each person that they needed to stay united. The lawsuit's days were numbered, he told them. We stick with the story. It worked once, and it'll work again. Before hanging up, Kauni told everyone that they should act surprised when the lawyer told them the depositions are cancelled. The last thing they needed was to draw more attention to each other. The plan was set and each player knew his role. Now all they had to do was to sit back and let the lawyers fight it out. Kauni felt like a hero. He was single-handedly saving his family. It was a tragedy what had happened to that girl, but nothing they did could bring her back and, after all, it was an accident.

CHAPTER 19

GAVIN KNEW THE next morning would come all too quickly. After hearing from the opposing attorneys that their clients would not be showing up, he spent the remainder of the day trying to find time to review the Harrington file between other projects that were beginning to pile up on his desk. Gavin was in demand. From day one at the firm, Duke saw something in him. Otherwise, he would not have given Gavin so much responsibility. He was grooming Gavin for partnership and the rest of the firm knew it. In the legal practice, perception is reality and the perception about Gavin was that he was headed for greatness. If Duke had so much confidence in his ability, the other partners should as well. It was contagious and Gavin was constantly being bombarded with project after project. The one saving grace was that the firm had a full kitchen and shower to accommodate the all too common late night research needed to keep up with the workload. At first, it was flattering and a much welcomed distraction from his big wrongful death case. However, as his time became more precious and fleeting, his other work loomed over his head like a dark cloud.

There were so many things that bothered Gavin about the case. The criminal trial gave Tyler and his friends such an edge that it was already an uphill battle even to point the finger at them civilly. Then, of course, there was the Jenny factor. She had every reason to be mad at him and even dislike him. Additionally, there were the photos and the strange numbers on the back. It seemed every clue came with a hundred additional unanswered questions.

As usual, Gavin got home after Hannah was already in bed. He went straight to the refrigerator and pulled out a plate wrapped in aluminum foil. It was now routine that Hannah prepared dinner only to eventually wrap it and store it away until he came home. Gavin pulled off the aluminum foil and put the plate in the microwave. There was a folded note taped to the foil. As his dinner heated, he got a fork from one of the kitchen drawers and took out a manila file from his briefcase and sat them on the kitchen counter next to the folded note. He would wait to open it until his dinner was ready. It was the closest thing to having a real conversation with his wife over dinner, and he didn't want to spoil it by reading it too soon. When the oven dinged, he took the plate and began eating. The food melted in his mouth. It was his first real meal all day. He skipped lunch to finish up some work, and he silenced the late afternoon hunger pains with some snack chips from the firm's vending machine.

After the second mouthful, he grabbed the note. He didn't want to rush anything. He could feel the void growing between the two of them. He knew in many ways, Hannah was being victimized twice by this case. First, because he was never home, and second because someone was indirectly threatening her. He couldn't think about that now. As callous as that sounded to him, he tried to dismiss it from his mind. There would be time to talk and time to mend whatever emptiness had crept into their relationship. Now, he needed to concentrate on this case. He smelled the paper first. There was a small hint of barbeque from the chicken on the plate, but he tried to imagine that it was Hannah's perfume. She always smelled so clean and fresh with a hint of lavender. He had seen her perfume bottle a thousand times but could never remember the name. Unfolding the paper, he began to read. *Sorry I missed you. My parents called and said hi. H.*

The note sat next to his plate, its words open and exposed as he continued to eat. Hannah's parents lived on the opposite side of the country, several worlds away from here. He read the note again before picking up the Harrington case folder.

He brought some materials home to review before tomorrow. He didn't want to be surprised by anything. He read his notes from the interviews with Paul and Casey. He couldn't help but hear the cries and the anguish of Sara's parents as they found out their daughter was shot, her organs torn apart by a bullet fired in haste. How helpless and desperate they must have felt as they boarded a plane to fly thousands of miles not knowing whether their daughter would be alive when they landed. How hopeless they must have felt when they arrived at the hospital, and were told they were too late.

A tear fell onto Gavin's notes. He wiped his eyes and took another bite of food. This case hit close to home. Gavin's mind turned to his father's lonely hospital bed. He could see him writing a letter to his son pleading to come visit him one last time. He could see his father licking the envelope closed, and handing it to the nurse in exchange for a cold unfeeling stack of unopened and unread letters marked refused. After his father's death, Gavin tried to find out what happened to all the letters that he sent back. They told him his father destroyed them, probably embarrassed by the fact that they were returned. Gavin ached to reach back in time and tell his father that he loved him, that he was sorry. He ached to have his father see how successful and happy he had become. Instead, he only had his incomplete memories, the same incomplete memories that must haunt the Harringtons.

He continued to flip through the papers in the file until he came across the photos. Right now, they raised the biggest question in Gavin's mind. He flipped back and forth between each photo trying to see the connection between the number on the back and the picture on the front. Gavin wrote out the symbols on a pad of paper: *9, 0, 7, 2, 2, 0,* and the letter *A*. The number two was on the back of a picture showing Jenny talking to him in the courthouse and Hannah at the grocery store. The other two pictures taken inside the courthouse had a zero on the back. The shots of their home had a nine and the letter A on the back. There did not seem to be any correlation.

Gavin couldn't think anymore. It was late and his head hurt. He finished his meal and put the dishes in the dishwasher. It was close to midnight and he had to be up in less than five hours. He put away his folders and made his way into the bedroom.

He tried to be quiet and sneak under the covers beside Hannah, but she always woke up. She was a light sleeper when he was gone and even the slightest rustling of the bed brought her out of any slumber. Usually when she felt his presence, she simply checked the clock with a resigned smile of relief. He hated the fact that she checked the clock because it reminded him of how much time that he spent away from home and away from her. Tonight, however, was different.

"Did you get my note?" She asked without opening her eyes.

"Yeah. Sorry to wake you. Did you tell them *hi* from me?"

"Of course. Don't worry, I didn't mention the photos. I wouldn't want them to worry."

Her words struck Gavin like a slap in the face. He was worried about her. He was worried that someone knew he was married. He was worried that someone knew where his wife worked. He hadn't said anything about it because he was also worried about this case. This was not a typical auto accident case. This was a complex wrongful death case with a grieving family putting everything on the line in the belief that their lawyer was doing the same. He needed to devote everything he had to the case, and he needed to devote everything he had to his family. Something had to give.

"Hannah," he said nudging her. "Hannah."

"What." She rustled slightly.

"Hannah, wake up." He nudged her again.

"What." Her eyes struggled to open and she turned on her back to face him.

"Sometimes I forget how beautiful you are," he said out of reflex. Her face sparkled in Gavin's eyes.

"You're sweet. I love you too. Can we discuss this tomorrow? I'm so tired and I have a long day ahead of me."

"I want you to go stay with your parents." He wanted to be subtler about it but she was too tired and not paying attention to him. He needed to discuss this now.

"What?" She struggled to lift herself against the headboard.

"Your parents. I think you should go stay with them. Just for a little while."

"Why?" She said with a yawn.

"I should've done this a long time ago."

"What are you saying?" She was awake now and engaged in the conversation.

"This case is getting dangerous and I don't want anything — I just think it might be better for you to be away from here."

"This isn't the time to talk about this. You're tired and I'm tired."

"We have to. I've been thinking about this a lot."

"*You've* been thinking?" She rubbed her eyes.

"Yes, and it's too dangerous."

"Is that what *you've* decided?"

"It is."

"No."

"What do you mean no? Are you listening to me?"

"I'm not going anywhere and this isn't your decision to make."

"What are you talking about? This case is dangerous, and I don't want you to be any more involved than you already are."

"Do you hear yourself? You've decided. You think. What about what I want? What about what I think? I don't work at your firm. I'm your wife and your partner."

"What are you talking about? I'm thinking about you."

"No, you're not." She rubbed the last bit of sleep from her eyes. "Okay, you wanted to talk about this now, then let's talk." She leaned into him. "I love you for your passion. And I'll put up with not seeing

166

you because I know you'd do the same for me, but you forget that I'm part of this marriage as well. I'm part of the us."

"I know that Hannah." He was taken off guard and needed a second to collect his response. "You're the most important thing to me and I don't want you to get hurt."

"Why didn't you think about that before you took the case?"

"What?"

"This case is not for us, it's for you. I want you to succeed, but don't try and tell me that you're doing all of this for us."

"This is my job."

"Yes, *your* job. What about the late hours, the dinners alone, the 'forgive me' phone calls? No, this is for you. If this is who you're going to be from now on, then tell me so I can adjust." The sincerity in her face scared Gavin. "What if I told you that you had to get out of town for awhile because of something that happened at work?"

"As a professor?"

Hannah was silent. He wished he could reach out and pull the words back in his mouth but they were already out there, circling the room hammering at the invisible wedge already between them.

"I'm sorry. I didn't mean that."

"Of course, you did." She took a breath. "You promised to walk with me, not in front of me." She got up and went into the bathroom locking the door behind her.

"Hannah." Gavin called out as he went to the closed door. "I didn't mean it."

"I know. I just want to be alone right now."

Gavin stood there for what seemed like an eternity. He knew that it was no use. He could only make it worse by trying to force her to come out. "I love you," he said finally and went back into the living room to sleep on the couch. His only solace was that in several hours, he would have to be up. His eyes closed with his thoughts jumping between Hannah, Sara, and the upcoming argument, each offering its own anxiety.

GAVIN'S NOSTRILS WERE FILLED with the smell of coffee as he opened his eyes. He could hear the pot churning away as it dripped hot water over freshly ground beans. As he began to stir, he could tell that he was still on the couch. The argument with Hannah flooded back into his head, reminding him of the ridiculous remarks he made to her. There was a blanket covering him that Hannah must have placed on him sometime in the night.

"Good morning," Hannah said. She was in the kitchen toasting a bagel.

"Morning." Gavin sat up. The argument weighed heavy on his consciousness. Hannah was fully dressed in a skirt and blouse. She did not appear to be mad, but Gavin was cautious. Hannah brought him a cup of coffee. "Hannah."

"Here you go. I gotta get going. I'm goin' in early today to get some stuff copied for my lecture."

"About last night."

"Don't worry about it." She stopped and faced him. "Just don't forget about me, and don't forget to shave," she said forcing a smile.

Gavin lost that argument. She was not going to stay with her parents or anywhere else and he knew it. She was a strong woman, and she was right. He was ignoring her while he focused on his work. She always seemed to win the fights between them. Probably because she had an uncanny ability to see right through him, and make him tongue-tied. He prided himself on his oratory skills. He had even been awarded for his ability to argue persuasively, but with her, he was lucky to rise to the level of a blithering idiot. He looked at the clock. It was just past six in the morning. He needed to get dressed and to the office. He took one last gulp of coffee and jumped off the couch.

CHAPTER 20

THE SUN ROSE over the horizon streaking the road with golden splashes of light. As Gavin approached the Narrows Bridge, Mount Rainier's snow covered peak towered in the background and offering its full spectacle for the world to see. Gavin was reminded on mornings like this one why he chose the Northwest as a place to live. Even the traffic was unusually light. He was over the bridge and to his firm within fifteen minutes.

Gladys was already at her desk rapidly typing up one of Gavin's legal memos that he had dictated yesterday before he went home. The firm gave all new associates a dictation machine and a note that read,

Use this wisely and often as it will save you that which we lawyers hold so dearly and costs our clients so much — time. Signed, The Partnership.

Truer words were never written by attorneys. Gavin's profession defined and justified human existence in six minute increments neatly logged and detailed on monthly billing sheets. Like the other associates, Gavin was immediately swamped with research projects, and made use of the machine in order to get his thoughts down on tape along with supporting case law.

"Good morning," Gavin said as he passed on the way to his office. He carried his morning cup of coffee from the break room.

"Morning, Mr. Brady," she said pulling one of the transcription earplugs out of her ear.

"You know, Gladys, even opposing counsel calls me by my first name." He always cringed when she used his last name, especially since he called her Gladys.

"And you call that a compliment? I say shame on them."

Gavin smiled. He enjoyed the banter, and she always had a quick comeback. "I'll be in my office if you need me."

"Once you get settled, you're wanted in the front conference room."

Gavin stopped short of his office door. "The conference room, why?"

"I don't know. Mr. Smithwick asked to see you briefly. May be another assignment. I guess you'll have even more work to put on your plate, lucky you."

Larry wants to see me? Gavin thought to himself. Even if Gladys suspected something bad, she would not have said anything to Gavin about it. She had been at the firm for years, and learned a long time ago that her job did not entail facilitating fear and doubt. The practice of law, especially for a new associate in a busy and demanding firm, was stressful enough.

"Okay, can you buzz him and tell him that I'll be down there as soon as I put my stuff down?" He jumped into his office and then quickly popped his head back into the hallway. "Oh, what time is it?"

"Seven-fifteen."

"Good." It was silly, but Gavin wanted to take advantage of every opportunity to point out to the partners, especially a named partner like Larry Smithwick, that he arrived at the office before the rest of the world's workday officially began at eight. He quickly put his things down, turned on his computer and walked down to the conference room. He stopped at the frosty glass entrance. Inside, Larry Smithwick sat next to Fred Meridiam.

"Morning," Gavin blurted out with a hint of reservation in his voice.

"Come in," Larry said with a smile. His demeanor was friendly but professionally formal.

Fred only stared expressionless as Gavin took a seat opposite the two men at the conference table in the room. Both men had notepads in front of them as well as several pages of what looked to be spreadsheet calculations.

"Is there something wrong?" Gavin's curiosity got the better of him so he cut right to the point. He started thinking about his billable hours. That couldn't be the issue here, he was on track to come close to three thousand hours in his first year, and partners seemed happy with his work up to this point. He had seen similar meetings like this one before. However, it usually occurred after the Monday partnership meetings and Duke was always present. Today was not Monday, there hadn't been a partnership meeting, and only Larry and Fred sat across from Gavin. The ambience, however, was just as grave.

"Not really," Fred said, "we just wanted to speak with you about one of your cases so we could stay on top of it."

"Okay." Gavin continued to be suspicious.

170

"You're new here with a heavy caseload, and we want to make sure you're getting all the help you need."

"We understand that you're working on a case called Harrington versus Titu — something?" Larry.

"It's actually Duke's case, but I'm working on it."

"Really," Fred replied, "how much is Duke working on it?" His tone sounded more like an accusation than a question.

Gavin was unsure of how to respond. He wasn't sure if they were checking up on him or on Duke.

"This is somewhat unusual because you're a first-year associate here and working on a case like this you see. It's our policy to closely monitor all cases that our newer associates are working on to ensure costs are balanced with the benefits to the firm."

"We do this with all new associates. It just usually takes a year before we get to you," Larry said.

Fred turned one of the pages in front of him. His demeanor showed no emotion. "I see you have quite a few hours in this case so far."

"It's a pretty big case with a lot of complex issues in it." Gavin felt somewhat proud of that fact. He knew that he was too young to be handling this case, and he knew that Duke had put his faith in him.

"And a lot of money in it as well," Fred said flipping through another page. "Any offers?"

"Not really, well nothing worth mentioning." Gavin was uncomfortable.

"Everything's worth mentioning," Fred stated.

"Okay." Gavin straightened himself up in his chair. "I got an offer of ten thousand dollars yesterday."

"And?" Fred asked.

"Don't you have some sort of motion to dismiss the case tomorrow?" Larry was a real estate attorney and not familiar with the terms in litigation. However, he understood the law, and was well-informed when it came to matters in the firm that involved money. For them, the law was about the bottom line.

How do they know that? "Well, the policy is half-a-million."

"And your costs are about ten thousand right now," Fred said.

"How confident are you about tomorrow's hearing?" Larry asked.

"Well, motions are always risky."

"Is that what you've been told?" Fred said interrupting him. It was a not so subtle reminder that Gavin was new to the business.

"Right."

"I'm familiar with the uncertainties of litigation. All that aside, how sure are you on the law? If there wasn't an argument tomorrow, do you win on brief?"

Gavin knew the legal argument cut against him. Lance had the law on his side, and now Fred Meridiam was asking him a direct question. He swallowed hard. "I think it's close." What he meant was that he hoped it was close.

Fred stared at him without changing the same expression he wore the moment Gavin entered the room. "Fair enough," he said finally. "I certainly like the sound of half-a-million better than ten thousand."

"Especially since it's seed money for the suit against, uh, you said you're going after the gun makers after this, right?" Larry interjected himself. He loved the idea of the larger suit and the publicity it would bring to the firm.

"Yeah. There are twenty-seven manufacturers that potentially hold a market share liability."

"Beautiful." Larry turned to Fred with the jubilance of a young boy. "Duke was telling me that the publicity alone could boost our revenues by forty percent. Plus, the damages are in the millions. We couldn't ask for a better dead girl."

"Her name was Sara Harrington," Gavin said matter of factly.

"Of course, it is," Larry responded almost as quickly as Gavin finished his sentence. "I'm sure she was a lovely person, and it's a tragedy that she's gone, but we're not here for the tragedy, Gavin, we're here to make the tragedy pay. I'm sure her family will find the necessary closure to their daughter's death by sticking it to a bunch of large corporations that profit off products that are designed for nothing more than to kill things that are living."

His colloquy showed a cynical disdain for Duke's practice. However, for Gavin, this was a case with specific facts and specific people who had escaped justice, people who had manipulated the legal system. The American criminal justice system's strength also stands as its own fallacy. Verdicts are the products of often pressured decisions of twelve human beings, all with their own pasts and biases, and who are subject to myriad influences.

"You're right," Gavin responded with as much false complicity as he could muster. "I'm just trying to get the highest settlement to help out the bigger prize."

"I appreciate the commitment, we all do," Fred said. "Our concern is not personal and it is unusual that we'd be talking to a first year, but this is the process. As Larry said, causes come and go but the bottom line makes or breaks us. Keep in mind that we've got thousands of dollars invested in this case, and we don't want to lose it. You say it's better to go forward than settle, then all we can do is trust you."

"We're all in this together," Larry added.

Gavin nodded. "Thanks." He was more uncomfortable than ever. Now the partnership was not only counting on him but they were watching him.

Larry and Fred chit chatted with him for several more minutes before letting him leave. Gavin survived his first case review meeting with the partners. However, he was not feeling particularly good about it. His case was tenuous at best and he did not like the idea of suing people simply to fund larger suits for profit. Somehow, he needed to find justice for Sara.

THE ELEVATOR MADE a loud ding before opening its doors. Marcus Kiuilani and his lawyer stepped into the lobby.

"May I help you?" The receptionist asked.

"Thomas McCullough and Marcus Kiuilani to see Mr. Brady."

They were led to the same room where Gavin earlier met with Larry and Fred. Gavin waited the expected ten minutes before entering the conference room. One of Duke's tricks was to always make opposing counsel wait a few minutes before a meeting. An attorney does not want to appear too anxious, and ten minutes conveys just the right amount of professional apathy conducive to high stakes negotiations.

"Good morning." Gavin extended a hand to Tom and then to Marcus. "Thanks for coming, I appreciate it."

Marcus did not appear as Gavin had imagined. He fidgeted nervously, and although he was just about the same age as Gavin, he seemed oddly young. Gavin took a seat across from the two men.

"Let me start by saying that my client has agreed to speak with you off the record to help you get to the truth of what happened that night." Tom's speech had a seasoned rhythm to it. "Marcus had nothing to do with the shooting. He didn't even know anyone had a gun that night until Tyler pulled it out."

"Is that true?" Gavin turned to Marcus.

"Yeah." Marcus only made eye contact for a split second before turning away.

"You were in the car though, right?" Gavin wanted to push his button a bit to see how he'd react.

"Yeah, but I didn't know what was gonna happen. I wouldn't have been there if I did." His answers were in short nervous bursts, and there was a ring of truthfulness to his tone. Gavin remained skeptical. After all, a jury believed that Tyler spent almost two years in jail awaiting trial in order to protect a kinsman, who, in the end betrayed his loyalty.

"Tell me about that night." Gavin wrote the date on his legal pad.

"Wait a minute," Tom said. "If my client agrees to talk to you about the events of that night, I want to talk to you about dismissing him from the case."

Gavin looked at Tom. This was a classic game of blind man's bluff. He knew that Gavin needed information from Marcus. He knew that there was a motion pending that might dismiss the only parties with money from the case. However, Tom needed to pass along Marcus' information because his client wanted to clear his name in the community. Both sides needed each other. Tom was now trying to see just how inexperienced Gavin was.

"I can't do that." He could not dismiss Marcus. Otherwise, the others would be pointing their fingers at the empty chair denying any knowledge of the gun at all. It was the exact theory that had been successful at the criminal trial, and it would be the obvious defense here. He needed Marcus in the case.

"Look, Gavin, you got my client in the car. The trial testimony will establish that much, but he wasn't the shooter, and he had no idea what was about to happen. He got wrapped up in Tyler's trial, and now it's happening all over again with the civil suit. You don't want him. You want the others. My client needs some type of guarantee. Otherwise, his best option is to take the Fifth and roll the dice at tomorrow's hearing."

The room went silent as Gavin and Tom looked at each other. Tom was right. Gavin's main objective was to get the others and Marcus was in the best position to give them to him. However, he also knew that making a deal to cut Marcus loose from the suit would allow the others to do exactly what they did at the criminal trial, point the finger toward Marcus. He needed Marcus to defend himself.

"You're right." Gavin finally said. "Your client's probably better off keeping quiet. I'm sorry I can't help you in that fashion." He got up and put his pen in his shirt pocket. "I just need the truth, but I can't dismiss your client. I'm sorry you wasted a trip over here. They can validate you at the front." This was a big risk for him. He had no idea how Tom or Marcus would react. He started to head to the door. Gavin counted the steps to the exit. He could hear his heart pound in his chest. Life always comes down to a few moments and this was one of them. He was taking a chance by leaving, but he knew it was the right move. He could not show weakness, not now, not here.

"Tyler's dad bought him the gun," Marcus said.

Gavin stopped dead in his tracks, almost out of the room. Silently he breathed a sigh of relief. It worked. Without turning around, he spoke. "How do you know?"

"Tyler told me. He told all of us."

Gavin turned around and faced him. "When?"

"I don't know. A while back."

"Were you guys drinking that night?"

"Yeah."

"What about drugs?"

"What about' em?"

"Were you taking drugs that night?" Gavin had him in his grips and he was not letting go.

"Just pot."

"So, do we have a deal?" Tom piped up as if to renew his offer to dismiss his client from the suit.

"No. But you're right, I don't want your client. I want the others." Gavin sat back down. "Let's start from the beginning."

Marcus began telling him about the night Sara was shot. He told Gavin they had arrived earlier in the evening at Tyler's house to celebrate that he got into college. Marcus and a couple of others brought over some marijuana, and they all smoked several bowls throughout the evening. They went out twice to get more beer even borrowing the car once from Tyler's father.

"Who drives a Trans Am?" Gavin asked.

"What do you mean?"

"I mean in that group. Who drives the Trans Am?"

"What Trans Am? I never saw no Trans Am."

Tom's ears perked up. "Could we have a moment? I want to confer with my client."

Gavin got up without saying a word and left the room. Outside the frosted glass walls, he reviewed his notes. He could feel his blood pumping through his body feeding the adrenaline rush. This is what practicing law was all about. This is what his law professors and Duke told him about. He had just bluffed with a losing hand and won.

He looked at his watch. How much time should he give them? It had been less than two minutes, and he was already getting antsy. He knew that he shouldn't seem too anxious by immediately going back inside. He needed to continue with the apathetic demeanor that he successfully displayed at the beginning. He decided to get a cup of coffee to give him something to do. It took several minutes to get to the break room and pour the coffee. He sauntered by several of the other associates' offices so they could see that he was conducting a witness interview. By the time he returned, Tom was already waiting outside the door.

"We're ready for you again."

Gavin entered and sat back down. He knew that Tom had grilled Marcus about any knowledge he may have about the vehicle. That was his job. The worst thing that could happen to an attorney was to be surprised by his client's own statements.

"You were telling me about a Trans Am." Gavin decided to push the topic again.

"I told you, man. I don't know nothing about a Trans Am."

"How about friends, anyone else in the community who may drive a Trans Am?"

"Look, I don't hang out with those guys anymore. I don't go to their church, and I don't hang out in the neighborhood, why would I?"

"I'm just asking questions." Marcus had a point. Tyler's family had done an excellent job at smearing his reputation within their community. By the time the trial had ended, no one was sure who had pulled the trigger. Marcus was a scapegoat and a pariah to his own people. Gavin just had to be sure. Marcus was the only one who was willing to talk to him.

"Okay, let's move on. Tell me about the gun?"

"I never really saw it. It was a nine millimeter."

"You said you knew that Tyler's dad bought it for him."

"Yeah. I knew he had one. I knew he had a nine millimeter. Everybody did. He told everyone, but I never saw it."

Marcus continued his story of the events of the night, and confirmed that Chillie was in the car before the shooting. Gavin knew that he needed Marcus to testify under oath if he had any chance of winning this case. He needed to confirm his allegations in the Complaint, and, given Chillie's permanent unavailability, Marcus was his star witness. The only problem was that he also needed him in the lawsuit. Gavin took copious notes of the meeting almost filling up an entire legal pad as Marcus talked.

"Why didn't the prosecutor ask you these questions?" Gavin asked. He knew from the trial transcript that the prosecutor didn't asked half the questions he did.

"I don't know. I don't think he knew very much about that night. Hell, he didn't even know about Chillie."

That was surprising because there was the memo that outlined an interview with Chillie by one of the investigating cops.

"Do you know an RB?" Gavin noticed before that there was a handwritten notation on the memo that read, *Route to RB*. He assumed that RB stood for one of the investigators on the case, and had made a request to the prosecutor's office for the names of all the individuals investigating or working on the murder case. What he got back was a type-written letter by the county's in-house counsel that such information was deemed privileged and confidential.

"RB? Who's that?"

"I don't know, initials I guess. One of the pieces of paper that mentions your buddy Chillie says route to RB."

"First off, Chillie wasn't my buddy and second off, I don't know anyone named RB."

"Maybe one of the cops you talked to or someone else?"

"No." Marcus chuckled. "Maybe RB is the guy in the Trans Am."

It was a possibility that Gavin hadn't thought about. If RB had a connection to the driver of the Trans Am, then someone from the original investigation was upset that Gavin was snooping around. The memo's elusive significance kept intensifying. He finished the interview without talking any further about cars or initials.

Marcus shed some light on the case but each answer only illuminated the many unanswered questions that were growing in number each day. Tyler's father knew about the gun. He bought it for him. He also knew that his son had dangerous proclivities because of his troubled past. Maybe that was enough to survive tomorrow's motion to dismiss, Gavin thought to himself. However, he had no proof. Marcus wasn't going on record as long as he was a defendant.

Maybe the photos had something to do with the initials. Jenny's confrontation in the courthouse was designed to get him concentrating on the memo. She obviously knew, or at least suspected, more than she was telling him. The questions swirled around Gavin's head as he reviewed his notes from today's interview. He was no closer to the truth than he was before meeting Marcus. However, now he knew in which direction to go.

Jenny knows something she's not telling me. That's the only reasonable explanation.

CHAPTER 21

THE CALL CAME from out of the blue. Gavin was sitting at his desk with the door closed sifting through the photos left by the mystery man when Gladys paged him on his intercom.

"Mr. Brady."

"Yes, Gladys." *Call me Gavin.*

"You have an incoming call. It's a reporter for the local paper."

"Really?"

"I think it's about your case." Her tone hid any inkling of pride that her boss was already getting media attention on his first case.

"Thanks, put him through." He was confused. Why would a reporter call him? This case had not received any publicity for several years.

"Mr. Brady." The voice on the other end had a sense of urgency about it. "This is Stephen Morrow, reporter for the *Tacoma Tribune.*"

"What can I do for you?" Gavin wanted to be cautious until he knew the purpose of this call.

"I'm doing a follow-up piece on the Harrington murder. I understand you represent the parents of the Harrington girl, and that they've brought a civil suit against several individuals."

"That's right. I represent Sara's estate as well as her parents." Gavin wanted to use her name. Everyone seemed to call her the Harrington girl. To Gavin, she was Sara.

"I covered the criminal investigation through the trial so I'm pretty familiar with the background. I'd like to ask you a few questions about the suit for a piece I'm trying to get out in Monday's paper."

Lance's motion was originally set for the regular Friday docket, but the judge had moved everything over to Monday due to an unexpected personal matter. Running a story about the case on the same day as the hearing was, he hoped, a sign of good luck.

"Sure." Gavin was excited for the attention. He'd never been interviewed before, and it made him feel a little like a celebrity. "What kind of piece are you running?"

"Just basic stuff. The criminal trial was big news around here, and the fact that there is now a civil trial is something I'm sure the public would like to know."

"Well, I don't know what I can tell you other than it's a wrongful death suit against the four boys who killed her as well as the Tutuila parents."

"You mean the four boys in the car the night she was shot, right?"

"That's right."

"What about Marcus?"

"What about him?"

"Well, let me ask it a different way. The jury didn't believe him at the criminal trial. Where do you stand?"

"He gave the same story that they all originally gave. It was the other boys who changed their versions of the facts." Gavin did not like defending Marcus, but he did believe him. "Look, it doesn't make any sense that Tyler admits to the shooting, spends eighteen months in jail, then changes his story just because he is trying to protect his good buddy, Marcus. No way that makes sense."

"So, you believe Marcus' story."

"I don't think he's a choir boy if that's what you're asking." Gavin was into the interview. The reporter had pushed the right buttons to get him talking. "I think right now he's as culpable as the others in the car. He was there. He was out with them to cause who knows what, and my client is dead as a result. Just because they all turned on each other doesn't make any of them the victim. That's just splitting hairs. There is only one victim in this case, Sara."

Gavin smiled to himself. He once heard to Duke say similar things once before to a reporter on the phone. It stuck in his mind because it was the truth. Besides, talking to reporters was already addictive, and Gavin was enjoying every moment.

"Now, I see both your name and Duke's name on the pleadings."

Officially, all court pleadings listed Duke's formal name, Jonathon Stewart. However, no one called Duke by his real name. In fact, he sometimes signed the name Duke above his signature line in a moment of forgetfulness. No one seemed to care. It was accepted and somewhat expected from him.

"However," Stephen continued, "when I called the office, I was told you were handling the case."

"That's right." Gavin felt ten feet tall. It didn't matter that Duke would have probably taken the call had he been in town. This was his case and now the community would know it.

"Let me ask you then, what do the Harrington parents hope to get out of this suit?"

"Justice," Gavin proudly said. "They were denied it in the criminal trial so we'll try again in the civil case."

"That brings up a good point. Where do you think you'll succeed where the prosecutors didn't?"

"Please, someone dropped the ball. You've got a guy who confesses to the crime and then gets acquitted. There were witnesses who were never called at the criminal trial who saw Tyler in the front seat, and proved that the change in the story was a lie."

"Has the prosecutor's office been cooperating at all with your suit?"

"No. They keep talking about putting together a secret investigation of their own."

"What are they investigating?"

"Don't know, wish I did. Hopefully not to figure out how to cover up for their past mistakes." Gavin spoke before he thought. Stephen had put him at ease right off the bat and he was excited at being interviewed. He brushed it off. They were investigating something and not cooperating. Besides, he got in a good quote about justice.

"What about tomorrow's hearing?"

"I don't know what will happen on Monday. What I do know is that the Harringtons are in this for the long haul. They want justice, and are committed to seeing this suit through to the end. Justice delayed will not be justice denied. I can promise you that." Gavin had pulled himself back together and come back with another good quote. "Is this gonna be in Monday's paper?"

"That's the plan. You were my last call, and now I have about an hour before my deadline."

"Well, anything else I can help you with ask away."

"I appreciate it. I think you were very helpful and I got everything I need."

"Okay, you know where to find me."

"Good luck Monday. Like I said, I covered this case and I think there was an injustice done. It's good to see someone trying to correct it."

Gavin hung up the phone feeling great about himself. He felt like he handled that reporter as if he had been doing this for years. He picked the phone again and dialed Hannah at work. Although he wanted to tell her about his first interview, he wouldn't mention it. He needed her to know he cared about her and hadn't forgotten their marriage. She didn't answer so he left a message. It felt as though they were communicating more and more through notes and voice mails.

After he hung up the phone, he silently flipped through the ominous photos that had been delivered to Hannah, turning each one over to look at the numbers on the back. The prosecutor's office dropped the ball and never reacted to the obvious lies during the trial. The photos were a part of the mystery, and the numbers on the back were there for a reason. This was not a random act. There was a message here. He just didn't know if the message was for him or not. He studied them, trying to make some sense of their meaning.

LANCE TOOK A SIP of his tonic water and lime as he looked around the restaurant for his clients. He sat at a booth next to a window overlooking Vashon Island. He was a regular here on Sundays and always sat in the same seat. Rusty's was his favorite restaurant. It was small and never crowded which appealed to Lance. He was not a fan of crowds. He liked his audience limited to twelve hand-picked individuals, who hung on his every word.

Lance was well known in the legal community, and was the author of one of the definitive treatises on insurance defense in the state of Washington. At the same time, he hated the recognition and prestige that came along with it. He was not comfortable hob-knobbing with the Seattle social elite and playing the name game. He was a serious litigator, who vehemently believed in his craft, nothing more.

"Sir, may I get you another tonic water?" The waiter asked as he walked by Lance's table. Lance had finished his drink quickly as he glanced over his notes.

"Yes, thank you."

"Mr. Penderson?" Palolo's voice and rough Polynesian accent was unmistakable. He and his wife walked around the back side of Lance from the front of the restaurant.

"Sit down." Tomorrow was the hearing, and Lance was willing to share his Sunday evening to meet with his clients one last time to go over any last minute details or questions. Also, Lance was paid by the hour, and his weekend rate was almost double his regular rate. They took their seats across from him.

"I'm glad you could make it out tonight. I wanted to go over tomorrow's proceedings with you, and give you a heads up on what to expect."

Palolo nodded his head in acknowledgment. His wife was stoically silent. There was an indefinable sense of pride and tradition in the way Palolo and his wife conducted themselves.

Lance looked them over once and continued. "All right, tomorrow's hearing will be a purely legal argument. That means you won't talk at all, and there won't be any testimony from witnesses."

"What do you want us to do?" Palolo responded in an uncharacteristic manner. Just then, the waiter appeared again.

"Can I get you something to drink or start you off with something?"

Lance shook his head. He had only taken a couple of sips of his tonic water since his refill.

Palolo looked at his wife and over to Lance. "We'll have two large colas."

"I'll give you a couple of minutes to decide on food while I get your drinks." With that, he disappeared.

"Nothing." Lance finally answered Palolo as if the waiter's interruption had not distracted his thinking at all. "Absolutely nothing. I want you and your wife to sit next to me at counsel table, and I want you two to look perplexed at the whole process."

"Perplexed?" Palolo had lived in the United States for a long time but his command of the language was still limited. He spoke Samoan at home and English only out of necessity.

"Confused. You know, *not sure why you're there type of look.* You see, we don't want to get caught up in the tragedy of the death that occurred because your involvement isn't really about that. Your involvement in this lawsuit is about money. Tomorrow's not about the death of a young woman. It's is about a legal system being taken advantage of by overzealous and gluttonous lawyers, who are trying to make a buck. They can't collect from the shooters, so they go after the only people with insurance to fund a verdict or settlement. Their justice is measured in greed."

"Shooters?" Lance recognized his mistake by the look on Palolo's face. "Our son was acquitted. He's innocent."

Lance knew the history of the criminal trial and did not want to go into it. It was true that Tyler was acquitted, but it was also true that he originally confessed to the shooting. Lance had his own doubts about Tyler's veracity, but that was not relevant to his representation of the parents.

"I'm sorry. I didn't mean to imply that your son was the shooter. What I meant was, as a matter of law, you can't be held liable for the death of Sara Harrington. You two could not have possibly known of the events that were to unfold that night regardless of who actually pulled the trigger. I don't want either one of you to worry about anything tomorrow, okay? Your job is to make the focus of the hearing about a law-abiding couple, confused as to why they are sitting in court. I'll do the rest."

For the next hour and a half, Lance continued to talk with his clients about tomorrow's argument and about the case. He discussed their attire and demeanor in the courtroom, and assured them that he would be there to protect their interests.

On the other side of the room, a small group of people were gathered in the bar taking advantage of happy hour. In the middle of the crowd at a single table sat Harold Benoit nursing a single malt scotch. He glanced over at Lance's table without any look of recognition. About halfway through the meal, Harold noticed four other males join Lance's table. He recognized two of them as Tyler and Kauni Tutuila. The other two males were older and wearing suits. Harold figured they were the attorneys representing them. The four of them pulled up chairs and sat down with Lance and Tyler's parents.

Harold stayed in the bar for most of their meal until his scotch was nothing more than a golden-colored liquidy ice. He took one final sip, plopped down a twenty dollar bill on the table, and headed out the restaurant. He sauntered behind the crowd in the bar out of sight from Lance's group to the front exit. The outside breeze was a welcome breath of fresh air. Harold looked around the lot. At the back, near a lamp post, sat a forest green Toyota Camry. It was virtually brand new and sparkled in the fluorescent light. Harold hit a button on his keychain, and the Camry's light beamed brightly unlocking the car. Harold's two luxuries in life were the occasional single malt scotch and the unmistakable smell of a new car. His police pension allowed him to live a fairly comfortable retirement. He didn't have a family so there wasn't anyone to spend his money on other than himself. He was one of those individuals who truly defined himself by his career. He needed to work to give meaning to his existence. Three months into retirement, he was hired as a private investigator for the prosecutor's office. The hours were good, the stress was low, and the extra money allowed him to purchase a new car every couple of years.

He took another breath of fresh air breathing in the night and the end of a very long day. As he walked across the parking lot, his peripheral vision caught the sight of a black Trans Am parked on the street on the side of the parking lot. The windows were dark, and he couldn't tell if there was anyone inside. He made a mental note of his observation before getting into his car and leaving.

CHAPTER 22

GAVIN WAS UP EARLY. He didn't sleep well. From two until five in the morning, he found himself flipping through everything that basic cable had to offer. His nerves were shot from a combination of worrying about his relationship with Hannah and over preparation for the hearing. All he could do was nervously channel surf, trying to focus on anything but his life. He spent the entire weekend poring over the Harrington file and preparing his oral argument.

Today was the big day and there was a lot riding on how the judge ruled. Gavin knew that a wrongful death suit that excluded the parents was problematic, and he knew that the partners in his firm, including Duke, wouldn't want to go forward on this case unless he was able to guarantee a monetary reward at the end. Lance thoroughly briefed the law, and his motion against Gavin was pretty solid.

The coffee maker sputtered as the timer activated the morning's brew. Hannah set it for Gavin last night to go off at 5:30. Next to the machine was a note that read, *Good luck today.*

Court was scheduled to begin at nine, which meant that the judge would show up around 9:20, and the docket would be called by 9:30. Gavin guzzled his coffee and jumped in the shower. The warm water revitalized his muscles, shaking off his adrenaline induced insomnia. Hopefully, the coffee would take over after that until he could get to court. Once there, his nervousness would keep him alert throughout the morning. This was a trick that Gavin learned early on in college while studying for finals. It served him well through law school. By the time his body realized that it had been fooled by a series of calculated acts, the crisis would be over.

Still damp from the shower, Gavin silently sneaked into the bedroom and picked out a suit. He dressed in the living room so he wouldn't disturb Hannah. She did an excellent job of pretending that she didn't hear him, but their house was too small to not hear Gavin's morning routine. By six, he was fully clothed and ready to head to the courthouse. He still had three hours before the county doors would be unlocked for the day's business, and there was no shortage of unfinished research projects on his desk to occupy his time. However, he wanted to get to the firm while it was still quiet and practice his argument out loud in his office. He softly kissed Hannah on the forehead without saying a word and left.

The traffic noise droned on in the background as he crossed the Narrows Bridge. Rounding the corner to his firm, he could see the county courthouse piercing the morning skyline with its formidable concrete structure. It was only eleven floors but it stood as solid and mighty as the tallest skyscrapers in the neighboring metropolis of Seattle. The outside was fittingly grey. There was no emotion or even optimism in the exterior décor. With neither pride nor regret, it simply sheathed the decades of strife and conflict played out in its bosom. It stood as blind power molded and harnessed by the men and women who walked its hallways.

He tried not to get too intimidated as the building shifted from his side to his rearview mirror. He could still see the massive structure as he pulled into the firm's parking lot. There were only a few cars, mostly associates trying to get a jump start on the day or ones who were still working from the previous night. Gavin slipped into the front entrance, and made a fresh pot of coffee without seeing anyone else. He was glad. He wasn't in the mood for company right now. The firm would be bustling with activity soon enough. For now, he wanted to get to his office and practice.

IT WASN'T LONG before Gladys arrived and interrupted Gavin's pre-game warm up. She flew through his office double-checking that his files were in order. After several minutes of her *help,* Gavin's stress level began to rise, and he needed to get out of the building. It was still early, but the courthouse doors would already be open to the public, and he figured there would also be other attorneys waiting for today's docket. He decided to walk. The morning air would revitalize him and it would help the time pass quicker.

Gavin crossed the street in front of the building with purpose and conviction. Each step was deliberate as if it had been perfectly scripted for his personal stride. Today was the day, he thought to himself as he walked toward the courthouse. There was a small crowd in front of him waiting to go through the metal detectors at the entrance. He could feel the presence of everyone around him. There were nineteen superior court judges and seven municipal and district court judges. On any given day, almost sixty trials were scheduled to be heard, which meant that the administrative staff had to constantly work overtime to prioritize cases so each litigant received his day in court within a reasonable time frame. None of this mattered to Gavin. Every inadvertent glance from the people in line seemed familiar as if they were all there just to watch one case, one argument. He assured himself that he was ready. He had fully briefed the issues, and Marcus shed some light on the case as a whole.

Gavin made his way through the entrance and walked to Judge Jose Velez's courtroom, where the hearing was scheduled to occur. Duke told him early on that Judge Velez had an affinity for the 'little guy' when up against the government or a hostile corporate defendant. Duke said the judge came to this country from Cuba as a young boy during the period of time that Fidel Castro was ousting dissidents. Mostly self-educated in Florida, he earned a scholarship to Duke law school, and then began private practice as a labor and employment attorney before coming to the bench. He was known to be a stickler for the rules, and had no problem holding an attorney in contempt if he thought he was trying to play fast and loose with the facts in his courtroom. Gavin had done his homework on the judge, and felt ready to appear in front of him.

He opened the courtroom doors and entered. Inside, the room was surprisingly bare compared to the lobby. There were no cameras or reporters waiting to document his hearing, only a judicial assistant and a court reporter seated directly in front of the bench. Lance was not present despite the fact that the hearing was fast approaching.

"May I help you?" The judicial assistant asked.

"Yes, I'm here for a hearing this morning." Gavin quickly suppressed the anxiety in his chest as he was reminded that this was his first solo argument. Sure, Duke let him to appear on the change of venue motion, but he never said a word. This time, no one was there to save him if he got into trouble. No one was there to give him advice.

"We've got a big docket today. What's the case name?"

"Harrington v. Tutuila," Gavin said as he walked up to the front trying to pretend he knew what he was doing. He remembered Duke signing in.

"Great, you're the first one here on this matter." She slid a sign-in sheet in front of Gavin. "Just sign in here."

Gavin looked at the sheet. There were three columns to fill in — *name, time arrived,* and *party represented.* Gavin put down his name and the time of 8:50, but hesitated when he got to the other line. The importance of this hearing flooded over him as if for the first time as he stared at the blank. Sara's memory, Sara's claim, all reduced to a simple line on a sign in sheet. He carefully wrote in *Sara Harrington.* Technically, he represented her estate and her parents, but today, he argued for her.

The judicial assistant flipped the sign-in sheet back around to face her and barely read the name. "Okay, Mr. Brandy?"

"Brady," Gavin said trying to reinforce his authority and legitimacy for being here.

"Brady, I'm sorry. You're the first one here," she responded without any inflexion in voice, "usually the attorneys don't arrive until about nine fifteen, so take a seat if you'd like or feel free to get some coffee outside in the lobby. Judge Velez will be calling the docket in about thirty minutes."

"Thanks." Gavin felt a bit like a child being turned away at an R-rated movie. He was too early, too prepared, and too nervous — a deadly trifecta because it gave him too much time to think about all the ways his argument could go badly. He started to walk back out of the courtroom. He did not necessarily want any more coffee, but he certainly did not want to be seen eagerly waiting in the courtroom when Lance showed up.

"Oh, by the way," the judicial assistant called out, "you're scheduled to be the second matter this morning. There's a last-minute emergency criminal motion that was placed before you."

"Great, thanks." That was the first bit of luck today. There is something to be said about not going first, he thought to himself as he exited the courtroom and headed over to the small espresso stand in the corner of the lobby.

Gavin stood next to the stand inconspicuously in sight of judge Velez's courtroom doors. He thumbed through his notes and briefing a final time waiting for someone else to enter the courtroom before he returned. The front lobby of the courthouse was bursting with seemingly displaced people milling around in every direction. Many of them found their way into a room marked *jury panel check-in* while others disappeared into the elevator. It was amazing the number of different lives that passed through the front doors, all praying for a favorable crack of the judge's gavel. This is where the fabric of society was sewn and, oftentimes, torn apart.

"Excuse me." A deep and familiar voice interrupted his musings. "Gavin Brady, right?"

Lance Penderson was standing to his side. He was pouring two packets of sugar in his coffee from the condiment tray next to where Gavin stood. He recognized Lance from one of his photos in the state bar magazine. Lance had been featured several times for cases he won against some of the best plaintiff's lawyers in the state. He was a major player in the legal field and way out of Gavin's league. Gavin registered his identity, and then pretended not to recognize him.

"Yes, I am," he said with as much artificial authenticity as he could muster.

"I'm sorry, Lance Penderson." He held out his hand. "It's good to finally meet you."

"Oh, yes. Good to meet you," Gavin said gripping his palm.

"Is Duke showing up today or are you handling this?"

Gavin shuddered inside. Already, Lance was playing some type of subtle intimidation game. "No, he's out of town so you're stuck with me."

Lance stirred his coffee and took a sip. "God, they make this too hot to drink. With all you plaintiff's attorneys around here, you'd think they'd be more careful."

"I'm just taking notes for the complaint," Gavin said, keeping up with Lance's quips. He was not going to be intimidated today, not today.

"I see you like to get here early as well," Lance said looking around the lobby. "When I first started out, I used to show up almost an hour early, and just stomp around the courtroom feeling out the space."

"Too bad you weren't here a little while ago. I could have used some pointers."

Lance liked Gavin despite being on the opposite sides of the profession. He played his intimidation game, and Gavin countered like a worthy opponent. Litigation is a living game of chess with each party making restrained, yet potentially deadly moves in the hope that their opponent's weaknesses will be exposed. Gavin and Lance were warriors just stepping onto the battlefield. However, they were also officers of the court, duty bound to advocate for their respective sides, but also duty bound to treat each other with respect. Lance was a true civil defense attorney. He was brilliant in the interpretation of the law and blindly callous in its application. For Lance, the law was not about people, it was about order, stability, and personal accountability. He was not out to change the world. He was out to apply the law and distinguish the facts, and he was a master at it. For him, today was not about people or an injustice that needed to be set right. It was about a strict interpretation of legal principles.

"I'm always so terrified that I'll show up late with the traffic from Seattle that I leave at an ungodly hour," Lance continued after a brief pause. He continued to slowly sip on his coffee carefully blowing away the hot steam each time.

"Yeah, for me I figured it was either sit in my office or sit up here."

"That's good."

"What's good?"

"The courthouse. It's already pulsing through your veins. I can see it in your eyes. It's the sign of a true litigator." Lance smiled at him. For the first time, Gavin felt like an equal, a professional advocate who demanded the respect and recognition of the title, *attorney at law*. Then he looked down at his cup and remembered Lance's remark about lawsuits and hot coffee. They were professionals but also adversaries, and, in the end, saw the world through completely different lenses.

Lance still had a full cup of coffee so he wasn't heading straight into the courtroom either. Gavin knew he had some time before he needed to be inside. He opened his folders and began reviewing his notes for a final time.

Behind his notes, he noticed a folder marked *mysterious photos*. Inside were the photos that were delivered to Hannah. He thumbed through them again. One of the photos caught his eye. It showed Jenny talking to him inside the courthouse, inside the front lobby. On the back was the ostensibly random numbering that continued to haunt him. Two photos of the outside of their home, three photos with the courthouse in the background, one photo showing the pier, and one photo at the grocery store. Each photo had a number on the back except the one showing their home, which had a capital *A*. He knew there must be a pattern, but it continued to elude him.

The large clock on the wall in front of the entrance to the building read 9:15. Gavin dumped the majority of his coffee in the trash next to the espresso stand, and headed into the courtroom. The photos would have to wait for now. Suppressing the churning butterflies in his stomach, he shook his head and focused on his argument.

CHAPTER 23

INSIDE THE COURTROOM, attorneys were beginning to gather. Gavin looked around at the area in front of the judge's bench, nicknamed *the pit.* It was an intimidating sight. Lawyers from both sides of the bar were chiding each other about past cases and current clients. Everyone seemed to know one another, which only accentuated Gavin's feelings of being an outsider. It was as if he was the new kid on the first day of school watching the popular crowd reunite to exchange stories about their summer break. Gavin did not feel like wading through the mass. Luckily, the judicial assistant caught his eye, and acknowledged that he had returned. Silently and alone, he took his place near the middle of the room. Lance entered shortly thereafter. His associate, Brian Thomas, accompanied him along with Tyler's parents and a young, somewhat stocky, female paralegal. The entourage took their seat across from Gavin on the other side of the courtroom as Lance went up to sign in. All of them had serious focused looks on their faces, like boxers on the way to a championship bout.

Within several minutes, Tyler and his attorney entered followed by Danny and his attorney and Sal and his attorney. The group sat in the same vicinity, but kept a respectable distance to avoid any appearance of collusion in front of the judge. Finally, Marcus entered with his attorney. Tyler, Danny, and Sal had all been told by their lawyers not to make any eye contact with Marcus when he appeared, and Marcus returned the favor by staring at the ground in front of his own feet. Although everyone refused to acknowledge each other's presence, the tension in the room gripped them, holding them tight like an uneasy embrace from a stranger. But that feeling was not new for these boys. They had been here before. Marcus and his attorney purposely sat on the same side as Gavin, just close enough to show adversity for the other defendants, but far enough away to keep a respectable distance from the plaintiff's position.

Gavin soaked up the moves made by each litigator. These men were professionals in their field and had litigated hundreds of complex cases. Gavin's client was not present, and could only be represented symbolically through his arguments. Sara's parents would only hear about the result of the hearing from Gavin when he called. The defendants, on the other hand, were local and showed up with a strong sign of solidarity and force.

One by one, the attorneys made their way to the front of the courtroom to sign in. Gavin nervously flipped through his notes one last time. He felt a small sigh of relief in knowing that he was not going first. He could hear his heart race as the time inevitably drew near. He gripped his briefcase and reiterated the argument in his head.

"All rise." The judicial clerk's voice echoed through the room.

Gavin stood up as the judge entered from his chambers. He was a serious man who looked quite at ease and comfortable in the position of final arbiter. Everyone sat back down, and the docket was called.

"We have nineteen matters this morning," Judge Velez said, "so let's not dilly dally around. I've read everyone's briefing, and I'll allow ten minutes per side for argument. Okay, let's call the first matter."

Like a well-trained regiment taking orders from their commander, everyone took their seats in unison. There was no doubt who was in control of this courtroom. The judge had a reputation for decisiveness and swift rulings. The first matter involved a criminal motion brought by the defense attorney asking for a bill of particulars, which is nothing more than a fancy way of requesting clarification of the facts that support a particular charge brought against an accused. Both sides were called before the judge.

The defense attorney started on the attack immediately. "Your honor, this case involves a contested charge of robbery in the first degree and assault in the second degree stemming from an encounter between —"

"I know the facts of the case, counselor, and I've read the briefing submitted by both parties. You want the state to outline what exactly they are alleging that your client did to substantiate the charge of robbery, is that right?"

The judge was being true to his reputation, thorough and direct.

"That's the cliff's notes version, correct your honor."

Gavin stopped listening to the attorneys, and looked back down at his notes. This was not exactly the best judge for the type of argument Gavin was making. He knew that his success very much depended on a broad policy reading of the law. He convinced his boss to sue Tyler's parents in order to collect money from their homeowner's insurance policy. It was the only way to convince Duke to keep the case. Duke had larger aspirations. He wanted to sue the gun manufacturers in a market share liability theory, but to do that, he needed money to fund the lawsuit.

"Counselor." The judge's voice reached out past the litigants standing before him and grabbed Gavin's attention in the middle of the room. "Isn't it true that the state can prove the charge in two alternative theories?"

"That's my point your honor. RCW nine A point three six point oh' two one states that the state can allege either substantial bodily harm or assault with a deadly weapon. I want to know which one they're alleging."

"Don't we all." A half-whispered voice from behind Gavin's head spoke.

Gavin turned around. He half-recognized the voice. Behind him sat another attorney gripping a handful of notes. It was Alex from his firm. Gavin's surprise was enhanced by the awkwardness of the moment. After all, Alex his firm fired Alex for not passing the bar.

"Hey, Alex, good to see you." Gavin wished that the two of them had become better friends before Alex was forced to leave.

"I hear you're up here on the Harrington case, good luck."

"How'd you know that?" Gavin gave him a puzzled look. Alex was a nice guy but he was now an outsider, and would not have that type of information.

"Hunter told me. He said you're some kind of rising star in the firm."

Hunter told him. Gavin felt a little embarrassed. He claimed to be concerned with the fate of one of his fellow associates and yet, Hunter, an associate in two classes ahead of him took the time to keep in touch with Alex. He quickly brushed off the thought. He was busy and had more pressure than the others. Ambition came at a price, and he would never be able to rise to the big cases unless he proved himself.

"I'm no rising star. It's all a façade," he whispered jokingly, brushing off the last remark. Alex smiled and, for a moment, Gavin detected a hint of affirmation in his expression. Perhaps, it was jealously, or, perhaps, it was acknowledgement that Gavin was indeed a fraud. Perhaps, Alex was secretly privy to information that Gavin jumped too early and too deep into a case that needed more investigation, more time. All the doubts of his case rushed back to the foreground as he continued to analyze each twitch of his ex-colleague.

"So what are you up to?"

"I'm doing some contract work for a local firm part-time. I come up here to watch arguments on my days off."

"The point I'm making your honor is that the merger doctrine is applicable depending on the state's theory." The defense attorney was feverishly defending his position.

The attorneys, embroiled in their own battle, grew louder and caught Gavin's attention again snapping him out of his conversation with Alex. "Under RCW 9A.36.021 subsection A1, the charge merges with the second count from the state. This is important, not only for the guilt phase, but for sentencing."

"What's he talking about?" Gavin wanted to show his ignorance to Alex. Rising star was more in line with teacher's pet, and he did not want to be either. Besides, he did not want to sound like he was somehow above Alex.

"9A is the criminal code in the state statutes; 9A.36.021 is the statute of assault in the second degree. That's all I've gotten out of it."

"Impressive." Gavin looked at him with astonishment.

"I'm contracting for a criminal defense firm, and, of course, still studying for the bar."

"Well, you're one up on me with that." Gavin was being polite. Alex was smart, and it was wrong how he was tossed out so early before getting a real chance to shine. The bar exam was no measure of an attorney's intelligence or potential. Some of the greatest trial attorneys in the country failed the bar exam on the first try. Gavin smiled at Alex and began to turn back around.

"Just remember," Alex continued forcing Gavin to focus on him and away from the courtroom. "Title Nine is the criminal code, and anything with an *A* after the nine is a crime." As he spoke, he reached over Gavin's shoulder and wrote *9A* on the margin of the notes in his lap.

Gavin nodded his head feigning interest in Alex's explanation. However, his nervousness had a choke hold on his attention span. Actually, he was trying to listen to Alex while replaying his own argument in his head.

"Anyway, good seeing you Gavin." Alex patted him on the shoulder. "Good luck today."

"Thanks." Gavin turned back around and watched the judge continue to interrogate the two attorneys. They were discussing something about the merger doctrine and how it applied to their case.

He wasn't entirely sure he still understood the merger doctrine, and he wasn't really listening to the argument. After the bar exam, he systematically purged from his brain all of the useless information he learned about contract law, securities law, land use law, and anything else not directly related to his goals as an attorney. Criminal law was interesting, but it, too, had gone to the wayside in his brain.

Gavin looked down at his watch. It had been twenty-three minutes since the argument had begun. That was three minutes longer than the judge allotted. This was a good sign. Perhaps his swift, cut-to-the-chase mentality would bend today, and he would be amenable to listening to why this case should stay alive based upon Gavin's broad public policy argument.

"Counsel, I've broken my own rule and allowed you to carry-on longer than your allotted time." It was as if the judge were listening to Gavin's thoughts.

"Your honor, I just want clarification on the statute," the defense attorney continued. "My client's on trial for his life, and he's supposed to be presumed innocent. I just want to know what the basis of the charge is."

"Your honor," the prosecutor responded as soon as the defense attorney paused for a beat, "the state is entitled to—"

"Gentlemen, I get it," Judge Velez said with exasperation. "Tricia, fetch me the statute will you?" His judicial assistant immediately got up and walked over to a stack of green books lining the east wall of the courtroom. She fingered the covers until she reached the one with a *9A* on the spine. She pulled it and handed it to the judge.

Gavin knew that a decision was imminent. The judge was reviewing the language of the statute with the two attorneys while giving his decision. Gavin began thumbing through his file to keep his mind off the fact that he was next. He had crossed out most of his notes to keep his argument concise and to the point. Behind his handwritten loose leaf pages were the mysterious photos. He started to glance through them again when he heard the judicial assistant calling out his case.

"Are the parties in the Harrington v. Tutuila ready?"

Gavin slammed his file shut and looked up at the front of the room.

"The defense is ready, your honor." Lance's voice pierced through the room. One by one, he heard the voices of each defense attorney call out to the court that they were present, and ready to proceed with the motion.

Gavin could now hear his own heartbeat. "The plaintiff is ready," he said managing to squeak out the words.

"I notice from the sign-in sheet that there are four additional parties appearing. I only have briefing from Mr. Penderson and Mr. Brady."

"That is correct your honor. The other parties have chosen to adopt my client's argument, and appear in support of the position outlined in my client's brief," Lance said.

"So, I'm only going to hear from you and Mr. Brady this morning?"

"Yes."

"Well good," the judge said with a smile. "If we can pull off having four attorneys appear before me without getting the opportunity to hear their own voices, I may have to start believing in leprechauns and unicorns again."

Like a pressured valve, a release of nervous laughter roared throughout the room. Gavin was still busy gathering his file and briefcase, and did not hear the judge's joke. He looked up and saw the guffaw coming from his colleagues. He saw that Lance had a big smile on his face as well, and was already at the front of the room before the judge. Had he done something funny? Was the room laughing at him? He quickly stood up, and began marching up to join the other attorneys. As he passed the front row, his arm slapped against the side rail knocking the file from his grip. It spilled onto the floor scattering his notes around his feet.

"I'm sorry, your honor." Gavin was truly embarrassed by his mishap.

"Don't worry about it, counselor. Happens to me every day. You've just stumbled on the very system used to judicially decide whose brief to read first."

The judge had a kindness about him that helped put Gavin at ease as he bent down and picked up the contents of his file.

"Here you go." One of the attorneys sitting in the front row handed him one of the photos that had spilled out along with his notes.

"Thanks." Gavin grabbed it and began to stuff it back into his file as he stood up. Something stopped him. He had viewed these photos a hundred times but, this time, something caught his eye. The attorney had handed him one of the photos with the backside facing up. Gavin stood there motionless, staring at the markings on the back. "Oh my God!" He murmured just under his breath. Everyone had originally thought that the numbers on the back were some type of categorizing system put there by the person or company who developed them. That wasn't true. He couldn't believe that he hadn't seen it earlier. These numbers weren't meant for organization. These numbers were trying to tell him something, like a message neatly wrapped in its own riddle. A riddle that was finally becoming clearer.

"Counselor, are we ready?" The judge asked.

"What? Yes." He shuffled his papers together and made his way to the front as the judicial assistant officially called the case.

"Now, Mr. Penderson, since this is your motion, you may go first."

"I'm sorry," Gavin interrupted.

"Yes, counselor, you'd like to go first?"

"No." There was a dull roar of chuckles from the attorneys in the room. "I'm sorry."

He was still organizing the photos trying to find some sort of order. There were two photos of the outside of his house, three photos of him at the courthouse, and two photos that contained single shots of his wife at the grocery store and himself at the pier. He glanced at the notation that Alex had made in the margin of his notepad, 9A.

"Uhm, I was wondering," he said looking back up at the judge. "Could I get that book you were using just a moment ago?"

"The criminal code, counselor?"

"Yes."

The judge gave him a quick stern look before turning to his judicial assistant. "Tricia, hand Mr. Brady title nine of our beloved revised code of Washington. I think he'd like to check my work on the previous motion."

Gavin started to speak, but the judge caught his eye and winked at him. Gavin smiled back with a sigh of relief. In his state, there was no telling what would have come out of his mouth.

Tricia handed the green book through Lance to Gavin's eager hands. He immediately checked the spine and flipped over one of the photos. There it was, smiling back at him, the letter *A* on the back of one of the photos of his house. He quickly flipped over the other photo of his house. On the back was the number nine. It was a message. He jotted down *9A* on the legal pad in front of him.

"May we begin now?" The judge interrupted his moment.

"Yes, I'm sorry." Gavin continued to turn his photos over.

Lance gave Gavin a final glance and began to speak.

"Your honor, I won't reiterate my brief here. I presume your honor has read it, and I'd be happy to answer any questions that the Court may have. Plaintiff's theory of liability turns on the application of the social host theory, which cannot be used against my clients because they are not commercial purveyors. We're not talking about a bar here where the bartender or even the owner may be held liable for over-serving someone."

As Lance continued his argument, Gavin hurriedly tried to solve the message that had been haunting him. There were three courthouse photos with the numbers zero, two, and zero on the back. The two remaining photos had a two and a seven on the back. If there was an order to the photos, he thought to himself, maybe the locations should be grouped together. All of the statutory crimes in the volume began with *9A* followed by a period, followed by two numbers, another period, and finally three numbers. The three courthouse photos must be the end numbers, he thought, which left a two and seven. Gavin quickly flipped through the book. There was nothing under Nine-A point twenty-seven. Switching the numbers, he quickly jotted down the number seventy-two on his legal pad and continued flipping through the book until he reached the section that he wanted.

His eyes widened. There it was; *9A. 72.020.* It matched the symbols on the back of the photos. The section defined the crime of perjury. That was the message. Someone was lying or someone had lied, but who? Tyler? That was too obvious. He flipped through the photos again. Whoever took these was sending him a message that he and his family were being watched, but why were there photos of the courthouse, and why was Jenny in one of them? Was Jenny involved? Was Randy involved? He didn't know.

"That's it." The words shot out of Gavin's mouth before he could stop them.

"Excuse me, counselor?" Judge Velez shot back. "You'll get your turn, but I do not put up with interruptions in my courtroom."

"I'm sorry your honor, it just slipped out."

"Well, put some tread on it. Go ahead, Mr. Penderson."

Lance wasn't rattled by Gavin's actions, but he was a little perplexed. "Well, I think Mr. Brady has said it quite succinctly. That's it. What we have is an allegation by the plaintiffs that my clients allowed their son to drink at home with his friends. The law is clear in this state. They cannot be held liable for the negligent acts of their son even if they knew that he was drunk and did nothing to stop him unless, of course, they were profiting from the party. They weren't. No money was exchanged, and this wasn't a party open to the public.

This was a group of dumb kids drinking at their parents' home. Nothing more. They were, at best, bad parents. Bad parenting, however, does not a tort make. This case should be dismissed."

"Thank you, counselor." Judge Velez turned to Gavin. "You must admit, your brief seems to concede many of his points."

Gavin was still trying to process his newest revelation. The message meant that he was on to something, and he was ruffling someone's feathers. "Your honor," he said regaining some composure. "This case is not about bad parenting. It's about a teenage girl and a fatal bullet ripping through her internal organs because those boys thought it would be funny." He pointed toward Tyler as he continued. "Or maybe they wanted to prove something or maybe they were too doped up to know any better."

"But it also has to be about the law, wouldn't you agree?" the judge said. He hadn't said a word during Lance's argument so Gavin did not see this exchange as a good sign.

"The social host theory was premised on the idea that we didn't want to create strict liability on people who were having get togethers at home and serving a seemingly innocuous drink. Alcohol is legal to buy for adults, and the law didn't want to be a harsh burden on the consumer. However, these parents didn't just allow their son and his friends to drink, they offered a safe haven for them to consume marijuana, which is always illegal, and they might have even provided the gun used in the shooting."

"I object to that, your honor," Lance said.

"Do you have any support for this accusation?"

Gavin turned his head and looked at Marcus, who was silently counting the tiles on the floor. He was in a Hobson's choice. Releasing Marcus from the lawsuit to confirm the marijuana and gun would seriously jeopardize his chances at trial. Keeping him as a defendant would ensure that he would remain silent. "I'm still investigating that aspect of the case," he said turning back to the front of the room.

"I've read your brief, counselor and I admire your passion." The judge was cutting him short. "But do you have any new evidence that might take this case outside of a social host liability theory other than conjecture?"

Gavin skimmed his notes. He had cut as much of his argument as he could, and the judge seemed to want to cut the rest. Lance was right. He needed more than just parents letting their son drink at home.

"As I see it," the judge continued, "you've got several problems. You've brought a lawsuit against four boys, and you can't establish who fired the shot or if anyone knew that there was a gun in the car before the shooting. Furthermore, the past criminal verdict is not helping you. Now, you want to bring in the parents of one of the boys to show what?"

"That Tyler was the shooter your honor." Gavin beamed as he spoke. The message from the photos was becoming clearer. "Your honor, they committed a crime and then conspired with somebody close to the case to cover it up."

Lance jerked his head toward Gavin in astonishment. "Your honor, I object. This wasn't in his brief."

"And I'm going to hear what he has to say Mr. Penderson. Who conspired?"

Gavin tried to organize his thoughts. Whoever sent these photos was careful enough to hide the message, as if it was too dangerous to say out loud. "The boys obviously needed help. Tyler's father is a powerful leader in his community. It's hard to explain but someone was trying to tell me something and I'm beginning to understand." Gavin was rubbing the photos in his fingers as he spoke. "These boys committed perjury, all except one, Marcus. But someone conspired with them to cover it up, someone close to the investigation."

The judge looked down at the photos in Gavin's hand. "Do you have any factual basis for your position, Mr. Brady?"

Gavin knew that the judge was listening to him, but he also wanted facts that would allow him to rule in Gavin's favor. His question was an opening to present some last-minute evidence. All Gavin had was heightened suspicion. Chillie Ki was dead and he was the only person who told anyone that Tyler had been waving a gun around earlier that evening. A horrific thought entered his head. The photos of the courthouse and of Jenny. What if she was involved? Someone paid off Chillie. What if she was the liar, and the bearer of the message was warning him to stay clear of her? She had been castigating him since the beginning about putting pressure on her. The only link right now to the parents being involved was the investigation.

"Nothing that I can tangibly put my finger on as I stand here today."

"Well, that's unfortunate, counselor."

"The prosecutor's office knows about the cover-up," he said in desperation. "They're aware of some inconsistencies and are conducting a secret investigation to get to the bottom of it." He slipped the photos back into a manila folder. He was treading on thin ice. If Jenny was involved, then she would hear about this argument and would react. Perhaps, even publicly disavow any investigation, which could get him disbarred for lying to a tribunal.

"Is this true?" The judge turned to Lance.

"I've only heard rumors, but my response would be so what? Legally, of course your honor. What does that have to do with my clients?"

"Everything, your honor." The judge seemed intrigued and Gavin was running with it. "Someone's pulling the strings to cover-up the truth." He spoke the words as they formed in his head. "If the prosecutor's office were to uncover, for example, that Tyler lied during the first trial, then he'd be guilty of perjury, and I would be able to prove who actually fired the gun. They might also uncover that the boys were smoking dope that night, which would take away Mr. Penderson's social host defense. They might even uncover evidence that Mr. Tutuila gave his son the gun that was used in the murder. There's more to this case your honor."

Gavin felt like a child who had just stood on his own for the very first time. He could see the long procession of attorneys stretched out to his right, their dark suits blocking out the light around him.

"Is that it?" the judge asked.

"Doesn't it strike this Court odd that a witness who actually placed Tyler in the front seat of the car as well as a gun in his hand just hours before the shooting subsequently disappeared?"

"Yes. It does," Judge Velez's response sounded almost sympathetic. "Unfortunately, odd occurrences do not always add up to facts supporting a lawsuit." His voice was calming and soothing as if he were a father speaking to a disappointed child. "I know you want justice son, we all do. But you're not there yet."

As the judge continued, Gavin could hear his own father's voice trying to reason with his young son. Velez's words transported Gavin back to his own tumultuous adolescence, and to the times when his own father would gently explain to him why he had to be on the road for the holidays. Tyler confessed to a shooting, and got away with it. The bench towered before Gavin and the room almost stretched to twice its size. He no longer commanded anything. He was once again the small child waiting by a front door that never opened.

"Mr. Brady," the judge continued. "Find me a link to the parents, someone, anyone. Right now, you don't even have enough to establish the identity of the shooter and you certainly do not have a legal basis to continue this lawsuit."

Gavin's mouth dropped. The judge was dismissing the lawsuit. How could this be? With the same deadly accuracy as the bullet that ended his client's life, Gavin was listening to the extinguishment of his case with each word from the bench. Then, the judge's tenor changed.

"What troubles me, counselor is this secret investigation by the prosecutor's office. If that's true, there might be more here than what is before me now." He lifted the thin legal brief titled, *Plaintiff's Response to Summary Judgment*, and then plopped it down with a heavy sigh. "I also don't want to clog my court with baseless claims. I'm giving you one week until next Monday's docket Mr. Brady. I'll reserve judgment until then, and I suggest you come with more than you brought here today."

"Your honor." Lance jumped in at the first beat of silence. "You said it yourself, there is no legal basis for this lawsuit to continue. I don't see—"

"Well then, counselor, you have nothing to worry about, do you?" He slammed his gavel down in a final gesture. "Who's next?"

Gavin's heartbeat was thumping in his chest. He had barely survived the morning. He could feel each corpuscle of blood pound through his veins as a rhythmic reminder of how close he came to utter failure. Beads of sweat welled up on his upper lip as he slowly gathered his notes. His legs were unusually heavy as he turned to face the room. It was full of other matters, but he could feel every eye piercing his chest. Slowly and deliberately, he dragged himself toward the back of the room. The exit sign shone especially bright as if to finalize the morning's events. A hand reached out.

"Good argument." It was Alex. His facial expression offered genuine selfless empathy. "You're really good. Most people would have caved under that kind of pressure."

"Thank you." Gavin gripped Alex's palm. No rivalry existed between these men. Their hands locked in mutual commiseration. For a split second, Gavin thought that Alex might be the author of the photos but dismissed it. A friendship was born in that moment, one that Gavin would grow to cherish and appreciate in later years. For now, the revelation itself was enough.

Gavin could already hear the next argument under way. This was his opportunity to slip away, and escape the area before anyone recognized him. He succeeded in turning his small wrongful death case into a conspiracy and cover-up involving a secret investigation by the prosecutor's office. He couldn't think straight yet. There was so much to do, and he had no idea where to begin. The photos saved him and delivered a vital message, but what was it? Was Jenny involved? And if she was, then who was helping her, and why?

CHAPTER 24

ALTHOUGH THE DOOR to Randy's office was shut, the sounds of muffled voices bled through the heavy wood into the lobby area where Jenny waited. She had been there for almost half an hour pretending to read the magazines that were laid out on the coffee table. Jenny thought it was odd for a prosecutor to have magazines in his front lobby area. It made him look more like a dentist than a prosecuting attorney. It was also odd because Randy's job was administrative in function, and he never dealt with the public. The only people who would be reading them would be his staff. There was a lot about Randy that did not necessarily make sense. She picked up the one of the latest news magazines and flipped through the pages.

Randy had left her a voice message the previous day to come to his office in the morning. He didn't specify a time, but that was typical of him. Randy never adhered to a strict schedule. He had never litigated a case, and had never been governed by court ordered deadlines. He filled his mornings with business group breakfasts and political golf games. His career consisted of hanging back in the shadows and making moves at the right time to advance himself. He was good at that.

Jenny figured she knew why Randy wanted to meet with her. Today was the day of defense's motion to dismiss Gavin's case. Randy was unusually interested in the case from the beginning, which raised Jenny's suspicions. She knew more than Randy thought she did, and she had to hold her cards tight now. Randy made her the face person for the prosecutor's office. Her role was to pretend to investigate a file that was closed almost three years ago. The political side of the law disgusted her, but it was a stepping stone within the office. He would be forced to promote her when this was all over. A promotion would mean bigger cases and more opportunities. Jenny knew that as a woman, advancement was meted out only due to a degree of perseverance. It wasn't enough to show up and win your cases. She needed to take every opportunity to show her skill and worth. Otherwise, she would end up climbing twice the rungs to reach the same height as her fellow male workers.

Part of her also knew that she had to stay close to Randy. Harold's ominous call to her on her day off had her on edge. For some reason, Randy went out of his way to stick his nose in a civil case. It was not a great surprise that the prosecutor's office did not want to dredge up an old loss. That verdict sent a shock wave throughout the community and rippled across the nation. However, it didn't make sense that Randy would be so sensitive about it. He was a junior prosecutor at the time, and the Tutuila murder case was the launching pad to his campaign as head of the department. If anything, he should be figuring out how to use the case to remind the community why they elected him to office. Randy's actions even had Harold acting strangely, and nothing rattled him. Whatever was going on, it had something to do with that memo.

She flipped the pages of her magazine to keep up the veneer of reading. She was really trying to focus on the heated conversation inside Randy's office. She thought she overheard some discussion of money and investigation. Perhaps he was just talking about the department's budget. She felt paranoid. She was not a conspiracy theorist, but this case was odd.

The door opened. A man stood in the doorway with his back half-turned away from her.

"I've done my part. Don't try to screw me on this one. I know too much," the man said with a raised voice.

Jenny could even see the veins in the back of his neck raised. Just then Randy came into sight making eye contact with her. He seemed noticeably disturbed by her presence at that moment.

"Close the goddamn door," Randy shouted at the man.

"No. You just get me my money." The man let go of the door handle that had been tightly clutched in his hand, and stormed out of the office. As he passed Jenny, he turned his head and looked at her momentarily. The man wore jeans and a cloth windbreaker.

An uneasy feeling came over Jenny. She thought she could see a hint of a smirk on the man's face. His eyes darted down her body and back up before making eye contact again. Normally, she would react with disgust to this type of chauvinistic behavior, but something about him disturbed her. There was something familiar about this man, but she couldn't place him. She didn't think they had met before, but he clearly seemed to recognize her. Within a second, he disappeared out the lobby and down the hallway toward the elevators. Jenny fought the desire to turn her head and follow his path.

"Jenny," Randy said. He stood at the doorway. His face was still beet red from his conversation. "Come in."

Jenny followed him in his office, and closed the door behind her.

"So, I guess you've heard," he said without hesitation.

"I didn't hear anything."

Randy looked at the door realizing that she was referring to his heated exchange with Nate.

"Oh, you mean my case. Sure." Jenny hadn't had a chance to go by the courtroom where Gavin was arguing before coming up to Randy's office, but she heard that the judge reserved his ruling for a week. That didn't surprise her too much. Judges often took matters under advisement. "Yeah, they told me, he's ruling next Monday."

"No, not that." Randy already seemed exasperated with the whole conversation. "That's just half of our headache." He slapped down the morning's newspaper. "This is what I'm talking about."

On the cover was a story about Sara's murder and the civil suit. Jenny hadn't seen the paper yet.

"I thought you were handling this. Now, your boyfriend's got himself a front page case."

"Excuse me?" How dare he flippantly throw Gavin in her face. She relayed their one brief encounter, and he was treating her like a rejected teenage girl.

"Look, I'm sorry." Randy composed himself. "But did you read what he's been saying?"

Jenny decided not to make an issue of Randy's remark. She chalked it up to his self-centered nature. She picked up the paper and found the article, which sat conspicuously on the right bottom section of the front page. It was titled, *An Old Wound Continues to Fester — A Family Cries Out For Justice.*

"You know what he says in there?" Randy began to pace behind his desk.

"Not yet," Jenny politely snapped back still annoyed at Randy's earlier remark. The article recapped the criminal trial and some of the evidence in the case. The reporter quoted the family as saying that they will continue to fight for the justice their daughter deserves. Randy's impatience was apparent in his quick strides back and forth behind his desk. She began skimming the piece to find Gavin's name.

"He says that we're starting a secret investigation about the case. Can you believe that? A secret investigation."

Jenny stopped reading and looked at Randy. "Aren't we investigating this case?" Randy himself called a meeting in his office with Frank, Harold, and her to discuss the implications of the civil suit on the office. He appointed her to review the file, and to watch the progress of the civil case. He even called the civil attorneys and told them their clients would be well-advised to watch themselves. She and Harold sifted through several banker boxes of evidence and discovery from the trial. Of course there was an investigation, and Randy put her in charge of it.

"There is no case. This is damage control."

"Damage control?"

"Yes. I'm not going to be dragged down by this case like my predecessor."

She was confused by Randy's tone and remarks. How could he be brought down by reopening the case and getting at the truth? This office was supposed to be about truth and justice. She brushed aside his paranoia attributing it to an inevitable byproduct of his nature as a politician. Still, there were a lot of questions unanswered, and this office wasn't treating this case like an ordinary matter. Even Harold sensed there was something odd going on. His cryptic phone call asking her to give him orders was out of character for the even-keeled retired detective. She made a mental note to call Harold for an update.

"Who does this young kid think he is?"

Jenny looked at Randy. "You only have one week to worry about him. From what I hear, the judge almost ruled against him today."

"I don't think you understand. I have a phone message from the reporter who did this story. He wants to know what this office is doing to get justice. Now, what should I tell him?"

"Tell him we're doing everything possible."

"I don't want this case to get out of control causing another embarrassment for this office."

"I'm all over this case, Randy. I'll take care of it."

"You'll take care of it?"

"Yes. I'll even call the reporter back if you want."

"No, I'll do that. I don't want the papers thinking I'm too scared to talk to them." He took a deep breath. "Just be on it. This is important."

With that, she left. Randy's comments were swirling around in her head. It was becoming clear that she was in the hot seat. If something went wrong, she would be the one holding the bag. She knew that losing the original trial was an almost fatal blow to Frank's career, reducing him to a senior deputy prosecutor with no power or responsibilities. All he did now was shuffle papers and draw up plea offers. His trial days ended the moment that verdict was read.

Jenny knew Randy could be cold and calculating. He took advantage of the Tutuila acquittal at the expense of everyone else, and to the benefit of his own advancement. He kept the media outraged throughout his campaign for chief prosecutor. He would never protect her if something went wrong. She needed to review the file again and she needed to call Harold for an update on his investigation.

SEVERAL MESSAGES WERE waiting for Gavin back at the firm. He wasn't in any mood to be confronted with questions about the morning's hearing so he sneaked into his office as quietly as he could. Fortunately, no one would say a word until he instigated the conversation. It is a superstitious tradition not to query about oral arguments amongst civil litigators. It didn't matter because everyone in the firm already knew what happened. Gladys received two messages from opposing counsel requesting copies of any additional discovery he uncovered from the prosecutor's secret investigation. She quietly handed him his messages, and ran interference in the office as he sifted through his email.

Although he would have liked to have hidden in his office for the rest of the afternoon, there was plenty of work that not only required his attention, but wasn't used to being ignored. His in-box had not been attended to in days, and was sprouting into an overgrown and almost unruly stack of papers.

He began sorting through the bottomless memos that had been routed to him, and needed to be researched and argued on paper. There was never time in the legal profession to take a break for conciliatory recuperation. The law was demanding and, more importantly, the firm's clients expected constant attention.

He sifted through each case memo detailing the endless tragedies of their potential clients. The memos told stories of neighbors bickering over the priceless inches between their properties, or carpets that might be linked to an outbreak of whooping cough, or prisoners suing the jail because it failed to treat an inmate for Hepatitis C. There was only one criterion for any potential new case, will it pay? The facts didn't matter and the law meant even less.

"Our job is not to abide by the law; our job is to create it," Duke would always say during associate training.

"You think that first lawyer, who dared to sue the neighborhood tavern because they turned a blind eye when one of their regulars, three sheets to the wind, left their establishment got in his car and ran over a young pregnant kindergarten teacher, had precedent to back up his complaint? What about ol' Rosa Parks? Which law gave her the right to refuse to move to the back of the bus?"

He loved to talk policy, and his training sessions were more like fiery sermons than legal discussions. Duke could joust with the best of them as he paced back and forth commanding the room's space, and utilizing hints of his blue collar southern ancestry for dramatic effect. By the end of his talks, he made everyone feel as if they were more than just stiff-collared, overly-educated attorneys interpreting the law. He made them feel like they were crusaders fighting for unattainable and larger than life ideals and principles.

After a couple of hours, Gavin had almost entirely forgotten about the morning's beating before Judge Velez. Gladys fielded phone calls while Gavin barricaded himself behind his office door catching up on the past week's work. It wasn't long before the cloud-covered Northwest sun was replaced by the dark blanket of the night outside of his window. The large inbound stack of papers had now been substituted with several smaller stacks complete with tabs and post it notes sticking out of the sides. The tragic morning had turned into a very productive afternoon, and Gavin was well on his way to mapping out the next month's late night research schedule. He stretched away the tension in his back and shoulders just as the phone rang.

"Hello."

"How was the argument?" Hannah said softly on the other end of the phone.

"Not great."

"I'm sorry to hear that. I have some wine that I just opened."

"That's the best news I've had all day. I'll grab some stuff and come home right now."

He hung up the phone and gathered his briefcase. It was still packed with the Harrington case file from the morning, and had no more room for the endless case memos on his desk. His workload at this point was daunting. It seemed almost irrelevant what he brought home to work on because there was so much work to do that he could easily spend an entire night on any of the piles on his desk, and he only had one week to save Sara's case from a fatal dismissal ruling.

He grabbed his suit jacket from the back of the chair, and headed toward the door as the phone rang again. He hesitated for a moment. *It could be Hannah making sure I'm leaving.* He grabbed the phone.

"Hannah, I'm out the door—"

"That was a good job today, counselor." Gavin didn't recognize the deep male voice on the other end of the line.

"Who is this?"

"I mean with the photos. I didn't think you'd ever figure it out."

"Who are you?" He didn't need the answer. Gavin knew he was talking to the person who delivered the message and the photos.

"A concerned citizen."

"Are you the one harassing my wife? You stay away from my family."

"I'm sorry about the delivery method. I just needed you to pay attention, and to be careful."

"What is this, some kind of joke?" Gavin was as confused as he was frustrated. He didn't know whether to be scared or angry at the voice.

"Conspiracy, fraud, murder. Those aren't jokes."

"Look, I don't know who you are or what you're trying to do."

"Just listen for a moment. You're doing a good thing with this case, but you're only part way there. Those boys lied on the stand, they lied under oath and they got away with a murder. Now, in my book that's perjury."

"I can't sue them for perjury."

"No, *you* can't."

"This is just a civil case, and not a very good one right now. I don't know if you saw what happened today. Actually, did you see what happened today? Were you in the courtroom?"

"This case is more than that, and there's a lot you don't know."

"Tell me about it. Oh, what was your name again?"

"I'm trying to help you, Gavin. I can just as easily hang up this phone, and then you'll never uncover the truth, and that little girl's family will never get any justice."

"No. No, I don't want to ruin our relationship now that we're on a first name basis so to speak."

"Good. Do you think those boys could have come up with such a plan, and pulled it off without help?"

"Whose help?"

"You have all the pieces. You're just not looking at them."

"Pieces, puzzles, if you've got something to tell me, then tell me. Why all the stupid games?"

"Because the truth is dangerous, and it needs to be your choice to move forward. I am gonna help you out, though. You know Nunzio's Pizza on sixth?"

"Yeah."

"I ordered you a pizza."

"What?"

"For you and your wife. Go pick it up, it should be ready by the time you get there. Hope you like pepperoni."

"How is that helping me out?"

There was a click followed by a dial tone on the other end of the line. The caller left Gavin with more questions and no answers. Maybe it was a trick or even a hoax designed to humiliate him in some way. He was already humiliated. He stood there contemplating the phone call for what seemed like several minutes, until he phone rang again.

"This is Gavin."

"I thought you were leaving to come home."

"I am. I ordered us a pizza. I'm picking it up on the way home."

"Oh, that's so nice. Thanks, sweetie, but hurry home, okay?"

Now he was trapped. The next stop would be Nunzio's pizza, and whatever lay at that location for him. At least whoever called saved him from the inevitable scolding he was about to receive for still being at the office. He hung up the phone, and hurried out of the building.

Nunzio's was only a short detour from his normal route home, and well worth the few extra miles. It was owned and operated by a Sicilian family, who immigrated to the United States after the Second World War. People drove from all over the county just to taste the homemade sauce, and the thick round crusts always smelled like fresh bread from a bakery.

The parking lot was full, which was not unusual for this time of the evening. Gavin managed to find a spot in the back of the building, and walked inside. He wasn't quite sure what to expect or if there really was a pizza waiting for him. As he made his way to the front counter, he looked around at the two dimly lit dining areas on either side of the entrance. Red colored booths lined the walls, and small checkerboard tables filled in the middle areas.

He didn't see anything out of the ordinary. Every seat looked occupied with couples and families stuffing their faces with the thick sloppy pies, and a dull roar of overlapping conversations competed with the piped-in music coming out of the speakers in the ceiling. A young man was manning the order counter as Gavin cautiously approached.

"Welcome to Nunzio's, what can I get for you tonight?"

"I think I ordered a pizza."

"You think?" He cracked a smile.

"I mean I did."

"What's the name?"

"Brady." *I hope.*

The guy disappeared into the back. Gavin continued looking around. Why would the voice on the phone want him to pick up a pizza, and why this particular location? This was, of course, the best pizza in town, but there was another reason he needed to be here right now. Then he saw something that caught his attention. In the back corner, a dark-haired body rose from one of the booths, and walked to the bathroom. Gavin froze. It was Tyler's older brother, Kauni Tutuila. He recognized him from one of the newspaper photos of the original trial. He was enormous. His body seemed to take up half the room as he walked to the back of the restaurant.

This was too much of a coincidence. *The voice on the phone must have known that he would be here, and wanted me to see him, but why? Oh my God, I hope he didn't want him to see me.* It was a chilling thought, and one he wanted to dismiss.

Gavin stretched his neck to see if anyone else was sitting with him. Perhaps, Tyler was there as well or even Danny and Sal. Perhaps, Jenny was there. Across the booth, Gavin could see the profile of another individual, but the shadowy figure didn't look Samoan. As Gavin stared at the human image, he could see it looked like a male in his late forties wearing a sports coat and a button down shirt. A half-eaten pizza sat in the middle of the table in front of an empty pitcher with the foamy remnants of beer.

Gavin was still locked on the male as he casually turned his head toward the front of the restaurant, and, before Gavin could react, their eyes locked. Gavin didn't recognize him but there was something familiar about his face. Something he couldn't put his finger on, or even articulate in his mind. Like a deer caught in the headlights, the man's eyes widened into a surprised stare.

"That'll be fifteen sixty-five," said the man behind the counter.

Gavin jerked. "Excuse me?"

"Your pizza. fifteen dollars and sixty-five cents."

Gavin pulled out a twenty-dollar bill, and handed it to him. Before he could even pull his hand away, the guy had placed four bills and some change in his palm along with the steaming cardboard box. This was a high-volume place, and good dexterity translated into more profits.

"Thanks."

Gavin had seen what he was supposed to see, and there was no reason to remain any longer. He gave the place one last look before slipping out the front entrance. There was a lot to consider as he traversed the sea of cars in the parking lot. He had partially solved the riddle of the numbers on the back of the photos, but he wasn't any closer to learning who all was involved. Additionally, there was now a connection to be made between Tyler's brother, Kauni, and the man at the table. Who was this man, and why did he seem so surprised to see Gavin? Of course, there was also the inescapable memo that had been haunting Gavin from the beginning of this case, and seemed to hold some great secret.

He bought a little bit of time with Hannah by telling her about the pizza, but soon she would be counting the minutes before he got home. As he weaved between cars, his eyes were fixated on the road and his mind on how late he was. He didn't even notice the black Trans Am with tinted windows.

He replayed the ominous phone conversation in his head over and over again on the way home. There was someone out there who had a stake in the outcome of this case, someone willing to help. This case hadn't made sense from the beginning. Even the prosecutor's office took a hostile position. Jenny chastised him about the Chillie Ki memo just about every time he saw her. That memo led him to Chillie Ki's mom, who told him that someone paid for her son's silence and unavailability at trial. There was more to it than that, and the voice on the phone confirmed it. At least he knew whoever sent the photos to Hannah wasn't a threat anymore. He still had to be careful.

He pulled into his driveway and saw Hannah waiting for his car behind the front window's half-drawn curtains. She smiled. It was another typical late night at the office, but they were trying to make more time for each other.

He walked up the driveway still deep in thought. Hannah opened the front door. Her eyes sparkled in the moon's rays, and her smile lit up the night sky like a welcoming beacon. As he looked up to see her, everything seemed to melt away. There were no more questions, no more dilemmas. He was home, and it was time to be a husband.

CHAPTER 25

THE BRISK AUTUMN air was rich with moisture as Gavin huddled in his car waiting for the thin icy layer of frost on his windshield to melt. The weather was quickly turning cold. Although the temperature in Tacoma would regularly drop below freezing, it rarely snowed, and when it did, the white flakes would almost instantly fall apart melting into the watery landscape. It did, however, rain — quite a bit. Northwest rain combined with freezing temperatures usually resulted in black ice, an almost invisible and deadly condition for unsuspecting drivers. It was also a lucrative business both for insurance defense lawyers and personal injury lawyers. Slippery conditions meant accidents. Accidents meant injuries, and injuries equated to billable hours and structured settlements.

Stewart Meridiam & Smithwick had dabbled in auto accidents in the past, but an attorney needed a high-volume practice to make any real money at it. Duke had, long ago, decided that the firm was above such ambulance chasing. There were bigger fish to fry — municipalities, state-run agencies, and corporations with pockets deep enough to justify his effort. His philosophy was, why waste time with fifteen auto accident cases when just one large case will yield the same amount?

That was where William T. Hanson came in. His father, the late Bartholomew Hanson, had been an extremely influential and popular congressman in the district. It was Senator Bart Hanson who gave Fred's father the anonymous tip that his copper smelting plant was under a secret federal investigation for environmental abuses. Bart even helped run interference as the Meridiam family sold the business for more than a hundred times what it would be worth once the investigation became public. In return, the Meridiams financed all of Hanson's future reelection campaigns, and recruited his son to the firm.

William Hanson's addition to the newly formed Stewart Meridiam & Smithwick was only natural. He was by no means a brilliant jurist, and allowed himself to get by on his name alone. However, no one cared too much because recruiting William instantly plugged the firm into the Hanson family's political connections in both Washingtons.

Almost overnight, Hanson's recruitment turned the small boutique plaintiff's firm into a powerful and political entity that could influence legislation and policy across the state. When William missed the statute of limitations on one of his early cases, the firm's clout was successful in persuading the state bar association to limit the punishment to a verbal admonishment. When he decided he was tired of the long stressful hours of his legal practice, the firm pulled some strings, and found a cushy out of state judicial appointment so that his local troubles with the bar association would not become an issue. They even found Gavin's father in San Francisco to help run his campaign.

Now Gavin sat shivering in his car as the next generation of quid pro quo by Stewart Meridiam & Smithwick. He had other things on his mind at the moment. It was still painfully early, and the black sky would not lighten to its normal dull grey for hours. Gavin somehow sneaked out of the house without waking Hannah. He hadn't told her about last night's phone call. He didn't want to involve her any more than she already was, and he was now certain that there was no further danger from whoever delivered the photos.

As he put the case together in his mind, the pieces kept multiplying. Tyler's brother was involved somehow, and he didn't know the identity of the other man at the table. He had no way of contacting the person who called him last night, and he wasn't even sure why he was helping. He had less than one week to figure this case out or judge Velez was going to dismiss it. The icy roads offered a welcomed distraction from his thoughts. There was very little traffic at this time of the day, though the convenience of the Narrows Bridge was slowly enticing more families away from the rougher environment of Tacoma to the upscale neighborhoods on the western side of the water.

This particular morning, the bridge was blanketed in a thick fog, and offered no spectacular vistas other than an endless sea of white. Gavin inched across the mile-long stretch of concrete and steel with his headlights straining through the thick haze to illuminate the upcoming few feet of asphalt. He divided his time evenly between the dark wet road in front of him, and how he was going to approach the next several days.

He didn't even know where to begin. All his depositions were cancelled, and of the remaining witnesses known to him, no one was talking. There wasn't time to send out interrogatories or requests for production of documents. Chillie Ki was dead and only existed through a suspicious memo that Gavin still didn't fully understand. He didn't trust Jenny at the moment, and had no clue as to the identity of the anonymous tipster, who led him to Kauni's meeting with the unknown man.

The visibility increased slightly on the other side of the bridge. Gavin could begin to see the dark silhouettes of Douglas Firs dotting the surrounding landscape. It was not difficult to understand why this area attracted so many residents. Despite the year-long down pours, the land must have been simply breathtaking to the early explorers with its clean pine smell, magnificent views of the water, and untamed wildernesses.

The firm's building pressed against the floor of the fog as Gavin drove toward the front entrance. There were a few cars still parked belonging mostly to the burned out third and fourth year associates, who were becoming antsy about partnership. They would secretly get picked up by their spouses, and leave their cars overnight to be conspicuously seen by any partner driving by the office after hours. It was a good system, but it was overused, and Gavin felt it was also a little dishonest. *Just do the work.*

The inside of the firm was still quiet when he entered. He made his way to the break room, and started a fresh pot of coffee. Soon, the hallways would be illuminated with the early morning lights from other over achieving associates' offices, but, for now, Gavin rested comfortably listening to the gentle gurgling of the coffee machine in the remaining few minutes of silence. He filled his cup under the steaming hot spigot, and headed to his office.

His door was wide open when he entered, which was unusual. The late night cleaning crew had explicit instructions to shut all office doors behind them after vacuuming and were usually very good about it. He walked inside, quickly inspecting the area. Nothing seemed out of place. His file drawers were still closed, but easily opened without the use of a key. He had no reason to distrust anyone in the firm, and the cleaning crew was bonded so he kept everything in his office unlocked. Satisfied that there was no mischief going on, he went to his desk to begin his day.

He set his coffee next to his phone and his briefcase on the floor next to his chair. He might as well review the Harrington file and get an early start. He opened the leather flap. *What in the world?* Inside was a spiral notebook and two textbooks. One was titled,

Methodological Issues and Strategies in Clinical Research, and the other titled, *Current Psychotherapies.* They were the books Hannah was using to teach her classes, which meant that he had Hannah's briefcase. It was hard to tell because it was identical to his. Her parents gave them matching briefcases as a graduation/moving present. He must've accidentally grabbed hers when he left this morning. *Great, just great.*

The blinking light on his phone diverted his attention from the mix up. There were several voice mails already. The first message was two seconds long, and consisted of the sound of someone hanging up the phone followed by the beginning of a dial tone. He figured it was Hannah making sure he actually left last night. The second message was from Duke.

"Hey, kid. Callin' for an update. Fill me in on my return."

Duke was a master at playing the uninformed overworked attorney. It was one of the tactics that he successfully used in litigation. However, Gavin knew better. Duke did not even turn on the television without a full briefing of what was happening in the world. His secretary, Becky, likely filled him in on what occurred in court, or perhaps, he spoke to one of the countless moles he had running around the county building. Gavin knew he had to face his mentor soon, but was glad it wasn't going to be this morning. He listened to third message.

"Mr. Brady, this is Steve Morrow from the *Tacoma Tribune.* We spoke a couple of weeks ago about your representation of the Harringtons. I'm doing another follow up story on the status of the case and wanted to get any updates from you regarding yesterday. I'm working against a deadline so I'll try and catch you in the morning."

Great. Now his failure would soon be in print for the entire community to read. It was still too early for anyone, who kept regular hours, to call him. It was also too early to call Hannah to apologize for switching the briefcases. He'd wait an hour or so. He pulled one of the large stacks of overdue projects toward him, and began working.

"EXCUSE ME PLEASE." Jenny squeezed herself between a couple of process servers in the ground floor hallway of the courthouse. The morning was always bustling with activity, and today was certainly no exception. She made her way across the front lobby past the espresso cart toward the elevators, where a throng of attorneys were waiting with their clients to head up to the fifth floor courtrooms.

She headed for the stairwell around the corner. Her office was on the ninth floor, but the steep long hike would be a delight compared to being trapped in an elevator with Robert. She also figured the exercise would be an added benefit. Her schedule had forced her to miss going to the gym last week, so she decided to attack the stairs before her with vigor. She glided up the first couple of floors like a well-conditioned athlete. She was in pretty good shape, but nine floors was an ambitious impromptu workout for a woman in high heels and a skirt. For the remaining floors, she resigned herself to taking the steps at a slower pace.

At the top, she took a moment to regulate her breathing, and wipe away the small beads of sweat forming on her forehead before opening the door to the hallway. As she exited the concrete spiraling tunnel, she could see the front entrance to the prosecutor's office, complete with a bullet proof glass door and security guard. To her right, the elevator lights signaled an oncoming car. She smirked at the idea that she had beaten the occupants, and felt as if she had just made up for splurging on the slice of blackberry cheesecake last week.

Next to the entrance sat Stephen Morrow. He was tapping a small reporter's notepad on his knee, and sipping from a coffee cup from the espresso stand on the first floor. Like a radar beacon, he spotted her as soon as Jenny entered the hallway.

"Jenny, you're here. Good, I've been waiting for you."

"Hey, Steve." She was well acquainted with him. He covered the legal news for the local paper, and spent several hours each day in the courthouse. He was also extremely handsome and single. He was a nice guy. However, he was also a reporter, and she didn't want to always wonder whether the man she was with was after her or the big story.

"I was wondering if I could ask you a couple of questions about the Tutuila investigation?"

"The Tutuila investigation?"

News traveled quickly. Normally, she would oblige his questioning, but this was out of her hands. The press was already after Randy. That was fine with her. She wasn't exactly the most media savvy person, and reporters scared her. She didn't like trying to describe the complexities of her cases in small quotable sound bites. She didn't go to law school to be interviewed, she went to law school to try cases, and put bad people away.

"I'd love to help you out, but Randy is the guy you should be talking to on this case."

"I already did."

"You did?"

"Yeah, yesterday. He didn't have much to say, you know administrative types and all. He told me that he didn't know anything, and that the investigation was your baby. You were in charge, so what can you tell me?"

Jenny wasn't sure how to react. Randy knew plenty, and was adamant yesterday about wanting to handle the media. Now, he was deferring to her. A cold chill ran down her spine. Randy was a political animal, and his morality came and went depending on whether a situation would benefit him or not. This case had a potential embarrassing sting to the office, and he wanted the fingers pointing somewhere other than at his door. She was being set up as the fall gal if something went wrong.

"Can you give me a quote on this secret investigation?"

"Did he say that?"

"Randy? Not in so many words. It was more of a non-denial denial. Very *pc*, but that's the scuttlebutt goin' round, and you seem to be the 'go to' gal."

"Well, that's the thing about secret investigations. Even if there was one, they're supposed to be a secret." She wasn't getting sucked into this quite yet.

"Okay, fair enough. Can't blame a guy for trying."

"No, I can't." All she could think about was how to get back at Randy. She wasn't going to lose her job to save him some public embarrassment.

"Maybe the Harrington's civil attorney will go on record. I spoke to him once, and he's a real talker if you know what I mean."

"Who's that?"

"Gavin Brady. He's new and kind of a climber from what I hear."

Jenny knew Gavin would be all too willing to talk to the press about his case. He was the loose cannon. He was the one who told the court that the prosecutor's office was looking at the case, and then turned it into some sort of *secret investigation*, which, according to Randy, she oversaw. Steve walked over and hit the down button on the elevators.

"Last chance." He smiled.

"I wish I could comment, but you know our policy. Good luck with Gavin."

She watched him disappear into the metal car before turning to the front entrance of the prosecutor's office. She could stare at his smile all day. As the elevator door closed, she swiped her card on the security panel next to the entrance and vanished from sight. She briskly weaved through the endless maze of hallways before emerging in front of an office door. Inside, a young man looked up from behind the desk.

"Can I help you?"

Her face turned red with embarrassment. "God, I automatically went to my old office. Sorry, still getting used to the move."

Every few months, the junior felony prosecutors rotated departments to gain exposure and experience in prosecuting a wide range of crimes. Jenny had recently been reassigned to the felony robbery unit from the property crimes unit. This meant longer hours, more responsibilities, and a move to the other side of the building. She turned around, and headed toward the opposite end of the floor.

As she approached her own door, she thought she heard a metal drawer slamming shut inside her office. The noise made her stop in her tracks. She wasn't expecting anyone this morning, and her colleagues were not known for making themselves at home in each other's offices. She stared at the closed door unsure of what to do next. She was in a relatively isolated spot so there wasn't anyone in the immediate vicinity to signal. Her heart skipped a beat as the door handle began turning.

Instinctively, she jumped back to the bend in the hallway, nervously spying around the corner to see who might emerge. With a quick jerk, the door flew open, and a man exited. She snapped her head back behind the wall before he could see her. By the time she mustered enough courage to stretch her head back around the corner, he was walking toward the back exit. He wore a baseball style cap and workman's coveralls. In his right hand, he was carried a metal toolbox. Something didn't feel right. No one said anything about any scheduled work orders, and government maintenance workers never came this early.

"Hey!" She called after him. She was only a quick dash away from the sexual assault unit, where people did come in this early. The man ignored her call, picking up the pace.

"Hey you!"

He flung the exit doors open. Without hesitation, he turned to the right and vanished. She saw his profile for only a split second, but she thought there was something familiar about him. Then it hit her. He looked like the guy leaving Randy's office yesterday. She didn't get a good enough look at him to be positive.

"My office," she said to herself as she hurried down the hallway to her now closed door. Cautiously, she opened it and entered. There were boxes on the floor and books stacked up against one of the walls. Everything seemed to be in the same state of disarray as she'd left it.

Oh my God. Draped behind her door was an extra suit for emergencies. Across the hanger was a pair of her stockings. She stood there naked and violated as if she had just been in a car wreck without first checking to see if she had clean underwear. This was supposed to be her sanctuary. She should be allowed to hang her private linens behind her door, and now, someone had violated her space. In order to enter the prosecutor's office, one needed a security card, which was only issued to prosecutors and their support staff. Everyone else, including police detectives and maintenance personnel, had to get buzzed in by the front desk.

She picked up her phone. *There's an easy way to solve this problem*, she thought to herself. "Hello, front desk, this is Jennifer Garrett back in property, I mean robbery. Did you buzz any repair people back here for any reason?"

There was a pause and some fumbling of paper. "No, no one's come through to your section this morning."

"Thanks."

As she hung up, she noticed that her filing cabinet's top drawer was ajar. It reminded her of the metal slamming sound she heard. The top drawer held her active case files, and was off limits to everyone except her and the paralegal assigned to her cases. She eyed the opening of the drawer like a police detective viewing a crime scene body. She didn't know exactly what she was looking for, but it seemed appropriate to run her fingers along the edges for anything out of the ordinary. At first glance, everything appeared in order. The files were alphabetized by the defendant's last name. She gently nudged the top tabs of each file with her hand trying to recount all her cases by memory. When she got to the back, she noticed something odd. The Tutuila file was slightly askew. It wasn't really an active file, but she set it up to store her notes and copies from the records room.

She pulled out the file and opened it. Inside were only three sheets of her handwritten notes from the first meeting with Frank and Harold in Randy's office. "It's gone!" She slammed the folder shut. Now she knew what the mysterious maintenance worker was after.

She bolted out of her office and down the hallway following the intruder's path to the exit and into the outer corridor. It was empty. The elevator lights were dark, and the stairwell doors shut. Whoever had been in her office was long gone.

Oh shit, she said to herself as the door leading back inside clicked shut behind her. In her haste, she forgot her security card on her desk. Her office lay less than twenty feet from the closed door behind her. However, without her security card, she would have to walk almost six hundred feet to the front entrance on the other side of the floor so that she could be buzzed back in, and then an additional eighteen hundred feet through the connecting hallways to her desk. *I've got a better idea*, she said to herself, and headed for the elevator.

IT WAS A short ride to the basement floor. Jenny could barely wait for the doors to open. *I've got to get there before he does.* She raced toward the records room. Gordy was in his usual spot behind his desk reading a book. A steaming mug sat next to him.

"Morning, counselor." He looked up as she reached the window.

"I need access to the Tutuila files."

"You just saw them a little bit ago," he said in a sluggish voice.

"Thank you for remembering, and now I want to see the files again." Jenny was not in any mood to play games with Gordy.

"Okay, it's your dime." Gordy slowly poured himself out of his chair. "You gotta sign in first." He pointed to a clip board on the counter.

Jenny quickly jotted down the word, *Tutuila*, under the appropriate blank along with some illegible initials as Gordy ambled toward the buzzer to let her inside. She raced past him toward the myriad bookshelves in the back room.

"Down the hall to the — well you know where they are." She was already gone before he could finish.

She stopped in front of one of the back shelves. The Tutuila files were neatly tucked away in ten red expandable folders, and looked like they had been undisturbed since the last time she saw them.

Her eyes glided along the reddish binders to review how the file were organized on the shelf. The files were already pulled the last time she was, and Harold put them back. She pulled several folders and took them to a nearby table. *It's got to be here.* She quickly flipped through each sheet, and immediately moved on to the next. *It's got to be here,* she kept saying to herself as she finished going through the last folder on the table.

It's not here. She let out a sigh of despair, and shoved the few remaining pages back into its cardboard binding. The memo was missing along with the privilege log. Someone it from her office and now the original was also missing from the official file. The maintenance man must have stolen the file from her cabinet, but how was he able to remove the original? Only authorized personnel were allowed down here, and it was a felony to destroy official court documents. Something was not adding up about this case.

"Finding everything okay?" Gordy said from behind her.

Jenny let out a startled high-pitched shriek.

"Hey sorry, didn't mean to scare ya."

"Yeah, I'm fine." She was still breathing heavy from being surprised. "I didn't hear you."

"Well, that's some set of lungs you got."

Gordy was a master at picking the most inappropriate comment at any given moment. Jenny was unfazed, and took two steps toward him to create some power in her body language. It was a tactic she had learned by watching her supervisors cross-examine tough witnesses in trial.

"Let me ask you something." She stopped and stared in his eyes. "Has anyone been down here to look at the Tutuila file since I was here with detective Benoit?"

"I don't think so, why would they?"

"That's not my question." Jenny took another step forward. "Has anyone been here to look at the files for any reason?"

Gordy saw himself as a rough and tough man's man, but the truth was he was all talk, and knew better than to directly challenge her.

"I don't think so." He defiantly forced the words out of his mouth. "If they did, they'd have to sign in."

"Do you keep the sign-in sheets?"

"It's a crime not to."

"Can you please show me all of the sign-in sheets from my last visit to this morning?"

Her voice softened a bit without losing its air of authority. Gordy silently led her to a filing cabinet in the front area next to his desk. He opened one of the drawers, and pulled out a manila folder.

"Got the whole month right here." He handed her the stack.

She quickly flipped through the first few pages without moving until she found her initials.

"Okay, it was here on this date," she said out loud but only for her benefit.

She took the mass of pages, and set them on top of Gordy's desk. He tried to snarl at her, but she was too focused with reviewing the sheets. One by one, she turned the pages looking for words like *Tutuila,* or *Harrington,* or even someone's initials she recognized.

"Damn. And you say no one's been down here to look at the file this morning?"

"Look, I'm not lying to you. The only people I seen today was the coffee gal, who comes by every morning to deliver my café leche, and the maintenance guy to change the light bulbs in the back."

"Maintenance guy, you didn't say anything about a maintenance guy."

"You said you wanted to know about people who were looking at files. He don't look at files, he don't sign in, he just changes bulbs."

"When was he here?"

"I don't know, a while ago. At least an hour before you got here."

She couldn't believe it. It must have been the same guy who stole the memo from her office. Why was it important to remove the memo from the official file? This was an old case, long since abandoned by her office until Gavin started snooping around. Now, some guy burglarized her office, and the same guy stole official documents.

"Did you see where the guy went?"

"Yeah, and we're having drinks later." Gordy was only cooperating out of necessity, and the unending interrogation obviously was grating on his nerves.

"This is important."

"I don't know. He came down here, I let him in, he went to the back, and then he left. That's all I know, okay?"

"Thanks."

She turned away and trotted out of the office leaving Gordy to clean up the papers on his desk. *Bitch,* he said under his breath.

Jenny headed up the one flight of stairs to the ground floor spilling out of the stairwell into the lobby. She looked around in a desperate attempt to stumble across the mysterious thief dressed up as a maintenance man. A line of people waiting to get through the metal detectors still stretched out of the glass doors at the entrance. The main area looked like a sea of black wool and leather satchels, but there was no sign of coveralls.

"Fancy meeting you again." Steve Morrow emerged from the hallway behind her.

Steve startled her. She forced a smile. "I thought you were working on that big story." It was becoming the understatement of the year.

"Yeah, I am. I was just lookin' something up in the clerk's office on another case."

"You must be busy." She kept looking around for her thief.

"The busier you are, the busier I have to be. Good seeing you again."

"Hey, Steve, he didn't say anything about the memo, did he?"

"You mean Randy?"

Steve turned back around to face her.

"Nah, Randy wouldn't say anything," she said just loud enough for Steve to hear. She wasn't sure who was behind the thefts, but she was the lead person on this faux investigation, and she couldn't afford to lose that document. "What about the Harrington's civil attorney."

"Brady?"

"He didn't say anything to you about a memo?"

"I haven't talked to him yet."

"That's right, I'm sorry."

"What memo are you talking about?"

"Oh, nothing. It's not important, don't worry about it."

She scanned the room with one last glance, and then disappeared back into the stairwell so that Steve couldn't continue his inquiry. *Screw you Mr. Maintenance Man.* After that performance, Steve would definitely ask Gavin about the memo. She was gambling on his weakness for the media to keep the memo alive for just a little while longer.

Who could make the memo disappear from her office and the official records? Who has that kind of power? She shuddered. *It can't be.* But Randy was acting strangely with her. Why would he be so scared of Gavin's investigation that he would risk his career by tampering with the Tutuila file? She had been pushing Gavin hoping he'd uncover something useful, but the case was beginning to hit close to home. She knew she needed to become proactive. Otherwise, she was going to end up suffering the same fate as Frank.

That's it, I need to find Frank.

CHAPTER 26

IT DIDN'T TAKE LONG for Steve to find Gavin's number from his list of recently dialed calls. He spent most days inside the courthouse chasing the big trials. Covering trials for the local paper wasn't the sexiest job at the newspaper, but Steve was a courthouse junkie. He once contemplated going to law school, but after watching the hours they kept, thought better of it.

The Harrington murder caught his interest from the beginning. There was a time when this case was the topic of every conversation in the community. When the verdict was handed down, people from all over were outraged, and cried out for justice. Randy's campaign kept the fervor alive for awhile. However, everyday existence began to creep back into people's lives, and soon, the entire debacle was forgotten. Within two years, no one could even remember Sara's name. She was reduced to being known as *that poor girl from out of town*. Still, editors liked the story because it sold papers. Steve ran a small article a couple of weeks back, and was successful in getting some nice sound quotes from Gavin. He hoped to do a follow-up piece on the hearing. He highlighted the number on his cell phone, and hit the call button.

"Mr. Brady's office," Gladys said into the receiver.

"Yes, is Gavin Brady available? This is Stephen Morrow from the Tribune."

"I'll check," she said without a hint of emotion.

Gavin's door was closed, but he wasn't hiding out from the world any longer. In fact, he was trying not to think about the case or about Sara at all. He decided to spend the morning catching up on several overdue research projects.

"Mr. Brady."

"Yes." Gavin knew the silence was too good to be true.

"A Steven Morrow from the Tribune is on the phone for you. Are you available?"

Am I available? He wasn't in the mood to discuss his recent legal defeat, but he didn't want to pass up any opportunity to get publicity for the case. Who knew where it would lead.

"Tell him I'll be right with him."

He clicked out of the current window on his computer screen, and cleared out a space on his desk between several opened law books to make room for the Harrington file. The files weren't there. He remembered that he left them in his briefcase, the briefcase that Hannah was undoubtedly toting around at work. He would have to make the best of it.

"Hello, Gavin Brady speaking."

"Mr. Brady, Steve Morrow from the Tribune, we spoke a while back."

"Yes, how are you?"

"Running up against a deadline I'm afraid. I was hoping to chat with you about your on-going wrongful death suit against Mr. Tutuila, his parents, Mr. Fause, Mr. Fuatimau, and Mr. Kiuilani. I hope I'm pronouncing the names correctly."

"Sure. What can I do for you?"

"Well, I was going to start by asking you where you thought this case was going, but, instead, I'd like to ask you something else."

"Okay, shoot."

"There's a rumor floating around the neighborhood about a memo, and I was wondering if you could enlighten me about it."

"A memo? Who told you about the memo?"

"Good, then it exists. I hear that Randy Bougainville knows about it."

"Well, he should. It came from him."

"So, he's the author?"

"No, I mean it came from the criminal file. I don't know who wrote it, and I also don't know why they didn't use it in the first trial."

"What do you mean?"

"It corroborates Tyler's original story, and rebuts the change he made."

"Tell me about it."

Gavin told him about the handwritten memo and how it corroborated Tyler's original confession to the police that he was in the front seat and fired the shot into Casey's car, killing Sara. He revealed to Steve that Chillie Ki was in the car less than thirty minutes before the shooting, and could place Tyler in the front passenger seat and Marcus Kiuilani in the back seat. He also told Steve that the memo showed that a liquor store clerk corroborated Chillie's story. It was powerful evidence yet was never used in the first trial, letting Tyler walked away with an acquittal.

"That's quite a bombshell you got there."

"It's no bombshell, it's the truth."

"So, are you saying that the lead prosecutor in the criminal trial, Frank Gilreath, knew about the memo, and suppressed it to conspire with the defendants?"

Steve's question went to the heart of the case. Gavin hadn't even gotten that far in his analysis. He didn't know Frank, but had heard that he wasn't very smart. He also knew that the case ruined Frank. What could he have to gain by conspiring with the defendants?

"I'm not making any accusations," Gavin finally said.

"Well, it sounds like you're pointing fingers at an awful lot of people, from the entire original trial team to the new district attorney."

"I'm not pointing fingers; I'm simply echoing what the community has been screaming for all along, justice. This isn't about someone dropping the ball. Those boys lied, and got away with murder. They have the evidence against them. They should file perjury charges against Tyler and the others for changing their story."

"Is that what you'd do?"

"If I were in charge, I wouldn't hesitate, and I'd guarantee a conviction. You can quote me on that."

"Are you offering your services as a special prosecutor?"

"Only if they're too scared to handle the case, then I'd be happy to step in and handle it for them."

"Can I quote you on that?"

"Mr. Brady." Gladys' voice grabbed his attention.

"I'm sorry, Mr. Morrow, can you hold on?" He hit the intercom button. "Yes, Gladys."

"A detective Cullison called from your residence. He was responding to a burglary call."

"Hannah!" Gavin immediately hung up the phone, and ran out of his office with Steve still on hold.

The drive to his house took a fraction of the time he spent on the way to the office in the morning. He sped down his residential street, and screeched in front of a police car parked in his driveway. Without saying a word, he bypassed the two uniformed officers in his front yard, and ran inside.

"Who's in charge?" he said still out of breath.

"Mr. Brady?" A sandy haired plain clothed detective turned to him.

"Yes."

"I'm detective Cullison. Here's the situation. About forty minutes ago, we responded to a call from a neighbor regarding a potential burglary in progress. When we arrived, we found the residence abandoned. Looks like they did a number on the inside though."

Gavin finally looked around his now ransacked home. The kitchen drawers were wide open, and all the living room furniture was overturned. There were items dumped out on the floor that Gavin didn't even know he owned.

"Oh my God! Who would do this?"

"We're a little baffled ourselves, I have to be honest with you. Our first thought was meth heads or punk kids, but it doesn't quite fit."

"What do you mean?"

"There's nothing missing. You got two easily pawnable TVs and two DVD players, and they're untouched. Also, there are no prints anywhere. We're dusting still, but we haven't found any yet."

Gavin thought about the photos. There were no prints on them either. "Wait a minute, no prints?"

"That's right, no prints. Whoever did this took the time to wipe down everything he touched. He probably also wore gloves. It's too professional for druggies out for a score."

"What does that mean?"

"It means they might have been looking for something specific. Maybe they were casing your house for a while, waiting for a time when they knew you'd be gone."

"Casing my house?"

"Didn't you call in a suspicious car a while back? We're just looking for anything that might give us a lead. Do you have any idea what someone might be looking for here? I mean, have you recently come into an inheritance or anything like that?"

"Inheritance? No." Gavin's cell phone began vibrating in his jacket pocket. He turned away from the detective, who immediately walked over to one of the other officers. "Hello."

"Gavin, are you at home?" It was Jenny Garrett.

"Jenny?" She was the last person he expected to call him.

"Yeah, are you at home?"

"Yeah, I'm at home. This is not a good time. Someone just destroyed my house."

"I know I just heard about it."

"You just heard about it?" Gavin was stunned. The police refer active investigations to the prosecutor's office, but not this quickly. They had just arrived.

"Over the police scanner. Old habit. Look, I don't have time to explain. Do you have the memo?"

"What are you talking about? I can't talk about the case right now. Someone just broke into my house."

"Listen to me. I think they're looking for the memo, you know the one that mentions Chillie Ki? Do you have it?"

"The memo?" Steve asked about the memo as well. "Who's looking for it?"

"I don't know." Jenny wasn't sure how much she could reveal to him. However, this case was becoming dangerous, and she needed to trust someone right now. "Someone broke into my office this morning, and took my copy. They also removed the original from the records room."

"They? Who's they?"

"You're the only one who still has a copy, so do you have it?"

"What's going on?"

"Please, there's no time. Do you have it?"

"Yeah, I have it. Wait. Oh my God!"

"What's wrong?" Jenny said.

"I gotta call you back."

He remembered his door being wide open when he arrived at the office. He didn't check to see if someone rifled through his files, but, if they did, they would have discovered that he removed the Harrington file, which contained the memo. Their next logical place to search would be his home. He stuffed his cell phone into his suit pocket, and turned his head toward the kitchen. On the wall was their answering machine. He called Hannah this morning while she was in the shower, and left a message about the briefcase mix up. She had the Harrington file with her, which meant she had the memo. If someone listened to the message, they would also know that.

"Mr. Brady, can we continue now? Anything you can tell us?" Detective Cullison spoke from the other side of the room. Gavin looked at the officers roaming around his house. They looked official. They also looked suspicious. Hannah might be in danger.

"I forgot about a meeting. I'll be back later."

"We're not done here." Detective Cullison called after Gavin, who was already out of the front door.

THE UNIVERSITY CAMPUS was located less than ten miles from their home. The bridge was free of traffic, and the morning fog had burned off. He weaved in and out of traffic like an undercover cop on the way to a silent alarm, and even ran a couple of red lights honking his horn. He tried her cell phone as he drove, but it went right to voicemail.

The campus parking lot was only half-full when he pulled in. He swung into a space near one of the walkways, and jumped out the car. He tried to think about where her office was located. He remembered her telling him about being housed in the Philosophy building, which was right in the middle of the campus.

Gavin's wool suit and wing tip shoes did not hinder his ability to sprint down the concrete path toward her building, only slowing to jump out of the way of the occasional oncoming student. He wasn't sure if she would be there or in class. He wished he'd paid more attention when Hannah told him her schedule. He sprinted inside and up a flight of stairs to Hannah's office. Her door was locked.

"You just missed her." He turned around to see the department's secretary sitting at her desk. "You must be her husband. I recognize you from the photos in her office."

"Yeah." He was trying to mask his desperation. "Do you know where she is?" He asked, still out of breath.

"Sorry. I only keep track of my department's schedule. I can tell you that the Psychology classes are all taught in the Psychology building. If she's in class right now, she's there. Do you know where that is?"

"I think."

"Two buildings down to your left."

"Thanks." He didn't bother making any further small talk.

He rushed out of the building, and raced down another path along the gothic architecture and ivy foliage. The buildings were grouped together so that students could easily walk from department to department in the allotted ten minutes between classes. The Psychology building was three stories high with classrooms on each floor. Gavin started on the bottom floor, running up and down the hallways peering in the doors looking for Hannah.

Nearing the end of the hallway on the second floor, he heard her voice. Without knocking, he threw open the door to her class. A room full of college students turned their heads in surprise to see Gavin standing in the doorway sweating and out of breath. Hannah was standing at the front of the room behind a wooden podium — unharmed and surprised to see him.

"Gavin?"

He was too tired to speak. He forced a smile to the countless eyes staring him down, and motioned Hannah over to him.

"I bet you're here for the briefcase." She smiled and grabbed the leather satchel, which was leaning on the other side of the podium just out of sight of Gavin's peering eyes. "I kept telling my parents that this would happen one of these days." She smiled.

Gavin stepped out of the doorway forcing Hannah to exit the room with him. He looked over each shoulder to make sure no one was coming, and wiped the sweat off his face.

"Did you open the briefcase?"

"Yeah, it's your stuff. I assume you brought mine. You're just in time too because I just started."

"No, did you take anything out of it?"

"Of course not." She noticed that he hadn't taken his eyes off the briefcase the entire time. "Is there something wrong?"

He looked around again. "We gotta get out of here, now." He tugged at her, but she resisted.

"Gavin, tell me what's wrong, you're scaring me."

There wasn't much time. He wanted to get out of there before anyone came looking for the briefcase, but he also knew that not telling Hannah would continue this game of tug of war. Besides, she deserved to know the story. He took a deep breath, and told it all.

"You son of a bitch." She shook her head at him.

"Hannah, please."

"I hope this is worth it for you. I hope they make you a partner because you're really earning your keep."

"I'm sorry, Hannah. You can be mad at me, but, right now, we have to get out of here."

"You're damn right I'm mad at you." She vanished back into her room to gather her papers, and excuse everyone for the rest of the class due to an unexpected family emergency.

Gavin grabbed the briefcase from Hannah as soon as she returned. They waited for the exiting mass of people to pour out of the room. As the last student left, he grabbed the inside of Hannah's arm, and followed the group. He wanted to take advantage of the crowd as they all moved down the stairs and out the door. As they walked, he continually peered to each side looking for anyone or anything unusual. Once they were outside, the students began to disperse in different directions leaving Gavin and Hannah relatively exposed in the open.

"Do you need anything in your office?"

"Why don't you just call the police?"

"I don't trust the police right now."

"Great."

"Please, do you need anything in your office?"

"No. You have all my stuff, remember? And I forgot my purse at home, which means it's probably gone, right?" Her tone was filled with disdain.

"We'll leave your car here." Its presence might also throw off anyone who presumed she was on campus.

He kept his loose grip on her arm as he began leading her back down the pathway toward his car. They had just squeezed past a slow-moving student when Gavin stopped suddenly, pulling Hannah backward.

"Ouch." She tugged her arm free from his palm.

"That's him." Gavin pointed to the Philosophy building, less than twenty yards ahead. Nate Bridges was walking up the steps. Gavin remembered him from the pizza parlor the night before. They watched him disappear out of sight into the building.

"Let's go, we gotta hurry." Gavin tucked the briefcase under his arm, and pushed on Hannah's back. They ran toward Gavin's car. Gavin figured the man would be directed to the psychology building by the secretary, and spend the next hour searching each room before figuring out that Hannah was gone.

Once they were in the parking lot, Gavin unlocked both doors. He placed the briefcase on his lap as he got behind the wheel, and the two of them sped away.

"Who is that guy?" Hannah asked as they raced toward their home. It was one thing to have Gavin explain to her what was going on, but to actually see someone searching in her building was quite another.

"I don't know who he is. I never saw him before last night."

"You're gonna drop this case, right? I mean after all of this, you're gonna drop this case."

Gavin looked at her almost shocked at her request. She saw the defiance in his eyes, and knew he was more determined than ever. He wasn't going to drop anything. They didn't speak the rest of the ride home. When they arrived, the police were still there. Gavin and Hannah gave statements. Both mentioned the mysterious man on campus as well as the possible connection to Gavin's case. However, Gavin didn't mention the memo. He held on to his briefcase the entire time he was talking to the detectives. He couldn't risk someone taking it as evidence only to have it disappear.

The police investigation was almost complete, and one by one, each officer left. They promised to send a car around the neighborhood for the next few nights in case the burglars returned.

That night, the months of loneliness and frustration that Hannah kept bottled up inside exploded into a sea of tears and a war of words. As the two of them began to pick up the pieces of their lives dumped around their house, she confronted Gavin with all of the recent events that had transpired. The silent dinners alone, the seven-day work weeks. It was as if she were renting a marriage. She accused him of being a one day a week husband who put work above her, allowing it to devour his family and endanger everyone around him.

At first, Gavin defended himself and his career by accusing her of not appreciating how hard he worked for their future. He raised his voice to give force to his argument, but he knew they were just empty words. He was allowing his work to define him. However, he couldn't just give up on the idea that justice existed for the Harringtons, for Sara. Finally, they run out of things to yell about.

When the air cleared, they silently sat in the living room pondering each other. Hannah came to realize that Gavin was fighting for something bigger than himself. It was his passion and drive that attracted her to him in the first place. Gavin also knew that pushing Hannah to the background in favor of his professional ambitions would only lead to the same plight as most of the divorced partners in his firm.

Gavin offered to make them some pancakes as a gesture of reconciliation. It was his way of reminding her that he hadn't forgotten their innocent Saturday mornings together. They settled on left over pizza and a movie.

Tomorrow he would call Jenny. She seemed to know what was going on before he did. She was aware of the break in, and was the one who told him that it was the memo they were after. Perhaps, she even knew the identity of the mysterious caller or the man he saw at Nunzio's Pizza.

He figured that Hannah and he were safe for now. Whoever showed up at her building would hear from the secretary that she was in class. She might have even told him that her husband had just been there, and was already looking for her. He might have even seen them running to the parking lot. At any rate, after today, the man would know that Gavin was on to him. He decided to rent a safe deposit box in the morning for the memo. Jenny said it was the only copy left, and someone wanted it badly.

CHAPTER 27

THE MORNING'S STORY was everything Jenny hoped for and more. Steve was a good writer, and knew how to craft the news in a way that was not only informative, but also dramatic. Even the headline tugged at the public's arm to continue reading. On the front page of the local section, *Civil Attorney Offers Services As Special Prosecutor.*

Gavin's comment about prosecuting the case was an off the cuff remark at best. However, since Steve only had second-hand hearsay and innuendo regarding a so called secret investigation in the prosecutor's office, he decided to focus his writing on Gavin and his statements about the memo. He made it sound as if Gavin was offering to prosecute the case for free, and could guarantee a conviction. Chillie Ki wasn't mentioned by name in the article, but Steve did allude to another passenger who could place Tyler in the front seat with the gun. He ended his article with a call to Randy's office for justice — for the victim and for the community.

Frank propped his feet up on his desk as he read Steve's article with interest. These days, there wasn't much for him to do except catch up on the news. With no case load, all he did was initial negotiation on files when they arrived at the office. He would read the police reports along with the criminal history of the defendant, then type up an offer that would quickly resolve the case. If a defense attorney tried to play hard ball or rejected the offer, the file was passed off to a senior prosecutor for trial preparation. It was a good system despite the fact that only the burned out and humiliated were subjected to such a fate. A defense attorney had no leverage with Frank, and couldn't scare him into a sweeter deal for his client. What did Frank care? He wasn't going to be the trial attorney anyway. He could make whatever offer he wanted without any consequences to a case load or win loss record.

"Knock knock." Jenny stood at his office doorway.

"Jenny." Frank quickly closed his paper and lowered his feet to the floor. "What can I do for you?"

"I see you're already reading the paper."

"Yeah, the press'll write just about anything to make a buck."

"Well, I guess it's their job. Did you read the article?"

"I perused it. What about it?"

"What did you think?"

"What are you getting at?"

"Nothing."

"No, not nothing. We're on opposite sides of the building, and I didn't even know you'd been hired until I saw your head shoved up Randy's ass at the meeting about the civil suit."

"Shoved up his ass?"

"Yeah, and now you're in my office the day this article comes out. You investigating prosecutors now?" Frank was demoralized by the criminal trial, and was the favorite target of the press.

"You're right," Jenny said, trying to defuse the moment. "I'm not investigating you."

"Come on Jenny. I was at the meeting. You were all over this case."

"I'm not saying I'm not looking into it. Randy told me to make sure the office's back is covered."

"Stellar job so far," he said holding up the paper.

"That's why I'm here."

"You want to know if I'm a screw up like this article makes me out to be?"

"No, that guy's an asshole. I'm just curious about what he wrote about Chillie Ki."

"You mean this report he's talking about?"

"Yeah. If I'm gonna counter his attacks on our office, I need information. You're the man with all of it, so I came to you."

"Okay. I didn't hear anything about this Ki fella' until after the trial started. No one did. I personally interrogated each lead detective, and they didn't know anything. You think I enjoyed the publicity?"

"What about the memo?"

"Never saw it. You'd have to talk to Randy about that one."

"Randy?"

"Yeah, he'd just started, and I had him doing some things here and there. He was just as outraged as I was."

Jenny's knees begin to weaken. So, Randy was involved with the Tutuila murder investigation. Was he covering for someone? This was a revelation she wasn't expecting. She quickly ended her conversation with Frank, and headed down to the first floor for an espresso. She needed energy to process this new information.

ALTHOUGH THE POLICE scanner was on the lowest volume setting, Jenny could still hear it as she approached her office. In law school, her roommate used to tease her for listening to it while studying, but the noise soothed her better than any radio station. She blew on her coffee as she walked down the empty hallway to her door.

Frank, unwittingly, gave her a wealth of information, but questions still remained. She was glad that Gavin exposed the memo's contents to Steve but she felt badly about setting him up. *I'll call him when I get into my office.* Her scanner revealed that Gavin wasn't hurt, but she still needed to talk with him again about the memo, and make sure he still had it. Randy was involved in the initial murder investigation under Frank. Perhaps, he overlooked the memo causing the trial to go sour. This would explain why he was so concerned about it now. However, Gavin said that Casey Goodman, the driver of Sara's car, told one of the cops about Chillie Ki. Nothing made sense to her as she entered her doorway.

"Whoa," she yelled spilling her coffee, when she saw Randy sitting behind her desk.

"I see you've read today's paper." He motioned to the paper she bought at the espresso stand, but his face was fixated on her eyes as if to gauge her reaction. His stare was making her uncomfortable, but she tried to act natural.

"I didn't expect you."

"I didn't mean to startle you. I just wanted to come down and chat about that article. I trust you read it."

"Yeah, you know, I didn't have anything to do with this." What she really wanted to do was run away and hide. He was her boss, but there was something eerie about his demeanor, and given Frank's comments about his involvement in the Tutuila murder investigation, she was beginning to have the same uneasy feeling that she had yesterday while hiding around the corner from the burglar in her office.

"I know you didn't. You're a team player. You wouldn't do that."

"Right." This was definitely not the usual Randy. "I was just telling Frank the same thing."

"I know."

"You know?"

"He just buzzed me, and told me you came to see him."

She tried to hide her surprise. Did Frank mention that he let slip that Randy had been involved in the Tutuila investigation? "He did?"

"Don't worry about Frank, he's harmless. He's like a puppy in a window looking out at the big world, without even knowing what he's barking at. He'll be okay. I see you like to listen to police scanners." His head turned to the small box behind her desk.

"Yeah, just a stupid habit."

"There's a lot of crime out there, huh?"

"That's what we're here for." He was starting to scare at her. She thought about screaming to see if anyone else was around.

"Yes, and you're doing great. Everyone says so." He got up from his chair, and walked across her office to where she stood in the doorway. "How well do you know this reporter, Stephen Morrow?"

"Not well. He's a little over dramatic at times," she motioned to the paper on her desk, "but, he has a good reputation. I'm sure you've seen him around."

"Well, he may ask you some questions, and I don't want you to answer them."

"Of course," she said trying not to let him hear her gulp. "I won't comment."

"I need you to do more than that." He turned to her. "He may ask you questions about this supposed memo that Mr. Brady has created in his mind."

"In his mind?"

"Yes, in his mind."

"Randy, there is a memo. I've seen it. It's out there."

"Is it?" He remained fixated on her eyes as if looking for any hint of betrayal or fear. "I haven't seen it. Do you see it anywhere here?"

Jenny could feel the blood rushing out of her face. The memo had disappeared from the building. Her hands felt numb as Randy spoke in an almost monotone voice like a serial killer calmly confessing to his crimes.

"I mean if this Gavin Brady wants to manufacture documents in some meager attempt to slander our office and exert political pressure on me, there are laws against that, laws that our office knows how to enforce, right?"

There was a moment of uncomfortable silence between them. He was talking about the memo as if it never existed. As if they never talked about it, and he never put her in charge of watching Gavin's investigation because of it. He knew that wasn't true. He was telling her that he would destroy Gavin's career if he pushed the issue.

"Randy, I don't think he's trying to do that."

"I don't think you understand. I need you to be a team player on this one, Jenny. I need you to pick a side."

"Of course." Jenny didn't know what to say. She knew that Gavin's case disturbed him but he was going too far. The man before her was no longer a boss; he was a stranger with dangerous propensities.

"Good, then we understand each other, right?"

Jenny wanted to argue with him, but she couldn't move. All she could do was open her mouth to let out, "Right."

"It's an old case anyway." Hints of the old Randy bled through his face as he smiled. "It's ancient history, why open old painful wounds? It's time to move on."

"That's what I told Frank."

"Well then, you just do your part, and I'll take care of the rest." He smiled and left. His visit was all the acknowledgment she needed that he was involved with the memo's disappearance. She remained frozen, the scanner lightly buzzing with activity of the morning's crimes in the background.

She was the one who armed Steve with the idea of the memo, and pushed Gavin to investigate its significance. In a way, she already betrayed everyone involved. Now, she was joining the conspiracy. Randy was, perhaps, an incompetent lawyer, but he was an extremely astute political operative. Defying Randy would have lasting and dire consequences, and she wasn't willing to throw away her career just yet.

Gavin would have to be on his own.

CHAPTER 28

GAVIN STRETCHED HIS arms and yawned. The sun was already bursting through the window as he sat up in bed trying not to disturb Hannah. The digital clock next to him projected a green beam against the wall that read, 8:15. Normally, he would have already put in a couple of hours of work by this point in the morning, but he decided to sleep in. Gladys would cover for him until he arrived. Besides, he thought to himself, he didn't punch a time clock at work, and for all anyone knew, he could be at the law library.

He took a few seconds to watch Hannah as she slept before jumping out of bed and into the shower. The morning light softly kissed her light olive skin and dark Irish hair.

He was fully dressed and already at the door with his briefcase in hand by 8:30. The morning paper was waiting for him on their front steps as he exited. He tossed it inside for Hannah when she awoke. He didn't read the paper at home. He always left for work before it arrived, and besides, he could read it on-line.

He stopped by the bank on the way into the firm, and opened a safe deposit box. Inside, he placed the last remaining copy of the Chillie Ki memo for safe keeping. He made himself the sole person authorized to access the box's contents. Even Hannah was excluded. It was time to separate his work from his personal life.

By the time he pulled into his spot at the firm, it was already 9:15. Jenny Garrett would be his first call of the morning. He needed answers, and he needed them quickly. He needed to know how Jenny knew that the burglars were after the memo, and why he was the only person left with a copy.

As he entered the front doors, the receptionist looked up and acknowledged his presence. "You're finally here," the receptionist said.

"Yeah. I was taking care of a few things." Gavin had never met the receptionist, and had no idea she could recognize him.

"Wait." She held up her hand to stop him, and pressed one of the countless buttons on her answering system. "He's here," she said into her headset. She looked up at him. "You need to go to conference room three, they're waiting for you."

"Waiting for me, who's waiting for me?" This was highly unusual, and Gavin wanted to go to his office first and check his messages.

"They are." Her voice conveyed immediacy and importance.

"Okay." Gavin wasn't sure what was going on, but he knew better than to question anyone at the firm. He took a deep breath, and headed down the hallway in the opposite direction from his office.

He could see several silhouettes through the frosted glass as he approached the large rectangle room. One of the shadows motioned him to enter. The back conference room was reserved for partnership meetings and high level depositions. There sat Fred, Larry, and Duke.

"Have a seat." Fred gestured toward one of the chairs across from the trio.

Gavin looked at the three partners across from him. It was never a good sign to be in the presence of all three of them at once. The firm had a board of directors that was responsible for the daily operations. However, all of the important decisions were still handled discretely behind closed doors with only the necessary parties privy to the proceedings.

Fred's scowl was typical, and offered no hint as to what he was in for. Larry's leathery skin and advanced age made it impossible to read his face. It was Duke who telegraphed the gravity of the morning's unlikely congregation.

"Good morning," Gavin said taking his seat.

"Have you seen today's paper?" Fred asked. In front of them was the local section. It was turned upside down so Gavin couldn't read the story.

"Not yet." He regretted not having read the newspaper on his front steps. "I normally read it around five thirty when I arrive, but I was taking care of some things this morning." Of all the days he could have picked to sleep in, it had to be today.

"That's right, you had a bit of — someone broke into your house as I understand it," Duke said with the first concerned voice of the morning. "Is everything okay?"

"Yeah, it was just, actually no. It's this wrongful death case. I think someone's been following me, and there were photos delivered to my wife and —"

"You've been under a lot of stress. We've all heard. There are no secrets in the firm, and we've been concerned about you. This is a tough business and unforgiving at times."

"It can make people do rash things." Fred turned the paper over, and slid the front page headline in front of Gavin.

"Wow," he said as read the headline.

"Wow is right. You want to be a prosecutor now?" Fred was not amused. "What were you going to do if they said yes? Ask us to let you take the next three months off, and pay for a free trial?"

"I didn't mean it that way, I was just talking."

"You mean lying?" Larry abandoned his grandfatherly tone.

"It was taken out of context."

"And what about this memo nonsense?"

"This memo is the key to the case."

"Pressure or no pressure, manufacturing evidence is not what we're about."

"Manufacturing evidence?" Gavin gasped, realizing the gravity of this meeting.

"Where is the Harrington case file?" Fred asked. "We looked in your office but didn't see it."

"Right here." He patted his briefcase. He could feel the tiny beads of sweat forming on his upper lip. "Why?"

"We were contacted this morning by the county's in-house counsel," Duke said. "He informed us that the memo referred by you in the article doesn't exist." He pointed to the newspaper.

"Can you show us the memo please?" Larry held out his hand.

Gavin started to open his briefcase. "I don't have it. I can get it." Gavin now felt stupid for opening the safety deposit box.

"We were also informed that if such a memo exists, then you or someone you hired wrote it." All three men stared at Gavin with somber expressions.

"That's not true. I don't know who wrote it, but I got that memo in discovery from the prosecutor's office. It was in their file. You can ask Jenny Garrett, she's seen it too."

"You mean the same Jennifer Garrett who is heading up the supposed secret investigation you mentioned to Judge Velez?" Larry asked.

Gavin's chest tightened. He could feel himself holding his breath.

"They've agreed not to turn this over to the attorney general's office, and they're willing to drop the whole matter as long as you drop the issue."

"The issue?"

"Yes, this whole memo business."

"But, there is a memo and I didn't write it. It's not my handwriting."

"We don't care whose handwriting it is. We care about not getting sued for fraud."

"Don't you see what's going on here?"

"We see what's going on here, do you?" Fred asked.

"Gavin, look, I gave you too much too fast," Duke said in a consoling tone. "This is political, and we can't afford an investigation or bad press."

"We want you to take the rest of the week off," Larry said.

"The rest of the week off? You're firing me?"

"No. Apparently Mr. Stewart here thinks you still have some redeeming qualities."

"This is what we worked out on the phone to make both sides happy," Duke said.

"Call it a short administrative leave," Fred added. "Get your family in order, and come back next week ready to work."

"This isn't happening. I don't need time off. Let me get the memo and show you."

"You're not hearing us. This isn't a request. Your work has already been distributed among the other associates. Now go home."

The three men's' expression conveyed the seriousness of their message. Gavin slowly pushed his chair back. They were clearly finished talking, and every second that ticked by was overstaying his welcome. He leaned down and picked up his briefcase.

"Leave the file," Larry said.

He slowly pulled the file out from his briefcase, and placed in on the table. "I didn't lie about anything. I swear I didn't lie."

With wobbly legs, he pushed against the frosty door, and made his way into the hallway. It was a long walk to the front lobby, and he could feel the receptionist's stare as he passed her. The outside sun blinded his eyes as he stepped into the parking lot. It was an unusually bright day for this time of year, but it was no consolation for Gavin. All he could think about was his meeting with the partners, and how they summarily exiled him from the firm. *There must be some kind of mistake.* He had to clear this up. How could he go back to his firm with them looking over his shoulder thinking he might do something unethical or even illegal?

THE COURTHOUSE WAS not far away. On dry days such as today, it was a nice walk, but he didn't have time. He needed to talk to Jenny. He jumped in his car, and steered it the two blocks to the parking lot behind the county building. Gavin flashed his bar card to the security guard at the entrance. Although attorneys were subject to the metal detector, they were often given special treatment by the security guards since they had to enter so often. The guard waved him through, and he joined the forming pack in front of the elevator just as the door was opening.

Once inside, he pressed the button for the fifth floor. Jenny's office was on the ninth floor, but he figured at this time of the morning, she was likely in the criminal courtroom with all of the other prosecutors for morning motions and pre-trial conferences. After a couple of seconds, the light above him illuminated his floor.

As anticipated, Jenny was sitting in the criminal court awaiting the judge to take the bench and call the morning docket. As Gavin entered the room, their eyes locked, and a surprised almost shocked look came over her face. She stood up even before he motioned her over to him. After a couple of seconds of confusing hand signals, Jenny figured out that he wanted her to meet him in the hallway.

"You need to get out of here," she said as she joined him outside the courtroom.

"What's going on, Jenny?"

"I mean it, leave," she said in a loud whisper.

"Not until you tell me why you're lying." For a moment, he displayed a hint of the undergraduate student seducing her.

"Get out of here."

"I almost got fired today. You know damn well there's a memo."

"There's no memo, you understand? It doesn't exist."

"I have a copy."

"No, you don't."

"Yes, I do."

"No, you don't. Now drop it and leave before I call security." She looked more frightened than angry. Her voice raised an octave. He noticed her head slightly moving to the side to see if anyone was watching them.

"What's going on?" Gavin could barely contain himself with anger. "I got people following me, following my wife. Someone broke into my house, and now my job is on the line."

"I can't help you."

"You're the one who told me about the memo. Now, I'm being set up as some kind of liar. You owe me."

"I owe you?" Her voice cracked and her eyes shot out years of hurt and anger. "I don't owe you anything." She lowered her tone, keeping the same message in her stare.

"Is that what this is about, payback?"

"Don't you dare. Does your wife know about us? Or are you lying to her the way you're accusing me of lying to you?"

Her words struck him like a bullet. The last thing he needed was to have some confusing confrontation with his wife regarding an encounter that occurred before they were even officially dating. "You're the one who pushed me to investigate this case. I don't understand."

"You think the next time they're gonna stop with just breaking a couple of pieces of furniture? I'm helping you. I won't have that on my —" she stopped herself. She wasn't ready to reveal that she had been threatened.

"What's going on, Jenny?"

"I have to work here too, and I don't know what else to do, okay? Now please leave." She turned around and went back into the courtroom.

He could see her through the small glass window in the door. She took a seat next to one of her supervisors without looking back at him. Someone had gotten to her as well, someone close to her at work. The memo was still the key to unlocking this mystery, and he had the only copy.

He was defeated as he made his way down the hallway to the elevators. The light above the doors showed that a car was heading up as he pressed the down button. The door opened to allow several people to get off before continuing upward. Gavin froze. In the back of the car stood Nate Bridges, the man he saw at the pizza parlor talking to Kauni Tutuila, and the man he saw entering Hannah's building on campus. His head was turned away from making small talk with someone wearing a suit, but Gavin was sure it was him.

"Oh, this is my stop," he heard the suited man say as he ended his conversation with Nate, and pushed his way out the door.

The doors began to shut, and Nate turned his body to the front toward Gavin. The two of them saw each other face to face before the door finally sealed shut.

"Excuse me." Gavin called to the man in the suit. He turned around.

"Yes."

"That guy you were talking to in the elevator, do you know him?"

"Nate? Yeah."

"Who is he?"

"Nathaniel Bridges, he's a retired cop."

Gavin's head was spinning. He stood in the hallway watching the light for Nate's elevator continue upward toward the top of the building. *That's why Jenny is scared. She works all day with the police, and she felt like there was no one around she could trust, especially if a cop was involved.*

He now knew the identity of the man at the pizza parlor. What he still needed to figure out was the identity of the man who delivered the photos to Hannah, and why the memo disappeared. Perhaps, Tyler and his brother were behind this.

Today was Wednesday and he remembered reading in the file that Wednesdays were family nights at the Tutuila's neighborhood church. The entire Tutuila aigu would be there. He churned that thought over in his mind as he hopped on the next elevator going down. Maybe even Nathaniel Bridges would show up. They had made the fight personal, and he wasn't about to back down. Someone was going to tell him why that memo was so important. Why it was worth covering up a murder, and powerful enough to reach through the prosecutor's office and into his own firm.

CHAPTER 29

GAVIN'S MEMORY ABOUT family night served him well. Palolo and Mauuaua Tutuila pulled into the church parking lot just behind his wife's cousin and Danny's mom, Kapaulana Fause. The two families got out, and embraced each other before pulling out the food they brought for the evening's festivities. They gleefully spoke in traditional Samoan, and pretended that they were still home on their beautiful island, where there was no need for English or American lawyers and judges. Family night was not the place to discuss work or business, it was the time to celebrate, which lately translated to a time to forget.

Palolo didn't discuss the civil suit with anyone in the aigu, and had only discussed the original shooting on one occasion with Danny's father. Danny drove the car the night Sara died. When he got home, he was already crying, but he never told his parents anything about what happened except that he never saw a gun until after he heard the shot. 'No one intended for that girl to die,' he told them. It was just a prank. His furtive remorse became masked by his loyalty to his cousin. He remained silent about that fateful night even after Tyler confessed to pulling the trigger, and he was the only one of the group who visited him in jail on a daily basis.

A week after Tyler recanted his original confession to the police and placed Marcus in the front passenger seat instead, Palolo visited the Fause home. By this point, Danny and Sal followed Tyler's lead, and, now, it was three boys against Marcus. The criminal trial was a regular front page story, and Tyler's attorney told Palolo that if the boys stuck together, there was a good chance for a hung jury or even an acquittal. His son was facing life in prison for a mistake that never should have happened, and all he could think about was his son. It was almost midnight when he knocked on their door, but there was no need to explain the lateness of the hour. He stood in his old friend's kitchen, and asked if Danny had told them anything about that night. He asked them for the truth. Danny's parents recounted their son's fragmented statements about not seeing the gun and wishing it had never happened. Danny's loyalty to his older cousin was as strong as the ties that bound each family to their shared heritage.

They talked for almost an hour about growing up in Samoa. Then, Palolo confessed his sins, and asked forgiveness. He asked forgiveness for Tyler and for himself for being too weak to teach his youngest boy the toughest lesson of all. The shooting was never discussed again between the families after that night. By the following evening, Marcus Kiuilani and his family's aigu were already enemies of the Tutuilas, and the peace-loving Samoan community would be torn in half forever.

THE SUN WAS already making its final descent behind the black forming clouds promising a dark cold evening, and the return of cool grey morning skies. Gavin's briefcase was on the passenger seat beside him. He reached inside and pulled out the memo he withdrew from the safety deposit box. He wanted to make sure it really existed. This was the cause of all his troubles.

As he left the interstate and headed toward the Tutuila's church, he realized that he had never actually been there. He had, however, almost memorized the investigative reports about the meetings and the fundraisers held for Tyler's defense during the criminal trial. The sheriff's department had staked out several family night gatherings in hopes of catching someone talking about the boys' change in testimony. They even went to a judge outside the county to get a warrant to bug Tyler's original attorney, Mike Davies' office, but heard nothing incriminating.

Gavin's mind was on the case, rather than the road in front of him. He almost missed the turn down Belany Street, which led to the church and his current destination. He placed his hand on the briefcase and the memo as he rounded that corner, and pulled his car alongside the heavily shadowed road.

With the memo in hand, he got out of the car. The church lights were shining brightly against the gray evening illuminating the numerous cars along the building. He crossed the already dewy road, and marched toward the brick house of worship. The front entrance was unlocked. Through the door, he could hear the dull rumble of voices and feet running around. He was still blind with rage, and all he could think about was exposing them for destroying his life all over a piece of paper. The room inside the entrance was large and spacious. Folding chairs stretched across the space, and a long metal table sat in the back filled with half-eaten casserole dishes and pies. Several kids ran around the center of the room playing tag, and most of the adults stood in groups along the back walls holding paper plates and conversing in Samoan. Gavin quickly eyed the room. He couldn't see Tyler or any of the others who were in the car the night Sara was shot.

"You all satisfied?" He yelled gathering everyone's attention. "Is this what you wanted?" He held up the memo, and stepped a couple of feet inside the room. In the back, he could see Palolo sitting by himself with a full plate of food. Tyler's mom was sitting across the room with several other women. A couple of large older men began walking toward him.

"Who are you? This is a private gathering," one of the men said with a thick Polynesian accent as they approached him. They looked to be in their fifties, but they were easily four inches taller than Gavin and twice his size.

"I'm not afraid of you guys. Not anymore."

Palolo yelled something in Samoan, which made the men stop. The younger kids ran to their parents clearing out the middle area of the room. Gavin smugly walked forward facing the entire crowd.

"Have fun in my house?" He turned around and addressed the entire congregation. They looked as if they were afraid of him and what he might do. "Surprised to see this?" He held up the memo. "Anyone have anything to say?"

"Why don't you just leave," the large man said.

"You're to blame. You bought him the gun. You didn't think I knew that did you?" He yelled indignantly at Palolo across the room. There was no reaction from the crowd. Gavin was filled with righteous indignation, but it was becoming clear to him that he had made a mistake. Whatever he thought he would find wasn't here. There were no monsters in this room, at least not tonight. The faces on the men and women showed only shock and fear.

"What do you want from us?" An anonymous voice said from the crowd.

"Justice." The people in the room remained still. "I just want justice," he said in a softer voice. He shook his head slightly and slithered out the same way he came in. It was a mistake to come here. He knew that.

"Hey!" Someone was calling his name. The voice came from the side of the building where all the cars were parked. Under a lamp post Gavin could see Tyler, Danny, Sal, and Kauni walking toward him.

"What are you doing here?" Danny yelled at Gavin as the young men approached him.

253

Gavin was beginning to realize how dumb his decision to come here had been. This was their neighborhood and their gathering. He was not only an outsider, he was an intruder. Tyler and his brother towered over the other boys.

"The lawyer's coming to pay us a visit," Sal said.

"I'm not looking for any trouble."

"Why'd you come here then?" Danny had a point. Gavin wasn't sure why he had driven over here and interrupted the community's family night.

"This ain't your courtroom," Sal said as the four men surrounded Gavin.

"If he still has one." Kauni laughed.

"You talking about your meeting the other night at the pizza place?" Gavin squared off in front of Kauni. He wasn't a fighter, and even if he were, he was still no match for Kauni, but he figured he might be able to back them down by pretending to know more about this case than he did. "With the retired cop?"

Kauni pushed him angrily. "You don't know nothing, little man."

The force from Kauni's shove, knocked Gavin back a couple of steps and almost into Danny.

"I know one thing. I don't need to hide in the shadows." The best thing Gavin could do right now was to keep quiet, but his blood was beginning to boil. This was his first time speaking to the defendants. He wasn't a lawyer cross examining a witness, he was speaking for a young teenager, who lost her life without anyone noticing. Now they didn't look so tough.

Kauni pushed him again. "No, you'll be hiding in the unemployment line from what I hear. Maybe your little wife won't think you're hot shit anymore. Maybe I'll pay her a visit, and show her what a real man is like."

Gavin felt his face turning red with rage. In the background, tires screeched to a halt in front of the church. Gavin glimpsed the outline of a dark green Camry. Time slowed. His hand squeeze into a fist and his fingernails dug into his palms. His arm flexed in the cool air as he lunged at Kauni swinging his knuckles at his face, and just missing his nose. He was still trying to catch his balance when the blow came. He felt a stinging sensation on his right eye following by the feel of skin against his face. As he hit the ground, he noticed how cool the grass felt, and how soothing it was against his throbbing cheekbone.

"That's it fellas!" Gavin turned and saw someone emerging from the Camry wearing blue jeans and dark shoes. The words reverberated in the slow-motion moment. "Show's over."

He saw the person running in his direction holding something metal. It looked like a gun. Then, he felt another stinging sensation against his ribs. He tasted the moist dirt and moss from the grass that had been uprooted by Kauni's shoe. Everything looked blurry as Harold Benoit leaned over him. His face throbbed, and his side hurt. Harold picked Gavin up and headed back to the Camry on the side of the street.

THE NEXT SEVERAL minutes were confusing, and filled with car doors slamming and the sensation of motion. He heard a female voice calling out to him. He imagined it was Hannah and they were on their honeymoon. The voice grew louder.

"Gavin, Gavin."

He opened his eyes and quickly regained focus. Jenny leaned over him in the back seat of a car.

"Gavin, you okay? Can you hear me?"

He tried to sit up, but his side was ached, and his head was throbbed.

"Where am I?"

"You were almost on your way to the hospital, kid. That was about the stupidest stunt I've ever seen and from an educated man," Harold said from behind the wheel.

Gavin listened to his voice. He recognized it from somewhere. "Where are you taking me?"

"There's a coffee shop just around the corner here. It's quiet, and the coffee always fresh."

He knew that voice. "It's you. You're the guy on the phone." Gavin closed his eyes, and cupped his cheek with the side of hand. He could hear Harold's voice on the phone talking about the photos. He was the mystery man.

"There'll be time for that."

"You're in on this with her? I thought you were on my side."

"I'm not on anyone's side, and you better take another look. That little lady's the reason you're sitting here and not in an ambulance."

"You have no idea what's going on here, Gavin," Jenny said.

Harold pulled his car in front of the coffee shop. "Here we are."

The three made their way into the brightly lit restaurant and to a booth near the back. Gavin sat across from Jenny and Harold. The waitress came by and Harold ordered three cups of coffee. Gavin was confused about a lot of things, and had a thousand questions for the pair across from him. However, the pain in his head kept him temporarily silent until the waitress retuned with the steaming mugs.

"I wouldn't go to any more family nights if I were you." Harold said.

"Who are you?"

"This is Harold Benoit. He's a retired cop."

"Great! Another cop."

"What do you mean another cop?"

"Your pal knows what I mean, don't you?"

"Yes, I do."

"I don't know what you're up to but you're a liar," he said pointing at Jenny before turning to Harold, "and I don't know what your game is, but I'm tired of it. The photos were cute and my wife sends her thanks for the pizza, but why all the cloak and dagger crap? You had something to tell me, why not just tell me?"

"You still don't get what you've stumbled onto, do you?"

"No, I don't because no one talks to me. All I get are answers in the form of questions."

"That's because it's dangerous. You're not playing with insurance companies and small settlements here. This is big boy stuff — fraud, corruption, covering up a murder. These people play for keeps. They can make people and documents disappear. He held up the memo. "Hell, you almost lost this thing tonight."

Gavin's eyes widened and a wave of desperation came over him. He didn't know the man across from him, and he wasn't entirely sure why Jenny betrayed him with his firm. That memo was all he had left. Without it, he didn't have a case, and he wouldn't have a job if he didn't hold on to it somehow. It also proved that he was not a liar and a cheat like everyone was saying about him.

"Give it back."

"Why should I?" Harold's gaze bore into him. "How do I know I can trust you with it?"

"I mean it. Give it back."

Harold smiled. "Now you're startin' to be smart, kid." He handed the memo across the table to Gavin's clutching hands. "Have you even read that memo?"

"About a hundred times," Gavin said as he straightened out the pages like a parent caressing a long-lost child.

"Then answer me this, who is RB?" Harold pointed to the notation on the front that read, *route to RB.*

"I don't know, someone working on the investigation maybe. It could be a department. Why is that important?"

"You already know why it's important."

"Because none of the other documents have *RB* on them," he said nodding his head in acknowledgment. The memo's cryptic notation had always bothered him, but he couldn't figure out what it meant.

"You're almost there. Who do you think wrote it?"

"A cop," Gavin responded without hesitating. He had read enough police reports to recognize the style a law enforcement officer uses when documenting facts in an investigation. "Probably RB, whoever he is." He pointed to the notation on the memo. "Wait a minute," he said staring at the notation as if he were seeing it for the first time. "A cop wrote this, a retired cop." *Nate wrote the memo.* "That's why you had me go to Nunzio's. You wanted me to see Kauni and Nate together."

"I told you they couldn't pull off an acquittal without help. Now Nate's good, but he can't make documents disappear from the records room, not without help from someone influential and powerful."

"RB," Gavin said.

"Mr. Bougainville himself."

"You knew this?" He asked turning to Jenny.

"I suspected it. I was hoping your lawsuit would make him do the right thing finally, or you would uncover something that showed it wasn't him. That's why I kept pushing you."

"Why'd you lie about me?"

"Randy threatened her." Harold took a sip of his coffee. "And you, by the way."

"That's when I called Harold, and he told me the whole story."

"So, you've known about this for a long time."

"Yeah, too long. I've been working on a plan to get both of them. Then you came along. That's why I decided to help you out."

"I still don't get it. Why would Randy hide a memo that could have guaranteed a conviction?"

"So there wouldn't be a conviction. It wasn't about the Tutuila family or the victim. It was about power, pure and simple."

The three of them sat in the coffee shop as Harold told them about the back story of the memo.

"Nate Bridges wasn't always retired. After the Harrington girl was shot, he was assigned as one of the secondary investigating officers, mainly following up on small leads and hunches, and reporting directly to the prosecuting office. On an anonymous tip, he went to a local convenience store, and interviewed a grocery clerk who sold Tyler and his friends beer that night. What Nate learned was that there was an additional person in the vehicle before the shooting."

"Chillie Ki."

"That's right. Nate drafted the now infamous memo documenting his discovery, and routed it to the prosecutor's office per protocol. At the time, he had no idea that internally, the memo would never reach Frank Gilreath's desk. It would first be routed to a young ambitious junior felony prosecutor, Randy Bougainville, and would set off a chain of events that would ultimately lead to Tyler's acquittal and our late night meeting here."

"Randy was involved in the investigation?"

"Just barely. His role was that of a kind of ghost investigator. He didn't ask for any recognition or even a seat at counsel table. Let's face it, he was always scared of the courtroom, and he probably saw Frank's case as a way of keeping busy without doing any real work. That he's good at. And Frank was lazy enough not to notice or even care. He was just happy to have the help."

"Frank never saw the memo. That's why he never used it at trial."

"By the time Frank heard about Chillie Ki, the trial was halfway over."

"He played right into the defense's hands," Gavin said.

"No, right into Randy's. That's not even the half of it, kid. When the memo came into the office, it first came to the front desk and was then routed directly to Randy along with all the investigatory leads. At first, he was probably unaware of the significance of the gift that fell into his lap. It was just a typical follow-up investigatory memo on an anonymous tip leading to someone else who was in the car confirming what they already knew — that Tyler was in the front seat. I'm sure he just stuffed it in the file, and forgot about it, until he ran across a tape-recorded statement from the driver of the victim's vehicle, Casey Goodman."

258

"The one from the hospital." Gavin said between sips of coffee. The warm brew was awakening his senses, and distracting him from the forming bruises on his face and rib cage.

"Randy must have listened to it. It was part of a list of items the prosecution was turning over to the defense as required by the disclosure rules of criminal procedure. He volunteered to compile the list for Frank and make sure all relevant documents were included. I bet he played that tape over and over while he came up with his plan."

"Cause, Casey couldn't recognize the driver."

"Come on, the guy looked over for a split second and a street light was shining in his face. All he saw was a big shadowy head. The problem was that Casey knew Tyler from school. He knew what he looked like so if it had been Tyler in that front seat, logic would suggest that he should have been able to identify him. At least that's what Tyler's lawyer argued."

"Eye witness testimony is probably the least reliable form," Jenny said.

"Tell that to a jury," said Harold. "Besides, it didn't matter. Randy had the driver of the victim's car less than four feet from the shooter looking at his face, and he couldn't recognize him. You see, Randy's opportunity had arrived. He planned to hold onto the tape, and leak it to the defense at the right time to embarrass the prosecutor's office."

"Why would he want to embarrass his own office?"

"The Orlich case," Jenny said. "The prosecutor's office had just been sued for withholding documents."

"And another scandal like that would be devastating to the elected prosecuting attorney in charge of the office. He'd be the fall guy, and it would give a young, well-connected prosecutor with friends in the state's capital the perfect opportunity to waltz right into the job."

"So, this case is just about politics." Gavin was disappointed to be hearing this. His idealism was bruising along with his injuries.

"Life is about politics, kid. This was about power. Just as Randy predicted, Casey was asked to review his statement prior to the trial. At first, the prosecutor's office could not locate the tape, and claimed it didn't exist. When the other side began screaming about it, the office blamed the police department for not turning it over. They were pointing fingers all over the place, and Randy was already three steps ahead of everyone."

"So, that's where Nate comes in."

"Yep, Lieutenant Nate Bridges was his ace in the hole. Randy knew Nate was close to retirement, and he also knew that he would never make detective. He was a good cop, but he had some trouble in the past with some of his supervisors, and got busted down a grade a time or two. Randy approached Bridges with an alliance. The deal was for Nate to keep his mouth shut about Chillie and the memo, then, resubmit Casey's taped statement into the property room as if it had always been there. The prosecutor's office had two alternatives, they misplaced it — or worse. In return, Randy would pay him twenty thousand cash, and help him set up a security consulting business catering to the state's political elite. With Randy's help, Nate could do a nice business in the influential circles."

"Wait a minute. How do you know all this?"

"Let's just say, I've been following this case for awhile. You want to talk about me or do you want to hear more?"

Gavin nodded his head to continue as the waitress approached with more coffee. They waited for her to leave before Harold spoke again.

"The plan was executed with perfect precision. Once the defense got wind of the fact that Casey was unable to identify Tyler, they began to scream mistrial and governmental misconduct. The memo would have probably been enough to grant a mistrial and cause the type of scandal Randy wanted, but he wasn't taking any chances. He had Nate approach Tyler's brother, Kauni, to hammer the final nail in the prosecution's case. I don't know how much money changed hands, but it was enough to help fund Tyler's defense. Within a couple of days, Tyler and the others changed their stories and placed Marcus in the front seat. Once the memo was finally released, it was too late, and the prosecutor's office was stuck back peddling on national television. The office was crucified in the media and the public cried out for change. No one really knew Randy, and only Frank knew that he had worked on the case so he escaped any of the back lash, and he won the following election by the largest margin in the county's history."

"And Nate got a security business servicing Randy's wealthy friends," Jenny added.

"If anything, Randy makes good on his promises. He withdrew twenty thousand dollars from somewhere, and funneled it through his campaign straight into the hands of a dummy subsidiary corporation of NB Security, owned solely by Nate Bridges. I think you know the rest."

When Harold finished, he sat back in the booth. Gavin sipped on his coffee, digesting the entire sordid tale.

"So, Randy's behind it all."

"He and his money. You're the only wrench in this story, and he's already scheming to get rid of you too."

"Why isn't there an investigation?"

"You can't prove this stuff. It took me years of quietly putting the pieces together. Randy's the kind of guy who covers his tracks. That memo's about the only evidence that links him to the case and the cover-up."

"You say you've been following this case for all these years? Why do you care? I don't get it."

Harold stared at him for a moment, and then took a deep breath. "Nate and I were partners, and I was part of that investigation too. I knew he paid off Chillie to disappear, and I didn't do anything about it. So, I listened, and I watched, and I waited. Let's just say you're not the only one who wants justice. For me it's also redemption."

Gavin's head began hurting again from an overload of information. "He seems to have covered his tracks pretty well right now. My firm thinks I'm a criminal, the memo's disappeared from the original file, and I got a case that's running out of time."

"Not your copy," Jenny said. "You still have your copy of the memo, and Harold and I think we may know a way to achieve all of our goals."

"I'm listening."

"We're gonna need to start trusting each other, and we're gonna need some help."

FROM GAVIN'S PERSPECTIVE, the plan was relatively simple. His current suspension from the firm combined with the coverage in the newspaper made him the obvious person with an axe to grind. Therefore, Harold and Jenny decided he should only have a minor role to play in their little scheme. It was an intricate plan that required precise teamwork. He would lay low the next day while Jenny and Harold put the pieces together. He would also have to give up the memo. Gavin wasn't too excited about the prospect of letting go of the only copy of the only document that could exonerate him with his firm. They spent another couple of hours at the coffee shop preparing for the next couple of day's events before he finally handed Jenny the pages. By the time Harold and Jenny dropped him off back at his car, and he made it across the bridge, he arrived home at about the same time he usually did on a work day.

It was impossible to keep the proceedings of the past twelve hours a secret from Hannah. Gavin couldn't hide the dried grass stains on his shirt and pants, and the skin around his eye and cheek was beginning to turn dark black and red. He sat her down on the couch when he arrived home, and told her the entire story. She listened without argument, having made her decision the previous night. She hated this case, but she loved her husband.

When he finished, she made him change into sweat pants and lie on the couch with a bag of ice over his eye. It wasn't long before she could hear him snoring underneath a quilt she threw over him. He would be an old man in a couple of years at this pace. She quietly put away the dinner she kept warm in the oven, and poured herself a glass of wine.

She changed the ice pack several times that night, and made herself comfortable in the recliner next to him. She knew that she couldn't stop the chain of events now set into motion. All she could do was offer her support. Secretly however, part of her rooted against Gavin. She wished the judge had dismissed the entire matter. She wanted the case to go away, and she wanted Sara to go away. She knew it wasn't rational, but Hannah was beginning to dislike her. It was as if her husband was having an affair with a woman against whom Hannah could never compete. Sara became an idea, a quest, and Hannah was simply skin and bones. Sara permeated his every waking thought, and like a scorned mistress, she was reaching beyond the grave and destroying their new life together.

She could never tell Gavin such thoughts. He wouldn't understand. She was jealous of someone who was dead, who could only speak to him through legal arguments. She was jealous that his attention and passion were redirected away from her. She sipped her wine and watched him sleep. She could hear the rain beginning to fall against their roof bouncing wet droplets of water on the ground outside the sliding glass door. The news predicted heavy rains for the next few days. She listened to the symphonic rumbling of thunder as the clouds began to burst like wet balloons. Soon it would be time to change the ice again.

CHAPTER 30

NATE'S OFFICE WAS located behind a seafood restaurant overlooking Olympia Harbor. The building was originally a small cannery for local fishermen, but the gentrification of the downtown area squeezed out the local sea trade, and brought with it franchised cappuccino houses and packaged seafood flown in daily from Alaska. Small fishing vessels were pushed westward through Hood's Canal toward the boundary of the Pacific Ocean, while the small capital's inlet harbor began sporting private sailing yachts and expensive house boats.

His building was part of the city's refurbishing project to attract new businesses to the area. Randy's seed money allowed him to grab two small rooms on the water side of the old cannery before prices became too expensive. He only needed enough space to store his surveillance equipment and read the mail in the morning, but the vaulted ceilings and old growth timber beams gave the space an old-world charm that impressed all the upscale urban tenants as well as their clients.

Nate steadied his latte in his left hand as he pushed against the outer door of his office. As part of the rustic charm, the heavy doors sometimes expanded in the dampness and needed an extra shove to open. It was raining heavily outside. Nate shook the water out of his hair as the door finally gave way against his weight. On the floor, lay a small stack of rubber banded mail from the last couple of days. Business was good, but Nate was too cheap to hire a secretary or even a part-time assistant to help keep him organized.

He kicked the stack of envelopes toward his desk, and shut the door. The front room was a true minimalist's vision of decorating. In the back corner, sat an oddly out of place metal desk just within reach of a matching grey filing cabinet. There was no art work and no certificates on the walls, probably because Nate had never earned any, and couldn't tell the difference between a Van Gogh and a velvet depiction of a man sparring with a bull. The back room was slightly more impressive. It was lined with dark metal shelves holding a plethora of electronic gadgets and gizmos.

He tossed his Gore-Tex jacket on the ground, and sat down to go through the mail. He figured that the last few days had earned him a relaxing slow-paced morning. In many ways, he despised Randy, but their unholy alliance kept the two bound together for years. His relationship with Randy turned him from a sub-par cop into a highly-paid law enforcement consultant. Nate's biggest problem was that he spent his money as fast as he earned it. He was always strapped for cash and looking to Randy for another hand out.

He flipped through the monthly bills and solicitors looking to pedal the latest in technological advancements in security. He owed forty-two hundred dollars this month. That's pretty good, he thought to himself, better than last month. Nate was just about to take an early morning break when he heard a knock at the door.

"Legal messenger!" The voice yelled from the other side of the wooded entrance.

"All right, I'm coming," Nate yelled back, kicking his feet off the desk.

Every law firm in the state as well as any investigative agency worth its weight in salt subscribed to Legal Couriers Incorporated or *LCI* for short. For a couple of dollars a day, LCI would guarantee same morning hand-delivered service from Seattle to Spokane and everywhere in between. Their couriers could even file pleadings across the state with returned conformed copies within hours of pick up. It was an extremely profitable business for everyone involved. In return for LCI collecting fifty-eight dollars a month from literally thousands of firms and solo practitioners, they amassed a delivery empire complete with a formidable fleet of Cessna style airplanes and delivery trucks that rivaled any national outfit. Additionally, the legal community saved the precious time it took a young associate to run up to the courthouse or a paralegal the time it took to deliver pleadings to opposing counsel, while still charging the clients two hundred fifty dollars an hour for the service. It was an all-around win-win situation.

Nate jerked his front door free from the frame to reveal a young college age student standing before him.

"Here you go." The young kid handed him a manila envelope. There was no return address, but the type-written label read, *Nathaniel Bridges, care of NB Securities.*

"Hold on a minute." Nate grabbed his coat off the floor and pulled out a folded piece of paper from one of the inside pockets. On it were two handwritten lines:

For services rendered by NB Securities for Mr. Randall Bougainville, esq. and consideration thereof, please remit the following amount owed in full, [   ].

The amount was left blank. He fumbled through the papers on his desk until he found the total he owed this month in bills. In the blank, he scribbled, *five thousand dollars and zero cents,* and shoved the paper into an envelope. The bill offered no explanation and none was needed. With the same care he took with filling out the contents, he wrote on the outside, *Randy Bougainville, Pierce County Prosecutor's Office.*

"And this is for you," he said exchanging parcels.

After the young courier left, Nate fished around for an envelope opener, and then resorted to ripping the package open with his hands. He hesitated a moment before pulling out the documents from the half-torn paper sheath. Gripped in his hands, was the dreaded memo that he had attempting to eliminate from existence. Is this some kind of joke? He scoffed to himself. On the front page, someone had taped a note using stationary from the prosecutor's office. It read,

> You missed this copy in my office. Meet me at six to discuss payment or read about it in tomorrow's paper.

Okay, Ms. Garrett, you have my attention.

JENNY WATCHED THE clock in her office trying to predict the exact moment that Nate would open the package. She wanted to see the smugness in his face turn to fear and concern. His first call would be to Randy's office. Fortunately for her, today was Friday and Randy's day to attend the weekly breakfast of the Rotary Club. He never missed it. On dry days, he would follow the meeting with a round of golf, but today's weather meant that he would be rolling in around 10:30 or 11:00 at the latest.

It was already 9:30, which meant she had a solid hour before he would be in the building. She was also late for the morning roll call in the criminal court. She gathered her case files, and headed toward the elevator. She had a full calendar of motions which would occupy most of her time through the early afternoon. It would also hopefully keep Randy away from her. Everything should be in place, she thought to herself.

After dropping Gavin off, she and Harold continued to finalize the preparations for their plan. She spent Thursday afternoon following up the leads that Gavin's investigation had uncovered. Chillie's mom identified Nate from a picture as the man who paid off her son. She also spoke with Casey Goodman, who confirmed that Nate was the cop who interviewed him after Chillie confronted him at the memorial service. She called Gavin a couple of times during the day to check up on him. He seemed to be recovering well.

It was 11:20 before Jenny had another chance to check her watch. She was completing her second plea agreement when she noticed the time.

"Janice," she called to the judicial assistant. "Can you call up to Randy's office and see if he's there?"

"You want to talk to him?" It wasn't unusual for prosecutors to call him throughout the day, especially during negotiations with a defense attorney. Randy had the final say on deals and sentencing offers, and enjoyed the feeling of importance when someone called for advice.

"No. You can buzz his secretary. I just want to know if he's arrived yet. I'll catch up to him personally."

She knew that Nate must have already called in a panic with the news of her extortion letter. She didn't know what Randy's reaction would be, but she needed to bide her time until lunch. That was when Harold and Gavin would come in and take over.

"He's not there yet, but she's expecting him any minute."

"Great. I mean okay."

She still had a few minutes before Randy spoke to Nate. She signed her name at the bottom of one of the plea agreements, and handed it to an attorney sitting at the table.

"Here you go, Jeff. You can fill in the deal. I'll be right back."

Randy's office was five floors above her at the top of the building. She excused herself from the courtroom, and headed for the stairs. Five flights barely caused her to break a sweat. She had other things on her mind and she had to beat Randy to his office.

"Hi, Ms. Garrett," Randy's secretary said as Jenny appeared in the tenth floor waiting area.

"Is he in?" Jenny played coy pretending that she was unaware of the Janice's recent call.

"Not yet."

Jenny innocently sauntered toward his closed door. Her real destination was the mail slot which sat next to Randy's office on a small mahogany bookshelf.

"Can I help you?"

"Well, I had a question for him." She was stalling for time to allow her to reach the door. "Do you know if the Providence case has been assigned out yet?" She could see several messages waiting for him. One of them had to be from Nate.

"I don't know," she said suspiciously extending her head to try and look around Jenny. "I'll let him know you came by."

Jenny couldn't see who the notes were from, and she couldn't pick them up to check in front of Randy's secretary. That would be too obvious and would cause an immediate confrontation.

"What case are you referring to?" Randy's voice startled her causing her to jump.

"Randy?" Jenny said spinning around.

"Didn't mean to scare you." His expression offered no hint of whether he knew about the letter to Nate. "What's up?"

Jenny was leaning against the side of his door with her hands clasped behind her back. "Uhm, nothing really."

"Well, it must be something important to get you out the courtroom." He started walking toward her.

"It's just a new case I heard about." She could feel the messages at the tip of her fingers. She just didn't know which one to grab. "I wanted to volunteer my services." She needed to act quickly before he got too close. Each step he took chipped away at her chances to grab the message without being seen. She fumbled with the small notes trying to pick the right one.

"What are you doing?" Randy cocked his head at her as he approached. He could see that she was leaning against his bookshelf in an unnatural looking pose.

"Nothing." She abandoned the idea pulling her arms back down to her side.

"Excuse me." He motioned for her to move away from the mail slot so she could grab the small stack of messages. "Don't you think you're in over your head already?"

"Excuse me." Jenny's heart sank. Did he know?

"With your current case load. You think you can handle another case right now?"

"Of course." He was flipping through the small telephone messages in his hand.

"Excuse me, Mr. Bougainville?"

Jenny turned her head simultaneously with Randy. Behind them stood several men in white shirts and holding clipboards.

"Yes."

"We're from the fire department. It's a surprise inspection."

Harold came through, and saved her. He had several friends at the fire department who owed him favors. He wasn't the kind of person to cash in on a debt, but this was a special situation.

"It's lunch time. Can't this wait?"

"I'm afraid not." The man seemed polite but insistent. "We're gonna need you to accompany us through the building."

Randy took a deep sigh, and shoved his mail back into his slot. "Okay, where do you want to begin?"

As he walked away from her, Jenny grabbed the messages from his box, and quickly slipped them in her jacket pocket without being seen. Harold left specific instructions to make sure that the inspection occupied at least two hours of Randy's time. She had until after two before Randy would return to his office. By that time, she would be out of the building doing witness interviews until Nate arrived at five. The rest was up to Gavin.

CHAPTER 31

RANDY LED the fire officials past every fire exit, and pointed out each fuse box and smoke detector. They even walked through the basement boiler room looking for fire hazards. Per Harold's wishes, it was 2:15 before the inspection was completed. Despite the hoax, they were able to find several minor items that needed repair, and left Randy with a written warning from the county, and a timeline to bring the building up to code.

By the time he made it back to his office, he forgot about Jenny and her suspicious behavior earlier in the morning.

His secretary stopped him before he could reach his mail slot.

"Sir, there's a gentleman who keeps calling for you."

"A gentleman?" He assumed it was Nate with some sort of complaint.

"He says it's urgent, and he's been calling every five minutes for the past half hour." She held out several telephone message slips.

"Did he leave a name?" Randy grabbed the pile from her and began flipping through them.

"Gavin Brady, he says it's about a recovered memo."

"Really." His response showed no hint of alarm, but her words made him stop what he was doing. "Did he say anything else?"

"No, sir. He left his cell phone number, and said you'd know what he meant."

"Thank you." Randy closed his office door behind him and couldn't reach the phone fast enough. Nate was supposed to have taken care of the memo. He sat down behind his desk and dialed the number.

Gavin was sitting in his parked car staring at his firm's building when his cell phone rang. The building went in and out of focus as his windshield wipers rhythmically mopped away the pouring rain. He wished he could go inside and explain about the cover up, but he had to follow through with Jenny's plan. It was the only way to really redeem himself, and the only way to give Sara's family any hope of justice.

"Hello."

"Mr. Brady, I believe you wanted to speak with me."

"Yes, thank you for calling. I wanted to drop off a document that I understand your office recently misplaced."

"If you're referring to the slanderous article in this week's paper, and I'm assuming you are, you should know that issue has been turned over to my attorneys to handle. My understanding is that they've already had a conversation with your firm about this matter."

Gavin could feel his blood begin to boil. He took a deep breath and regained his composure. He needed to stay calm if this was going to work.

"That's correct, but they don't know what I know."

"Oh yeah, what's that, Mr. Brady?"

"A payoff. A payoff by a junior prosecutor to a cop to cover up a murder." There was silence on the other end of the phone. Gavin waited several seconds before continuing. "Are you still there?"

"I'm listening."

"I'm referring to the money paid to Chillie Ki to make him disappear, and to Nate Bridges for God knows what all."

Randy paused, then let out a gregarious laugh. "Is this a joke, Mr. Brady? Are you recording this conversation to manufacture more evidence?"

"I assure you this is no joke, and it would be a felony to record this conversation without your consent. I'm a lawyer and an officer of the court."

"Well, Mr. Brady, you're playing a dangerous game."

"I'll be in front of the courthouse at five p.m. At five o' one, I head straight to the newspaper with what I know." He hung up the phone without giving Randy a chance to respond.

Randy continued to hold the phone in his hand as his mind raced. There was no way Gavin could have any proof about his dealings with Nate. He made sure to destroy any documentation linking the two men, and besides, he owned Nate. Something was up, and he wasn't about to walk into it blind. He quickly hit the next line and dialed Nate's office, who answered on the first ring.

"Where the hell have you been, Randy?"

"I've been busy figuring out why I'm still hearing about this memo."

"What do you mean?"

"The lawyer just called me. I thought you took care of it."

"I tried. He didn't have the file in his office or at his home, and he got to his wife before I could get it from her."

"From his wife?"

"It's a long story. We got another problem."

"I don't pay you for problems."

"The girl knows."

"What girl?"

"Your girl, Ms. Jennifer Garrett. She just sent me a little love note to meet her today."

It was beginning to make sense. He remembered Jenny acting peculiar. She must have been feeling him out.

"What does she want?"

"What does everyone want? Money."

"What does she know?"

"I assume everything."

"Okay." Randy needed to collect his thoughts. Jenny and Gavin must have made some alliance to extort him for money. He liked the boldness of their actions, but there was no way he would pay out one cent to them. If he gave in now, he'd be paying them forever. "What time are you supposed to meet her?"

"Five, at her office."

It was the exact same time Gavin told him to be in front of the courthouse. *They were at least smart enough to split up.*

"I think you need to make that meeting. And this time try and get it right if you know what I mean? It's time to tie up loose ends."

"What about the lawyer?"

"It's funny you should ask. He wants to meet me at five also. I think it's time to call our friend, and cash in on what I've already paid good money for. He owes us. A life for a life, you know what I mean?"

THE COURTHOUSE WAS already emptying out when Nate entered the building. He was twenty minutes early, but he hoped to steal into Jenny's office before she returned. Randy paged her after his conversation with Nate, and found out that she was out conducting witness interviews. Randy reached into his desk and grabbed his cell phone. He silently exited the building and walked across the street to call Nate back and tell him. He also wanted to make sure that Gavin's demise had been properly purchased, and didn't want to talk in his office.

Nate swiped a security card that Randy gave him months earlier, and entered the inside lair of the prosecutor's office. He was careful to avoid the surveillance cameras, and kept his head down as he made his way back to Jenny's office located in a remote section of the department. He opened the door, and silently slid his body through the frame.

"Come in." Harold sat behind Jenny's desk. "Long time no see."

"Harold?" Nate was shocked to see his old partner. After the Tutuila acquittal, they never spoke again.

"I've been expecting you. Sit down."

"This must look strange."

"Sit down."

Nate sat across from him and smiled. He had no explanation for being in Jenny's office, but then again, neither did Harold.

"What is this, a shake down?"

"You know, Nate, I never cared that you were a lousy cop or that the only way you ever got laid was to entrap prostitutes."

"Harold, you jealous that you're still working in this dump?"

"No, what I can't stand is the fact that you're willing to throw everything away for a two-bit scumbag like Randy Bougainville."

"Is that a wire under your shirt?" Nate motioned toward his button up shirt.

"No, it's not." He pulled out a small digital recorder from his inside jacket pocket, and placed it on the desk between them. "It's a tape recorder and it's off."

"Refreshing."

"What happened to you? We were friends once, partners."

"I got smart. I realized that the only brass ring out there was the one you go out and get for yourself."

"I want the memo."

"I don't know what you're talking about."

"I sat across from you at the station house probably no further away than we are now, and watched you write it."

"That was a long time ago."

"Not that long ago."

"That memo's dead and buried, just like that case. You'd be smart to leave it there."

"I tried that. It didn't work."

"That's disappointing." Nate stood up and pulled out a silver handgun from under his jacket. It had been intended for Jenny. "It's dangerous to live in the past."

"What are you doing?" There was no fear in Harold's voice as he shook his head.

"It was a long time ago and I'm not willing to go back. Stand up." Nate motioned for him to get up. Harold slowly opened his sport coat to show that he didn't have a weapon.

"It's over, Nate."

"Not till I say it is."

"The driver in the murdered girl's car ID'd you. It seems an Asian guy approached this Casey Goodman fellow, who said he was in Tyler's car just before the shooting, and placed him in the front seat. That must have been the anonymous tip that led you to interview Chillie Ki."

"Casey, huh? It looks like I got another stop to make after I leave here."

"I'm sorry about this, Nate."

"Me too."

"Have you heard enough?" Harold called out to the office door. Before Nate could turn around, the door swung open revealing two uniformed officers with guns drawn standing in the hallway.

"Police! You're under arrest!"

Nate looked back at Harold in amazement. "You set me up?"

"No. You set yourself up. I just couldn't live with it anymore."

The officers cuffed Nate without a struggle. Harold walked up to his former partner, who was standing before him in defeat.

"Like I said, I'm sorry." He reached into Nate's jacket and pulled out the security card. "You might want to trace where he got this," he said, handing it to one of the officers.

GAVIN WAS THE final piece of the plan. He stood under an umbrella next to the small brick retaining wall outside of the courthouse. The rain was a downpour by noon, and showed no signs of letting up. Gavin wasn't sure what he would do if Randy didn't show, and he had no idea how Harold was making out upstairs with Nate. He also didn't enjoy standing out in the rain. He didn't have to contemplate the possibilities very long. Randy opened an umbrella as he exited the front of the building at exactly fifty-five seconds past five. Gavin pretended to be calm and relaxed as he waited for Randy to walk up to him.

"Okay, let's hear what you've got to say."

"Just what I said earlier. I want to give you something that I know your office is desperately searching for." He pulled out a damp copy of the memo, and handed it to Randy.

"What's this supposed to be?" Randy smirked. "Manufacturing evidence is a crime."

"It was written by a Lieutenant Nathaniel Bridges, and it corroborates that Tyler was in the front seat of the car, and lied on the stand during his trial. You know, this notation always bothered me," he said pointing to the initials on the front page. "RB. That kind of ties you into the whole scandal, doesn't it?"

Randy stared at Gavin with an intense look. "It doesn't mean anything to me."

"I can prove it came from the original file too." He flipped the memo over. Stamped on the back were the numbers, *PC100124*. "My understanding is that you created this ingenious system of stamping the back of each archived document with sequential numbers so that they could be identified at a later date. I bet you're rethinking that decision right now."

Randy gripped the memo. "What do you think you're doing, counselor?"

"Getting at the truth. That's what we're all here for, right?

"You can't prove any of this."

"Maybe I can, maybe I can't. I don't need proof with you because the scandal will go on for years, and your name will always be attached to a cover up and a murder." You can keep that copy," he said, pointing at the document Randy was crumpling with his grip. "I've got another." Gavin turned around and left. Randy didn't move from his spot until Gavin's car was out of sight. *He won't get very far.*

GAVIN'S FIRST CALL was to his wife to let her know he was on his way home. He didn't talk long because he still needed to call Jenny regarding Harold's encounter with Nate. He was ecstatic with energy as he sped down Pearl Street toward the on-ramp to the freeway. The rain slowed traffic considerably. His windshield wipers shaved off sheets of water as fast as they formed. He dialed Jenny's number as he approached the underpass. He hoped the bridge wasn't backed up. It was the only way across the water, and delays often turned a twenty-minute commute into an hour-and-a-half delay.

He put on his left blinker, and prepared to turn onto the ramp once the oncoming wave of cars cleared. Behind him, a vehicle approached.

He adjusted his rearview mirror to counter act the car's high beams in his eyes. The car didn't seem to be slowing down as it grew nearer. Gavin flicked his lights off and back on again in the hopes of getting the driver's attention. The car seemed to be gaining speed. Gavin hit his horn a couple of times, but the vehicle kept coming. There was going to be an accident. He dropped his cell phone, and braced himself against the steering wheel. A loud booming noise rolled across the water as his car lunged forward from the impact.

Luckily, it was a solid hit, and he wasn't thrown into the oncoming lane of traffic and Gavin had his seatbelt on. He didn't think he was hurt. He unbuckled himself and opened the door. When he stood up, the rain immediately ran down his head into his eyes. He wiped his forehead to survey the damage. Behind him sat the black Trans Am. The windows were tinted, and the droplets of rain acted as an extra layer making it impossible to see inside. The car started pushing against Gavin's car.

"Hey, stop!" He jumped back behind the wheel, and slammed on the brake. "What are you doing?"

The car continued pushing against the back bumper sliding Gavin's locked wheels forward. There was one chance to escape. Gavin saw a small break in the traffic. He quickly turned his wheel to the left, and floored the gas pedal. His wheels screeched against the wet pavement barely missing an SUV on his way to the on-ramp. He leveled out the wheel, and merged into traffic without slowing down.

In his rearview mirror, he could see the Trans Am was still gaining on him. He tried to reach his cell phone, but the impact threw it under the seat just out of reach. He weaved past several cars toward the bridge trying to maintain control on the slick asphalt.

The rain poured down, causing the water to slosh up on the windshield in large waves as the tires cut through it. He could see the bridge ahead. The Trans Am closed in on him. 'Who the hell is this guy?' He knew it wasn't Randy or Nate, but he must have some type of connection to them. He was almost at the bridge. The traffic was heavy but moving at a steady pace in the pouring rain.

His exit was just on the other side bridge, but he knew he couldn't take it. He wasn't about to steer whoever this person was to his home, to his wife. Just then a large pickup truck passed him in the opposite direction, and shot a wave of water over Gavin's windshield. For a moment, he was blinded. He tightened his hands across the steering wheel until his knuckles turned white from the pressure. His arms tensed as he tried to maintain control of the car. He breathed a sigh of relief when the blades cleared an opening for him to see the road. The water was still shooting over his vehicle from his own tires as he finally reached the Narrows Bridge.

Gavin heard the clatter of his tires as they contacted the metal grates. Again, the Trans Am rammed his car from behind. Gavin lost control momentarily, and began to slide across the metal grating on the bridge.

"Oh, my God!" Instinctively, Gavin turned into the direction of the slide and finally regained control. He was drawing dangerously close to the edge of the bridge and the almost six hundred-foot drop to the water below. He began to slowly turn the wheel away from the edge trying not to panic.

For a third time, the Trans Am slammed into the back of his car. He turned the wheel to the left to no avail. His car collided into the side railing like an explosion, and bounced back across the lanes to the other side of the bridge into the oncoming traffic. A large diesel truck was barreling down on him. There was nothing Gavin could do but watch. The trucker jerked his trailer away from Gavin's vehicle just barely missing him, but as the trailer whirled past the front tip of Gavin's front door, it jackknifed into a v-shape, and turned on its side. Gavin's car slammed into the other side of the bridge finally coming to a halt. The truck kept sliding across the bridge against the traffic, and toward the black Trans Am. Gavin turned his head just in time to see the explosion as the front bed of the truck ignited into a fiery ball of flames upon impact with the car.

A black cloud of smoke mushroomed into the air. Several other cars collided around the truck and Trans Am creating an orchestral ambience to the fire and rising smoke. Traffic came to an instant standstill. Gavin checked himself and looked back at the damage across the bridge. It was hard to see anything through the white and black smoke and flames. He unbuckled himself, and got out of the car. There were cars lined up and down the bridge, and some people were scrambled around, trying to help. Others tried to get off the bridge. Something in Gavin pulled him toward the flames. He crossed the lanes, and approached the trailer, turned on its side and halfway through the railing. He tried to go around the right side to the front, but the flames were too hot and the smoke too thick. He put his shirt over his mouth to stop his lungs from filling with burning diesel.

Near the back of the trailer, was a crushed back fender of a blue car lodged between the trailer and the broken railing. He ran around to get a better look. Apparently, the trailer hooked the vehicle as it jackknifed passed him. Gavin hurried to the side of the bridge, and tried to see if anyone was trapped. Who could survive such a crash? He leaned over the edge. The vehicle was flipped on its side and turned backwards. The trailer crushed back half of the vehicle and left it hanging off the edge. It looked like a man was trapped in what used to be the passenger side. Gavin made his way along the side of the railing to the man. He was still breathing, but his lower torso was crushed under the massive weight of the steel trailer. Behind the car, flames engulfed the Trans Am.

"Can you hear me?" Gavin said calling to the man in the blue car. He could see his head turn slightly but there was no reply. He climbed onto the railing, and squeezed between an opening to the side of the man's face. His eyes were open, and he was breathing. Gavin looked down and saw that the trailer had flattened the vehicle below his waist. It was amazing that he was even still alive.

"Can you hear me?" The man looked at him and nodded. "Are you in any pain?"

"I can't feel anything."

"It's okay. Help's on the way." Gavin had no idea when any help would arrive, but it seemed the appropriate thing to say. "You'll be okay. I'll tell them you're here." He began to wiggle backwards through the opening.

"I'm scared." Gavin stopped. "I don't want to die alone." Gavin didn't know how to respond. He looked around him at the small opening.

"Don't worry. I'm not going anywhere." Gavin crawled forward again next to the man's face. The man smiled at him.

"My name's Gavin. I'm gonna stay right here with you."

The man took a deep breath and the fear in his face lessened. His voice, now calm, echoed in the small metal cage as he began to tell Gavin about his life. The pattering of the rain outside echoed gently throughout the vehicle. He talked about his wife of eleven years and their two children. He told Gavin about how he proposed to her on the very same bench where they had met during college. Gavin learned about the family's trip to Disneyland last month to celebrate their youngest son's seventh birthday.

He listened closely to the man speak about his life, a memoir that would survive only through Gavin. This was closer to reality and truth than anything he had ever experienced, and within a few minutes, it was as if the two of them had known each other all their lives. Gavin laughed as the man told him stories about his children, and about his hopes and dreams for his family. In these brief fatal moments, the two of them became brethren.

As the man continued talking, Gavin's eyes filled with tears. There was a comfort in the man's face at the prospect of passing this world in the company of someone else. Gavin turned his thoughts to his own life and his own world. He thought of Sara and he thought of his own father both of whom spent the last days and last moments of their lives completely alone in a hospital. This was his penance. He knew it the moment he saw Sara's father weeping at the loss of his daughter. Gavin's betrayal doomed his father a cold and lonely death, and he would spend a lifetime making it up to him through others.

The man now gasped for air.

"It's starting to hurt."

"What do you need?"

"Nothing."

"Try to breathe," Gavin said fighting back the lump in his throat. It did not matter what the man wanted, there was nothing to do but wait. Death was near and they both knew it. "Think about your wife."

"I see her smiling." The man's eyes began to roll gently back in his head.

"I bet she's smiling at you." Gavin was trying to maintain control. He was helpless to do anything, and knew his job was to not let him die alone in the darkness.

"She is."

"Go to her."

"Ow." The man's breathing was louder. "Don't leave me."

Tears streamed down Gavin's face. "I'm right here. Go to your wife."

"I see her."

"Go to her. Hurry, go to her. Run. I'll be here with you. Run to her."

A look of calm came over the man's face. He looked over at Gavin and gave him his last gaze. Gavin was terrified as he stared into the eyes of mortality. An ignominious end to such an illustrious life. The slight smile was on the man's face as he breathed his last. Gavin reached out a trembling hand and touched his forehead. "Go to her," he said again out loud.

The silence ended as the railing next to him jerked. A hand reached into the darkness, and pulled Gavin back through the opening. The light was blinding, and the soot-drenched sweat dripping down his face was stinging his teary eyes. Someone grabbed his back. Just as he came out of the opening, the trailer collapsed completely against the railing, crushing the remaining portion of the vehicle, and the man who was no longer in this world.

Gavin now wept uncontrollably. The memories of his father and his death flooded his mind as the tears poured down his face. As if by reflex, his mouth opened and released deep repressed cries of loss. He never remembered crying this hard before, not even when the actual news of his father's death came. Now, he couldn't stop, and he couldn't cry hard enough. He didn't even realize that someone was holding him. After several minutes, he felt the tight fabric of a coat pressed against his face and someone's arms around him, holding him as he sobbed.

"Are you okay now?" The voice asked. Gavin looked up and saw a man in a fireman's coat. The man had a gentle smile on his face as he looked down at him. The rain dripping down Gavin's forehead masking his tears.

"Yeah, I'm okay. Thanks."

"You hurt?"

"No," he said as he wiped his runny nose on his shirt.

The fireman looked at the now collapsed trailer. "You're lucky, a few more seconds."

Gavin swallowed hard. "I know."

"I came over here cause I heard voices."

Gavin looked at the man. He tried to speak but couldn't find the words.

"Was there someone else in there with you?"

Gavin paused before answering. "His name was Bill Langston." Gavin could feel the lump in his throat. "His wife and two children were with him. They were crushed in the crash. He was alive for a while but —"

He stopped. There was nothing else to say. The fireman helped Gavin to an aid vehicle that had just arrived. He felt empty and alone as the rescue personnel asked him questions about his health, and peered into his eyes with small lights. He heard them say something about calling his wife and taking him to the hospital. A couple more seconds, and he would have died alongside Bill and his family. On another day, he could have been in Bill's place. It was all so random and unfair. Today no longer seemed to matter as much, and life became a little more fragile and precious as Gavin leaned back in the gurney and braced himself for the ride to the emergency room.

CHAPTER 32

"HEY SPORT." Gavin turned his head as Duke entered his room.

"Duke, hi."

"They said you'll be out of here in a couple of hours, good as new."

"Yeah, that's what I hear." Gavin wasn't feeling very lucky. He had watched a man die whose only mistake was to be crossing the bridge at the same moment as Gavin.

"You got a pretty little wife out there too."

The hospital called Hannah as soon as Gavin arrived. The accident had crippled the middle section of the suspension bridge so crossing traffic was diverted thirty miles south toward Olympia where the land finally connected.

"Thanks."

"I got a call from a reporter this evening just before I heard about your accident on the news. You're being called a hero by the way."

"I'm not a hero."

"Anyway, this reporter wanted to fill me in on a few things."

"You know everybody, Duke." Gavin smiled.

"I know a lot of people. Anyway, this reporter also wanted to let me know that the police ID'd the driver of the Trans Am."

"Really?" Gavin perked up.

"The car was registered to Kauni Tutuila. They're matching dental records right now, but they're pretty sure it was him."

Gavin let the news sink in. It was Kauni who followed him for so long. He was the person who rammed his car, and tried to run him off the road, the one who helped Randy destroy the prosecution against his brother, Tyler. Kauni had met with Tyler's group, and told them to change their stories, putting Tyler in the back seat and Marcus in the front seat. 'Flip the script,' he said. It's so easy that it'll work. The difference was that he didn't do it for money or power and he wasn't out to destroy the system. However misguided, his actions were understandable.

"Someone also anonymously delivered some photos of him with a retired cop. You wouldn't happen to know anything about that would you?" Gavin smiled. Harold drove the final spike into Nate's coffin.

"I didn't think so."

"I never lied about the memo."

"I know. You got spanked a little bit by the system. That's the way it works sometimes. Hell, the case was never there to begin with. But you sure rattled some cages, and made as much noise as you could. That's all you can hope for in this business. Now, school's over, and it's time to get back to work."

"So, I'm not fired?"

"You were never fired." Duke patted his arm. "If you're up to it, why don't you join me in court on Monday? It's technically still your motion. Take the weekend to rest up, and I'll see you bright and early."

"Okay."

"Don't expect anything, this is still a losing fight." He smiled at Gavin and walked out of the room with the same momentum as he had entered.

Gavin was released within the hour, and Hannah drove them home. For the next couple of days, she made him stay inside and sleep as much as possible. They didn't talk very much about what nearly happened. She even made them pancakes on Saturday. The only time he left the house that weekend was to pick up the rental car that Gavin's insurance company paid for until they settled his claim. Monday would be a big day for both of them. Gavin would be back in court fighting for the woman who became his obsession, and Hannah would be helplessly awaiting the result as well as his return home. She stroked his head as he lay with his head in her lap, softly snoring. There were still remnants of their life that she owned. For now, he needed his rest.

JUDGE VELEZ'S COURTROOM was filled with attorneys already waiting for the morning docket when Gavin entered, not too early this time. The bridge was still closed to the public. There would be numerous lawsuits springing up out of the accident, and a lot of attorneys would be trying to make a name for themselves on both sides.

Although he was dressed in a suit, the bruising under his eye and fresh scrapes on his face made him look more like a defendant than an attorney. As the doors shut behind him, every head turned, and a hush fell over the room. Even Duke, who was standing at the front bench talking with Lance Penderson, fell silent. At first, he wasn't sure how to react. He hadn't read the paper over the weekend, but had a pretty good idea that his name was mentioned in more than one story.

He didn't see Randy anywhere in the room, and hadn't talked to Jenny since Friday afternoon. He hoped things went as planned with Nate. She must have heard about what happened. He hoped she was all right. Along the side walls, stood several uniformed officers. One of them offered Gavin a sympathetic nod. He slowly walked through the silent crowd feeling the faces turn with him as he joined Duke.

"I told you I'd make it."

Just then the courtroom doors swung open as if for dramatic effect and in walked Randy Bougainville. He immediately made eye contact with Gavin and began walking toward the front of the room motioning for the uniformed officers to join him. Less than two feet behind him trotted Jenny. Randy's steps were purposed and firm, and his police escort was an intimidating sight for anyone. Gavin's heart began to race, and he felt like Kauni's car was about to slam into him again. He could feel his hand grip the steering wheel, bracing for the impact. Randy walked right up to him before turning to his right.

"Excuse me," he said as he continued past with his entourage. Jenny stopped and faced him.

"I hear you had quite a day." She tried to hide her emotions behind her thick professional exterior.

"I've had better."

"Maybe it'll be today." She smiled and winked at him before catching up to Randy just as he reached Tyler, Danny, and Sal. The boys didn't move and remained seated.

"Ms. Garrett." Randy moved aside to make room for her.

"Tyler Tutuila, Aleni Saulo Ga Fuatumau, a.k.a, Sal Fuatimau, and Daniel Fause, the state of Washington charges you with hindering an official investigation, and perjury in the first degree." She pulled out three documents from a folder. "I am handing you indictments outlining the allegations against you. You have the right to remain silent, you have the right to an attorney. At the end of these proceedings you will be taken into custody to await arraignment, which will occur within forty-eight hours. I'm sure your attorneys can answer any questions you may have." She turned toward Gavin to catch his reaction. Justice at last, but at a heavy price. Randy and Jenny exited as quickly as they'd entered. He had his legs cuts out from under him, and this was his way to gain some damage control in the public and in the press.

In the back of the courtroom, Gavin saw Tyler's parents sitting behind their attorney. The couple was silent, and didn't even look over as their youngest child had his rights read to him. Mauuaua quietly wiped tears from her eyes. It seemed inappropriate to celebrate any victory here. There were no winners in this courtroom, only loss. Gavin took a couple of steps toward them. He stopped when Palolo looked up at him. It was the same look he gave him in the church, one of hatred and distrust.

"I'm sorry for your loss."

Mauuaua slowly turned her head to face him. She took a moment to wipe her nose. "What more can you do to me?"

She was nothing like the defendant he described in his original complaint. She was a grieving mother, who had lost a child, and now, a family. It didn't matter how or even why. He could see the same emptiness in her eyes that he had seen in Bill Langston's eyes as he lay helpless next to his crushed family on the bridge. It was the same emptiness he saw in Louise Harrington's eyes as he stood in her family kitchen convincing her to put her trust in his firm. Even Chillie's mom was filled with the same empty void as she told him of her son's payoff.

Tyler, Danny, and Sal sat in their seats as they read the charges along with their attorneys. It was over, and Sara's death would not go unpunished. In the back, Marcus sat silently with his lawyer, Dennis Handling. Gavin stepped back to join Duke and Lance, who were already picking dates on their phones to reschedule the hearing.

"No," Gavin said. Both men looked up.

"What's that?" Duke asked.

"I'm ready to proceed today."

Lance looked flabbergasted. "I don't think you understand the gravity of the circumstances. Did you just see what happened?"

"I think I understand the gravity of the circumstances, Lance." Gavin was tired, and had finally earned the right to look at both men on equal footing. He turned to Duke. "I'd like to handle the hearing if that's okay."

Almost on cue, Judge Velez entered the courtroom dressed in his black robe with a stern earnest look on his face.

"All rise!" The bailiff waved the gallery to their feet until the judge took the bench.

"Good morning everyone. We have a full docket this morning so let's try and practice brevity in our speeches." He scanned the list of cases. "I'd like to begin with a set over case from last Monday, *Harrington versus Tutuila.*"

Gavin moved in front of Duke to stand at the front bar. Lance took his place beside him along with the other attorneys. Even if the judge had not already been informed about last night's events, it was written on Gavin's wounds and the somber looks on the defendants.

"Mr. Penderson, please extend the court's condolences to your clients for their loss."

"Thank you, your Honor."

"I also understand we've already had some activity in this matter this morning in the form of criminal indictments for perjury."

"That's correct."

I assume that you are looking for a continuance, correct?"

"Correct, your honor. Given the recent tragedy, and the developments by the prosecutor's office, I'd ask for a one month set over."

"Mr. Brady, when I said bring me something by Monday, I certainly didn't expect this. I expect you'll accept a short delay to prepare some additional briefing."

"No, your honor." Gavin could hear the gasp from the gallery. "Plaintiff objects to any continuance, and wishes to proceed today." He turned around and looked at Duke, who was squinting at him in disbelief.

"Mr. Brady, I'm not sure you quite understand what I'm saying. You won. Perhaps you'd like a moment to confer with Mr. Stewart behind you?"

Gavin looked over at Kuani's parents who were still sitting in the front row, defeated and unable to grieve or show any pain and sorrow. He fought hard for this win and all he had to do was stay as quiet as he did the first time he appeared in court with Duke. He could hear his words in his head, *sometimes the winner is the one who knows when to shut up.* "This is my case your honor. I'm handling the argument." He didn't even turn around to allow Duke the opportunity to respond. He was no longer intimidated by his youth or the caliber of his adversaries.

There was a long pause as the judge contemplated how to proceed. Gavin was new to the bar, and there were compelling reasons for a continuance. However, he was a licensed attorney and knew the risks of what he was doing.

"Okay counselor, very well. You understand that there has been no additional briefing submitted since Monday?"

"I do, your honor. You asked for additional evidence to support plaintiff's claims."

"Yes, I did."

He looked over at the parents one last time. "There hasn't been any new evidence that I could find." He couldn't hide behind legal maneuvering any longer. It was time for the truth, and it was time to let go. Lance was wrong when he said Gavin was trying to punish the parents for the sins of their son. However, Palolo and Mauuaua were already paying the ultimate price for their transgressions. Their crime was loving their children so much that they were willing to look the other way when one child set himself up to be sacrificed while trying to protect his sibling.

"What about the new indictments?"

"I don't practice criminal law, but I'm pretty sure they're innocent until proven guilty. I apologize to the court, but I stand on my original briefing."

Lance looked back at Duke to see if he was going to interject. Gavin was literally throwing the case away.

"You understand that without new evidence and without a continuance, I'm left with no choice but to dismiss the entire case?"

"I do, your honor."

The judge locked eyes with Gavin. He looked at the attorneys who were standing at the front bar in shock about what was happening.

"Very well. Mr. Brady, without any new evidence to support your claims against the defendants and without the benefit of what seemed to be an agreed upon continuance, I am left with the unfortunate decision to grant the defendants' original motion. Case is dismissed."

Gavin turned around and faced his mentor. The hero worship had already washed away. He expected a scowl, but Duke was half-smiling.

"You call that justice?" Duke asked.

"No. It's closure. They'll get justice when the convictions are handed down."

"Excuse me," Lance said coming over to him. "I don't know what you just did back there, but my clients thank you."

"No, they don't," Gavin said looking over at them. "How could they?"

"You're probably right. I will say that took guts, and it was an honor standing in the same courtroom today." He shook his hand and went over to Tyler's parents.

Enough lives had been destroyed over this case. Sara would find the justice she deserved, but it wouldn't be in the civil courts. Tyler and the others would be tried for their wrongdoings by a jury of their peers in the criminal justice system — this time, without the benefit of Randy's money. They would also have to face Jennifer Garrett, a young prosecutor, who was quickly climbing the ranks in the office.

THE CASE WAS dismissed. The leaking of the memo was all the ammunition the prosecutor's needed to indict Tyler, Danny, and Sal for perjury. Harold's final act was to lean on Freddie Aureue, one of Tyler's seedier friends, and the one person who was at his house when Danny pulled into the driveway after the shooting. While Kauni was chasing Gavin across the Narrows Bridge, Harold had Freddie in a police interrogation room until he finally got him to admit that he saw Tyler get out of the front passenger seat, and Marcus get out of the back passenger seat. The prosecutor's office gave Freddie full immunity, and he became their star witness against the other boys. It was a betrayal that he was all too happy to take part in after hearing his potential prison sentence for perjury. Marcus and his family would finally be vindicated in the community, and Sara, however indirect, would finally receive the justice she deserved.

Unfortunately for the firm, no money flowed through their thick oak doors, and hundreds of valuable associate hours were spent on an unprofitable case. However, after Steve's follow-up articles in the Tribune, Gavin and Duke were painted as heroes of the common citizen, and the firm was hailed as a steward of justice. "Empty words on a page," Fred yelled as he reminded his partners about the ten thousand dollars Lance offered and Gavin turned down. He was in the minority, and the favorable publicity convinced the partners to cough up the dough themselves to fund the suit against the gun manufacturers.

Gavin closed the door on his way out of Duke's office. The hanging photos and framed settlement checks that lined the walls were now blurred in Gavin's vision as he made his way down the corridor. Becky, sat perched as always at her desk typing away on something Duke dictated that morning. She hardly noticed him as he silently slipped down the hallway and out of sight.

As a direct and proximate cause of Defendants' acts, Plaintiff has suffered damages in an amount to be proven at trial.

Gavin could almost predict verbatim the language being tapped out with lightning speed as she continued polishing Duke's next civil complaint. It was the next case in line demanding a yet unspecified amount of compensation for the victims — demanding justice for the unrepresented in our society. She didn't hear Gavin say goodbye. She probably wouldn't notice his absence for several days. There were pleadings to file, and new associates to help create them.

He turned the corner of the building just as Gladys hung up the phone with Becky wanting to know what happened. "Well?" Gladys asked.

Gavin was silent, prolonging the suspense as he ducked into his office and grabbed his briefcase. "Would you do me a favor, Gladys?"

"Of course."

"Call my wife. Tell her I'll be home early."

She smiled her first endorsement he had ever seen from her. "I'd be happy to, Mr. Brady."

"Thanks."

"Now, what happened?" She was not going to let up. She wanted to know what Duke offered Gavin to stay.

Gavin straightened himself up. "Are you ever gonna call me Gavin?"

"Not ever, Mr. Brady. It wouldn't be proper." She smiled at him. "And besides, you're an attorney."

There was a brief pause as he stood there contemplating her words. It was the biggest compliment she could have given him at that moment, and, perhaps, the biggest compliment of his life.

"I guess I am." Gavin stood before Gladys a taller man. He gripped his briefcase. "Please, tell my wife I'm on my way home."

"You have a wonderful evening, Mr. Brady," she called to him as he made his way to the exit.

"I will." He smiled back at her, "Thanks for everything, Gladys." His voice echoed as the door slammed shut behind him.

Gladys stood there unable to hide the smile growing on her face as she stared at the closed door. "Good for you," she said to herself, "good for you."

Gavin turned down a three hundred thousand dollar a year salary and all the perks that went along with working at one of the most powerful and politically connected firms in the Northwest. He had made an enemy of the man who was probably slated to be the state's governor one day, and had given up the opportunity to be involved in a large complex suit against the gun manufacturers that was sure to draw national attention and media coverage. Gavin felt great. Justice had been done, and he fulfilled his promise not only to Sara's parents, but to himself.

Today would be the first time in months he'd arrive home before the sun went down, and would mark the beginning of many early days coming home to his wife. There was no office yet, but he could already picture the nameplate that would don the front of the building. He was officially a solo practitioner. That meant more freedom to devote to what was important in his life. A lesson learned by one fateful shot and one wrong turn of the wheel. He learned that moments were fleeting, and that the memories built on a foundation of time were more valuable than the billing statements that document that time. Gavin decided to define his life not solely by the successes of his professional accomplishments, but also by the successes of his personal life.

He stopped in front of his old firm's entrance. A tinge of doubt hit him as he took a deep breath. The world he knew just moments ago was already staring at him from behind. His time at the firm had already come full circle. Duke knew his young protégé's decision before they even met that morning. But, true to his nature, he offered him a bundle of money to sell his soul to a life of shoveling out complaints and demanding high settlements. Gavin learned there was a price to Duke's justice, and it was too high for him. In the end, Duke never actually expected him to accept the firm's offer, and Gavin certainly didn't disappoint him. Their parting was amicable and optimistic. Gavin always saw the best in Duke. After all, he built a practice bringing claims on behalf of the oppressed during an era when corporate America waved a banner of personal responsibility that allowed them free reign to act with impunity.

However, Duke's motives were, to some degree, fueled by the same greed that drove his adversaries. Although he successfully chanted for the underdog, Duke forfeited his purity long ago in a tantalizing sea of huge verdicts and upscale restaurants. Gavin walked through the front doors of his old firm's entrance. A cool breeze cut across his cheeks like an invisible blanket alerting him to the world around him. Perhaps, this was the same breeze that touched Sara the night she left the party — a breeze that failed once to warn of the impending dangers ahead, a breeze that waited more than five years for justification of its own existence.

Alert and refreshed, Gavin made his way down a Frostian, less-traveled path, past the rows of foreign luxury cars parked in the firm's parking lot to his rental car. He thought about his friend Alex, who offered his hand in professional friendship at one of the lowest points of the case. He wondered what he was doing right now. They spent many long and late night hours here in the hopes of solidifying a future as eventual partners. Their paths diverged very early in seemingly opposite directions, and, yet, their destinations were identical. Gavin stopped and looked back one last time at the entrance to his former firm. The difference between him and Alex was that Gavin didn't have any regrets. His path was paved out of choice like a beckoning ray of hope and opportunity.

He continued to his car, passing Duke's on the way. He stopped and took a close look at his license plate. The lettering of *JUSTICE* gleamed in the afternoon sun. "Justice," he said. Perhaps, he would give Alex a call to see if he was interested in helping to forge a small civil rights practice, one that cared about clients and allowed for a life outside of work. Perhaps, he would just go into practice alone. The world was wide open as he contemplated the last year and all the things he learned. Everyone involved had, in one way or another, leveraged a lucrative career on the death of a seventeen-year-old girl.

Randy's career was now on extremely shaky ground though his family name would probably pull him out of trouble. He would end up becoming a judge in some small town somewhere until everyone forgot about the Harrington case. Then, he'd run for the state legislature, perhaps even governor one day. Nate come into a small bundle of money to hire a prestigious criminal defense attorney to defend against allegations of fraud, embezzlement, and obstruction. In the end, he'd probably be Randy's fall guy, allowing some judge to throw the book at him publicly so everyone else could silently disappear into the woodwork. It would be a true political punishment, and one that the public could accept. It was, after all, the age of comebacks. Randy would ensure Nate's place alongside the other fallen heroes of the world. He'd write a book or end up as an on-air enforcement expert on important national cases.

Careers were advanced and destroyed, secret deals were made, and money changed hands. It seemed that everyone involved had received a payoff. In the end, only the Harringtons didn't receive any money for the death of their daughter. The system successfully came full circle. Each payoff helped to launder the taint of corruption before finally bathing itself in a salvation of criminal justice. It was a lesson in irony that mocked all its critics. Somewhere in the sea of legal arguments and motions, everyone forgot the horror that took place on that lonely road. No one focused on the tragedy that ripped a beautiful young life from the world, denying her and her family the future that lay ahead, and sent a wave of tragedy that culminated in a young man watching his family die on a bridge. The truth would eventually be known and those involved finally punished, but the victims outweighed the benefits. Sara, Bill Langston and his family, and even Kauni were forever gone, and the legal system was at least briefly turned upside down, exposing it weaknesses.

Gavin shook his head still focused on Duke's license plate. The snow-white edges were beginning to show the hints of rust. It was almost unnoticeable unless one took a close look. The rust had already covered the back side of the plate where there was no protective coating and where it was hidden from view. One day, the rust would finally bleed through, eating away at the lettering and exposing the façade.

Gavin brushed the plate lightly with his hand, paying final respects to a lost ideal that even the fresh coat of wax could not revive. He made his way to his own car and opened the front door. The sun was just beginning its evening descent, marching the hands of time forward into night. He stood there for a moment staring at his, now uncertain, future and contemplating the past. He thought about Jenny and how she sucked him into an unwitting fight with the prosecutor that helped save the case. He would never fully understand why she helped him. Perhaps, she, too, saw the opportunity to advance in the wake of the murder. Perhaps it was simply her way of getting closure on an old wound between recently reunited strangers. It didn't matter. He owed her a debt of gratitude.

He thought about Sara Harrington, and the future that she would never have. He thought about her parents and how their unwavering faith in the memory of their daughter strengthened them. He thought about the man on the bridge, who befriended him in the last moments of his life as his family lay crushed to death by his side, and Kauni's desperate attempts to save his little brother from a life in prison. Gavin's goals and ideals were so clear until a small seemingly insignificant case came across his desk. What began as a simple quest for advancement, resulted in redemption from himself and those early ideals. His trial advocacy professor was right. True justice always comes with a high price.

The sun peeked through the dark grey clouds illuminating them against the blue backdrop. Another cool breeze touched his face as if to alert him to his surroundings. For the first time since his father's death, he could feel his presence. Just as Sara's spirit reached through the heavens and touched her parents in their kitchen, Gavin's father now comforted him. It was a feeling of hope and peace. The breeze filled his lungs as he tried to inhale every ounce of this moment. His thoughts ran to his wife and the one request she made at the beginning of their journey together, *don't forget to come home to me.* His eyes welled up as he got in his car to fulfill that promise. *Thank you.* For the first time, he sat confidently between that which was and which was yet to be.

The sky softly spoke to him in small puffs of air, and he felt his father's proud loving embrace in the warmth of the sun's rays wrapping around his face. He looked up amongst the clouds and knew his father was smiling down on him.

Don't miss Stone Grissom's exciting new novel BONDS OF FRIENDSHIP.

Coming from Moonshine Cove Publishing, LLC in 2018.

Read the first chapter beginning on the next page.

Chapter 1

THE VOICES FADED in and out as he struggled to open his eyes. He could feel his back resting against something solid, the floor. The voices grew stronger now.

"Are you okay?" He could tell that someone was leaning over him, but he was still struggling to see. Everything looked like it was covered by a thin blanket of fog. Several figures were milling around the room. They were wavy and nondescript. "Are you okay?" The voice asked again.

The words echoed against his skull. There were other voices in the room as well, other figures wandering about. He concentrated on the words coming from the figure above him. He could tell it was a man. Suddenly, he began to feel a sharp stinging sensation on the side of his head.

"Where am I?" He barely mustered enough energy to utter the words. The room still looked hazy, and the light seemed to be forcing its way through the dense air. The pain from his head was becoming more intense now, shooting through his forehead down his spine.

The figure was still leaning over him. However, he couldn't make out the words. He tried to focus on the shiny object attached to the voice's waist. As he moved his head slightly, bits of the previous evening suddenly flashed in front of him. He remembered the tiny bar downtown. He could see himself sitting on a stool in front of a large mirror. He remembered drinking a lot of alcohol, and he could hear people laughing around him.

"Do you remember anything? Hey, Buddy, stay with me." The cloudy figure shuffled from one side to the next. The pain shot back through his head. The shiny object was just about in focus. There were words written on it, *Detective Seattle Police Department.*

He could hear the dull rumbling of other conversations more clearly now. He softened his stare to make use of his peripheral vision. The room was full of uniformed officers walking around. He could see that one was taking notes on a pad while looking at the wall.

"Mr. Manning, can you hear me? Do you understand where you are?" The detective's voice pounded his head like a drum, intensifying the already sharp pains that were circling across his forehead. "Do you know your name?"

"Heyden Manning," he said mechanically. "That's my name." He was still shaken up, but at least he knew who he was.

"That's good Mr. Manning." The detective's badge came in and out of focus. "Now, do you know where you are?" Heyden slowly looked up. He couldn't tell exactly what the man looked like. He thought he could see a moustache, but nothing was clear enough to make out. The detective leaned down. The smell of cheap Brut cologne mixed with the detective's coffee breath hit Heyden like a bullet. "We're in your living room. Can you remember what happened last night?"

Heyden took another breath , this time internalizing the smell ruminating from the detective. It reminded him of visiting his grandfather in the Delta of Mississippi. He didn't even feel the detective's hands as he was helped to his feet. He took another breath, and felt the throbbing pain across his skull bringing him back to his dazed reality. The fumes from the detective continued to surround him, drenching his senses and adding to the already pounding sensation in his head. The simple recollections of his youth were no longer sufficient to keep him from wanting to vomit. Heyden covered his mouth. He could feel the involuntary tensing of his neck trying to hold down the contents of his stomach.

"You okay?" Heyden nodded his head as he swallowed a tangy liquid lump.

The room was beginning to come back into focus. 'My living room,' he thought to himself. He could see that the entire area was in shambles. The couch was turned on its side and the coffee table looked as if it had been broken in half. Once Heyden was sure his stomach has settled enough to move, he finally looked the detective straight in the face.

"Who are you?" The words slowly drifted out of his mouth.

"I'm detective Tom Reagan with the Seattle Police Department." His six-foot frame stood eye to eye with Heyden, and his tweed coat barely concealed the gun and badge on his waist. "Do you remember anything?"

Heyden just shook his head and, without any recognition or emotion, looked at the melee around him. Heyden looked down at his clothing. He was wearing a white tank top and boxer shorts. The shirt was torn in a couple of places and he thought he could see reddish stains on the front.

"We'll get that looked at," Tom said motioning to Heyden's head. Heyden raised his arm and could feel the jagged edges of the dried blood on the side of his scalp. His head was throbbing and he was in no condition to ponder his predicament. He was just now beginning to acknowledge the figures as they continued to blur and refocus in sync with the pulsing veins in his head. "Follow me," Tom said nudging him to the other side of the room. Heyden felt almost detached from his body as he got to his feet and glided behind Tom to the other side of the room where another plain-clothed officer was standing.

"This is my partner, Detective James Figgs."

"How's he doing?" Jim asked as the trio came together. Heyden stood with the two detectives while they openly talked about him in the third person. He tried to focus on what they were saying, but it was easier and less painful to simply allow their conversation to echo through his skull in the background. After a moment, the two detectives gently grabbed Heyden's arm and nudged him down a hallway. They passed several uniformed officers, all with somber expressions. At the end of the corridor was what looked to be a brightly lit room breaking through the light-streaked haze. As they continued forward, Heyden thought he heard a woman's voice coming from inside. He stopped to listen. He could hear her giggling, and, unlike the other voices around him, it didn't echo through his head; rather it cut through the air in a clear distinctive tone.

"What's wrong, son, are you sure you're up to this?" Tom asked.

Heyden looked forward to see both men facing him. Suddenly, the giggling stopped and all he could hear was his own head pounding in rhythmic unity with his beating heart. Tom's coffee breath slapped Heyden in the face as the question was repeated to him. Although he nodded to continue, there was almost no acknowledgment behind his eyes. The three continued to the end of the hallway. Tom and Jim stopped and turned to him. The light from inside the room was almost blinding, drowning out their words in a sea of iridescent white. After a moment, the two detectives turned and entered the room.

Inside, the atmosphere looked sterile and bright. A Japanese paper lantern hung from the ceiling illuminating the room with a hazy glow. As Heyden looked around, he saw more police figures. They were all lumped around the center of the room. Tom signaled him to continue forward. As if on cue, the officers in front of him parted to each side to reveal what they had all been concealing. A queen size bed came into view. His eyes danced around it before honing in on what seemed to concern everyone. He blinked several times to bring the scene into focus. On the bed lay the naked body of a young woman.

"Amber." Heyden whispered the name without realizing the full extent of what he was seeing. She a beautiful late twenties woman with lifeless blue-green eyes. Her neck had been slashed open, and dried blood stained her naked breasts and stomach. There were deep gashes along her sternum and thighs. Heyden turned expressionless to Tom, who had rested his hand gently, albeit uncomfortably, on his shoulder. Heyden's forehead ached from a large gash that stretched across it. He looked at the dried blood splattered across his own torn shirt and boxer shorts, and then back to the blood across the top of the bed.

"I know this is difficult," Tom said in as soothing a voice as he could muster, "but can you tell us anything about what happened here? Anything at all would be greatly appreciated."

Heyden didn't say a word. After what seemed an eternity to everyone in the room, Heyden finally turned back toward Amber's bloody corpse, and slowly reached out his hand to touch the sheet bunched up at the foot of the bed. As his fingers made contact with the fabric, he could hear the woman laughing again. His head jerked around. The giggling was coming from the hallway. No one else was reacting to it. It was as if they couldn't hear the beautiful sweet voice dancing around inside of Heyden's head. He didn't acknowledge anyone in the room as he turned toward the giggling. It was the only voice he could hear with any clarity. None of the officers moved as Heyden stepped back out of the room. He stood at the edge of where the light of the bedroom and the darkness of the hallway met. He looked at the ground and teetered back and forth on his wobbly legs as if standing on a cliff overlooking a vast sea of black. The woman giggled again, this time louder and more clearly. He raised his head in the direction of the sound. At the end of the dark tunnel in front of him, he could see a woman. It was Amber, still naked, but very much alive. She smiled at him and then disappeared back into the living room.

Heyden followed her down the hallway. The dull ambient rumbling from the investigation going on was hauntingly silent, and the hallway seemed to stretch on forever. As he rounded the corner, the police officers who had been scattered throughout the house, had

299

disappeared from his vision, and he wasn't in pain any longer. The living room was empty and nothing was out of place. Something pulled him back toward the bedroom. As he entered, he noticed the room was clean and the sweet smell of potpourri filled the air. Amber stood next to the bed. There was no blood anywhere in the room, and she had a soft innocent glow about her. Heyden could just see hints of her bare skin through the thin slip she was wearing. He could smell the freshly painted walls. Heyden and Amber had been dating on and off since college. Their relationship had become more serious within the last six months when she agreed to finally move in with him. Her only condition was that the entire inside of the house had to be repainted. Much like an exorcism, she wanted the interior to be fresh and new with walls that had never been tainted with previous memories. Part of what he loved about her was that irrational superstitious side, so he had agreed to this baptismal exercise. Now, as he found himself back in their bedroom, the fresh paint smell was as real as the vision of Amber standing in front of him.

She moved over to a small vanity in the corner of the room and sat down in front of the mirror. Heyden didn't need to think about how to react. He was back at their first night as a couple living together. He instinctively moved toward her, smelling the sweet dried flowery scent as he came up behind her. He almost couldn't wait to wrap his arms around her, touching her soft freshly lotioned skin. She turned around to meet him as he reached her, and the two met in a passionate embrace. His tongue danced around her neck, and he felt her body tense in his arms with every new touch. He finally found her lips.

"We can't," she said between her deep breaths.

"Yes, we can," Heyden shot back, not paying any attention to her objections. Their kisses became deeper with each moment. They were always at their best in this room. All of their inhibitions vanished in each other's arms. Heyden struggled to take off his shirt.

"Baby, we - can't," she meekly retorted again, not resisting any of his advances. Heyden's hand moved across her thighs to the base of her slip, lifting it up and disappearing underneath the slinky fabric. Her moans were acquiescence enough. "Oh, my God," she said in a breathy voice.

"I thought we didn't have time." His arm continued to move back and forth underneath her slip as the moment began to quickly consume them. Finally, he picked her up in his arms and took her to the bed. She wrapped her legs around his waist and pulled him in tightly. As he continued to kiss her, her moans began to grow in strength.

"Oh, Amber," he said over and over, kissing her neck and shoulders. He always loved feeling how soft her freshly lotioned body felt. As she was losing herself in the moment, Heyden began to feel uneasy. Something was wrong. He began to feel a resistance instead of acceptance coming from his lover. He raised his head from her chest. Her face was filled with what looked more like fear than love. She wasn't looking at him anymore; rather she was looking over his shoulder. Her mouth was open and she wanted to scream, but no sound was coming out. Panicked, Heyden pushed himself back.

"What's wrong?" He looked back over his shoulder to see what could have frightened her so much. Her arms pushed him further away. Suddenly, her scream found the right octave and filled the room with a terrible shrill. Heyden immediately turned around. All of the feeling left his body. In front of him was a dark shadowy silhouette swinging something at him. He closed his eyes as the figure followed through with a full thrust to his head. Suddenly, everything was black and then bright again. He opened his eyes. The throbbing pain continued to pulse through his head. The light of the bedroom was almost blinding.

"Can you hear me?" Tom asked. "Heyden, can you hear me?" Suddenly he knew where he was. There was no mistaking Tom's breath and cologne smell. The echoing rumbling of the investigation had returned. He could hear the dull ambient conversations bouncing off the caverns of his head.

"Is he okay?" Jim asked taking a position on the other side of Heyden.

"Yeah, I guess it was too much too soon," Tom said with forced concern. "Hey kid, just take it easy. There's no rush. You just take it easy." Heyden moved his head to the side. Next to the bed, two officers zipped up a black body bag sealing Amber within it. Heyden was emotionless. Nothing was registering.

"Let's get a medic over here," Jim said to the officers as they carted the human-sized plastic coffin out of the room.

"Hey Figgs." One of the officers holding the bag turned around at the door toward Jim. "Captain's here."

TOM AND JIM headed back down the hallway leaving Heyden with one of the uniformed officers. The two detectives met up with Captain

Paul Seward who was standing in the living room talking to another officer.

"Captain," Jim said.

"What do you got?" Paul turned to his detectives.

"The victim's name was Amber Jenkins." Tom responded without missing a beat.

"Was?" Paul asked, almost annoyed.

"No, 'is' named Amber," Tom said.

"Is," Jim interjected, "was – she's dead, right?"

"Yeah," Tom said, "she still has a name, right, captain?" Tom knew the captain was a stickler for such details and often perseverated on points that others felt were mundane or even morose, like whether the past or present tense is more appropriate when referring to a deceased person's name. He had been the head of homicide for the past 11 years and Tom sucked up to him despite despising his eccentricities. Paul was also well-connected in the political arena and if Tom had any hope of one day running his own department, he had to stay in Paul's good graces.

"What else you got?"

"Hey, captain," Jim said smiling, trying to soften Paul's impatient glare. "She lives here, or lived here, with her boyfriend, Heyden Manning. He's in the back room and looks like he took quite a beating himself, probably trying to stop whoever did this."

"Forced entry?"

"No sign of forced entry," Tom piped in.

"No broken glass, no muddy prints," Jim said as if finishing Tom's sentence. The two of them often parried back and forth like an old married couple completing each other's thoughts. It came from years together trusting their lives to one another. "Just walks in here like nobody's business and slashes up the place."

"Have we talked to the boyfriend yet?"

"Tried," Tom said. "He's still in shock. He's just sleep walking at this point." It was the part of the job Tom despised. He could handle severed bodies or bloody crime scenes, but he wasn't used to the fragility of human emotions that went along with it. He was the perfect model of self-restraint and self-denial. Relationships were foreign to him. It was the job that got him going each day. By the tender age of 33 he had already been shot twice in the line of duty, been decorated by the mayor, and was lead detective on most of the biggest cases in his department. He was also known for having a bit of a temper, and had several citizen complaints regarding the use of excessive force during arrests and interrogations.

"There's one more thing," Jim said, "we found this." He raised his hand to display a metal object.

"What is it?"

"That Heyden fella's key. It was in the front door."

"His key?" Paul quipped.

"Yeah, apparently, he must've left it there."

"Perfect," Paul said in exasperation.

"Excuse me, captain." One of the uniformed officers interrupted their meeting. "We've got a woman -"

"Hold it. What time is it?" Paul's mind spun at a different rate than that of the average person.

"Uhm," the officer looked at his phone. "4:30 in the morning."

Paul shook his wrist. "Damn watch." Paul was old school. He still wore a watch, the kind that still needed to be wound up on a weekly basis. "You were saying."

Jim shot Tom a glance as the officer continued. "Captain, we've got a woman outside who claims to have maybe seen someone exiting the house early this morning."

"What do you mean maybe?" Paul snapped back.

"Maybe. She said maybe. She's old. She lives across the street. I think she's the one who called this in."

"Now we're getting somewhere," Paul said.

"We'll go talk to her," Jim volunteered, "right?" He nudged Tom.

"Absolutely," Tom said.

"Hey wait," Paul called after them, but they had already disappeared. "Okay, the case is yours."

CPSIA information can be obtained
at www.ICGtesting.com
Printed in the USA
BVOW03s0427050817
491149BV00003B/199/P